The ghter

The Collector's Daughter

A Novel of the Discovery of Tutankhamun's Tomb

Gill Paul

HARPER LARGE PRINT

An Imprint of HarperCollinsPublishers

This book is a work of fiction. References to real people, events, estab-
lishments, organizations, or locales are intended only to provide a sense of
authenticity, and are used fictitiously. All other characters, and all incidents
and dialogue, are drawn from the author's imagination and are not to be
construed as real.

HarperCollins books may be purchased for educational, business, or sales
promotional use. For information, please e-mail the Special Markets
Department at SPsales@harpercollins.com.

FIRST HARPER LARGE PRINT EDITION

ISBN: 978-0-06-311791-4

Library of Congress Cataloging-in-Publication Data is available upon request.

21 22 23 24 25   LSC   10 9 8 7 6 5 4 3 2 1

For Karen Sullivan, publisher extraordinaire
and the very best of friends

The Collector's Daughter

Chapter One

London, July 1972

Eve opened her eyes a fraction and saw an old man sitting a couple of feet away. He had silver hair that receded on either side of his brow, leaving a widow's peak in the center. She shut her eyes again and watched the fuzzy shapes that glimmered and danced in her visual field.

The next time she opened her eyelids the man was still there. Behind him she could make out a white room and the rectangular shape of a window.

"You're back," he said with a choking sound, as if he was overcome.

She tried to focus on him, blinking against the light. His eyes were red-rimmed behind wire spectacles. He was wearing a suit and tie. She looked down and realized he was holding her hand. At least, the hand was attached to an arm that led up to her body so it must be hers, but she couldn't feel it, couldn't make the fingers respond. That wasn't good.

"You've had one of your funny turns, Pipsqueak," he said. "You're in the hospital. You've been here before and you've always come bouncing back so I'm sure you will this time." His voice was wobbly. He had been crying.

She looked around. There was a tube in her other arm, attached to a bag with clear liquid in it. She remembered she'd had one of those before.

Who was the man? Was he her father? She frowned. That didn't feel like the right answer. He couldn't be a doctor because he wasn't wearing a white coat. Maybe he was her husband.

"Hu . . ." she said, but the word wouldn't come. She remembered that too. She must have had a . . . what was it called? A stroke. Strange word. Strokes should be gentle, the way you stroke a dog or a horse, but the type she had were cruel. They stole bits of her brain and didn't always give them back again.

Her husband—that's who the man was, she remembered now. And his name was Brograve. Sir Brograve Beauchamp. He was saying that she had been good as new after previous funny turns, but he was lying. She remembered the tedious weeks of rehab, when people spoke to her as if she were a child. She had to learn to talk and walk again, and afterward, when she got home, she always felt a bit less herself, as if a chunk had been taken out of her.

She closed her eyes, exhausted at the thought of all the hard work ahead, and slid into drowsy sleep.

It was five to six when Brograve left the ward. Their daughter, Patricia, would be waiting outside the entrance at six, hovering on the yellow lines. If he was late, one of the parking attendants would tell her to move on. At least this time he had good news for her—that Eve had regained consciousness. It had been almost two days. He stopped to blow his nose and lifted his glasses to dab his eyes before stepping into the revolving glass door.

"Oh, thank god!" Patricia said when she heard the news. "Did you talk to the doctor? What happens next? When will they start the speech therapy? And physio?"

Always impatient, just like her mother, Brograve thought. He allowed himself a faint smile. "When they think she's ready. You know how it is."

"I'll come in with you tomorrow. Thank god she's awake. Did she know who you were?"

"I think so," he said. "I hope so."

"I went to your flat, by the way. Watered the plants

and picked up the post. There were a few letters that have been redirected from Framfield. They're all on the back seat." She clicked the indicator and pulled out into the traffic.

Brograve turned and saw the pile. He tried to reach back through the seats but a twinge in his lower back stopped him. They would wait till he got to Patricia's.

"I should move home to give you and Michael your privacy," he said.

"Nonsense, Dad. I won't hear of it. You'll stay with us until Mum's ready to be released from hospital. You know you're useless at looking after yourself."

Useless? he thought. *That was unfair.* "Mrs. Jarrold does the cleaning and laundry, and I'm sure she would leave me supper on a tray." His voice tailed off. Eating on his own, in front of the television set, was not an appealing thought. He pictured himself doing the washing-up, then having a nip of whisky in front of the ten o'clock news, and it made him sad. No, maybe he'd stay with Patricia and Michael awhile longer, if they'd have him.

He sat at their kitchen table opening his letters while Patricia prepared dinner. There was an electricity bill, a bank statement, their tickets to a forthcoming dinner at the House of Commons . . . One letter addressed to Eve had an Egyptian stamp on it, and had been sent to the country house in Framfield they had sold the previous year. He hesitated, then opened it.

"Dear Lady Beauchamp," it began. The letterhead was that of a university in Cairo, and underneath was typed: "Dr. Ana Mansour, Faculty of Archaeology." He skimmed the letter.

We have recently discovered the tomb of an Ancient Egyptian man known as Maya, in a site at Saqqara. As I'm sure you know, he was the overseer responsible for the burial preparations for several kings of the Eighteenth Dynasty. He left detailed notes on papyrus that we have been interpreting in my department.

We are puzzled because there are several key anomalies between the items Maya says he left in the burial chamber of Tutankhamun and the catalogue of the excavation made by Howard Carter in the 1920s. Since you are the only person still alive who was present at the opening of the tomb, I would very much appreciate an opportunity to ask you some questions. I will fly to London at your earliest convenience.

Brograve put down the letter and scratched his brow. Before this latest stroke, he knew Eve would have been happy to talk to Dr. Mansour. She was knowledgeable about Egyptology in general and could cite chapter and verse on the discovery of Tutankhamun's tomb in 1922, which had been funded by her father, the late Earl of Carnarvon.

What did Dr. Mansour mean by "anomalies" though? The records would never match up after three millennia. Weren't there supposed to have been a couple of robberies in ancient times? And everyone took souvenirs back in 1922. He thought of the gold box Eve had kept as a memento from the tomb—a stinky old thing with some kind of ancient ointment in it. That wouldn't have appeared in Howard's catalogue.

How should he reply to this letter? He glanced at the date and realized it had been written in April—three months earlier. There was no rush. Academic studies tended to take years to complete. He would wait until Eve was better and then she could reply herself.

Chapter Two

London, July 1972

A nurse bustled in to change the plastic bag attached to Eve's catheter, which was full of amber-colored urine. Two more nurses came to give her a bed bath, rolling her onto one side, then the other, like a slab of beef they were browning for Sunday lunch. They massaged her legs and feet, slapping them to encourage circulation, and Eve felt grateful that she could feel the slaps. The only bit of her body she couldn't feel, or move, was her right hand, which was numb and useless as a dead fish.

Midmorning, a therapist came to teach her to swallow. She'd been swallowing perfectly well for seventy-one years but now it seemed her throat had forgotten how. The woman gave her a spoonful of something with the texture and taste of thin wallpaper paste, then told her to let it slide to the back of her tongue and to massage the sides of her neck, just under the jawbone, till it went down. Eve coughed and choked and the woman bent her forward and thumped her back, then they started all over again. Afterward her throat was raw, but Eve vowed to keep practicing. Until she mastered this, she wouldn't be allowed proper food.

She'd been hoping to start speech therapy straightaway but instead the therapist—the same one as last time, a sparky, friendly girl, name of Katie—brought an alphabet chart, the kind children used to learn to read. She could communicate by pointing to the letters but it was painfully slow.

"What daughter name," she spelled out. It had completely slipped her mind and she didn't want to hurt her feelings when she visited.

"Your daughter is called Patricia, and you have two grandsons, Simon and Edward."

Eve knew that. She could picture them. Handsome, strapping lads with sunny personalities. They got Brograve's height, thank goodness—he was six foot four while she was teensy, only five foot one. That's why Brograve called her "Pipsqueak." She was excited she could remember so much.

"Try to say your name," Katie said. "Eee-ve." She enunciated, exaggerating the movements of her lips.

"Eeee," she managed, but the *v* sound wouldn't come. Her mood plummeted. It seemed she would have to lift herself up from quite a low starting point this time.

After the nurses had left, but before Brograve came, Eve fumbled in the bedside cabinet for her reading glasses and perched them on her nose, then reached for a laminated page of medical instructions one of the staff had left behind. She mouthed the words, following them with a finger: "Oropharyngeal airways should be used in unconscious patients as they stimulate a gag reflex." She read the whole page, then tried to say the words out loud. It was frustratingly slow, but she persevered.

When she was a child, everyone teased Eve for being a chatterbox—as an adult too, come to think of it. She was one of life's talkers. She could live without the use of her right hand if need be, she could even manage if she had to use a wheelchair for the rest of her life, but she couldn't possibly manage without speech.

Brograve brought a photo album to the hospital that afternoon. He'd compiled it after the stroke before last, interleaving shots of family and friends from over the years to try and nudge Eve's memory. He was aware he shouldn't rush her—the doctor had emphasized that—but he needed to know for himself that the brain damage wasn't too great. She might have a few gaps in her memory, but if she remembered most things, and if she was her bright, funny self, then he could wait for the rest.

Eve smiled crookedly when he arrived, the left side of her mouth not lifting. "Lo," she said, and he kissed her on the lips before pulling up a chair.

"The nurse gave me this alphabet board in case we need it," he said. "I'm hoping you won't make me do all the talking. What on earth would I say?"

"O-kay?" Eve asked out loud, then spelled "sorry" on the board.

"Goodness, you have nothing to apologize for. *I'm* sorry I wasn't there. I got back from my walk and found you unconscious. You could have been lying there as long as an hour."

He shivered, remembering the horror of the moment. Eve was slumped facedown on the kitchen table and breathing noisily, with a rattling sound a doctor had told him was called stertorous breathing. He'd gone into overdrive: turning her head to the side so she could breathe more easily, telephoning an ambulance, then calling Patricia, all the while his heart thudding as if it would burst from his chest. His hands were clammy and there was a rushing sound in his ears. He opened the front door so the ambulancemen would be able to get access if he collapsed before they arrived. And yet, when they got there, he was lucid enough to explain Eve's medical history, to tell them that she had been prone to strokes since a serious accident in 1935, and that she had been treated in the past at St. George's, Tooting.

With previous strokes, Eve had come around reasonably quickly—within a few hours, a day at most. The doctor had warned him that the fact it took longer this time meant the damage could be greater. She might not recover all her faculties. He wasn't to get his hopes up.

You don't know my wife, he thought. *If it is remotely possible to recover fully, then Eve will do it.*

And here she was, sitting up in bed and smiling at him with one side of her face. He told her that he was staying at Patricia's because it was closer to the hospital. He told her that Patricia was coming to say hello when she picked him up later but they didn't want to tire her out. The boys sent their love.

She smiled at that. "Edwa . . . Si-mon."

"Edward and Simon. Jolly well done!" He grinned.

She pointed at the glass of water by the bedside and he held it to help her take a sip, watching the way she massaged her neck to make it slide down.

"Are you in the mood for some photos?" he asked, holding up the album bound in Black Watch tartan, a birthday present to her from someone or other a few years ago. Eve bought birthday gifts for dozens of friends, never forgetting the dates and choosing the gifts with great care, so when her own birthday came around each August an avalanche of parcels arrived, even now that she was in her seventies and their friends had started dying off.

He opened at the first page. The Earl of Carnarvon stood outside the main entrance of Highclere Castle, holding a rifle, with his three-legged terrier Susie beside him.

"Pups," Eve said, quite distinctly—her name for her father. She ran her finger along the stonework above the doorway, then used the board to spell "*Ung je Serviray.*" It was the family motto that was engraved there, meaning "One will I serve."

Brograve shivered. What a thing to remember! "Very impressive," he said out loud. "You're definitely all there, aren't you, Pipsqueak?"

"Ope ssso," she managed.

He turned the page to a glamorous photo of Eve's mother, the Countess of Carnarvon, in full evening gown with a tiara perched on her dark hair. It looked as if she was in the drawing room at Number 1 Seamore Place, the magnificent Mayfair townhouse she had inherited from her godfather, Alfred de Rothschild.

"Ma-ma," Eve said, quite clearly.

Usually they called her Almina, Brograve thought. She hadn't been much of a mother. As parents, he and Eve had believed in spending time with their daughter, to teach and nurture her, but Almina had left Eve and her brother, Porchy, to be raised by a nanny, and had shown an interest only when it was time for them to marry. In later life, Almina had leaned on Eve—both emotionally and financially—until her death just three years ago. She hadn't been Brograve's favorite relative, suffice it to say.

On the next page was a picture of Porchy at his wedding to Catherine Wendell, his first wife. Eve stared at it for a long time, then turned the page without a word. She flicked past a picture of her three closest friends, Maude, Emily, and Lois, and Brograve couldn't tell if she remembered them or not. He didn't want to make her feel as if this were a test. She'd remembered the family motto, after all.

"You'll know these lively fellows," he said, when she turned to a page with pictures of their racehorses, Miraculous and Hot Flash. Eve loved horses. She'd grown up in the saddle at Highclere, galloping around the estate's five thousand acres from when she was a nipper. "Do you remember when Hot Flash took the St. Leger at odds of eight to one? You yelled yourself hoarse. Your voice was husky for days afterward."

He looked into her eyes and saw confusion. She didn't know what he was talking about and it was upsetting her. He turned the page quickly.

Next there was a grainy black-and-white photo of Egypt. He recognized the Nile from a felucca in the foreground and some palm trees on the opposite shore but couldn't work out where the image had been taken.

"Luxor," Eve spelled on the board. "View from Winter Palace."

"Ah, I only stayed there a couple of nights," Brograve said. "But you spent three winters there, didn't you? You must have known it like the back of your hand."

Eve slid her finger under the photograph and slipped it free of the photo corners. She gazed into the picture, then looked up and smiled.

"Goo . . ." she said, then a word he couldn't make out. "I kee . . ." She tried to form another word, frowning with the effort.

"You want to keep it?" Brograve guessed, and she nodded. "Of course you can! It's your photo. Probably taken by your father."

He put the album away after that and sat, stroking her good hand, describing the episode of *Dixon of Dock Green* he had watched with Patricia and Michael the previous evening. A nurse came to feed her some god-awful gruel and Eve turned to him and made a comic face. She was her old self, she definitely was.

But lying in bed later that night, Brograve was worried. Her mother, father, and Egypt were the only images she had responded to. Did that mean the rest didn't ring any bells? Or was she just too tired to comment?

What's more, he'd been watching her face when Patricia came into the room, and there had been no sign of recognition. By the time she reached the bedside, waving a bunch of pink roses, Eve had arranged her face into a lopsided smile of welcome, but Brograve was pretty sure she hadn't recognized her own daughter. And that was sad beyond words.

Chapter Three

Luxor, November 1919

After Brograve left, Eve stared at the photo of Luxor. The scene felt as familiar to her as her husband's face, but it must be ages since she'd been there. She remembered she was eighteen years old when she first visited. She'd traveled with her parents and two ladies' maids on the boat train to Paris, then they took another train to Marseilles, from where they crossed the Mediterranean on a steamer to Alexandria. Her mother went straight to Cairo, where she loved the expat social scene, but Pups took Eve and her maid to Luxor with him. *What was the name of that maid?* It escaped her.

Since Eve was a nipper, Pups had kept a collection of Egyptian artifacts at Highclere Castle and she loved to be allowed to examine them and imagine the lives of the pharaohs they had adorned in ancient times. Her brother, Porchy, wasn't interested, so at first it had been her way of wangling time on her own with her beloved Pups, but as she grew older, and read more about Egyptology, she had become determined to visit the country. "When you're old enough!" her parents said—and then the war got in the way, so it was November 1919 before she first saw the place she had dreamed of for so long.

They arrived by night, under velvety black skies studded with brilliant white stars. As Eve stood on the platform gazing up, two bats glided past, blotting the light for a split second. A donkey-drawn cart took them from the train station to the Winter Palace Hotel, where they checked in and were shown to their suite. Eve fell straight into bed, but she slept for only a few hours and woke as soon as light began streaking around the edges of the curtains.

She flung them open, then pried back the heavy wooden shutters, before gasping in surprise. The River Nile was so close she could have thrown her shoe into it from the narrow balcony of her third-floor room. She hadn't imagined they would be so near. The water was the deepest of blue colors, like liquid sapphires twinkling in the morning light. On the opposite bank were spiky green palm trees and low white houses, backed by reddish-gold hills that she knew enclosed the Valley of the Kings. It was the most thrilling moment of her life so far.

There was a basket chair on her balcony so she slipped on a pale silk robe and sat outside to take in the view. Tiny boats with single white sails flitted across the water at astonishing speed, and the air was filled with noise: traders calling their wares, a donkey braying, a cart clattering past. Even so early—she saw from a mantelpiece clock that it was only six-thirty—the shore was bustling.

It wasn't yet hot but the air was humid, with a sweet flower scent, overlaid by another, ranker smell that reminded her of blocked drains. Dozens of gray birds with yellow breasts were chattering in a tree, and suddenly they rose in a rush of wings, so close she could feel the ripple of air on her cheeks. Watching them, Eve hugged herself. She knew beyond a shadow of a doubt she was going to fall in love with Egypt.

Howard Carter came to the hotel reception at eight a.m., wearing a baggy suit that looked as though it was made from old potato sacks and a straw boater with a black ribbon around it. Eve rushed to greet him with a squeal of delight.

"Look! It's me! I can hardly believe I'm here in Egypt at last!"

She'd known Howard since she was six years old. He used to come to Highclere bringing artifacts he'd purchased for Lord Carnarvon's collection, and Eve would corner him and attempt to impress him with her knowledge of Egyptology. At that age, it consisted of the ability to recite all the kings and their dynasties in date order, plus an encyclopedic recall of her father's treasures.

Howard recommended books to fill out her understanding and always stopped to chat. What she liked most was that he never talked to her as if she were a child, but answered her questions plainly and factually. Her mother said his manners were "lacking" and he didn't show "proper respect for his superiors," but as far as Eve could tell, he treated everyone the same, young or old, family or servants, and she liked that.

"Shall we have breakfast?" Pups asked, but Howard insisted they should cross to the Valley straightaway, because it would be too hot to remain outdoors past eleven-thirty.

They followed him through the hotel's lush gardens and down some steps to the riverside. He approached some fellows with dark-brown skin and spoke to them in Arabic before turning to beckon her and Pups.

"Your first trip in a felucca," he told Eve, holding her arm to steady her as she climbed in. "The Egyptians are born sailors. They can take these craft upstream, down-stream, or east bank to west and vice versa no matter what the wind direction."

She gazed around, drinking it in: a man with a crocodile tattoo on his arm feeding nuts to a blue-and-yellow parrot perched on a fence; a border of jet-black mud where the water lapped the shore; some wooden crates stacked precariously on the dock, stamped with the names of impossibly distant lands like Siam and the Dutch East Indies.

Their sailor balanced on the edge of the felucca, his toes curled around the rim like a bird's claws, and angled his sail to catch the wind. In an instant they were whisked from the bank, zigzagging around other boats with just a tilt of the sail. Eve imagined this must be what fly-ing felt like. They got to the other side in minutes, and she wished it had taken longer because it was such fun. Howard slipped their boatman a few coins, then walked over to a group of men with donkey carriages. Voices were raised, as if he was arguing with them.

"Is there a problem?" Eve whispered, sidling up, curious.

He smiled. "Just getting the best price. Everyone haggles here. You'll get used to it."

She decided she very much wanted to try her hand at haggling.

The carriage took them up a twisty road with deep potholes and ruts that made them jolt alarmingly. The verdant land flanking the Nile soon gave way to reddish sand and dust, and the air grew quieter, stiller, and hotter. Eve opened the white lace parasol she had brought; her mother would be furious if she got freckles.

"This is the Valley," Howard told them, as their driver took a sharp left turn onto a dirt track. "You will be able to make out various tomb entrances set in the hillsides."

"I've seen a map of it," Eve said, jumping down from the carriage. "The tombs all have numbers, don't they? Like houses in a London street."

"Indeed. There are sixty-one of them, with numbers starting KV for King's Valley or WV for West Valley. We are in the East Valley."

All she could see were sand hills and piles of rubble without distinguishing features; no plants or animals, just red sand on rock. How could anything be found here? She scuffed her toe, writing her name in the sand.

"Let's have a look at an empty tomb, KV17," Howard said.

They walked down some steps to a low-ceilinged passageway that led to a long, narrow chamber hewn in the rock. Lord Carnarvon had to crouch to get in.

"I am the ideal height for a lady archaeologist," Eve

remarked. "Look! I can stand up straight." Being tiny wasn't often an advantage.

The interior of the tomb was hot as a furnace and the air was stale, as if it had been breathed by hundreds of souls across the millennia—into their lungs and out again, over and over. Eve shivered, thinking of the weight of the sand mountain above them and hoping it would not collapse, trapping them for eternity.

Howard pointed to a row of hieroglyphics painted on the wall, but they were faded and hard to make out.

"The colors survive if they are undisturbed, because there is no air or water to cause decay," he explained. "But as soon as human beings enter and start breathing, the fragile pigments disintegrate."

"I shall hold my breath in that case," Eve said, "to play my part in the preservation of antiquities." She tried, but couldn't manage for long because she had too many questions to ask. Whose tomb was it? How old? Had anything significant been found there? Any treasures?

"Poor Howard," her father remarked. "If he's not already used to your loquaciousness, he soon will be."

Eve caught Howard's eye and smiled. She knew he was happy to talk from dawn till dusk if the subject was Egyptology; anything else, and he'd be bored senseless.

They had a stroll around the Valley, looking into

two more tombs and surveying the concession Howard's team was currently excavating. A primitive hand-operated railway carriage was taking rubble out to the road for disposal. The site looked no more promising than anywhere else, Eve thought, but who knew what lay beneath the sand and rock?

"Will you teach me how to dig?" she asked. "I'm simply dying to learn. It's my lifelong ambition."

Howard glanced at Pups before replying. "Certainly. You'll have to wear clothes you don't mind getting dirty, and bring a wide-brimmed hat because you won't be able to hold that parasol. But I don't see why I couldn't teach you some basics."

Eve jumped in the air with an ecstatic whoop. If her mother had been there, she would no doubt have said it was unladylike, but Pups had always been happy to let his daughter be her own person. He adored her. She could wind him around her little finger.

Their carriage driver had waited, and when they finished the tour he took them down the hill to the house where Howard lived, which he had named "Castle Carter." It was white-painted and one story high, with a dome in the center, and it was almost completely surrounded by trees, making it feel cool and fresh after the scorching, enervating heat of the Valley. They sat in his sparsely furnished drawing room and he brought a whisky and water for her father and a lemonade for Eve that his houseboy had made with fresh lemons from a tree in his garden and heaps of sugar.

"Don't you have ice?" Pups asked, fanning himself, but Howard explained that he did not possess a refrigerator. Even if he did, the electricity supply was so erratic he doubted it would stay cold long enough for water to freeze.

Eve heard a bird whistling outside the window, a tuneful creature putting its heart and soul into its song. "What type of bird is that?"

"It's my pet canary," Howard told her. "The Egyptians think its song brings good luck."

"I'm sure they're right," Eve said. "What's his or her name?"

"Bulldog, believe it or not." He laughed at her bewildered expression. "It's the nickname of a friend of mine."

"You'll give that poor creature neurosis," Eve teased. "How would you like it if I called you Dentist or some other such thing that you're not?"

"That would certainly be odd," he agreed.

His home was very much a bachelor's: books lay open on dusty tabletops; a pair of binoculars rested on a window frame; the upholstery was worn and had clearly been chosen without any notion of a design scheme.

"Don't you get lonely here?" she asked, for it seemed miles from any other habitation.

"Howard doesn't get lonely," Lord Carnarvon chipped in. "He has the pharaohs for company."

"And Bulldog," Howard replied.

Eve wanted to ask why there wasn't a Mrs. Carter but she supposed it might be difficult to find a woman who would want to share his spartan lifestyle. She couldn't imagine being quite so isolated and hoped it wouldn't be essential if she were to be a lady archaeologist. She was definitely more of a sociable type.

The next morning, Eve and Pups crossed to the Valley at dawn. Howard took them to the concession and showed Eve how to sift debris with a trowel and sieve, looking for anything out of the ordinary, before throwing it onto the spoil heap. If she struck hard rock, he told her to mime for one of the Egyptian boys to break it up with a mattock. They didn't speak English but would understand. If she found anything apart from sand and rock, she was to call him immediately.

Eve worked her patch with great diligence, daydreaming about the Ancient Egyptians who chose this spot as their burial ground. They walked on this earth, saw the same views she was seeing, felt the same baking heat. Millennia apart, they probably experienced the same emotions—love, fear, irritation, happiness—although their worldview had been so very different, peopled by gods and spirits, slaves and rulers.

She didn't find anything except the bone of an animal, which Howard thought was a jackal, but still she loved the experience.

"Can't I come and work in the desert with you?" she asked. "I'll be your trusty assistant. It's my dearest ambition, the one thing I want more than anything else."

Before Howard could reply, her father spoke: "I'm afraid your mother has other plans."

"Yes, I know," Eve said, with gloom in her heart. "A prestigious marriage." She adopted her mother's clipped tones: "No one of lower rank than a viscount, and no second sons, only the eldest."

Both men burst out laughing at the uncanny accuracy of the imitation.

Chapter Four

London, July 1972

When Eve wakened in the hospital the following morning, there was a moment when she thought she was back in Egypt, lying in bed at the Winter Palace. There was something about the sharpness of the sunlight blinking through the window and a disinfectant smell that reminded her of another scent she couldn't quite put her finger on, one she knew was to do with Egypt.

A nurse came to take her temperature and at first she mistook her for the lady's maid who had accompanied her to Egypt in 1919 to look after her wardrobe and style her wayward hair. *Marcelle! That was her name!* Then she glanced down at the wrinkled, age-spotted skin on the back of her hand and knew she wasn't eighteen anymore, not by a long shot.

"Is your husband coming today?" the nurse asked, fitting a blood pressure cuff on her arm.

"Fink so," Eve managed to reply. Her tongue felt heavy, making the *th* sound difficult.

Mornings were devoted to mechanical functions: bowels, urine, washing, stretching, massage. The doctor came by on his round and told her she was doing very well.

"Ow long?" she asked.

"It's impossible to say right now," he replied, "but perhaps we can transfer you to a convalescent home in a few weeks." He caught her expression of shock. "Don't be impatient. I know you've always made a miraculous recovery from previous strokes, but you're in your seventies now and it could take a while longer."

Not if I can help it, Eve thought. As soon as he'd gone she pulled out the page about ventilators and did her best to read it out loud.

Brograve came at two, when visiting hours started, and she knew he would stay till six, when they ushered all the guests out for the night. He hadn't brought a photo album this time but there was a newspaper tucked under his arm.

Katie, the speech therapist, arrived shortly after him, full of apologies because she was running late. She should have come before lunch but she'd left her notes in the office and had to go back for them, then the traffic was hideous. Eve smiled, remembering from last time that she was a chaotic sort, but very likable.

"I don't want to banish you when you've just arrived," she said to Brograve. "Maybe the three of us could have a conversation so Eve can practice her talking?"

"Certainly," Brograve said. "If it's helpful."

Katie did some warm-up exercises with Eve first—*"Muh, Wuh, Huh, Tuh, Duh"*—demonstrating the way she should move her lips for each consonant, then she asked, "Why don't you tell me how you two met? I don't think I've ever asked."

"Cai-ro," Eve said straightaway.

"I believe it was something to do with a lace sleeve." Brograve smiled. "Some kind of devious female trickery."

Eve took a deep breath and spoke slowly. "One . . . of . . . usss . . . had . . . to." It was her longest sentence yet, and she clenched her left fist, pleased with herself.

"I would have been too shy to approach her," Brograve explained. "She was by far the most popular girl at the party—and the prettiest too."

"You met in Cairo? Did I get that right? How romantic!"

"Chriss—mass," Eve said. "Cai-ro."

The grand ballroom of the British Residency was festooned with holly and ivy garlands and a plump fir tree stood in one corner. Waiters were hovering with glasses on silver trays, and candles glowed on every surface, their flames licking dangerously close to the paintings on the walls above. The guests were a handful of soldiers from the local military base and some titled folk of Eve's parents' generation, all dressed in evening finest, the women weighed down by heirloom jewels.

Eve and Pups had arrived by train from Luxor only the previous evening, and so far all she had seen of the city was the very smart area around the Continental Savoy Hotel, where Eve's mother had reserved a suite for the season. Apart from the sticky heat, it felt as if they could be in England, with neatly planted gardens, Christian church spires, modern cars on the roads, and European-style architecture. It seemed incongruous to Eve to be celebrating Christmas in a Muslim country situated not far north of the tropics, but it must be the norm here because all the buildings in that quarter had festive decorations.

She was delighted to see her uncle Mervyn with his new wife, Mary. Mervyn, her father's younger half brother, had recently been appointed first secretary at the British Embassy in Cairo. He had been a fun uncle when Eve was growing up, always arriving at Highclere with imaginative presents: cat's-eye marbles, board games, and a slingshot that their mother confiscated as soon as he left. He had Eve in stitches with his repertoire of jokes and funny faces, and she was pleased he had married a woman who seemed to share his sense of fun. Mervyn and Mary whispered and giggled like children, and were clearly very much in love.

A footman announced that the carol singing would begin shortly, and everyone shuffled toward a grand piano. Eve took the song sheet she was handed and stood between her father and Uncle Mervyn. Her view of the pianist was entirely blocked by a tall soldier in a scarlet tunic directly in front of her.

When the singing began, Eve caught eyes with Pups and almost chortled out loud because the man was tone deaf; he sang every word of "Silent Night" on the same flat note. What's more, he didn't seem aware of his shortcoming because he sang along with enthusiasm. Eve pinched her nose to contain her mirth and saw Uncle Mervyn doing the same.

Once the carols were done, Eve's mother led her to the front of the crowd to introduce her to Lady Allenby, wife of the British high commissioner.

"So *this* is your girl," she exclaimed. "What a beauty!

That dark hair and amber eyes—just like yours, Almina. She'll certainly be a hit with the young men."

Eve had absolutely no idea whether she was pretty or how young men would react to her. She'd spent an isolated childhood at Highclere with Nanny Moss and a succession of tutors who coached her in French, mathematics, music, and literature, but never told her anything about the world outside. She hadn't yet "come out" as a debutante; that had to wait till the following year because there was a backlog of girls waiting to be presented at court after the war.

A buffet was laid out in the Residency's dining room and Eve's mother stood at her elbow instructing her which foods to select: "Have a cucumber sandwich—salmon will make your breath smell. No cake—you don't want to get porky. And don't think of touching the champagne; men flirt with drunk women but they never marry them."

Once her mother was ensconced with a group of older women friends, Eve was at last free to wander around. She couldn't see any girls her own age, but she spotted the tall soldier in the red tunic standing on his own by some potted palms. He was younger than she'd imagined from his back view, and looked uncomfortable, as if he would rather be anywhere but there. Eve felt the urge to talk to him, but knew from her mother's strict instructions, as well as the romance novels she read, that it was frowned upon for women to initiate conversation with a stranger.

Around her wrist she wore a slim diamond bracelet with a safety catch, and earlier the lace of her sleeve had become caught in the catch. Her mother had freed it without tearing the lace but it gave Eve an idea. She pulled back the safety catch until it caught the lace again, and gave a little twist to secure it. Then she wandered toward the potted palms, pretending to be so absorbed in disentangling her sleeve that she nearly walked straight into the man.

"Oh, I beg your pardon!" she cried. "This blasted bracelet will keep getting caught . . ." She smiled up at him. "I don't suppose I could prevail on you . . ."

"I'll do my best," he said, putting his drink down on a side table. "I hope I don't make matters worse." He stooped to peer at the delicate cream lace.

"It's most awfully kind of you," Eve said, at the same moment that he exclaimed, "That's it!" and freed the bracelet. His hair oil had a spicy scent.

"Evelyn Herbert," she said, thrusting out her hand and tilting her face toward his with a grin. "Can you hear me all the way up there? Exactly how tall are you?"

"I'm six foot four."

"Five foot one," she said. "But I have three-inch heels, which help somewhat." She lifted a foot to show him. "I'm so small that I get lost in a crowd without them, like a Chihuahua in a cornfield. Which bit of the army are you in? Is it an especially tall brigade?" His scarlet jacket was trimmed with gold epaulettes and buttons, and worn with slim-fitting dark trousers that had a red stripe down the outer leg. She should probably have known what that signified but regimental dress held no interest for her.

"The Life Guards," he said. "And no, height is not a particular requirement because we are a cavalry regiment."

"I *love* horses," she said. "My father has a stud farm and I could ride almost before I could walk."

"You're lucky. Mine is a banker and a politician who tried his best to groom my brother and me for life in the House."

"Is your brother here today?" Eve asked. "Or is he stationed elsewhere? Mine is still in India with the Seventh Hussars." She stopped, sensing a change of mood. "Have I said something tactless?"

He shook his head, but his expression was stiff. "My brother died in 1914. At Givenchy-lès-la-Bassée." He spoke as if it were a name she should recognize.

Eve's eyes filled with tears. "Oh no, I'm so dreadfully sorry. How awful for your family. Was he an older brother?"

"Yes, there were just the two of us."

She blinked hard. "I feel a total idiot for speaking so thoughtlessly. Many families here must have suffered losses, but I blundered on regardless."

"Please don't apologize," he said, but Eve still felt clumsy. Her mother had warned her to avoid speaking about the war, saying that those who had fought did not want to talk about it, but she couldn't just drop the subject, not now.

"I suppose I feel a sense of unreality because I was stuck safely at home for four and a half years being bored to distraction. My mother ran a hospital at our house for a few months and I helped there, but I never saw the trenches, never heard a shell explode. Men just left for France and some didn't come back."

He nodded as if he understood. "I was on the Western Front and saw men dying all around me, but I still find it hard to accept that Edward won't turn up at our door one day. My parents and I went to France to find his grave last summer, in the hope that would bring some kind of acceptance. But it's just a wooden cross with his name on it, in the middle of a muddy field with thousands of wooden crosses as far as the eye can see. It's very difficult to believe he's there . . ." He shook his head as if to clear the image. "Forgive me. This is not a suitable conversation for a Christmas gathering."

A dance band struck up in the next room and when Eve turned she saw a few couples traipsing onto the floor. It felt incongruous and disrespectful given their conversation.

"Tell me about your brother," she asked. "What were his interests?"

Brograve smiled with pursed lips. "Motorcars. He was passionate about them. He knew the details of every make and model. I think, had he lived, he would have worked in the automobile industry."

"I can drive," Eve couldn't resist telling him. "My father taught me. It's a wonderful feeling. But please don't mention it to my mother. She'd be horrified. Not ladylike, don't you know."

He seemed impressed. "You must be rather a daring sort."

Eve considered. "I don't particularly know what 'sort' I am yet. I led such a sheltered childhood that I feel as if I am only just starting to live, and finding out who I am along the way. Whereas you—you've been to war. You've lived through the worst thing imaginable. Losing a brother must be like losing a part of yourself."

Brograve was about to answer when Eve's mother suddenly appeared and interrupted them. "*There* you are, Evelyn. I've been looking everywhere. There is someone you simply must meet." She tugged on Eve's elbow.

"Might I finish my conversation first, Mama?" she asked. It felt rude to abandon Brograve at such a sensitive moment.

"I'm afraid he's just leaving. My apologies, Lieutenant, but I must drag her away." She smiled politely, but with steel in her gaze.

Eve held out her gloved hand to Brograve, and he bowed his head as he took it. "Pleasure to meet you," she said.

"Likewise."

As they walked through to the ballroom, Almina hissed to Eve: "I know him and he won't do. His father is a Liberal and his mother is American." Both, in her view, were unforgivable.

"L–long . . . time . . . till . . . we . . . m-m-m . . ." Eve struggled over the word *married* and Brograve leaped in to explain to Katie.

"There were dozens of other men who were crazy about Eve, some of them much richer and more deserving than me, so I never thought I stood a chance." He looked at her fondly.

Eve rolled her eyes. That wasn't the real story and

Brograve knew it, but she was too tired to say more. Everything was an effort: thinking of the words she wanted to say, shaping her lips into each syllable, shifting her tongue, which felt too big and heavy for her mouth, then finding the air in her throat to push the sounds out in the right order. All the muscle strength had gone.

She lay back on her pillows. A quick nap, then she would try more talking later.

"You're doing so well," Katie said. "I can tell how hard you're working. Keep it up and you'll be chatting away in no time."

Damn right I will, Eve thought before she drifted into sleep.

Chapter Five

London, July 1972

Brograve rested his elbow on the edge of the bed and laid his head on his hand as he watched Eve sleep. Thinking back to the girl he'd met in Cairo at Christmas 1919 made him melancholy. She'd been so effervescent, those amber eyes sparking, and she'd looked at him intensely, as if she wanted to know everything about him. He scarcely ever talked about Edward back then—he was a reserved person by nature, and the grief was still raw—but somehow he had found himself blurting out to her that his brother had died even though it was only their first meeting. And when her eyes filled with tears in response, he felt the early stirrings of what would gradually become love.

Almina had made it very clear she didn't consider him worthy of her daughter. Her curtness spoke for itself. He had become heir to a baronetcy on his brother's death but that obviously wasn't good enough for her precious Eve, who was the daughter of an earl.

Brograve had followed them to the doorway of the ballroom and watched Almina introduce Eve to Lord Tommy Russell, son of an earl who was at least as wealthy as her father, Lord Carnarvon. Tommy had the reputation of a hard-living, untrustworthy cad, and Brograve's stomach gave a twist as he watched him cling to Eve's hand far longer than was customary. There's no question he would fall for her, but would she for him? Brograve turned and left the party rather than wait to find out.

He looked at her now, head resting on the pillows, snoring very faintly. She would be horrified if she could see herself in a mirror. Her hair was usually immaculately set and tinted a rich mahogany shade, but now it was unruly and there was a hint of gray at the roots. Her skin was pale and dry as parchment. Perhaps he should bring her face cream next time he visited. He liked the creases at the corners of her eyes that had been earned with laughter, the faint lines scored across her brow, the deeper grooves like parentheses around her mouth. She had such a narrow nose that her reading glasses often slid down. The long neck was hardly wrinkled at all and he knew she was proud of that. She liked to wear a pearl necklace he had given her one birthday, which drew attention to her neck.

Can you feel how much I love you? he wondered. *Have I told you often enough?*

Was it luck that they chose each other? Or fate? Suddenly he could hear Eve's voice in his head: *"No, you dunderhead. It was all down to me. I chose you early on, but I couldn't get you to realize it. You were so blinkered that it took me four years to get you down the blooming aisle."* He chuckled. He had a memory of her saying that one time.

Brograve closed his eyes and drifted off. He hadn't been sleeping well at Patricia's, unused to a single bed, unused to being without Eve.

Eve dreamed that she was driving an old-fashioned car with open sides. It was a left-hand drive, like the Panhard & Levassor in which her father had taught her. He'd given her her first-ever lesson on Armistice Day, the eleventh of November 1918, as their own particular form of celebration.

She had been upstairs in the schoolroom at Highclere, with Nanny Moss, when they heard the church bells ringing in the village and knew it meant that the war had ended. It gave her a shivery feeling. She hoped Porchy would be home soon. Several estate workers had died in the fighting, including the two Harrys—Harry Ilot and Harry Garrett—teenage boys who had worked on the grounds, and used to mumble shyly if Eve addressed them. It was wonderful to think the killing was over now and life could go back to normal.

The Times that morning had said that ships would be honking their horns at eleven a.m. and huge crowds were expected to gather at Trafalgar Square, but at Highclere it felt like any other day: remote, silent, and tedious.

Eve rushed down the red staircase to her father's library, to make sure he had heard the bells. He was sitting at his Napoleon desk, the one that an ancestor had purchased from the estate of the French emperor. His hands were resting on the eagles' heads that decorated the arms of the matching chair, and the racing pages of the paper were spread in front of him.

"I heard," he said. "Thank god."

"We should do something to celebrate, Pups," Eve said. "In London people will be taking to the streets and here we are, stuck at home as if nothing's changed."

"What do you suggest?" he asked.

She shrugged. "I don't know. Perhaps drive into Newbury to see if anything's happening there?"

Pups regarded her for a moment. "I suppose fresh air is a good idea. . . . Tell you what: how do you fancy your first driving lesson?"

Eve shrieked. Never in her wildest dreams had she thought she would be allowed to drive. "Are you serious? That's too exciting for words! I can't think of anything I'd like more. Can we start now? Straightaway?"

Pups sat beside Eve in the Panhard, pointing out the gear pedals, throttle, and brakes, and positioning her hands on the steering wheel. They had to adjust the seat as far forward as it would go so her legs could reach the pedals. One of the old men who worked in the stable came out to hand-crank the engine and it juddered to life, the vibrations traveling up her arms and down through her whole body. She released the brake and the car lurched forward, like a greyhound let off the leash. Lord Carnarvon reached across to straighten the wheel, then left Eve to get the feel of it for herself.

They were on private estate roads with no traffic, but she had to be wary of grazing cows that could suddenly wander out from among the ancient cedars of Lebanon. She found that the slightest pressure on the steering wheel caused the car to veer left or right, and that she had to be very gentle with the pedals or it bounced erratically. It wasn't long before she was cornering, gliding, and braking with confidence. It felt natural, as if the car were an extension of her body. She adored the wind in her face, the sensation of speed, and the feeling of being in control.

"I love driving!" she yelled over the rumble of the engine, and her father grinned.

"I rather thought you would. But whatever you do, don't tell your mother. Let's keep it our little secret, eh?"

It was the dichotomy of her teenage years: her father offering her freedom while her mother tried to rein her in and teach her the rules of "polite society." Each wanted a different daughter, and while she struggled to please both, it was her father's vision that appealed the most.

Almina's main goal as a parent was to turn her tomboyish, horse-loving daughter into a young lady worthy of a great match. When they traveled to Paris to purchase Eve's coming-out wardrobe, it was their first trip alone together. Eve would have liked to wander around taking in the sights but instead they spent most of their time in fashion-house ateliers. It was a serious business. Everything from the length of her neck to the circumference of her ankles was measured by the elegant ladies who bustled around them. Her mother chatted knowledgeably about the Empire waistline, the flounced and draped skirts, and the above-the-ankle hem, while Eve flitted in and out of curtained cubicles, trying on gowns of taffeta and satin, crêpe de chine and Chantilly lace, along with soft kid shoes with high heels and jeweled decorations. The ladies told her she would have to return daily for fittings until each garment was like a second skin. She felt exhilarated and terribly grown-up, but at the same time there was a twinge of loss for the carefree childhood she had spent in cream serge smocks, with comfortable lace-up boots that were perfect for running around.

Over dinner at the Paris Ritz, Almina suggested, almost offhand, that she should pick Eve's husband for her.

"Girls your age have no common sense when it comes to men: a few fancy compliments and you're all a-flutter. But it is the most important decision of your life, and will affect everything that comes after: the home you are able to provide for your children, your social standing, and thus your happiness."

Eve was horrified. "What about love, Mama? What about passion? Goodness, would you have me marry someone I don't have anything in common with, so we will struggle to make conversation over the breakfast table?"

"Conversation over breakfast is not the most challenging aspect of a marriage by any means." Almina scrutinized her daughter. "And I can't imagine you ever being lost for subjects to talk about. But of course your feelings will be taken into account—so long as you recognize that I am a better judge of what will work long-term."

Eve knew her parents' marriage had been arranged. Porchy had told her. The family's not-so-secret skeleton in the closet was that their mother was the illegitimate daughter of Alfred de Rothschild, a stern Victorian gent with a bushy walrus moustache who Eve had previously been told was her mother's godfather. She looked at him with new respect once she heard he'd had an affair with her grandmother. At least there must be passion in his soul.

"It was common knowledge," Porchy said. "They didn't try to hide it. Mama's name, Almina, is a combination of their names—Alfred and Mina. It was a huge scandal at the time, and it meant Mama would have struggled to get a husband if Alfred hadn't offered a vast dowry of hundreds of thousands. And

Pups was forced to accept because Highclere needed the money."

"Will you have to marry a girl with money?" Eve asked him.

Porchy made a crude gesture, miming the exaggerated shape of a woman's figure. "Maybe money will be the secondary consideration," he sniggered.

In Eve's opinion, her parents' marriage wasn't an enticing example of matrimony. They spent much of the year apart—her mother in London, her father at Highclere—and when they were together, she frequently heard raised voices behind closed doors. Her mother liked city life: parties and fashion, and running her private hospital. Her father liked the countryside—horses and shooting, motorcars and photography—and he loathed parties. Two more different people was hard to imagine.

Eve was in her early teens when she made up her mind about the type of man she wanted to marry. Handsome, of course, and cultured, so he was a sparkling conversationalist. He would have to love travel, because she planned to travel widely, and he would have to be willing to let her be a lady archaeologist. That was essential.

She opened her eyes and saw Brograve asleep on

the hospital bed beside her. Thank god she'd married him and not Tommy Russell, the man her mother had selected for her. Tommy had become a drunk, or so she heard. Bad luck for his wife. What was her name again? She couldn't for the life of her remember. . . .

A nurse popped her head around the door, and Eve raised a finger to her lips to shush her. Her husband looked as though he needed the sleep.

Chapter Six

London, August 1972

Three weeks after arriving unconscious in an ambulance, Eve confounded her doctors by being ready for discharge from hospital. She couldn't walk and her right hand was still weak, but her speech had come on by leaps and bounds. As they wheeled her out to the hospital van that would transfer her to a convalescent home, she pleaded with the nurse to stop for a moment and let her feel the breeze on her skin.

"Thash wunnerful!" she slurred, closing her eyes and breathing in. It was an overcast day but the air still smelled of summer. To her it was heaven after the stuffy room she'd been stuck in, with a window that wouldn't open and the persistent smells of disinfectant, rubber, and overcooked food. She felt a rush of happiness.

Brograve had booked her a garden room at the Pine Trees convalescent home, and the first thing she saw when she was wheeled in were French windows opening onto a delightful little terrace. She had her own en suite, a television, two armchairs, and a table, so she would be able to get out of bed and sit with her visitors. Every morning she would have speech therapy and an intensive physiotherapy session but, aside from that, friends could drop by anytime they liked.

"It's p-p-erfect," she told him.

Once the nurses left her to settle in, Brograve produced a bottle of medium-dry sherry from his briefcase, along with two crystal glasses brought from home, wrapped in an old tea towel.

"I bet you've been missing this," he said. "Fancy a tipple?"

"How . . . did . . . you . . . know?" She sighed.

The sherry was delicious: fruity, full-bodied, and complex, by far the nicest taste she'd had in her mouth for ages.

"I'll hide the bottle in your wardrobe," he said. "We can have a sherry before your dinner every evening."

"Don tell the nurshes," she slurred. "I might get f-frone out."

After she ate her dinner—a meal that was a huge leap up the gastronomic scale from hospital food—they watched a television program together: *Dad's Army,* a comedy about some bumbling home guards during the war. Brograve pulled an armchair to her bedside and held her hand, the good hand, playing with her fingers idly.

And then, when the program finished, he said, "Time to go, I suppose. You need your beauty sleep."

That was the moment that killed her every time. He kissed her goodbye and turned for the door, his shoulders drooping. Before he was out of sight he turned and tried to give a cheery wave but she could see in his face that he was upset, and knew he could see it in hers too.

Brograve felt as if he was smothered in a cloak of sadness, and it only lifted slightly during the hours he was with Eve. He knew from her previous strokes that most progress was made in the early weeks, and after that it tended to stall. Last time and the time before, she had been walking within a week or so, but this time she couldn't seem to take her weight in her legs, even when supported by a walker. Her speech was still slurred as if she were drunk, and her memory gaps concerned him. She was adept at covering up when she didn't remember something, but he knew her well enough to spot the momentary hesitation, the blank look that flashed across her eyes.

The hospital doctors had discharged her because there was nothing more they could do. As far as they were concerned, she was a seventy-one-year-old woman and if she never walked again, that was a shame but not the end of the world. They didn't realize how desperately Brograve needed her home. He'd moved back to their London flat but it was dark and echoey. He couldn't see the point in opening the curtains in the morning because he'd only have to close them again when he got home from visiting Eve. Despite the best efforts of Mrs. Jarrold, it smelled of neglect.

The morning after she was installed at Pine Trees, another letter arrived for Eve from Dr. Ana Mansour, the Egyptian archaeologist. In it, she said she had telephoned the new owners of the Framfield house and been given the London address.

"Perhaps you didn't receive my last letter?" she wrote. "I am most anxious to speak to you about your memories of the opening of Tutankhamun's tomb. Might we set a date for me to visit? I'm sure you will understand the importance of making the historical record as accurate as it can possibly be."

Brograve wondered whether to mention it to Eve. Maybe setting a date to meet Dr. Mansour in, say, a month's time would give her a goal to work toward. But he wasn't sure if she even remembered the discovery of the tomb. Perhaps he should take some photographs and newspaper cuttings to nudge her before replying to the letter. Then again, he hated to upset her by asking something she didn't know and he couldn't imagine what Dr. Mansour wanted from her. That phrase about "anomalies" came back to him. What was she getting at?

He wavered for a moment, then put the letter on a pile by the kettle.

The telephone rang, and he recognized the cheery tones of Eve's best friend, Maude.

"How is she enjoying Pine Trees?" she asked. "I'm simply *dying* to see her. When can I visit?"

"She's . . ." He hesitated, trying to think of a tactful way of saying it. "She's not fully herself yet. Don't get your hopes up."

"I'll be fine," she said firmly, and he knew that of all Eve's friends, Maude was the steadiest, the least prone to overreaction. She was also discreet.

"Alright. Would you like to go this afternoon? Around two? I'll leave you to chat together in peace and delay my visit till three."

"Thanks, Bro. I want to see you too, of course. I miss you both *terribly*."

When he hung up, Brograve felt pleased that Eve

would have someone new to chat to. She'd enjoy that. But it gave him another hour to fill till he saw her, and the morning stretched ahead like a vast cavern.

One of the great joys of Pine Trees was that a nurse bathed Eve and dressed her in her own clothes every morning. It felt wonderful after weeks stuck in a nightdress. Brograve had brought some elasticized-waist skirts and button-up blouses that were easy to slip on, as well as her favorite pearl necklace, and it made her feel a lot more human.

She was sitting in an armchair by the window, trying to squeeze a physio ball in her right hand, when there was a knock on the door and a familiar face peeked in.

"Yoohoo!" a voice called. "Guess who?"

Eve looked up, startled. "My goodnesh, how . . . kine . . . you . . . come."

The woman had short silver hair and she wore an eccentric combination of colors—olive green, magenta, and orange—that somehow worked. Eve knew this person, knew her well, but the name escaped her. Hopefully it would spring to mind soon.

The visitor hurried over to hug her. "You look wonderful, Eve darling. Good as new."

"Can't . . . walk," Eve replied. "Soon . . . I . . . ope."

The visitor sat down and took Eve's left hand in

hers. "You are an inspiration to us all. The way you fight back is incredible. I'm proud to be your friend."

Tears came to Eve's eyes. She kept getting emotional over the littlest of things. "How's . . . you . . . famly?" she asked, to distract attention from herself.

The woman began chatting about her children, her husband, Cuthbert, and then a friend of theirs called Lois, who had recently come to visit from the country.

Suddenly a phrase came to Eve and she struggled to pronounce it: "Un-ho-lee . . . quad-rum-v . . . v . . . vir-ate."

Maude laughed. "Goodness, I had completely forgotten we used to call ourselves that, way back in the nineteen twenties. The four of us had a blast, didn't we? All those wild parties, and then—equally important— the forensic analysis of the parties the next day. Do you remember we used to give men marks out of five? You gave Brograve low marks. How wrong could you be?" She chuckled.

"You . . . like . . . his fren . . ." Eve had a clear memory of this woman falling for a friend of Brograve's, someone who had been in the war with him. And then the name came to her in a flash. This was Maude. Maude Richardson. Of course. Her best friend in the world. The one who had coined the term *unholy quadrumvirate* in the first place.

Chapter Seven

London, May 1920

Queen Charlotte's Ball was Eve's first formal dance as a debutante. There were oodles of rules to remember and strict etiquette to follow, and she felt as though there was a swarm of bees in her tummy when she arrived and contemplated the crowded room.

She had only come out the week before, at Buckingham Palace. The whole uninspiring event consisted of one queue after another. First of all, her car crawled in a line waiting to get into the Palace forecourt. Hundreds of girls queued up the steps inside, all wearing the obligatory ankle-length white evening dress with a long train, and ostrich feathers secured in half-veils.

"We look like brides-in-waiting," she remarked to the girl next to her. "I suppose that's what we are."

Next they queued to have their formal photographs taken, posing on a gilt-backed sofa. And then there was another queue in the antechamber before they were led into the throne room to curtsey to Queen Mary.

Eve repeated the instructions in her head, nerves knotting: *step, step, deep curtsey, reverse without turning your back on Her Majesty.* Afterward, she was grateful to have gotten through it without being sick on the Queen's pearl-encrusted shoes.

At Queen Charlotte's Ball, once again dozens of girls dressed in white had to line up and parade into the ballroom. Eve felt self-conscious because the ones in front and behind her were several inches taller, making her look like a child dressed as a grown-up who had wandered in by mistake.

After the parade, she was handed a dance card. She stared in dismay at the blank spaces alongside the twenty dances of the evening. It looked as though she would be sitting them out, because the men huddled on the opposite side of the room were not paying her the slightest bit of attention.

"You look as though you need to borrow my brother," a voice remarked over her shoulder, and Eve turned to see a girl with short dark hair and a glint in her eyes that signaled amusement at their predicament. Straightaway Eve knew she wanted to be her friend.

"Oh, yes please!" She extended her gloved hand. "I'm Evelyn Herbert."

"Maude Richardson. Stay there and I'll fetch him."

Maude dashed off and returned only moments later dragging a thin lad with a toothy smile. "This is Charlie. Charlie—fill in three of her dances, won't you? And ask your friends too."

"Won't you take the first dance?" Eve begged, handing over her card. "I'm terribly nervous and want to get it out of the way so I can start to enjoy myself."

The card was signed, the orchestra struck up a foxtrot, and they took to the floor. Charlie wasn't a proficient dancer—Eve would have a bruised toe the following morning—but he was chatty and natural and she enjoyed herself.

As the dance finished, a girl with sandy blond curls and pretty doll-like features approached and asked, "May I poach him? Maude said it was alright."

"Of course," Eve agreed. "He's all yours."

Charlie was good-natured about it: "I don't mind being passed on like a used book. Maude tells me that's what little brothers are for."

"Emily Bramwell," the girl called by way of introduction, before swinging him onto the dance floor. It rather looked as if she was leading, but Charlie gamely did his best to keep step.

Maude joined Eve, followed by a girl with wide green eyes, auburn hair, and perfectly shaped eyebrows. "This is Lois Sturt," she explained, "and she has a cousin James who has promised to dance with all of us. Give me your card and I'll get him to sign."

Eve handed it over and Maude dashed off. "She's terribly efficient," Eve commented to Lois. "I should have been sitting out the entire evening without her."

"Goodness, I'm sure you wouldn't, not with your looks," Lois said.

"I was about to say the same about you," Eve replied. "I love the way you've done your eyebrows. I saw it in a magazine and didn't dare try in case I made a fearful mess, but it's very fetching."

"Come for tea and I'll show you how it's done," Lois promised. "We need to keep in touch."

At the end of the evening—which Eve found exhausting and exhilarating in equal measure—Lois presented her "at home" card to Maude, Emily, and Eve, and invited them for tea at four o'clock on Friday.

Eve was beside herself with excitement. She had always longed for female friends. None of the men she had danced with had made much of an impression, but she already knew she was going to *adore* these girls.

Two days later, her mother's chauffeur took Eve to Lois's family home in South Kensington, where tea was set out in a formal drawing room decorated in shades of rose pink and gold.

"We've survived our first ball," Maude said, helping herself to a scone. "But this Season could prove tricky, given the ratio of about four girls to each eligible man. We need to stick together and pool our resources."

"Is your mother putting pressure on you to find a husband?" Eve asked. "Mine has said she will consider me an abject failure if I'm not engaged by Christmas. Frankly, I intend to put off the dreaded decision for as long as I can."

"My mother wants me to marry the son of some family friends," Lois said. "We've known each other since we were children and I like him a lot, but I'm not sure I feel about him the way one should about a husband."

"Try kissing him," Maude advised. "That's the crucial test. You'll either feel 'it' or you won't."

Eve wondered if Maude had experience of this test. What must it be like to kiss a man? Wouldn't his moustache prickle against your lip?

"My mother died when I was a baby," Emily said. "And my aunt doesn't have the first clue about the Season. I'm relying on you girls to advise me on etiquette, dress codes, the whole kit and caboodle."

"We will," said Maude. "Although it seems the dress codes our mothers swear by are changing. Hems are creeping ever higher and gloves are no longer the be-all and end-all of civilized life."

They talked about the new fashions—coat dresses were said to be au courant but it was hard to think when you might wear them. Lois lent Eve a magazine that described how to pluck the eyebrows into inverted V shapes that made the eyes look much bigger, and Eve announced she would try as soon as she got home.

"If I'm wearing a low-brimmed hat next time you see me, you'll know why!" she said. "The style makes you look intriguing, Lois, but I may just appear startled."

It wasn't all fashion and frivolity. Their conversations roamed through the topics of the day: the Spanish flu, which had caused mass panic the previous year but now seemed to have tailed off; the Paris Peace Conference setting terms for the war's end; and Sherlock Holmes author Arthur Conan Doyle's new book, *The Vital Message*, in which he claimed that human beings were on the verge of discovering an entirely new way of understanding life and death.

"Sir Arthur is a friend of my father's," Emily said.

"He told us he has absolutely no doubt that he communicates with his son Kingsley, who died in 1918 at the Somme, as well as his brother Innes, who passed last year. He thinks God has sent us new revelations about the afterlife at precisely this moment to comfort those who lost loved ones in the war."

"My mother's a believer," said Lois. "She's forever attending séances."

"My father too," Eve admitted. "He has a Romany woman called Sirenia who holds séances at Highclere. I've been to a couple but I have to admit I'm skeptical." She described to them a night when she watched Sirenia surreptitiously tug on a string to make a vase of flowers topple over. And she had seen her stuff gauze into her mouth, then regurgitate it, pretending it was ectoplasm. "But my father is utterly convinced he's communicating with his late mother, so it would be cruel to contradict him."

They agreed there were charlatans in every trade, and it seemed especially far-fetched that so many self-proclaimed "clairvoyants" were appearing out of the woodwork.

"We are clearly heathens," Maude announced. "And there are four of us. So I christen us the 'Unholy Quadrumvirate.' Such will be our name forever after."

"Can you be a heathen and still talk about christening?" Emily quibbled. "Alright, why ever not!"

Eve felt like the luckiest girl in the world to have made such interesting friends so early in her first Season. After the isolation of her teenage years at Highclere, it felt as if she had struck gold.

One of the Pine Trees nurses brought a tray of tea for Eve and Maude, with some digestive biscuits on a plate decorated with painted bluebells. Eve was glad that Maude poured the tea because her left hand was shaky. She'd had many a spill trying to pour herself a glass of water from the jug by her bed.

As they sipped the tea, Maude told Eve about Lois's visit the previous week. She rarely came to town so they had had a lot of catching-up to do. They'd gone shopping on Bond Street and then to see a show, and they scarcely stopped talking for ten hours straight.

"How's Em-m-ly?" Eve asked. "Have you seen her r-rec-ently?"

Maude frowned, twisting her lips to one side before answering. "Emily died, Eve. Over twenty years ago. It was breast cancer, like her mother before her. You came to her funeral, at Holy Trinity Brompton. Remember?"

Eve clutched her face in shock and burst into tears.

How could Emily be dead? She could picture her as a young girl, swaying to the music of a jazz band, with her pretty blond curls and wide brown eyes. Poor Emily. The first of them to go.

Brograve bustled in at that moment, carrier bags in hand. He took in Eve's tears and glanced at Maude for an explanation.

"She'd forgotten Emily had died," Maude told him, passing Eve a hankie and patting her hand.

Brograve put his arm around her and stooped to kiss her forehead. Maybe now wasn't the time to ask her about Egypt and Tutankhamun. Loads of people died after that, and it would be cruel to remind her while she was still so fragile. Imagine how awful it would be if she mourned each one anew—like losing all your loved ones in one fell swoop.

Chapter Eight

London, October 1972

Brograve was reading his newspaper in the sitting room of their London flat when the doorbell rang, making him jump. It was one of Mrs. Jarrold's days—she came on Mondays, Wednesdays, and Fridays—and he heard her talking into the intercom. She popped her head around the door.

"Dr. Ana Mansour to see you," she announced. "She says she's written."

"Oh god!" It had been on Brograve's mind to reply to her but he couldn't think what to say. Eve was still showing signs of improvement but he didn't think she was ready to be quizzed by a stranger. "You'd better let her in," he said, folding his paper.

He heard the lift arriving on their floor and the clatter of the lattice metal doors being pushed apart. "This way, please," he heard Mrs. Jarrold say, then a woman was standing in the doorway. He leaped to his feet.

"Dr. Mansour," he said, holding out his hand.

She was attractive, with dark shoulder-length hair curled up at the ends like Jackie Kennedy's, lightly tanned skin, and black lines painted around her eyes. Brograve wasn't good at women's ages but guessed she must be somewhere around forty.

"Lord Beauchamp." Her hand was warm, with slim fingers. "I apologize for dropping in uninvited, but I leave London tomorrow and I was keen to speak to your wife." She glanced around as if hoping to see her there.

He let out a long sigh. "Please sit down." He gestured to a chair. "Can I offer you tea?"

While Mrs. Jarrold made drinks, Brograve explained about Eve's health setback, and his reluctance to overburden her while she was still piecing her memories together.

The woman was sympathetic. "I'm sorry to hear that. Strokes can be devastating. I looked after my father for years after his stroke, so I know what a strain it can be." Her expression was warm. "Is her memory affected, or is the damage mostly physical?"

Brograve thought back to Maude's telephone call the evening after her visit. She had a theory that while Eve could remember details of events from the 1920s as if they happened yesterday, her memories seemed to fade in the 1930s and become vaguer the closer you got to the present day.

Brograve suspected Maude was right. The same thing had happened with previous strokes but most of the memories returned gradually as she recovered. The question was how you went about filling in the missing pieces. He couldn't bear to see her upset, as she'd been when she heard about Emily.

"Her memory is patchy so I haven't pushed too hard," Brograve said. "Her speech is much improved, but I haven't asked her about Egypt yet. That might be difficult for her."

Ana Mansour paused, weighing her words. "I remember from my father's case that our first instinct is to wrap them in cotton wool. It's entirely understandable. But the scientific advice is that stimulation helps the brain to regain function more effectively than rest. I know your wife used to be an extremely knowledgeable Egyptologist."

Brograve nodded. "Indeed, she was."

Ana's eyes fixed on his. "If that knowledge is still there, accessing it could help to refresh her neural connections and give her confidence." She paused. "I might be able to help."

"How do you mean?" He was wary.

She smiled. "What if you took me to meet her and introduced me as a visiting Egyptologist? I could say that I was keen to shake her hand, given her important role in the history of archaeology. She needn't feel under any pressure that way."

In normal circumstances Eve would enjoy that, Brograve thought. She'd be thrilled. But was it fair to bring visitors she didn't know when she wasn't at her best? Maude had arranged for a hairdresser to visit Pine Trees every week to wash and set her hair, but Eve couldn't apply makeup with her weak right hand, so she wasn't as well turned out as she had always been before. Besides, her speech was still slurred and unclear.

Ana Mansour continued: "I have a few photographs with me of Egyptian artifacts we're working on. I could show them to her—not to challenge her, just to see if there is a reaction. If there is none, at least we have tried. But if she recognizes them, it might help to open up her brain." She cupped her hands and mimed the opening of a flower. "'Use it or lose it.' Isn't that what they say?"

Brograve pondered that. What she said had a certain logic, especially since Egypt had a special place in Eve's heart. She had taken the photo of the Nile from his album. Was that a sign? But then he remembered about the mention of "anomalies" in Ana's letter.

"You know Eve wasn't present when the tomb contents were catalogued, don't you?" he asked. "That was nothing to do with her."

"I'm aware of that," she replied. "I'm interested in her memories of the opening of the tomb. Perhaps our discussion will trigger something that could be useful, but if not"—she spread her hands—"it will be an honor to meet her all the same."

He supposed that sounded fine. "When were you thinking of visiting?" he asked. "She has good days and not so good days." Sometimes she was exhausted after her morning physio sessions, with a woman whom Eve jokingly called "Sally the Sadist," and she always seemed more forgetful if she hadn't slept well.

"I am flying to Cairo tomorrow. We could either go this afternoon, or it will have to wait till my next visit. It's entirely up to you."

Suddenly Brograve felt impatient to see if this strategy would work. "Let's go today," he said. "Let's give it a try."

Brograve normally walked to Pine Trees but when he suggested it, Ana glanced down at her boots, which were elevated on platforms at least two inches high.

Why did women wear such treacherous footwear? If she went over on her ankle, it would probably break. "I'll get the car," he said, and went to fetch it from the car park beneath their apartment block.

When they got to Pine Trees, he greeted the receptionist and waited for her to buzz open the door that admitted visitors to the rooms, all the while worrying that he might be making a mistake and this could upset Eve badly.

She was sitting in her chair by the window, and she beamed at him as he walked in. "I've been w-watching a shquirrel," she said, then noticed the woman behind him. "Oh, hello! A v-visitor!"

Brograve made the introductions and invited Ana to sit in the other armchair while he perched on the bed, wondering how to bring up the reason Dr. Mansour was there. He didn't have to, though, because Eve took over the conversation.

"You're from C-cairo?" she asked. "M-my husband and I m-met there. It's a w-wonderful city but I expect m-much changed from my d-day."

Since the stroke, Brograve had never heard her speak so clearly. She must be making a special effort for their visitor.

"You were there during the transition from British rule, were you not?" Ana asked.

"Yes." Stumbling over her words, Eve described an incident from her first visit, when an Egyptian man ran up to the donkey cart they were traveling in. He was wearing a headdress and his eyes and teeth sparkled white against his dark skin. She had smiled, thinking he was being friendly, but instead he shouted, "English out! Death to imperialists!" and spat at her. Eve smiled. "I was r-rather shaken, as you c-can imagine."

Ana nodded. "The British called it a protectorate rather than part of the empire, but their hold on the army and police force made it paternalistic."

"I always th-thought you should have your f-freedom," Eve said. "They said it was German spies who had encouraged n-nationalism during the w-war, but Egyptians h-have such an ex-tra-or-din-ary . . ." She paused, unable to think of the word.

"History?" Brograve suggested. He was stunned at how articulate she was today. Where on earth had this come from?

"C-culture," she continued. "Unique culture. They should c-clearly have b-been s-self-governing." She took a deep breath and he could tell the stammer was driving her crazy. "T-tell me, what is your area of s-study?"

"The Valley of the Kings." Ana smiled. "I under-stand you know it well. I did my first digs there as a young archaeology student, and now I am engaged in a research project. Perhaps you would like to see pictures of some artifacts we're studying?"

"I-I'd l-love to," Eve said, leaning forward.

Brograve braced himself. This might be the moment when she got distressed if she couldn't recognize anything. In that case, he would intervene and change the subject.

Ana opened a slim document wallet she'd been carrying and passed across a sheet with a colored image printed on it. Brograve couldn't see what it was.

Eve smiled as she took it. "Amun-Re," she said. "I know this f-fellow. He was in my father's collection at H-Highclere. He was found at K-Karnak and H-Howard thought he was Eighteenth Dynasty."

Ana nodded. "We've been reassessing and think it might be later than Howard Carter believed, perhaps after the reign of Ramesses XI." She pulled out another sheet of paper and passed it across.

"Opening of the m-mouth ceremony," Eve said straightaway, squinting at it. Brograve rose to fetch her glasses from the bedside table and helped her to put them on. "So the d-deceased can eat and drink in the afterlife."

"Do you recognize where the image comes from?" Ana asked, then, without waiting for an answer, she passed another picture. "Perhaps this will help."

There was a simple cartouche drawn in black on the white sheet of paper.

Eve gave a broad smile. "That's the b-bird for 'u' and the ankh for 'l-life.' Tu-t-ankh-amun." She pointed to each of the elements in the hieroglyphic. "The opening of the m-mouth p-picture was on the wall of the b-burial chamber. I could never forget that. It was one of the d-defining experiences of my life."

Brograve turned so neither of the women could see the tears prickling his eyes. All these months, it seemed he'd been underestimating her. Everything was in there, locked away. Ana had been right; all she needed was stimulation.

Chapter Nine

London, October 1972

E ve was overjoyed to have passed the tests Ana Mansour set for her—they were clearly tests. Of course she remembered Tutankhamun! How could she not? She watched Ana slide the images back into her document wallet, thinking that she seemed very fashionably dressed for her profession. Archaeologists tended to wear practical clothing, both in the field and elsewhere.

She thought of Howard Carter's baggy three-piece suits with patched elbows, the shirts with fraying cuffs, and the sloppily tied bow ties. By contrast, Ana was wearing a slim skirt and matching belted jacket, and some gold earrings and a necklace with a twisted knot design. There was no wedding band on her ring finger, no rings at all. Eve didn't know if Egyptian women wore wedding rings; she'd never been close enough to check. The ones she used to see in the streets of Cairo wore veils that covered their hair and faces, leaving only the eyes visible.

She guessed Dr. Mansour's age to be late thirties, maybe forty. Surely she must be married. She had beautiful eyes, a golden leonine color, and her skin was unlined, her figure trim. Some man was bound to have snapped her up.

"Did your interest in archaeology come from your father?" she asked Eve.

"Pups and Howard C-Carter both indulged my c-curiosity from a young age. And H-Howard taught me how to dig during my first w-winter in the Valley. I loved it from the s-start."

Recently, Katie had been teaching Eve to slow her speech right down. "You attack a sentence like my Labrador attacks her food bowl," she commented. "But if you space the words out more, your tongue will have time to find the vowels and consonants."

It was true, Eve thought. She'd always had a lot to say, but if she tried to speak fast now she tripped, helter-skelter, over the words.

"My father was a dealer in antiquities, based in Cairo," Ana said. "He and Howard Carter sometimes did business together."

"Really?" Eve was excited. "Perhaps he knew my f-father too?"

"He would have loved to meet your father and shake his hand," Ana said. "He was only a young man when Tutankhamun's tomb was discovered, just starting out in his trade, and he said it made him very proud to be Egyptian. The fact that it happened only months after Egyptian independence was particularly special—as if we were at last demonstrating to the world the greatness of our heritage."

"I think the world has always r-recognized the genius of the Ancient Egyptian c-craftsmen," Eve said. "I was bewitched by their work at an early age. D-did your f-father visit the tomb?"

"Not till much later. It was hard for ordinary Egyptians to get access. My father told me many stories of digs in the years before the discovery, though, and I know you were present at some of them. Weren't you there, for example, when Mr. Carter found the Merneptah embalming oil jugs?"

"It was me who found them!" Eve exclaimed. "My one true c-claim to fame!" She was overjoyed that Ana had asked about them. They weren't important in the scheme of things, but they'd always been special for her.

It was the twenty-sixth of February, 1921. Eve and her father were digging with Howard in the Valley. She'd been working on an area near the eastern edge of the concession when she spotted something pale glinting in the sand. She felt with her gloved fingers and was thrilled to realize it was an object, about six inches long, and it seemed more substantial than an animal bone.

"Howard!" she called, with a ripple of excitement, and he was at her side in an instant.

"You've got something there," he said. "Well done, Eve." He eased it out slowly, using a delicate-pointed probe, and brushed it down with a fine brush. It appeared to be some sort of vessel, long and narrow, with the remains of a handle on one side.

"Alabaster," Howard said. "Probably used for embalming oil."

"Might I hold it?" Eve asked, and was breathless when he passed it to her.

"No other hands have touched it for thousands of years," he said, grinning. "How do you feel?"

"Like a proper archaeologist." She cradled the vessel as carefully as she would a newborn baby. "This is the best feeling in the world."

———

"**It was** the first significant find in that concession," she told Ana. "There were th-thirteen jars altogether, engraved with the name Merneptah and that of his father, Ramesses II."

Brograve was staring at her with astonishment and she realized she had barely stumbled in the whole sentence. Ana Mansour was smiling encouragement.

"Howard had ex-excavated Merneptah's tomb in . . ." Eve forgot the date. Damn. Katie said just to keep talking if she couldn't remember a word. "KV8," she said. "That was the tomb number. He said it had some rather lovely w-wall paintings, though much faded."

"But it was you who found the jars. I'll make a note of that. You should be credited in the archives!" Ana took out a notebook and turned to an unmarked page, where she scribbled something down.

"It was Pups's concession," Eve said, secretly pleased her name would appear in the records. "Tell me, have you done much fieldw-work? Where have you dug?"

Ana closed her notebook again but kept it on her lap. "I was honored to be part of the team that discovered the Lighthouse of Alexandria four years ago. That was a special moment but, as you know, no one person can claim credit for finds of that magnitude. There were several of us involved, all researching different aspects."

Eve shook her head. "In the case of T-Tutankhamun, it was definitely Howard's find. He just knew it was there. Theodore Davis, the American archaeologist, had sponsored a team that dug within six feet of it and gave up, but Howard had a plan . . ."

She paused. There was a word she couldn't think of. Howard had drawn a huge scale map of the Valley, charting the areas of each previous excavation, including the depths to which they had dug. What had he called it? What was that word?

"He worked out there was an area beneath some old w-workers' huts that hadn't been explored." Suddenly it came to her. "A gridblock plan!"

"And he suspected Tutankhamun's tomb might be there?" Ana asked.

Eve nodded. "He was quietly confident it was in that v-vicinity."

Howard spread the roll of paper across his table, weighting down the edges with books. It was like an engineer's drawing, in pencil on squared paper, the writing tiny and barely legible. Eve and Pups stood to watch as he explained.

"In 1905, a faience cup engraved with the name

Tutankhamun was found here," Howard told them, pointing to the spot, his fingernail encrusted with what looked like centuries' worth of dirt. "As you'll remember, Eve, he was an Eighteenth Dynasty king who ruled for nine or ten years. Theodore Davis assumed that KV54, which he and I had excavated in 1907, was the tomb of Tutankhamun, because it contained embalming oil jars with his name on them. In 1913, he decided there were no other tombs to be found in the Valley, and that's why he retired when he did, but I disagree. I think Tutankhamun's real tomb might be somewhere in this vicinity, as yet undiscovered." He circled an area of the plan with his fingertip.

"Crikey!" Eve felt a shiver down her arms. "And you plan to find it?"

"Your father and I are negotiating the terms of the concession with the Egyptian government—but of course it is moving slowly, as everything does out here. Negotiations for the country's independence somewhat muddy the waters because the nationalists are insisting that all artifacts found on Egyptian soil should belong to the state. But they know they need our expertise and investment, so I'm sure we will prevail."

"An undiscovered tomb in the Valley!" Eve exclaimed. "Isn't that the holy grail of every archaeologist in the world? You'll be famous, Howard Carter. Gosh, I really hope I'm there when you find it."

"I think I knew that day in Castle Carter," she told Ana. "Howard inspired c-confidence. Pups always had total faith in him, although he s-struggled to find the money." She paused. "Everyone th-thought he was wealthy because he was an earl, but places like Highclere take an enormous amount of . . ." Damn. The word had gone.

"Upkeep," Brograve helped her, and she smiled her thanks.

"While you've been talking, I've had an idea," Ana said. "You clearly have remarkable recall of events that happened fifty years ago. Would you be prepared to talk me through the whole story if I return with a tape recorder? It would make an invaluable record for the Egyptian Museum in Cairo. Perhaps they could make it available for visitors to listen to."

Eve turned to look at Brograve, feeling unsure. "I'd probably forget bits."

"I could ask you questions as we go along, and bring some images to prompt you. . . . Although you've proved to me that you are a good raconteur and need little prompting." She smiled warmly.

Eve liked the idea, but what if her speech let her down? She would sound like an idiot if she forgot words and stammered all the way through.

"We can edit out any hesitation and pauses," Ana said, reading her mind. "You'd be amazed what they can do with tapes."

Eve's second worry was that there were things her father, Howard, and she had agreed never to tell about the discovery of the tomb. What if she forgot and blurted them out by accident? She would have to stay on her guard.

"Take your time to decide," Ana said. "I'm flying to Cairo tomorrow but I'll be in London again before Christmas and I'll get in touch to see if you want to chat. There are some questions I would very much like to ask you. It should only take a couple of hours, if that."

"I hope my speech will be better by then," Eve said. "I'm w-working hard at it."

"It sounds fine to me already," Ana replied. "I know from your husband that you are making remarkable progress." She glanced at her watch. "I mustn't intrude on your visit any longer, but I just wanted to say it's been an honor to meet you—a great honor. My father would be very envious."

She shook Eve's hand firmly, and Eve could see how genuinely pleased she was. It was nice to make someone happy.

Brograve saw her to the door, and returned a few minutes later, his eyebrows raised.

"Well," he said. "That was quite something."

"Wh-what do you think?" Eve asked, her lips stretching into a grin that she could feel was only slightly lopsided now.

"I think I haven't seen you so happy since . . . since before you were admitted to hospital."

He never called it a stroke, Eve noted. He always found some other form of words.

"I suppose it will g-give me a goal to aim at," she said, taking her time between words. "I need to be speaking per-perfectly before she comes back. I'll tell Katie to keep my nose to the g-grindstone."

She was like a new woman, Brograve thought. Egypt had always had that effect on her. She became luminous, lit from within. Back when he first knew her, she used to be animated when she told him about digging in the Valley of the Kings with her father and Howard. It set her head and shoulders above other girls in that era, who in his experience had rather limited conversation about new gowns and romance novels.

Then a shadow crossed his brow. It was all very well talking about the discovery of the tomb, but he very much hoped Ana Mansour didn't want to talk about what happened *after*. That wouldn't be a good idea in Eve's current state of health. Not good at all.

Chapter Ten

London, November 1972

Katie came to visit Eve at Pine Trees twice a week, invariably late and breathless. She never wore a bra and her breasts jiggled as she spoke, nipples poking through her cheesecloth blouse like fabric-covered buttons. Eve forced herself to look at her face and not let her gaze drift lower.

Katie started their sessions with some warm-up exercises, in which Eve pronounced letters in exaggerated fashion, then went on to some tongue twisters: "Peter Piper picked a peck of pickled peppers" or "She sells seashells on the seashore."

"Can you think of some words that start with 'w'?" Katie asked one morning. It was a letter Eve still had difficulty with.

"W-wit, wealth, allure," Eve replied, quick as a flash.

"I know 'allure' doesn't have a 'w,' but those were the q-q . . ." She'd forgotten the word. ". . . the things my girlfriends and I looked for in a man. We gave them marks out of five." And then the word came to her. "Qualities."

"Wit, wealth, and allure? Sounds very wise. I always go for the good-looking ones and get my heart broken." Katie gave a rueful smile.

"I didn't follow those rules, though," Eve said. "Brograve wasn't wealthy when I married him, and he wasn't flashy the way some other men were. My mother w-wanted me to marry a man called Tommy Russell. She bent over backward to bring us together. She had no idea how w-wild he was."

"That sounds like an interesting story," Katie said. "Wild in what way?"

"Booze, fast cars, loose w-women . . . Tommy was fun to party with, but I knew instinctively he wasn't the kind you should ever think of m-marrying. My m-mother knew nothing about love, I'm afraid."

In March 1920, three months after meeting Eve at the Residency Christmas party in Cairo, Tommy Russell returned to London, and he came to call on her and her mother at the family home in Berkeley Square. On being shown into the drawing room, he bowed and presented Eve with a book of Rupert Brooke poems bound in blue leather.

"My sister tells me he's very popular. I believe dying is essential for a poet's career these days."

"'There is a corner of some foreign field that is forever England,'" Eve recited. "Thank you. Are you a fan of poetry?"

"Not really. I don't have much time for reading," he replied.

Eve's mother interrupted. "It must be hard for you to hold a book, is it not?" She turned to Eve. "Lord Russell's shoulder was shattered by a bullet in the trenches. He was treated at my hospital, which is how we met."

Now that she looked more closely Eve could see that his right shoulder hung lower than the left. "I'm sorry. How ghastly for you!"

He shook his head. "Not ghastly at all. It was what we soldiers call a 'blighty'—a wound severe enough to get me sent home, because I couldn't hold a gun anymore. I probably wouldn't be here otherwise because my unit was decimated in battle after I left. Luck of the draw, I guess."

Eve wanted to ask how he got shot, what it felt like, and whether he had lost many friends—but they were all questions she knew her mother would disapprove of. "I hope you enjoyed the care in my mother's hospital," she said instead. "When it was based at Highclere, it was my job to wheel around a trolley at four o'clock and serve glasses of stout or sherry to the men. They were terribly grateful."

"They must have thought they were hallucinating." He grinned. "A vision of beauty bearing alcoholic beverages is every man's dream as he crouches in the mud of Flanders."

Beautiful, was she? The compliment slipped out so easily that Eve guessed it wasn't the first time he'd called a girl beautiful and that it wouldn't be the last. His conversation was entertaining, though. He had spent a year in America, with some cousins, and disagreed with Lady Carnarvon's view of Americans as crass and ill-educated. She was forced to admit her opinion was based on a month's stay in Boston so her experience was less extensive than his. It wasn't like her mother to back down, Eve thought—in fact it was almost unprecedented. She clearly wanted to impress Tommy.

He stayed just half an hour, but before he left he asked if Eve would like to come to a party a friend of his was throwing that evening.

"I'm afraid I'm not available to chaperone," Lady Carnarvon said. "I must be at the hospital this evening as a patient is coming around from surgery."

"It's not a formal party," Tommy insisted. "Mostly young people. Perhaps you would like to bring some friends?" he asked Eve. "Then you could look out for each other. And I will, of *course*, vouch for your safety."

He caught eyes with her and his look had clear mischief in it.

"I'd love to," she replied.

Eve invited the other three members of the unholy quadrumvirate to Tommy's friend's party and they arrived together at the address in Hanover Square. Straightaway Eve realized it was a world of difference from the formality of Queen Charlotte's Ball: there were no dance cards, no buffet supper, and no string quartet; instead a jazz band was playing loudly in a corner of the drawing room, the trumpet notes strident. Each of the reception rooms that led off a central hall was crowded with young people smoking cigarettes in long holders—even the women—and drinking what were clearly alcoholic drinks from coupe glasses.

"Mama would have a conniption fit if she could see this," Eve whispered to Maude. "Yet it is her doing because she is so desperate to match me with Lord Russell."

Eve felt out of place, like the gauche country girl she

was, and sensed Maude and Lois did too, because they huddled together. Only Emily seemed at ease. When a Black woman, with a dress falling off one shoulder, began to sing with the band—"Sweetheart, won't you please come home"—Emily swayed to the tune, mouthing the words, and Eve wondered how she knew them.

"There you are!" Tommy cried, appearing through a doorway. He motioned to a passing footman to fetch them drinks and Eve made the introductions. "My god, your friends are visions of loveliness," he whispered, his lips brushing her ear. "My pals will simply *gobble* them up."

She took a sip of the drink she was handed and shuddered. She'd tried her mother's gin before, so knew what alcohol was like, but this was fiercer. It tasted poisonous, the way she imagined Lysol would taste.

Tommy introduced them to a group of his male friends, then led Eve to a quiet alcove in the hallway where they would be able to hear each other speak. But what should she talk to a gentleman about? The war was taboo, according to her mother, and Tommy had said he didn't read books.

"You weren't at Queen Charlotte's Ball, were you?" she asked.

He pulled a face. "I loathe the pretentiousness of the formal events of the Season. This kind of thing is more up my street. But I imagine you will be dragged around them all. Your mother is formidable."

Eve laughed. "I suppose you saw her in action at the hospital. She's tiny—two inches shorter than me—but utterly indomitable."

He described an argument he had overheard when her mother had wiped the floor with a doctor who disagreed with her diagnosis of a patient, and he mimicked her: "I know liver disease when I see it and if *you* don't, I suggest you go straight back to medical school."

"Imagine what it's like having her as a mother!" Eve exclaimed. "Almina doesn't ever admit to being in the wrong. She's constitutionally incapable."

Tommy leaned in close so she could see the pinkish veins in his eyes, and his dark blond lashes. His breath was so alcoholic that she imagined it would catch fire, like a dragon's, were he to strike a match.

"I can't think about her," he said. "I'm too busy trying to decide how I can impress her daughter. What would it take?"

Eve had never been asked a question like that before so it took some thought. "Do you drive?" she asked, in a moment of inspiration, and squealed with delight when he told her he had one of the new Model T Fords, just released that year.

"I read Ford has begun making cars that are not hand-cranked but operated with a starter motor," she said. It had been in her father's newspaper.

"You do know a lot for a girl," he said. "Yes, she has a starter motor and runs like a dream. Do you fancy a turn? She's parked outside."

"Gosh, I'd love to," Eve said. "I adore driving."

"Come on then. What are we waiting for?"

He took her arm and pulled her toward the door, staggering over the edge of a rug and bumping into a metal lamp stand that teetered back and forward before deciding to stay upright. Eve had never seen a drunk man before, at least not to her knowledge, but she could tell Tommy wasn't in a fit state to drive.

"Perhaps I'll just have a peek inside," she said. "I don't want to abandon my friends."

The car was shiny and black, with a roof and proper glass windows at the sides, so it would be cozy and dry in the rain—unlike her father's Panhard, which just had a canvas top. Eve squeezed into the front passenger seat, which was upholstered in soft gray leather. The controls looked very modern, with three floor pedals, which Tommy told her were clutch, reverse, and brake, and a small round button set alongside them.

"How do you start it?" she asked.

"Easy," he said. "Pull up the ignition lever, then the throttle, pull the choke handle, then step on the starter motor."

He demonstrated each move for her, then pressed his foot against the button in the floor. Even though her hands weren't on the wheel, she felt that familiar sensation of pent-up energy as the engine rumbled to life. The car leaped forward, hitting the bumper of a car parked in front.

"You idiot! Turn it off!" she cried, and when he didn't obey immediately, she stood and stretched her foot across his leg to push down on the brake pedal. He closed the throttle and the engine fell silent.

"Thank you for the demonstration," she said, pulling her leg back, embarrassed it had pressed against his in such an intimate way. "It's a beautiful machine."

"And sho are you," he slurred, looping an arm around her shoulders and yanking her toward him.

Eve had never found herself in a situation like this before. All thoughts of politeness flew out the window. "What are you doing? Stop it!" He leaned forward to kiss her and she pushed him away but still his lips landed on her cheek, at the corner of her mouth. "You clearly don't know how to behave yourself so I'm going back inside." She reached for the door handle, but Tommy wouldn't let go.

"Don't be a spoilsport," he said, and his palm cupped her left breast, a thumb stroking the nipple.

"Lord Russell!" she cried, smacking his hand away. "I think you have mistaken me for another kind of girl entirely. Get off!"

He slumped back with a shrug, muttering to himself. Eve swung the door open, jumped out of the car, and ran inside to hunt for her friends. Did all men do that to girls they barely knew? She spotted Maude first and grabbed her arm.

"You'll never guess what Tommy just did!"

"Does he have a case of wandering hands?" Maude asked. "I had a feeling he might be that sort."

Eve laughed, although she was still feeling flustered. "You've got it in a nutshell."

A letter of apology arrived the following day. Tommy wrote that his behavior was the result of an old army friend forcing him to drink whisky over a long luncheon, and he hoped it would not permanently taint Eve's opinion. She forgave him, and the unholy quadrumvirate went to many more of Tommy's friends' parties. But Tommy's chance of marrying Eve never got out of the starting gate, not after that.

Chapter Eleven

"It may not seem much to your generation but for a man to touch your breast in 1920 was a very shocking thing." Eve laughed at Katie's expression. "I knew I could never trust him again, although we stayed friends for some time afterward."

"Had you already met Brograve by then?" Katie asked.

"I had, but I didn't see him often. He was a recluse. He wouldn't come to parties or balls unless his mother positively forced him. The only time I bumped into him was at horse races. He was always at Royal Ascot in June. He gave me a tip on a horse once—Diadem." She smiled, pleased to have remembered the name. Tiny details like that were particular triumphs. "We both won a few pounds that day."

———

Eve had gone to Ascot with the unholy quadrumvirate but as soon as she spotted Brograve, she left them and dashed over to say hello. It was the first time she had seen him since their Christmas meeting in Cairo.

"Evelyn Herbert," she reminded him, holding out her hand.

"Of course, how could I forget?" He took her hand and gave a little bow.

"I'm very glad to meet you again, especially since our social circles don't seem to overlap in London."

"That's because I don't have a social circle," Brograve admitted. "I'm not a fan of balls and soirees."

Eve was surprised. "How do you ever meet anyone?"

He gave a self-deprecating smile: "I try to avoid it whenever possible. Present company excepted, of course."

"Goodness, we're total opposites in that case," Eve said. "Making new friends is my absolute favorite pastime." Her voice was drowned out as last bets were called for the King's Stand Stakes. She smiled. "I know you're a cavalry man so I hope you can give me a tip for this race that will make my fortune."

"My money's on Diadem," he said. "Odds of seven to three."

"Perfect! Might I ask you to place the same bet for me?" She opened her purse and handed him a guinea. "I'll wait here to watch the race with you. You've picked rather a good spot."

As soon as the starting pistol fired, Eve began cheering for Diadem, and Brograve laughed out loud at her exuberance. He was handsome when he laughed, Eve thought. Shame it didn't happen more often.

Diadem took the lead in the last furlong and when she crossed the line first, Eve couldn't contain herself. "We won!" she yelled, her voice hoarse from shouting. She beamed at Brograve. "From now on you must be my racing tipster. We'll make a killing together."

"I have to confess that the tip came from a friend," he said. "But I'm glad to be of use."

Maude, Emily, and Lois found them afterward and Eve made the introductions, feeling a prickle of annoyance when Emily monopolized his attention, even placing her hand on his arm.

Brograve went to fetch Eve's winnings and brought them to her, but she didn't get another chance to talk to him alone for the rest of the afternoon. Just before leaving, he issued an invitation and she fancied he was looking at her.

"I don't suppose you ladies are interested in polo, are you?" he asked, blushing slightly.

Eve smiled encouragement. "We could be, so long as you don't mind our complete and utter ignorance of the rules."

"I'm playing at the Hurlingham Club next Saturday. At two o'clock. You'd be welcome to come, but please don't worry if you have other plans."

"That sounds fun," Emily cried. "Count me in."

"And me," Maude said.

"I'm afraid I shall have to check with my mother," Eve said. "She rather rules the social calendar. But if it's at all possible, I should love to watch you play a . . . a chukka, isn't it?"

He laughed. "Well done. We'll make an aficionado of you yet."

He tipped his hat to the four of them, then Eve watched his back as he left.

"I think Eve has a pash for someone," Maude told the others in a teasing tone.

"No, it's not that," Eve said. "He lost his brother and I like trying to cheer him up."

The girls exchanged knowing looks. "It's a slippery slope," Maude remarked.

When asked, Lady Carnarvon point-blank refused to allow Eve to attend the polo. "It's not appropriate," she said. "I'm too busy so who would chaperone you?"

"Oh goodness, Mama, the other girls would be there. And no one bothers about chaperones these days. It's a positively Victorian concept."

"Maybe others don't, but we do." Her mother had made up her mind and would not be swayed. Eve knew it was because she had mentioned Brograve's name, and that it would have been another matter entirely if Tommy Russell were playing.

Maude and Emily went to the Hurlingham Club and reported back that Brograve was a talented player, and had been a convivial host after the match finished.

"We gave him your apologies," Emily said, and Eve felt a curious twinge of jealousy.

"You said it was ages after meeting Brograve before you got married?" Katie asked. "Why was that?"

"It was!" Eve shook her head at the memory. "After the w-war, the men who'd fought were all damaged by their experiences, but it came out in different ways. You got the ones like Tommy Russell, who turned to the demon drink, or to drugs, or who took crazy risks as if, having survived the trenches, they were somehow invincible. One man we knew died after diving off Waterloo Bridge, convinced he'd be able to swim the Thames." She pursed her lips. "Then there were others, like Brograve, who closed in on themselves and were almost impossible to reach." She laughed. "It's just as well I relished a challenge."

"Do you realize you're not stammering?" Katie said. "I'm sorry to say it, but I'm not sure you need me anymore. Perhaps I need you, though. Can I bring my boyfriends around for you to vet? You can pick out the good guys and tell me which to ditch."

Eve laughed. "I would adore that. I'll prepare a q-questionnaire. Come anytime."

When Brograve arrived that afternoon, Eve looked at him with fresh eyes, remembering the man he had been in his early twenties. His face had had a guarded quality, and his brown eyes were masked and difficult to read. She'd never known where she stood with him right up until they got engaged.

Now she noticed he'd lost weight. His cheeks were gaunt, and there was a grayish tint to his skin. If she knew him, on the nights Mrs. Jarrold didn't leave supper he would just have cheese and crackers washed down with a whisky. She would telephone Maude and ask her to invite him around for a proper evening meal.

I have to get home, she thought. *He needs me.*

Christmas was only four weeks away. Come what may, she was determined to be back by then.

Chapter Twelve

London, November 1972

Brograve was worried when Eve started talking about coming home. He missed her terribly; life was miserable without her smile first thing in the morning, her bright chatter around the house forming the accompaniment to his day. After he had retired from work, he often found himself following her from room to room as she tidied and rearranged drawers and chatted on the telephone, happy simply to be in her presence.

But he was concerned that she hadn't accepted the extent of her disabilities. She was still a long way from being able to walk, and couldn't even lift herself out of the wheelchair, because her right hand was too weak to be of much use. That meant she couldn't go to the toilet on her own. She couldn't get in and out of bed or dress herself without help. She certainly couldn't have a bath. Was he capable of helping her with those things?

Most alarming of all, she still had the occasional choking fit. It happened without warning. A morsel of food went down the wrong way and suddenly she was coughing and clutching her throat, panic in her expression. When it happened at Pine Trees, she pressed her personal alarm and a nurse rushed in to help. Brograve had watched the way they did it, clutching her around the waist from behind, fist clenched, making her bend forward, then pulling backward in sudden jerky movements until the food dislodged. But what if they were at home alone and he couldn't manage it? She might choke to death in front of him.

It was Patricia who came up with the solution. She found an agency that hired out private nurses who could either live in or visit for a few hours a day. Eve and Brograve had a large guest room where a nurse could live comfortably, so that might be a solution. He rang the agency, inquired about fees, and asked them to send details of suitable candidates.

Next he spoke to the matron at Pine Trees and asked if she thought it was a workable idea. Between them, they agreed that Sally the Sadist could visit Eve at home to continue her physiotherapy. If it didn't work out, she could always come back to Pine Trees, although there was no guarantee her garden room would still be available.

And finally Brograve told Eve what he had been planning.

She covered her face with her hands and for a moment he thought she was upset. Maybe she wasn't ready to leave, or felt she should have been consulted. When she looked up, her eyes were glistening with tears.

"That is the best Christmas present I've had in my entire life," she cried. "I like this room but I can't wait to be back with you, in my own home. Oh, that's p-perfect."

A nurse called Sionead was hired, a flame-haired, green-eyed Irish girl, and the date of December fourteenth was set for the move. Brograve had a lot of arrangements to make. He asked Mrs. Jarrold to prepare Eve's favorite lemon sole for her first dinner at home, taking special care to remove the bones. He bought bunches of chrysanthemums in shades of mauve and gold for every room. He bought a huge box of Terry's chocolates with mixed centers, a bottle of Gordon's gin, and another of Eve's favorite Tio Pepe sherry. Everything had to be perfect.

The day before the move was to take place, Ana Mansour telephoned him.

"I'm back in London and wondered how Lady

Beauchamp is getting along? Did she decide about when I might come to interview her?"

"I'm afraid it's not convenient this week," Brograve told her, and explained about the move. "She'll need time to settle in and get used to being at home. We're taking each day as it comes."

"Of course," Ana said. "I understand. It's just that I brought her a gift from Egypt. I wonder if I might drop it off today so it's there to greet her when she gets back? I won't get in your way."

Brograve hesitated. "Certainly. If I'm not here, my housekeeper will be able to accept your gift. That's very kind."

When he got back from Pine Trees that evening— the last evening he would spend on his own, he hoped— there was an arrangement of exotic pink flowers in a vase on the kitchen table along with a card addressed to Eve. It wasn't sealed so he opened it.

"Dear Lady Beauchamp," the card read. "You will remember the beauty of lotus flowers from your time in Egypt. I hope you enjoy these ones, which have survived a plane journey perched on my lap. Wishing you and your husband a wonderful Christmas. Yours sincerely, Ana."

He felt very touched that she would go to such an effort. It was thoughtful, and made him warm to her.

Eve was as excited about going home as a kid going to the seaside. She hoped their gardener had kept on top of all the chores without her prompting him. She loved her mature garden, a whole acre of it with different areas: the alpine rockery, the apple orchard, the vegetable patch, the rose garden she had planted herself, the wild strawberries, the rhubarb, the lupines. Their gardener took care of the heavy jobs but she did a lot herself: pottering around with her pruning shears to keep on top of the dead-heading, dealing with greenfly and slugs, watering the beds on summer evenings. Of course, hardly anything would be flowering in December. Sometimes a late rose or two survived the early frost, a defiant blast of color against the backdrop of crisp brown leaves that littered the lawn.

When the day arrived, she was wheeled out to a special van in which her wheelchair could be secured. Brograve sat in the front seat and kept swiveling around to smile encouragement. She gazed out the window, watching a father cycling along with a small child perched in a basket in front of him, then a tramp sitting on the pavement who caught her eye while they were stopped at a traffic light.

The drive should have taken more than an hour, but

in less than five minutes, the driver pulled up and Brograve got out of the van.

"Where are we?" Eve asked when the driver began unfastening the straps that held her chair. She turned to Brograve. "I thought we were going to Framfield."

His face fell. "Pipsqueak, we sold the Framfield house last year, don't you remember? It got too big for us, and it was too far away from everything. We live here now. It's a lovely apartment. You'll remember when you see it."

She was quiet as they wheeled her into a lift with metal gates, which took them up to the third floor. She missed her Framfield house as if it were a lover; she had an ache in her heart for it. Why had they left?

It was a shock to find she didn't recognize the apartment at all. She remembered the furniture—her favorite armchair, the bureau that had been her mother's; she recognized paintings and ornaments, but the layout was unfamiliar. She wheeled herself down the hallway, checking inside rooms and cupboards, getting her bearings. It was spacious at least, and there was a lot of natural light. The windows overlooked a park along one side. Regent's Park? Hyde Park? She didn't like to ask. Oh, but she yearned for her Framfield garden. She mustn't let Brograve see how disappointed she was.

"I have a new trick to show you," she told him, wheeling herself into the sitting room. "Come and watch." She'd been practicing with Sally the Sadist, saving it up to surprise him. She drew up alongside an armchair, put the wheelchair's brake on, and lifted herself slowly, leaning her weight on her left hand, before stepping sideways and lowering herself into the chair.

Brograve cheered. "Hooray! I didn't know you could do that! You *are* clever, Pipsqueak!"

"It seems they were wrong about old dogs and new tricks," she said, pleased with herself.

Brograve lifted the lotus flower arrangement that Ana had left and placed it on the table beside her. She stared at it for a long time, sniffing the delicate scent and examining the intricate design of the pink petals curled around yellow stamens.

"There were many lotus flower carvings in Tutankhamun's tomb," she said. "It was believed they gave strength and power. Perhaps that's why Ana brought them for me." And then she remembered something: that gold box she had taken from the tomb had a lotus flower carved on the lid. She shuddered involuntarily.

The nurse, Sionead, came into the room holding a cake with a candle burning on top, one hand cupped around the flame. "Welcome home, Lady Beauchamp," she said. "I know it's not your birthday but I thought we should celebrate all the same."

"What a pretty cake!" Eve cried. "Thank you." It had lemon icing and slices of sugared lemon on top.

"Make a wish!" Sionead urged, holding it in front of her.

Eve closed her eyes. Lots of wishes flooded her mind: to see her Framfield garden again, to get the rest of her memories back, but one was foremost. She wanted to walk by Christmas. That's what she wished for as she blew. The flame sputtered for a moment, then vanished in a puff of smoke.

Chapter Thirteen

London, December 1972

Christmas was around the corner, so Eve threw herself into the arrangements. Maude very kindly agreed to do her shopping at Harrods from a long list she'd handwritten—fifty-four gifts for friends and family, including a bottle of Rive Gauche perfume for Sionead, a new Barbour jacket for Brograve, and a box of cigars for Porchy, which would be delivered direct to Highclere. She managed to gift-wrap everything herself, sitting at the dining-room table, and she scribbled her wobbly signature on dozens of Christmas cards but left Brograve to address and stamp them and stick them in the postbox. They had a tree in the corner that Sionead festooned with the mismatching decorations they'd collected over the years, and Brograve nailed a festive holly wreath on the front door.

She invited Maude and Cuthbert for dinner on the twenty-third to thank them for all their help during her illness. Mrs. Jarrold rose to the occasion and produced a spectacular menu of coquille Saint Jacques, beef Wellington, and a bread and butter pudding. There was champagne to start, a different wine for each course, and Napoléon brandy, which always reminded Eve of the smell of Pups when she sat on his lap as a child.

Cuthbert and Brograve had served in the war together, so their friendship went back even further than Eve and Maude's: fifty-six years as opposed to their fifty-two. Brograve had retired long ago but Cuthbert was working for the British Council and had just returned from a trip to Cairo.

"Did they have Christmas decorations everywhere?" Eve asked. "I remember finding that very odd when I was in Cairo one Christmas."

"None that I noticed," Cuthbert said. "Fifteen percent of the population is Christian, but they fast in November and December and celebrate on the seventh of January."

"It's a sensitive time for Anwar Sadat in the aftermath of the Israeli war," Brograve said. "Did you encounter any problems?"

Cuthbert made a face. "It's frightfully difficult politically, but we steered well clear. We were there on a cultural mission, to reach out the hand of friendship and invite collaborations."

Maude chipped in: "Yes, and to persuade them to educate their children at British universities, while refusing to send back any of the Ancient Egyptian treasures our ancestors stole from them."

The men laughed. "That's my job in a nutshell," Cuthbert agreed.

Eve knew there was a school of thought that they should hand back antiquities to the countries they had come from during the colonial era, but it wasn't straightforward. Some of these countries didn't actually exist anymore because maps had been redrawn; others didn't have the facilities to care for antiquities properly. She would be sad to see everything returned. The British Museum was an extraordinary archive of world culture, and she loved to hear the gasps of schoolchildren seeing a mummy for the first time, or a haunting Easter Island statue, or the Rosetta Stone, which had made it possible for scholars to translate hieroglyphics. She didn't say anything though; it was too hard to get her thoughts in order.

Mrs. Jarrold called them to the dining room, where she was serving the first course. Brograve wheeled Eve through in her chair, while Maude took Cuthbert's arm to help him stand up. He was stooped from a spinal condition and Eve noticed him wincing.

"How did we all get to be so old?" Maude asked. "It seems only yesterday when Eve and I were flitting around town, our only concern being which frock to wear to that evening's party."

"That was never one of my concerns," Brograve quipped.

"You used to hate parties," Eve said, then turned to their guests. "His mother practically begged me to invite him out, but more often than not he turned me down. It's a wonder we ever got together."

"How did you know his mother back then?" Maude asked. "I can't remember. Were they friends of your family's?"

She shook her head. "Not at all. They turned up at the Winter Palace in Luxor in the winter of . . ." She hesitated and glanced at Brograve. She still had trouble remembering dates.

"February 1921," he said.

Eve continued: "I'd been digging in the Valley all day and got back to the hotel, covered in sand from head to toe, bedraggled as a street urchin. Imagine my horror when I saw Brograve standing in reception with an older couple, who I assumed were his parents. I tried to slink behind a screen, but he spotted me, called me over, and made the introductions." Eve pulled a face. "Betty was a delightful woman but I made a terrible blunder over cocktails and upset her badly."

"It wasn't your fault," Brograve murmured, and she was grateful, but all the same she knew it *had* been.

Brograve's father, Sir Edward, was formal, shaking Eve's hand briefly without smiling, but his mother was instantly friendly.

"Do please call me Betty," she said in an American accent. "I never understand English titles and how you're supposed to use them. Am I Lady Betty or Betty, Lady Beauchamp? Frankly, I just prefer Betty."

"In that case you must call me Eve. How lovely to meet you. Are you staying here long?"

Betty explained that they were on a Nile cruise and had fancied a couple of nights on dry land while they explored Luxor. "I can't wait to see Karnak and the Valley of the Kings," she said.

"I've just come from the Valley," Eve explained, gesturing at her grubby gown. "And I appear to have brought some of it back on my clothing."

At that moment they heard the sound of raised voices coming from outside. Men were shouting in

Arabic, and they sounded alarmed. Brograve hurried to the door to see what was going on.

"Probably some local dispute," Sir Edward said. "If you ladies will excuse me, I'm going up to our room to read some telegrams I've received." He bowed and told Eve it had been a pleasure to meet her, before heading for the stairs, swinging a room key.

"It's the office," Betty told Eve. "They can't leave him to vacation in peace."

"Am I right in thinking he's in politics?"

Betty nodded. "He's a member of parliament, and he's also chairman of Lloyd's of London, the insurance company. The telegrams will be from them."

Brograve returned. "There's a snake in a tree. A cobra, I think. Some men are trying to knock it down with forked sticks."

"Which tree?" Eve asked, the blood draining from her face.

"A palm tree by the staircase up from the garden."

"You mean the tree I just walked under?" Eve asked, having visions of a snake dropping onto her head, or uncoiling to strike as she passed.

"Oh my, was it there when we arrived?" Betty asked, an edge of hysteria in her voice.

"I think I should buy you ladies a drink," Brograve said. "I'm sure they won't allow any snakes indoors."

Eve was about to excuse herself, feeling too scruffy to enter the hotel's very smart salon, with its cool marble floors, white blinds, and aquarelles of ancient sites on the walls. She considered going upstairs to let Marcelle tidy her hair at least, but the lure of a drink was too powerful.

"Perhaps I'll join you for a quick freshener," she said. "I could murder a gin rickey." It was a drink she had been introduced to by Tommy Russell—gin with ice, soda, sugar, and lime.

"How do you two know each other?" Betty asked as they sat down, and Eve explained while Brograve went to the bar to place their order.

Betty admitted she had found it difficult to make friends since she had arrived in London. Everyone seemed to have their own social group and did not include outsiders. "It means I don't have many acquaintances with sons or daughters of Brograve's age who might invite him to social events," she said, then looked at Eve. "Perhaps you would be so kind as to include him in your gatherings once in a while? He hardly goes anywhere and I'd love him to make more friends."

Brograve was returning from the bar and overheard her. "Mother!" he exclaimed, his cheeks coloring.

"I'll do my best," Eve promised, smiling at him. "But I suspect I might need to hold a pistol to his head."

A waiter brought a tray with three gin rickeys served in tall glasses dripping with condensation. Eve and Betty kept up an effortless flow of conversation without Brograve uttering more than a few words. It seemed he would never get a sentence in edgeways if she didn't ask direct questions, so she turned to him.

"Are you still playing polo?" she asked. "I was sorry to miss that match at the Hurlingham. My friends said that, from the little they could understand, you seemed to be a skilled player."

He gave an embarrassed laugh. "Not at all. In fact, I've had to retire from the team as my work doesn't allow me time for sport."

"What work is that?" she asked. "Are you a career officer in the Life Guards?" She sipped her drink, brushing away a drop of condensation that landed on her skirt.

"My commission has recently come to an end," he replied, "and I am starting my own business."

"Goodness, that sounds intriguing. What kind of business?" The conversation was hard work because Brograve never volunteered information, leaving her to dig for it.

"I'm sure you will find it terribly dull, but I plan to manufacture a new kind of copper cable. It's the type required for the telephone network to be expanded, and will have many other uses, I hope."

"Well, far from finding it dull, I can tell you I will be your biggest customer," Eve told him. "I love telephones! I spend far longer on them than you can possibly imagine. How did we ever manage without them?" She shook her head, smiling at Betty. "I also remember you mentioning that your father wanted you and your brother to go into politics. Will you combine the two careers, as he has done?"

Brograve glanced at his mother, seeming uncomfortable, and Eve wondered if she'd spoken out of turn. The terrace doors opened and she turned, momentarily distracted by the thought of the snake in the garden.

"Am I misremembering?" She turned back. "You said your brother would have made a better politician than you, because he was more outgoing."

Betty made a slight choking noise and clutched the triple strand of pearls at her throat.

"I'm so sorry," Eve said, realizing too late she had strayed into difficult territory. "I shouldn't have mentioned Edward. I can be horribly tactless sometimes."

Betty's eyes filled with tears, and Brograve whipped a handkerchief from his pocket and passed it to her. She covered her face with it, shoulders heaving.

"*Please* forgive me . . ." Eve's voice tailed off in horror as Betty stood up abruptly. *What had she done?*

"I'm sorry," Betty said, her voice choked with tears. "I have to get better at this. I *must*."

Brograve half-rose from his seat, reaching out a hand, but his mother hurried through the bar toward the stairs before he could stop her.

"Please run after her," Eve begged. "Tell her I'm a complete dolt and am heartily ashamed of myself. I remember now you warned me that she couldn't bear to talk of your brother."

"Don't concern yourself. She'll be fine," he said, but he didn't sound convinced. "Perhaps she will compose herself and return to join us soon."

Eve thought how hard it must be for him to live in an environment where he had to curb his own grief because of his mother's distress. All the pressure rested on him as the son left behind. No wonder he had the air of carrying the world on his shoulders.

She decided then and there to take him under her wing. She felt drawn to this tall, reserved man. She sensed she could be good for him—if only he would relax his guard for five minutes and let her.

Chapter Fourteen

London, Spring 1921

After the discovery of the alabaster vessels of Merneptah, Eve's determination to become a lady archaeologist was stronger than ever, but back home in London, Almina had other ideas.

"Ideally you should have been engaged after your first Season," she said, regarding her daughter critically. "But to be single after your second would look as if there's something terribly wrong with you. Shall I invite Tommy Russell for dinner this week?"

Eve cringed. "Please don't, Mama. You would embarrass us both. He has his eye on many other girls apart from me and seems content to sow his wild oats."

"There are subtle ways a girl can encourage a man," Almina said, looking coy. "Perhaps he doesn't realize you are interested."

Eve snorted with laughter, wondering what methods her mother had in mind. "Believe me, Lord Russell knows exactly where he stands."

Her mother's expression clouded over. "Such a shame. He would be perfect. If you're too fussy, you'll miss the boat entirely. How about Wilfred Beningfield?"

Eve gave a mock shudder. "He's inoffensive, I grant you, but . . ." She screwed up her face, and Almina couldn't help but laugh.

"We're counting on you, Eve," she said. "Porchy's the mischief-maker in our family, but you're a good girl. You won't let me down."

Eve knew what had sparked this conversation. Porchy had fallen in love with a girl called Catherine Wendell, who was spectacularly beautiful, with strawberry blond hair and the darkest blue eyes she'd ever seen. Pups was vehemently against the match because she was virtually penniless and he'd been hoping the estate would get an injection of cash from Porchy's wife's dowry. Almina was against it because she was American, and, what's worse, it seemed her father had been an actor before his early death.

Eve liked Catherine enormously and couldn't imagine a sweeter sister-in-law, so she was doing her best to change her parents' minds. Porchy was so headstrong that she knew he would marry Catherine with or without their approval, and she feared that could cause a family rift.

Eve loved Highclere and knew that Porchy did too. They'd had an immensely privileged upbringing, but the price was high if they couldn't marry for love. Sometimes she wished she wasn't Lady Evelyn Herbert, daughter of the Earl of Carnarvon, but just plain Eve, from a normal family, who could pick any man she wanted as a husband, be he a lord or a chimney sweep.

All around her, friends were settling down. Lois had agreed to marry her childhood friend after the "kissing test" proved successful, and she was the first of the unholy quadrumvirate to walk down the aisle. Emily was engaged to a flashy friend of Tommy Russell's. She chased around town in taxis following him from one party to the next, breathless and giddy, in no mind to listen to her friends urging caution.

Maude was Eve's closest confidante in those years as they scrutinized the available men and endlessly discussed the type of marriage they wanted—and then Maude found Cuthbert, leaving Eve the last one on the shelf.

Fifty-one years later, over dinner with Maude and Cuthbert in the dining room of her London apartment,

Eve smiled to remember that they had met because of her.

"Do you ever think of all the coincidences that brought the four of us to be sitting here tonight?" she asked. "I met Brograve by chance at the Residency in Cairo; I met Maude when she saved me from social humiliation at Queen Charlotte's Ball; and, Maude, you met Cuthbert because I pressed Brograve to bring a friend to your party. Otherwise we could all have married quite different people, and where would we be now?"

"I think I deserve some of the credit," Cuthbert said. "I had a deuce of a time persuading Brograve to go to that party. He made every excuse under the sun to bow out, and finally agreed only to stop me from throttling him."

"If you and I hadn't met that night, I'm sure we would have found each other on another occasion," Maude murmured.

"But you might have been swept off your feet by another man by then, and I would have had to worship you from afar." He turned to Eve. "I had the strangest feeling when Maude greeted us at the front door. Right from the start I knew—I just *knew* I had to marry her."

Maude smiled at the memory. "By the end of that evening, I felt the same way. After all the agonizing you and I had done, Eve, when the time came it was simple."

Mrs. Jarrold brought the main course of beef Wellington and there were gasps of admiration. The pastry was golden and flaky, the beef pink and tender. Eve had hesitated over the choice of beef because it was tricky for her to cut meat. She could hold cutlery in her right hand but not firmly. She saw Brograve wondering whether to offer to cut it for her, but she was determined to manage herself. She stabbed her fork into the beef and sawed with the knife in her left hand until she had a mouthful.

"I remember chatting to you at the end of that party," Eve told Maude, "and you couldn't wipe the grin off your face."

For her, the evening had not had such a happy conclusion.

Chapter Fifteen

London, July 1921

As the friends' second Season drew toward a close, Maude's parents agreed to throw a party for the younger set at their Hampstead house. Eve decided this was a good opportunity to fulfill her promise to Betty Beauchamp to tempt Brograve into society. The invitation was sent, and a reply came two days later offering his apologies. He said he would not be able to attend, but gave no reason.

Eve resolved not to let him off the hook so easily. She asked the operator to put a call through to his family home in Putney, South London, and got Betty on the line.

"I think he's worried he won't know anyone," Betty confided. "Perhaps if he could bring a friend, that might persuade him?"

"Of course he can bring a friend!" Eve exclaimed. "I

know I speak for the hostess, who is my dearest chum. Please will you pass that message on?"

Formal balls were completely out of fashion in their set, so they had decided that Maude's party would be a "Fun and Games" one with card tables, a roulette wheel, and childish pursuits like Pin the Tail on the Donkey.

Eve was doing rather well at roulette when she looked up and noticed Brograve had arrived with an equally tall man by his side. Maude was chatting to the friend, while Brograve hung back, looking uncomfortable. Eve collected her chips and slipped them in her evening bag, then hurried over.

"You're here!" she exclaimed to Brograve. "Wonders will never cease!"

"And he's brought his friend Cuthbert Delauney," Maude told her.

Eve shook hands with them both and addressed Brograve. "Are you going to stay awhile or are you already devising excuses to escape?"

He chuckled. "Am I so transparent? I have no skill at the kind of talk people seem to make at parties. I find myself tongue-tied and thinking with longing of the book I could be reading in the garden at home."

"That's precisely why this kind of party is ideal," Eve told him. "There's no need to talk. We can just play games."

Maude was deep in conversation with Cuthbert so Eve led Brograve to a sunny parlor that had French doors leading out to the garden. "Let's see what mischief they're getting up to in here."

A lively group were huddled around a card table, laughing raucously.

"Come join us," a young man beckoned. "We're playing Answers and Commands."

"That sounds alarming." She glanced at Brograve.

"We take turns to throw the dice and if you get a six, you select a question from this hat." The young man indicated a top hat filled with folded slips of paper. "Should you refuse to answer your question, you must perform a forfeit taken from the other hat." It was a brown homburg that reminded Eve of the one Howard Carter often wore.

"Perhaps we'll observe for a while," she said, worried that Brograve might find it too intrusive. "I'd like to see what kind of forfeits you have in store before I commit myself."

"You're either in or you're out," the man said. "No half measures. Are you a lion or a mouse?"

Brograve and Eve caught eyes. He was waiting for her to decide. "Shall we give it five minutes?" she suggested, and he agreed.

The dice was passed around, each person taking a

turn. Eve was relieved to get a four but immediately afterward, Brograve threw a six.

"On the first throw. Just my luck!"

"Take a question!" the young man ordered, and two of the others chanted, "Ques-*tion!* Ques-*tion!*"

Brograve dipped his hand into the top hat and pulled out a question. Eve watched him and could have sworn he blanched as he read it.

"Read it out!" the young man ordered.

"'What is the thing you are most ashamed of?'" He took a deep breath. "I am going to plead the Fifth Amendment, as the Americans say, and surrender myself to your forfeit instead."

He dipped into the homburg, pulled one out, and read it. "It seems I am to sing the national anthem in a style of my choosing," he declared to the company, with a sheepish grin.

Eve remembered his singing in Cairo, and worried that everyone would laugh at his appallingly flat voice. Was he aware he was tone deaf? He hadn't appeared to be.

Brograve stood, placed his right hand on his heart, and began to sing, in the style of an opera singer: "God Save Our Gracious King . . ." all on the same baritone note. He gesticulated dramatically with his left arm but his singing was completely tuneless.

The guests around the table looked at each other in bemusement, then one girl laughed, followed by another, and soon the whole table was in stitches. Eve couldn't help joining them. It seemed Brograve was able to laugh at himself, thank goodness.

He paused at the end of the first verse, glanced around his audience, then launched into the second with even more gusto: "O Lord our God arise, scatter our enemies . . ." More partygoers wandered in and gathered in a circle around them, enjoying the spectacle. When he finished there was a spontaneous burst of applause.

Brograve bowed, then sat down. Eve caught eyes with him and grinned. It was wonderful to watch him enjoying himself. She hadn't seen that often enough.

The game continued. One young woman was challenged to do a handstand and she complied bravely, skirts falling over her head to show peach silk bloomers. Another was ordered to recite the alphabet backward while eating a bunch of grapes. The forfeits were getting increasingly outlandish, so Eve decided she would answer the question if she threw a six unless it was completely impossible to do so.

When her turn came, she opened a slip of paper from the top hat. It read: "Tell everyone around the table the initials of the one who is your secret pash."

What should she do? If she said she didn't have a pash, they might force her to do a forfeit.

"AE," she said, adopting a mysterious tone.

Everyone around the table began speculating. Algernon Edwardes? Andrew Eglinton? Eve shook her head at every suggestion.

Only Brograve guessed the truth. He leaned close to her ear and whispered, "Ancient Egypt, I presume?"

She laughed. "How very clever of you! Shall we leave the table now before they finagle any more secrets from us? I think we've been decent enough sports."

It was one of those soft July evenings when it stayed light well beyond ten o'clock. They wandered into the garden and picked up glasses of champagne from a table covered in white damask. At the far end of the lawn, a wooden door was flung open leading onto the famous Heath, at a point halfway up Parliament Hill.

"I've never been to the top," Eve said. "Would you like to go and look at the view over London? It's said to be spectacular."

They strolled up slowly, glasses in hand. Birds were squawking like children who have been allowed to stay up past their bedtime and are expending a last burst of energy before sleep. There was a summery scent of greenness and a faint buzz of insects.

At the brow of the hill, they paused. The view was

hazy and Eve peered out, trying to detect landmarks.

"That's St. Paul's." Brograve pointed to the distinctive dome. "And I think that's St. Bride's just right of it. The one shaped like a wedding cake."

"I'm surprised we can see green hills to the south of the city," Eve said. "It makes London feel small, yet it takes forever to cross when you're driving."

"Would you like to sit awhile?" Brograve asked. He whipped off his jacket and laid it on the grass, then held her glass while she sat. Impressively, he lowered himself to sit beside her without spilling either of the drinks he held in each hand, and they sat regarding the view. His shoulder was touching hers, and she was intensely aware of it but didn't move away.

"How is your mother?" she asked, remembering the awkwardness last time they met.

"Better," he replied. "It will be seven years this December since Edward died. I suppose the grief will never go away but she is learning to live her life despite it."

Eve shivered. "I don't think I would ever recover if my brother, Porchy, died. Even though he's the family troublemaker!" She told him about Porchy's unpopular choice of bride, then an idea came to her. "You should meet him! We're having a shooting party at Highclere on the twelfth of August and he'll be there. Why not join us?"

"I don't shoot," Brograve said, gazing at the horizon. "I did quite enough of that in the war."

"I don't either," Eve told him. "It's not obligatory. But do come. Stay a few days. I'd love you to see Highclere."

He hesitated for so long she sensed he was searching for a polite excuse to refuse. Perhaps he thought she was making advances to him and he wasn't interested. She felt simultaneously disappointed and humiliated.

"I'm afraid I have work commitments that won't let me escape," he said at last. "But thank you for the invitation."

Eve asked him to tell her more about his magical copper cables and they sat awhile longer, but the atmosphere had changed. He had shrunk back from their earlier intimacy and raised the shutters and she had no idea why.

The light was fading and the sky had turned the color of tobacco before they headed back to the party. Maude grabbed Eve's arm and drew her into a corner where Emily and Lois were chatting.

"Well?" she asked, her eyes flickering toward Brograve. "Did he try to make love to you?"

"Not even remotely," Eve replied, trying to keep the hurt from her voice.

"But you wanted him to?"

Eve furrowed her brow. "I think I did."

Maude embraced her. "I predicted it a year ago at Ascot," she said, with irritating smugness. "You *are* slow on the uptake, Eve Herbert."

"Do you think he might be one of them—you know, like Oscar Wilde?" Emily asked. She was just back from her honeymoon, glowing with contentment and superior in her knowledge of the joys of the matrimonial bed.

"I don't think it's that," Eve said, but she didn't know for sure. It was totally beyond the scope of her life experience. Perhaps he was simply content to be single, like Howard Carter.

And yet, she sensed he liked her. She knew his eyes followed her when she walked across a room, and that he listened when she was speaking. It was a mystery, but short of throwing herself into his arms—*could she? no, she wasn't brave enough*—Eve had no idea how to solve it.

Chapter Sixteen

London, Christmas 1972

E ve and Brograve went to Patricia's for Christmas Day. Her sons, Simon and Edward, were home from university for the holidays, and looking taller than ever—like beanstalks, Eve said. Patricia's husband, Michael, was a generous host, handing them glasses of champagne as soon as they took their coats off. They had made space for Eve's wheelchair, but she transferred herself to an armchair, hating the visible reminder of her disability.

They exchanged presents, leaving the sitting-room floor strewn with crumpled balls of shiny paper, and they all watched the Queen's speech on television at three o'clock. It had been Elizabeth II's silver wedding that year and she thanked the public for the good wishes they had sent, before referring to the suffering in Northern Ireland. Eve glanced at Michael, knowing he had served there with the army, but he didn't comment. He seldom spoke about his work.

Patricia was dashing in and out of the kitchen. Eve heaved herself up from her chair, grabbed the back of the sofa, and shuffled to the kitchen door, using the sofa for support as she inched her way along cautiously. She was proud of this new achievement, which she'd been practicing at home.

"It was my goal to be walking by Christmas," she said, "and I think this counts, don't you?"

"You're amazing, Mum!" Patricia exclaimed, rushing over to hug her. "I'm so proud of you."

At four on the dot, Patricia ushered them into the dining room. A bronzed turkey sat at one end of the table, waiting for Michael to carve, and the boys helped to bring in myriad dishes of vegetables and sauces. Patricia flopped into her chair with a sigh.

"My work is done," she said. "Someone hand me a drink."

Brograve filled her glass from a decanter of wine. "A toast to the hostess with the mostest," he cried, raising his glass, and they all joined him.

After eating, they went back to the sitting room and Michael came to perch by Eve, holding out a Sunday supplement.

"Before I forget," he said, "there's an article in here

I thought might interest you." He turned to the page and handed it over. "It's about an archaeological dig in Saqqara in Egypt, and it mentions your boy Tutankhamun. I saved it for you."

The first thing Eve saw was the picture of the gold funeral mask with the striped headdress and uraeus. "Thank you," she said. "I wonder what they've dug up this time?"

The boys wanted to watch *The Morecambe & Wise Show* Christmas special on television, so the set was switched on to warm up. Eve dug her glasses from her handbag and began to read the article while Simon fiddled with the aerial to get a sharper picture.

On one of her trips to Egypt Eve had visited Saqqara, site of some ancient step pyramids dating back to the Third and Fourth Dynasties. This new discovery was the tomb of Maya, an Eighteenth Dynasty bureaucrat who had been in charge of royal burials in Tutankhamun's day.

Eve remembered Howard Carter talking about him. He'd described him as a powerful figure with his finger in many pies. He was treasurer of the kingdom, responsible for raising tax revenues, he was fan bearer to the king, meaning he had the king's ear, and he organized the festival of Amun every year, as well as making the arrangements for burials in the Valley of the Kings.

"He would have known Tutankhamun well," Howard had said. "And probably had a lot of influence over him since he was so young when he took the throne—perhaps just sixteen or seventeen."

The article said that Maya's tomb had first been discovered by a German archaeologist in 1845 but then it was lost again, covered up in a Saharan sandstorm, and it had only been rediscovered this year. Among the tomb contents were detailed papyrus records Maya had kept of his work, indicating that he was a man of great precision.

Eve wondered if his writings would answer the question she and Howard had often pondered: Was Tutankhamun murdered? His skeleton had shown signs of a head injury, but three thousand years after his death it was impossible to tell if it had been caused in an accident during the burial or if it was a deliberate killing.

She read that Maya had fancied himself a necromancer: his writings seemingly spoke of magic in Tutankhamun's burial chamber that would bring "discord and unnatural death" to tomb robbers. That rang a bell. She remembered something about that. Maybe Howard had mentioned it? Threats to deter any who might consider plundering the treasure were common in Ancient Egyptian tombs, but had there been something specific?

According to Maya's record, some early robbers had been caught in his lifetime, after betraying each other. The penalty for tomb robbery in that era was either beheading or drowning in the Nile. Maya decreed drowning on this occasion, and the bodies of the six men were tied to rocks and toppled into the river. Eve shivered. There was something about the story that made her uneasy, and she wondered if she used to know more than she was remembering.

The author of the article couldn't resist mentioning, in a side panel, all the "unnatural" deaths that had been associated with Tutankhamun's tomb in the modern era, but Eve had long since learned not to read such things. Journalists loved the "curse" story, but she found it distasteful the way they used genuine human tragedies as popular entertainment.

"Are you alright?" Brograve asked. "You should watch this. Eric is playing Prince Albert while Ernie is Queen Victoria."

Eve put down the magazine and watched the pair clowning around. Her grandsons were chortling. Patricia looked pink-cheeked and glowing as she sipped a glass of ruby dessert wine, and Michael reached across to squeeze her hand. She had chosen her husband well, just as Eve had. She hoped the boys would find similar happiness in their marriages. Their grandmother, Almina, hadn't, and neither had Porchy. It wasn't a given.

Eve drifted off into a micro-sleep, in which she

was still conscious of the sound of the television in the background, but she was in Cairo again, and there was a clamor in the streets. Was it nationalist protests? The River Nile was wide and muddy as it flowed under the Qasr El Nil Bridge and men were shouting in Arabic, their voices strident and full of alarm.

Christmas 1921 was spent at Highclere, then, in early January, Eve and Pups sailed for Egypt. He had some business to attend to in Cairo before he proceeded to Luxor, and Eve made use of the free time to go sightseeing. It was on that trip that she visited the step pyramids at Saqqara, as well as the monumental pyramids of Giza, which she rode around on a camel's back. The following day she decided to explore the Egyptian Museum.

The concierge at her hotel hailed a carriage driver to take her the short distance to the imposing building in Ismailia Square. She bought a guidebook at the entrance kiosk, politely rejecting the services of the official guides. Consulting the map, she headed for the Eighteenth Dynasty collection, because in her opinion that was the epitome of Ancient Egyptian artistry.

Straightaway she came upon a glorious painted chair, which had belonged to Sitamun, a daughter of Amenhotep III, with dancing scenes in plaster and gilt relief, and armrests finished with the heads of birds, just like Pups' Napoleon chair. She gasped at the limestone statues of Amenhotep with his wife and three daughters, which stood over twenty feet high. There were several lifelike heads of Nefertiti, wife of Akhenaten, who was rumored to have been a great beauty; she had pronounced cheekbones, almond eyes, a slender nose, and full lips. The wealth of the collection left Eve overwhelmed. She could take in only a small part of it; several return visits would be needed to do it justice.

When she left, carriage drivers jostled for her custom, but the day was not oppressively hot and she decided to walk back to the hotel. It gave her a sense of daring to be walking on her own in a foreign city. She was slightly apprehensive because of the pro-independence protests, but the English quarter was said to be safe. She wondered what Egyptian men made of her as she strolled by, wearing only a picture hat tied with a ribbon rather than the full veil that their women wore.

"Lady Herbert!" a voice called, and she turned, startled to see Brograve hurrying across the road toward her.

"How extraordinary!" she greeted him. "Have you followed me all the way from England?"

He laughed. "I've only followed you for the last few seconds. But I'd be happy to walk with you, if you like. Where are you heading?"

"Pups and I are staying at the Intercontinental," she said. "But don't let me waylay you if you have other plans." He looked very smart in a slim-fitting gray suit and a jaunty boater.

"I'm going in that direction as it happens," he said. "I've been in a meeting and now I'm joining my parents for lunch at Shepheard's Hotel. But tomorrow I return to London. My business is demanding all my time."

Eve felt a stab of disappointment. It was odd to be in his presence again when she had been thinking about him so much since Maude's party.

"Is all well in the world of copper cables?" she asked. Out of the corner of her eye she noticed an Egyptian child, a curly-haired boy who looked around three or four years old, wandering into the road. She turned to look for a parent in pursuit but couldn't see one. At least the traffic was quiet.

"It's fine, thanks," he said, and she saw that he had also noticed the child, then he looked the other way. They could hear some kind of commotion. At first Eve couldn't work out what was going on and she asked Brograve, but instead of answering, he suddenly set off at a run. In an instant she understood: a donkey had become untethered and was careering down the road at speed, the cart behind it swinging wildly from side to side. Her heart began pounding. Brograve was running straight into its path.

A few Egyptian men leaped out and tried to catch the donkey's reins but it swerved out of reach and they had to jump back to avoid being struck by the cart. Others stood well clear. The donkey was terrified, Eve guessed. All the yelling was causing it to panic.

Brograve was standing in the middle of the road now, between the child and the donkey, and she could tell he was calculating whether he would be able to catch the reins and bring it to a stop.

"No, don't!" she yelled. It was too dangerous.

At the last moment he seemed to realize this and instead he grabbed the child. The donkey was almost upon them when he dived out of its way in an athletic leap, landing on his shoulder and rolling onto his back, while holding the child in the air above him.

The donkey cart hurtled past and Eve dashed across the road toward them, at the same time as an Egyptian man who appeared to be the child's father. The boy was completely unhurt but started crying from shock as Brograve sat up and handed him over.

"*Shukran, shukran*," the man kept repeating, bowing and holding the child tightly. Eve knew it meant "thank you." Brograve replied with a few words of Arabic. She hadn't known he spoke the language.

"Are you hurt?" she asked when father and son left.

He was still sitting on the curb and he put his hands over his face and didn't reply.

"Did you land on your shoulder?" she asked. "I hope it won't be bruised."

Still he didn't reply. She picked up his hat, which had fallen off, and laid it on the curb beside him, then she crouched and placed her hand on his shoulder.

"That was the bravest thing I've ever seen," she said. "You saved that boy's life."

His shoulders were shaking and he made a strangled noise in his throat.

"Don't call me brave," he muttered. "Don't ever call me brave."

The words were muffled and his voice was strange. It was only then Eve realized he was crying.

At first she couldn't decide what to do. He would be embarrassed for her to see him like this. Should she leave him alone, walk back to the hotel and give him time to compose himself? Or should she offer words of comfort? Instead, she sat on the curb beside him and stayed silent.

There was a mosque opposite. Men were starting to file in for the lunchtime prayers so she knew it must be almost one. Pups would be expecting her—they were having lunch with Uncle Mervyn—but she couldn't leave Brograve while he was struggling to control himself.

After several minutes, he wiped his eyes and sat up straight, placing a hand on the ground for support. She put her own hand on top of his. He didn't try to push it off and they sat like that in silence for a while longer.

"I'm sorry," he said at last, but she hushed him.

"Please don't apologize. You have nothing to be sorry for."

"I can't talk about it," he said. "I just can't." He cleared his throat and stood up, reaching out his hand to help her to her feet. "Please don't ask me to."

She nodded. "Alright, I won't."

He brushed the worst of the dust from his suit, and she did the same with her skirt, then he held out his arm, his eyes not meeting hers.

They walked the rest of the way to her hotel in silence. His manner was businesslike as he guided her through traffic, and for once Eve was at a loss for words.

At the entrance to the Intercontinental, he released her arm. "I hope you have a successful digging season," he said. "I assume that's why you're here. Please give my regards to your father."

She felt a rush of disappointment. It had felt as if this might be a breakthrough moment, when he confided in her and they grew closer, but instead he was shutting her out, definitively, and there was nothing she could do about it.

"Oh," she said. "Well, I wish you all the very best of luck with your business endeavors."

He turned as if to go and she shook her head in astonishment. Was he really going to leave her like this, after what had just happened?

As if he could hear her thoughts, he turned back. "I'm sorry if it was distressing for you to witness."

She didn't know if he meant the rescue of the boy, or him crying. "I am quite a plucky sort," she said. "Don't worry about me."

Up in her hotel room, though, she shed a few tears: of delayed shock and of frustration. What an impossible man he was! She wished she hadn't let him get under her skin, because he was clearly never going to be any more than a passing acquaintance.

"I'll simply have to find someone else," she said out loud, as if trying to convince herself.

Chapter Seventeen

London, Christmas Day 1972

Brograve drove them home from Patricia and Michael's at ten on Christmas evening, leaning so far forward in an effort to see the road ahead that his nose was almost pressed against the windshield. Eve knew he was tipsy. A steady stream of alcohol-filled glasses had been pressed into their hands all day long. He drove through a red light at one point and exclaimed, "Oops-a-daisy!," which made Eve giggle.

"What was that article you were reading?" he asked. "The one Michael gave you."

Eve described it to him. Michael had said she could take the magazine home with her so she'd packed it into a shopping bag along with all the presents they'd been given, and a slab of Patricia's Christmas cake wrapped in silver foil.

"I wonder if that's what Ana Mansour was talking about?" he said. "She mentioned new information had come to light about the tomb."

"Did she?" Eve couldn't remember her saying that.

"I think it was in the first letter she wrote to you, way back when you were still in the hospital. She said there were amomalies . . . no, amon . . . no." He laughed at himself and tried again. "An-om-alies. Between the new discoveries and Howard's catalogue."

"She did? I don't think I saw that letter."

"I'll look for it tomorrow." He hiccupped, and excused himself. "It's around somewhere."

Eve leaned back against the seat. She liked getting letters, but she hardly ever wrote them these days because she couldn't hold a pen for long with her weak right hand. It was so much easier to pick up the telephone. As a young girl she'd been trained to write letters for every occasion: thank-yous for dinners and gifts, sympathy when someone was sick, congratulations on a new baby, condolences, apologies for leaving a party early . . . the list was endless. Sometimes it was easier to express yourself in a letter because you had time to think before you wrote.

And then she thought of the letter Brograve had written to her in Egypt, the one that finally broke the impasse in their relationship. She'd heard from Maude, long afterward, that Cuthbert had talked him into writing it. He would have buried his head in the sand otherwise. She must look for it sometime and have another read.

It had arrived at the Winter Palace Hotel in March 1922, a few weeks after their inauspicious parting in Cairo, and no letter had ever meant as much to her as that one. Knowing him as she knew him now, she could imagine how much effort it must have taken to write it. But thank goodness he did!

There were three sheets of paper, covered on both sides in neat handwriting.

"I feel I owe you an explanation for my behavior by the roadside," he began, "but it will not be easy for me to admit the cause, so please bear with me."

Eve was tempted to race to the letter's conclusion—*would he admit to having feelings for her?*—but forced herself to slow down and read carefully.

The first thing I need to explain is that when my brother, Edward, died, in December 1914, I was halfway through my officer training, and due to be shipped to France three months later. I was given compassionate leave, which I spent with my mother and father at home in Putney. You are an intuitive sort so perhaps you can imagine the scale of my mother's grief. There were times when my father and I thought she would not survive.

It had been almost seven years after Edward's death when Eve saw her break down in the hotel bar, so goodness only knows what she had been like in the immediate aftermath.

She tried to persuade me to pull out of officer training and escape to a noncombatant country or to become a conscientious objector. I could not stomach the notion of letting other men risk their lives on my behalf, and having white feathers thrust at me in the street. I insisted I would do my duty in the war, and I would do it to honor Edward. It's what he would have wanted.

There was much weeping and pleading, but my father took my side. Eventually my mother said I could go if I promised on my honor that I would come home again—and, to pacify her, I agreed. Ridiculous promise! None of us wakening in the morning on the Western Front knew whether we would see out the day. Death came stealthily, and completely at random. You didn't have to be in no-man's-land, or taking part in a raid; it found you in your bunker as you slept, or on a bench as you ate a tin of bully beef.

But I knew I must honor this promise to my mother to the best of my abilities. I needed to do all I could to come home alive. And so we get to the part of this letter that I am going to find hardest to write. I don't think there is another soul in the world I could tell this story to, Eve, so I pray you won't judge me too harshly.

The truth is that I kept my head down for the three and a half years I spent in France. I didn't volunteer for anything. I took extra precautions, never removing my helmet and staying well away from danger spots in the trenches. I earned no promotions, no medals for bravery. I entered the war as a second lieutenant and I stayed a second lieutenant. My commanding officer viewed me as a coward and so, I suspect, did the men, but I had promised my mother I would come home alive. That was at the forefront of my mind. She couldn't lose both her sons.

Eve had goose bumps all over. Of *course* he had to try and survive for his mother's sake! It was heroic to do that. Two phrases in particular echoed in her head: "You are an intuitive sort" and, even better, "I don't think there is another soul in the world I could tell this story to." He must care for her. *He must!*

She turned the page. "Now, I have to tell you the worst, so brace yourself and please try not to think too ill of me." She blinked, nervously.

My best friend in the trenches was a fellow officer called Oliver Hill—Oli. We were as close as can be, talking about our families, our fears, and our plans for the future once the war was over. Someday I hope to tell you more about him, Eve, but for now all you need know is that he was the best friend I have ever had.

Perhaps you have heard of the Battle of Poelcappelle, which took place on the 9th of October 1917. It had been raining for weeks and the mud was so thick that men drowned in it. When we were told we must go over the top to attack the German lines less than half a mile away, I felt a grim clenching in my stomach. It was always going to end badly. I'll spare you the details, but suffice to say the Hun were waiting for us and opened fire once we were out in the open. I had made sure I was not at the front of the pack—I told you I was a coward, Eve— and I turned and crawled back to our trench, slipping down to safety. But Oli was not so fortunate.

He was hit—in the stomach, in the legs, I don't know where else—and injured so badly that he couldn't get to us.

Another man—not me—tried to slip out to rescue him but the Hun had kept their guns trained on the spot and he was killed instantly with a shot to the head. They did that, you see: when they knew there was a wounded man, they kept a gun trained on the spot to see if anyone would try to rescue him.

Eve was horrified. Stricken. She felt sick to her stomach at the inhumanity.

For the next six hours, well after dark had fallen, Oli kept calling to us. He was in terrible pain but he knew why we couldn't come out for him. He understood. Every now and then I stuck up a helmet on a pole to test if the gunman in the other trench was still aiming there. Always a shot bounced off it. I stayed in that spot, under cover, calling to Oli, trying to calm him. He gave me messages for his family, his fiancée. He knew he was dying.

Around four in the morning, all was still and silent. I raised a helmet and there was no shot. I stepped up to the wire and there was no shot. I threw a stone against a tin can to make a noise but it did not draw fire. It seemed the Hun were asleep and that I could take the opportunity to creep out and rescue my best-ever friend. But I couldn't do it. My nerve failed me. I stood there willing my legs to move and they wouldn't. Instead I slid back down into the trench. By dawn, Oli was no longer responding when we called. I don't know exactly when he died but I know he was brave to the last and I was a coward.

Eve's heart dissolved. Poor Brograve. To listen to your friend's last words and be powerless to help must have been devastating for him.

You will wonder why I am telling you all this. When I was running to rescue that child on the road, and I saw how close the donkey cart was, there was a moment when I nearly ran away. That's what my mother would have urged. But instead, I leaped to save the child and because of my hesitation, we only just made it.

And then I broke down. How could I risk my life for a child I had never met before, yet I didn't do it for Oli? I could have saved him too. When I think back and relive that moment, I am sure of it.

To my dying day, I will live with regret that I didn't try.

So please don't think of me as brave. I don't want you, of all people, to have any false illusions. I will understand if you do not want to reply to this letter or invite me to any more of your friends' parties. You would be sensible to forget me. I thank you for your friendship, which has meant a lot, and wish you the most exciting discoveries during your time in Egypt.

There were tears streaming down Eve's cheeks as she finished. At last she'd found out what made him so guarded, so difficult to get to know. At last, he had opened his outer shell to let her see inside.

Eve sat up till the early hours of the morning writing and rewriting her reply until she felt it struck exactly the right note. She wrote that she felt honored he had shared his experiences with her, and she appreciated how hard it must have been for him to write about them. She said it sounded as if Oli would not have survived the night anyway, and chances were, the German sniper was still there, biding his time, so he made the right decision. When he ran toward the child on the road, he made a split-second calculation that he could save him, and his instinct was correct. She had no doubt that the instinct in 1917 that stopped him rushing out into no-man's-land had also been correct, but she could only imagine how harrowing it must have been to listen to his friend's last words.

She sent her letter first thing the following morning. Brograve's reply came three weeks later—faster than she had expected. He was loath to accept he couldn't have saved Oli but thanked her for her generous response. He told her that when he visited Oli's parents, they had said the same thing, but it didn't make it easier to bear.

They corresponded till the end of the digging season, then met once she was back in London in April. Without telling her mother, Eve accepted an invitation to the races at Newmarket with him, then another day they went riding in Hyde Park and had a picnic on the grass. Eve never worried about being alone with him because she knew he was a gentleman through and through. Sometimes she wished he would try his luck with a quick kiss; she would have reciprocated without hesitation. Didn't he realize that a girl had expectations when she spent so much time alone with a man? What was he waiting for?

She invited him to Porchy and Catherine's wedding on the 15th of July, hoping the romance of the day might spur him to action, but it was an odd occasion in many respects. Her mother had been somewhat mollified about Porchy's choice of bride after learning that the extended Wendell family had substantial holdings of land in New York City. Eve's father, on the other hand, was still furious. Eve knew he was worried about money and concerned that Porchy was not taking his responsibilities to the estate seriously, but it wasn't fair that his attitude cast a pall over the day.

When they emerged from the church, Catherine threw her bouquet directly at Eve, and she caught it with ease. Glancing around, she saw Brograve watching her with a thoughtful look. Did he know what it meant to catch a bride's bouquet? Would it finally nudge him to propose?

The wedding party was to be held at 31 Grosvenor Square, a grand mansion lent to them for the occasion by a friend of Pups's, but straight after the ceremony her father told Eve he was driving back to Highclere, and nothing she could say or do would induce him to stay. He didn't like parties at the best of times and he had no intention of celebrating this particular wedding.

She was upset about that as she and her mother drove the short distance from the church, but she cheered up at the sight of the magnificent house with its white and gold Louis Quinze–style public rooms, which had been festooned with rare hothouse orchids borrowed from the Rothschild collections at Gunnersbury Park and Tring. Their delicate pink, white, and green colors complemented the eighteenth-century French art that lined the walls, while their fragrance mingled with the scents worn by guests. Liveried footmen trickled champagne into towers of coupe glasses, stacked six tall, and groups of guests stood to watch, holding their breath in case they should come crashing down. Doors were flung open to the garden square opposite, where flushed guests could cool down after dancing.

During the evening Eve drank more champagne than she was used to. Guests were gossiping about her father's hasty departure and his disappointment in Porchy's choice of bride, always stopping abruptly when they noticed her nearby. Brograve didn't like to dance—he said he feared he would injure her with his heavy-footedness—so she took to the floor with a string of others, including Tommy Russell. She glanced around, wondering if it would make Brograve jealous, but he gave no outward sign.

As guests began to leave, she panicked, fearing the moment might be lost entirely.

"Would you mind coming to the library with me?" she asked Brograve. "Just for a few minutes."

He looked puzzled but followed her down the corridor to the high-ceilinged, book-lined room lit only by a few Art Deco lamps.

"Sit down," she said, pointing to a leather armchair.

When he obeyed, clearly bewildered, she waltzed over and sat on his lap, leaned in, and kissed him firmly on the lips. After an initial hesitation she could feel him responding and it became a long kiss, a delicious kiss.

When she broke away, she looked him in the eye and said, "*Now* you have to marry me."

"Are you sure that's what you want?" he asked, and she almost screamed in frustration.

"Of *course* I'm sure!" she cried and kissed him again.

Fate had brought them together with three chance meetings in Egypt, but she couldn't rely on fate alone. Sometimes it was necessary for a girl to take matters into her own hands.

Chapter Eighteen

London, January 4, 1973

Sally the Sadist was delighted when she saw Eve hauling herself to her feet and inching along, clutching onto furniture.

"This is how toddlers learn, isn't it?" Eve laughed. "I remember Patricia doing this when she was eighteen months old."

"You've been working hard over the holidays!" Sally said. "I've never met anyone so determined."

She fetched a metal walking stick with three pronged feet from her car and adjusted it to Eve's height, then showed her how to walk around using it for support.

No longer being dependent on the wheelchair made a huge difference in Eve's independence. Once she'd mastered walking with the tripod stick, she could get herself out of bed in the morning, she could go to the toilet alone, and she could potter through to the kitchen to make a cup of tea, although she relied on Brograve or Sionead to carry it for her. She still used a wheelchair to go outside because she didn't want to risk a fall, but every day her confidence grew. She remembered blowing out that candle and making a wish to walk again, and here she was, six months after the stroke, her ambition achieved.

Walking around the flat, she frowned at the way objects were arranged on the shelves and bureaus. She had lots of pretty ornaments that had been given to her by friends over the years. In Framfield, she'd taken great care to display them attractively, but here, it seemed they had been placed without any thought. Why were her eighteenth-century enamel snuff boxes hidden away in a corner cabinet? The cabinet should display taller porcelain ornaments that could be seen through the glass doors. Her bejeweled Fabergé cigarette case should be on a side table, filled with cigarettes so guests could help themselves. And she certainly hadn't put that ugly old ship's sextant on the mantelpiece; that's where the gold carriage clock Brograve's father was given on his retirement from Lloyd's usually sat, ticking away. All the family photographs in decorative frames were muddled too.

She began to rearrange everything, working one

surface at a time. It was slow going but she could lean on her right elbow for balance while lifting items with her left hand. Oh, to be fully ambidextrous again! That would have to be her next goal.

Dr. Ana Mansour rang in mid-January and Eve hobbled out to the hall to answer the telephone.

"I'm so glad you called," she said. "I wanted to thank you for the divine lotus flowers, but you didn't leave an address. I hope you had a good Christmas?"

Ana answered that she had been in London, with friends, and that she was hoping it might be possible to come and talk to Eve again soon.

"Anytime you like," Eve said. "I'm feeling much better than when you last saw me, so I will have a good stab at answering your questions."

"I can hear how much your speech is improved. I'm delighted for you," Ana said.

They agreed on a date to meet just a week later, and Ana said she would bring a tape recorder.

"Will you stay in the room while we're talking?" Eve asked Brograve later. "Clear your throat or interrupt me if I start to say anything I shouldn't. I do have a tendency to babble on."

Brograve agreed that he would hang around in case Eve needed any reminders, but said he was sure she would be fine. Her memories of Egypt were as detailed and vivid as if it had all happened last week, not fifty years ago.

She narrowed her eyes as a thought occurred to her. What if there were things Brograve didn't know about? Who would help her then?

Ana was wearing a slate-gray suit this time, with a pair of black platform boots and a black polo neck, a fine silver chain around her neck with an ankh-shaped pendant. As they shook hands, Eve noticed an unusual perfume—sweet and musky—and made a mental note to ask about it later. But then she changed her mind. Her sense of smell had been playing tricks on her since the latest stroke. She kept smelling things that weren't there: strong smells like onions, or smoke, or iodine. Sometimes she only had to think about something to be able to smell it as clearly as if it were right next to her.

Ana had brought a Sony tape recorder, which she placed on a side table between her and Eve, before slotting in a cassette. She pulled a sheaf of typewritten notes from a briefcase and arranged them in her lap. "Don't worry," she said. "These aren't all questions I'm planning to ask! Just a few facts to remind myself."

Brograve sat on the other side of the room, by a window, his newspaper open on a table in front of him. He could make the paper last all morning, and by the time he'd finished with it the pages would be out of order and some would be stuck together with marmalade. He was a fastidious man in most respects but his treatment of newspapers always amused Eve.

Ana switched on the machine and began by introducing Eve, explaining that she had been one of the team that discovered Tutankhamun's tomb in November 1922. That wasn't quite accurate and Eve opened her mouth to interrupt, but Ana gestured with a raised finger to let her finish.

Once the introduction was over, she asked Eve to confirm that she was happy to answer questions, and Eve said she was always delighted to talk about Egypt and hoped that her contribution would be helpful. Ana played back a section to check that the recording was clear and Eve winced, hating her voice on the tape. She sounded plummy, like the Queen.

"I wasn't there when the steps to the tomb were first discovered," she said, to clarify.

"Don't worry. You'll have a chance to explain all that later," Ana replied.

She switched the recorder back on with a click and asked Eve to talk about Howard's gridblock plan and his conviction that Tutankhamun's tomb was in the area of the old workers' huts in the Valley. That was easy. Eve described him showing her and Pups the plan over drinks in Castle Carter, and her strong feeling that he was onto something.

"Do you know when he started excavating under the huts?" Ana asked, her expression encouraging.

"I think it was at the start of the winter 1922 season, around October maybe," Eve said. "Before that, he came to Highclere and Pups told him that he had run out of money and wouldn't be able to fund another season."

"Howard must have been upset to hear that," Ana commented.

Eve nodded. "He was. He paced up and down the library, as if absorbing the news, then he turned to Pups and said in that case he would fund the season himself, from his life savings. He said if there had been little prospect of success, he would have withdrawn gracefully, but on the contrary, he was so confident of a major find in that area that he was prepared to stake his own money."

"Interesting," Ana commented. "There is a theory doing the rounds that he had already started excavating in that area and knew more than he was letting on." Her look was penetrating. "Perhaps he had even discovered the steps at that stage and that's why he was so determined to proceed."

Eve dismissed the idea. "Goodness, no. Howard didn't keep secrets from Pups. They were thick as

thieves. It wasn't a normal employer-employee relationship; they were friends too. Pups used to stay with
him in Castle Carter for weeks on end." She wondered
why Ana would ask that. "If he had already found the
tomb, he would have told Pups. But they talked about
the money problem over the course of a couple of days
and eventually Pups agreed that he would somehow
raise the cash for one more season. He couldn't let
Howard risk his own savings."

"Howard Carter was well-off in his own right, I believe," Ana said. "He'd taken a dealer's commission on
several major purchases he made for the Metropolitan
Museum in New York, and other museums too. He was
quite the businessman."

"I suppose he was," Eve said. She glanced at Brograve but he shrugged. He didn't know any more than
she did about Howard's financial affairs.

"So . . ." Ana consulted her notes. "He went back
to Egypt and you received a telegram from him on the
sixth of November, saying that he had made a 'wonderful discovery,' I think that was the phrase."

Eve smiled. As long as she lived, she would never
forget the thrill of that moment.

She and Pups were eating breakfast when the butler
brought in the telegram. As he handed it to her father,

Eve's heart skipped a beat. During the war years they had dreaded receiving telegrams, in case they brought news that Porchy had been injured—or worse.

Her father tore it open and read, his expression changing from concern to—could it be amazement? He looked at Eve, then back at the telegram.

"Good god!" he exclaimed. "It's from Howard!"

"What is it?" She could tell it was good news before he spoke.

Pups read it out: "'At last have made wonderful discovery in the Valley; a magnificent tomb with seals intact; have preserved for your arrival; congratulations. Carter.'"

Eve dropped her fork, her eyes filling with tears. "This is it. This is what Howard has been longing for. Can I read it?"

Eve took the telegram and read the words for herself. "Seals intact." Who knew what might be inside? The Ancient Egyptians wouldn't have sealed an empty tomb. Her mind was running wild with possibilities. Could it be Tutankhamun's?

"I'm going to reply that we're on the way," Pups said. "You're coming with me, aren't you, Eve?"

"You bet I am!" she cried, spilling some tea in her enthusiasm.

They threw clothes into steamer trunks and set off in

the car for London to catch the boat train. She couldn't wait to be in the heat and dust of the Egyptian desert, to see with her own eyes whatever it was that Howard had found.

Frustratingly, the trip to Egypt took longer than usual. They had to wait in Marseilles for a steamer going to Alexandria, and then it was a slow one that stopped in every port around the south of Italy, then Greece. Eve strained her eyes for a view of the North African coast, and when they disembarked on the twenty-third of November, seventeen days after receiving the telegram, she hustled Pups straight to the train station. They had cabled their arrival time to Howard and, as the train crawled into Luxor station in the early evening, Eve looked out the window and saw him pacing up and down the platform in a brown homburg and a crumpled beige suit.

As soon as they got off the train, he hurried across and began telling them the story, so eager that the words came out in a rush.

"A young waterboy called Hussein tripped over something solid in the sand. On examination, it turned out to be a step," he said. "We excavated and found a staircase leading down from it. Of course, it could be a tomb that was built and never used. Or it could have been looted in antiquity and the seals cleverly resealed."

Eve had never seen him looking so excited. "You wouldn't have sent that telegram if you didn't think it was significant. And I know you; you don't get excited over nothing." He grinned, and she could tell he was optimistic. "Any sign of a name?" she asked.

"I'll show you in the morning," he said, refusing to be drawn further no matter how much she pestered him.

While they were speaking the sky had turned copper and the stars were appearing. Day transformed to night fast in the desert, as if someone had turned off a light switch. A solitary bat glided past.

"Can't we leave our trunks at the hotel and go straight to the Valley now?" Eve asked, consumed with impatience. "I'm never going to be able to sleep."

"We old men don't have your energy, Eve," Pups said. "I need to rest after the journey."

She glanced at Howard, wondering how he felt about being called "old." He was eight years younger than Pups, only in his late forties.

"I'll meet you first thing in the morning. Five a.m.," Howard said. "Keep your hair on till then, youngster."

Chapter Nineteen

Valley of the Kings, November 24, 1922

Dawn was only the faintest streak on the horizon when Eve and her father walked down to the shore of the Nile and woke a man who was sleeping in his felucca, motioning that they wanted to cross. He leaped to raise the sail and whisked them over the shadowy water in no time. A solitary donkey cart driver beckoned and seemed to know without being told that they were heading for the Valley. A heavy mist hung in the air, making it feel ghostly, and Eve shivered in the chill.

Howard was standing at the Valley entrance with Pecky Callender, a young English assistant he had hired. They walked to the concession and Eve saw a huddle of Egyptian boys, eyes huge and dark in the pinky-gold light of approaching dawn. Howard introduced her to Hussein, the water boy responsible for the find. Like the other workers, he was dressed in the long white tunic they called a thawb, over some loose white trousers. She shook his hand warmly, congratulating him effusively, although it was clear he didn't understand a word she was saying.

"How old is he?" she asked.

"Eight," Howard told her, and Eve raised her eyebrows. It seemed terribly young to be working.

After they found the staircase, Howard had ordered his workers to pack it with rubble in order to protect it from looters, so their first job was to unpack it again. Eve helped, passing smaller rocks back to the boys behind her. The sun rose above the horizon and suddenly the temperature leaped from cool to sweltering. A long sand-colored lizard arranged itself on a flat stone nearby to absorb the heat, so still and well camouflaged that Eve could only tell it was there when it blinked.

A plastered doorway emerged at the foot of the stairs and Howard beckoned for Eve and Pups to come and look.

"Do you see this seal?" He pointed. "The bird is the 'u' sound, and that's the symbol of an ankh." He pointed to each syllable as he spoke. "Tut. Ankh. Amun."

"Howard! You rogue!" Eve punched his arm. "You're so secretive! Why didn't you tell me last night?" She peered at the other seals. "What does this one say?"

"That's a jackal guarding nine captives. It's a common protective seal in official tombs."

"So this looks genuine?" Pups asked, his voice hoarse. Eve had a pang of worry about him. He seemed very tired from the journey.

"It does. But look." Howard pointed. "The seal in the top left corner has been broken and replastered, on what looks to me like two separate occasions." He traced it with his finger. "The materials used indicate robbers entered in antiquity, but I can't see any sign of a modern robbery."

"Are you sure?" Pups replied. "That's rather good news, isn't it?" The men exchanged glances.

"Let's take some photographs," Howard said, and there was a delay while Pecky Callender set up the camera on a tripod and took the shots.

"What now?" Eve asked, when he had finished.

"Now we break through," Howard told her, with a grin. He stopped to swig from a stone water bottle, then signaled to the Egyptians to use their picks on the plaster surface.

Eve held her breath, hoping a treasure-filled tomb would appear right there in front of their eyes, but instead they came upon a long downward-sloping corridor packed full of limestone chips. After examining a few, Howard told them the chips dated from antiquity. The corridor would have to be excavated very slowly and carefully in case anything was preserved within.

"How long will it take?" Eve asked, hopping from foot to foot.

"A few days," he replied, and she tutted her impatience.

Pups chuckled. "When you were younger, I tried to teach you that anticipation of a treat could heighten the pleasure, but I see that lesson didn't sink in."

On the contrary, Eve remembered arguing to be allowed to open her birthday presents the day before so she could spend her entire birthday playing with them. It was an argument she never won.

At four in the afternoon on November twenty-sixth, the excavators finished clearing the corridor and came upon a second plastered-over doorway, this one engraved with more oval seals. Eve recognized the Tutankhamun ones from the bird and the ankh shapes.

Howard used a small pick to chip a hole in the doorway. "Don't get your hopes up," he warned as he worked. "We might find yet another long corridor beyond. The

Egyptians designed these tombs specifically to confuse intruders."

Once the hole was big enough to admit a man's hand, Pecky Callender lit a candle and passed it to Howard. Pups and Eve huddled close as he inserted it through the hole and waited a moment before pulling it out. The flame was flickering and sputtering but still burning.

"We always have to test for foul gases," Howard said in response to Eve's questioning look. "But this seems safe. It didn't extinguish the flame."

Pecky handed him a small battery-powered torch and he pointed it through the aperture, then leaned his face against the rock, his eye to the hole. Eve stood on tiptoe, straining for a glimpse, scarcely breathing in her longing to know what lay within.

"Can you see anything?" Pups asked.

There was a long pause. *Why was he taking so long? Was it empty?*

When he spoke, Howard sounded utterly awestruck: "Yes. Wonderful things."

Eve's skin prickled from the top of her skull right down her spine, and she gave a little skip.

Howard widened the hole, then stepped back so they could each take a turn to peer through. Pups went first, and he exclaimed, "Good god!" After a minute or so he turned and handed the torch to Eve, an expression of incredulity on his face.

She poked the torch through the hole, leaned her face against the stone, and looked inside. At first it was fuzzy but when her eyes grew accustomed to the dimness, she saw a jumble of golden objects, some strange animal heads, and lots of shadowy shapes that she couldn't identify, all heaped up together. It looked like a picture of Aladdin's cave in a child's storybook. She shivered.

"Can we go inside?" she asked, turning to Howard.

Pups and Howard glanced at each other and Howard shook his head. "The Egyptian authorities have to be here before we go any farther," Howard said, looking around at the workmen who were clustered behind. "It's a legal requirement. I'll ask the men to fit a gate across the doorway, to keep it secure, then I'll telegram Pierre Lacau, the director of antiquities in Cairo."

"How long will it take for them to get here?" Eve asked, feeling as if she might burst if it were more than an hour or so.

He shrugged. "A few days, I imagine."

"Days!" she squeaked, her voice rising to a high pitch. "How can we possibly wait for days?"

Her father laughed. "We'll manage somehow."

Eve sat on a rock to watch as they used a clay-type mud to seal the hole Howard had made, then fitted an iron gate across the doorway, drilling into the bedrock so it was held securely. It was early evening when Pecky Callender headed off to his hotel, while the Egyptians went to their homes for the night. Howard, Pups, and Eve got a donkey-cart driver to take them to Castle Carter, feeling a mixture of frenzied excitement and crushing anticlimax.

We still had no idea what we had found," Eve told Ana Mansour. "As I'm sure you know, it was three days later, the twenty-ninth of November, when the official opening took place. Do you want me to describe that as well?"

"No, not yet," Ana replied. "Let's retrace your steps. First of all, I want to ask how closely you examined the doorway into the antechamber? Can you vouch for the fact that the seals were intact? I ask, because some of my colleagues suspect that Howard Carter might have entered *before* the official opening."

"Pecky took photographs of the seals," Eve insisted. "I was there. That was just three days before the official opening."

Ana nodded. "I've seen those photographs. It's useful that you can confirm the date they were taken, but I still think Howard broke into the antechamber before the twenty-ninth, and that he entered the burial chamber too. That means it must have happened on the twenty-seventh or twenty-eighth, presumably by night."

Eve stared at her, wondering what to say. She had never been good at lying. She usually blushed and gave the game away. But she couldn't tell Ana the whole truth. The three of them had agreed that night that they would keep it to themselves forever. She glanced around at Brograve and he cleared his throat. He knew. She hadn't been able to resist telling him, in the absolute confidence that he would never breathe a word.

"As I told you, there was evidence of two break-ins in antiquity," Eve said. "And it's clear from the disarray in the antechamber that there had been robberies. The Ancient Egyptians would never have left it like that. Perhaps that has led to c-confusion."

"All that is mentioned in Mr. Carter's records, of course. But were the rest of the seals intact on the twenty-ninth? Do you remember that?"

"I . . . I'm sure . . . they m-must have been," Eve stammered.

"Perhaps this might be a good moment to pause for refreshments," Brograve interrupted. "Eve needs a break. Can I offer you a sandwich, Dr. Mansour? Some cake perhaps?"

Ana was watching Eve with a puzzled smile, as if wondering why she had hesitated to answer. Eve bent to pick up her tripod stick from the floor as a way of avoiding her gaze.

"I'll come to the kitchen to help you," she said, straining to push herself up from the sofa. Her heart was beating faster than usual and she was sure her cheeks were scarlet.

Chapter Twenty

London, January 1973

Brograve found some York ham in the fridge and made ham and mustard sandwiches, while Sionead prepared a pot of tea and set a tray with side plates, napkins, and some slices of Victoria sponge. Sionead carried the food into the sitting room and offered Ana Mansour a sandwich, but she shook her head, saying, "Not for me, thank you." It was only then Brograve remembered that if she were Muslim, she wouldn't eat ham.

"Would you prefer cheese and pickle?" he asked, but she said no, she had eaten before she came. She shuffled her papers and scribbled something on top of one sheet, lost in thought.

While Eve and Brograve were eating, Ana carried on talking. "We know Howard Carter took several items from the tomb and gave them as keepsakes to his friends. Many have since been donated to museums. British Egyptologist Sir Alan Gardiner gave an amulet to the Cairo Museum, saying that Howard Carter had given it to him as a gift but he felt uncomfortable keeping it. Howard's niece, Phyllis Walker, sold some small items to the Metropolitan Museum after his death, and donated the remainder of his estate to the Griffith Institute in Oxford."

Brograve expected Eve would leap to Howard's defense. She had adored him and usually wouldn't hear a word against him. Instead she agreed with Ana's comments.

"You have to remember the context of the time," she explained. "The Egyptian government was newly independent and kept changing the rules about ownership of artifacts every five minutes, or so it seemed. A decade earlier, archaeologists could keep their own finds, then a new law was passed that they could only keep half, but under the terms of my father's concession to dig at that site . . ." She paused, and Brograve could tell she was making sure she got it straight in her head before she spoke. "If a tomb was untouched, the entire contents belonged to the Egyptian authorities, but if there was evidence of previous break-ins, then the archaeologists who held the concession got a share. So it was unclear."

Ana nodded agreement but continued: "Howard

Carter claimed to have made the most accurate and comprehensive records of any archaeologist to date, yet he neglected to catalogue the items that he purloined. Don't you think that taints his records somewhat?"

Brograve objected. "The term 'purloined' is a bit strong. As my wife pointed out, the case was not at all clear-cut."

"I'm sure he didn't take anything significant," Eve said. "Just little jars or *shabti* figures. There were hundreds of them lying around."

"On the contrary," Ana replied. "My colleagues suspect he *did* remove some significant items, and that's what I hope to get to the bottom of—perhaps with your help." She smiled. "You're the last person alive who knows what really happened, so I'm deeply grateful you agreed to talk to me."

Brograve knew Eve would be alarmed by this line of questioning, so he interrupted again. "Howard was a very close friend of my wife's. We don't want to be part of any campaign to accuse him of theft when he's no longer around to defend himself."

Ana corrected herself. "Of course not! I certainly wouldn't use the word 'theft' for what was common practice in the old days. Everyone knows Heinrich Schliemann treated the gold found at Troy as his own personal treasure chest, and I'm sure my father didn't question too closely where items brought to his dealership came from. He just bought and sold them to make a profit. But now, in the present day, we aim for more transparency." A strand of Ana's hair had tumbled forward and she smoothed it back, patting it into place. "Some new developments have raised questions about the whereabouts of several important items."

"What new developments?" Eve asked, pushing her half-finished sandwich to one side. "Do you mean the discovery of Maya's tomb?"

Ana smiled. "Ah, you heard about that. I might have known you would be up to speed. Would it be alright if I turn the tape recorder on again?" When Eve agreed, she pressed the button with a click.

"Did you ever come across the name Maya in connection with the tomb?" Ana asked.

"Of course," Eve replied, watching the tape loop across the window on the top of the recorder. "Howard often spoke of Maya, the overseer in charge of the burial. He said it looked as though Maya had been rushing, perhaps because the death was unexpected. It appeared he had borrowed objects from other tombs because he didn't have time to create enough treasure for Tutankhamun. That's why different names were found on items."

"Yes, that seems to have been the case," Ana said.

"Among Maya's writings was a comprehensive list of the items that he placed in Tutankhamun's tomb. Over five thousand of them! We've been translating it and comparing it with Howard Carter's records, and there are many unexplained differences. Several valuable treasures seem to be missing and it is my job to find out what happened to them."

"How do you know they weren't taken by tomb robbers in antiquity?" Eve asked.

"Maya writes about those early robberies, but he is very clear that the robbers did not breach the burial chamber, where many of the missing items were placed. That hadn't been accessed until Howard Carter got there." She sounded stern.

Eve pulled her cardigan tightly around her body. "What kind of items?" she asked, a tremor in her voice.

Brograve grew concerned. He couldn't see her expression from where he was sitting but he hoped the tone of this questioning wasn't upsetting her. Should he ask Ana to stop? The doctor had said Eve was to avoid stress.

Ana consulted a list on her lap: "Some quite distinctive ones: a wooden goose varnished with resin; and this . . ." She pulled a color photograph from among her papers and handed it to Eve. "This wishing cup should have had a twin because Maya said it was a set of two."

Brograve stood and walked across to look over Eve's shoulder. Shaped like a flower head, it had hieroglyphics around the rim. Eve had gone very quiet and he sensed she recognized it.

"It's a shame you didn't speak to Howard's niece, Phyllis, about these," Brograve said, in an attempt to deflect attention from Eve. "Unfortunately she died just a couple of years ago."

"Oh no!" Eve exclaimed. "Is Phyllis dead?"

Brograve patted her hand. "We went to the funeral, darling," he said, and Eve bowed her head. Phyllis had been a couple of years younger than she was. How sad.

"I've tried to track down everyone who visited the tomb in the early months, and it seems you are the only one left," Ana said. "That's why your recollections are so crucial. There's a particular mystery I'm hoping you might be able to solve. Maya is very clear that he left a solid gold unguent container just inside the doorway to the burial chamber. It had a lotus flower engraved on the lid. It sounds distinctive, and yet Howard Carter doesn't mention it. How could he have missed such a thing?"

Eve turned to Brograve with panic in her expression. How ironic it should come up after all these years. He wanted to urge her to tell a lie, just a white lie, but couldn't think how to communicate that without giving the game away to Ana.

Ana was watching Eve closely. "Did you see anything like that?"

Eve opened her mouth to answer and stammered a little: "I-I d-d . . ." It was the first time in ages that Brograve had heard her stammer. And then she laid her head back on the sofa and closed her eyes. Her cheeks seemed very pale.

"Are you alright?" he asked, shaking her shoulder, and grew alarmed when she didn't answer. He asked again. Eve was breathing slowly and deeply but she didn't seem able to hear him. "Sionead!" he called, trying not to panic. "Can you come here, please?" He stroked Eve's hair, murmuring words of comfort.

Sionead was there in seconds, and Brograve stepped back to let her get close.

"Can you hear me, Eve?" Sionead asked, speaking clearly in a professional tone. She placed two fingers on the pulse in Eve's neck.

Eve's eyelids fluttered and she nodded her head slightly. That meant she was conscious. Thank god! Brograve clutched his face. Ana stopped the tape recorder with a click.

"Can you open your eyes?" Sionead asked.

Eve opened them slowly, as if it took some effort.

"Follow my finger with your eyes," Sionead instructed, moving her index finger from one side to the other. Brograve watched Eve's pupils following the movement.

Please don't let it be another stroke, he prayed. *Please, I beg you.*

"Now could you smile for me?" Sionead asked, and Eve curled the corners of her mouth.

Brograve didn't think her face was lopsided, the way it had been in the hospital, but it was hard to be sure. "What do you think?" he asked Sionead, his throat tight with fear.

Sionead didn't answer him straightaway but asked Eve to raise her left arm. Eve managed to lift it above her head. "Now the right," Sionead said. It wouldn't go so far. Eve hadn't regained full mobility on that side.

"I think she's just overtired," Sionead said, looking him in the eye. She clearly had more to say but didn't want to alarm Eve. "Let's get her to bed for a rest."

Brograve slipped an arm around Eve's waist on one side while Sionead supported the other side and between them they helped her to her feet. She was astonishingly light, like a child—always had been. They walked her slowly to the bedroom and Sionead pulled back the covers, then they laid her down and tucked her in.

"Should I call a doctor?" Brograve asked, under his breath.

"Can't do any harm," Sionead said. "But I don't think it's anything to worry about."

Brograve walked through to the hall telephone. His legs were trembling as he dialed the number so he sat down on the chair. The receptionist promised that a doctor would drop by on his round that afternoon and he felt close to tears with gratitude.

There was a sound from the sitting room, and Ana Mansour appeared in the doorway, clutching her tape recorder. He was startled. Why was she still there? What had she been doing while they were putting Eve to bed?

"I'm so sorry your wife is unwell," she said, touching his arm. "I hope it's nothing serious. Might I telephone tomorrow to ask after her?"

Brograve nodded.

"You seem shocked. Is there anything I can do?" Ana asked. "Shall I make you a cup of sweet tea?"

"I'm fine." He shook his head, wanting her gone. "Thank you."

He stood to help her on with her overcoat, then ushered her out of the flat, leaning his forehead against the wooden doorframe as he listened to the clanking sound of the lift approaching. The old grandfather clock that had belonged to his great-grandparents gave a mechanical click as it reached the hour, then the gong rang out, muffled and doleful.

Chapter Twenty-One

London, January 1973

Eve was awake when the doctor arrived but she felt drowsy. He was a young doctor, one she hadn't met before, and she would normally have chatted while he did his examination but she couldn't seem to wake up enough.

After he left, she lay in bed, thinking about the questions Ana had asked. Maybe it was time for her to tell the truth about what happened in November 1922. If it were true, that she was the only one left who was there at the beginning, before the tomb was dismantled, that gave her a responsibility.

She didn't want the reputations of either Howard or her father to be tarnished by this new investigation. If she confirmed they had taken items from the tomb, would they be labeled thieves? Might she even be arrested as an accomplice to crime?

What would Pups want her to do? He had been shy of publicity so would probably want it kept quiet. But Howard was a scientist first and foremost, so perhaps he would urge her to tell the truth, especially now it couldn't harm anyone.

If only she could reach out to them in the afterlife and ask their wishes. It felt wrong for her to make the decision all on her own about something that concerned them all.

After that first torchlit glimpse into the tomb on the twenty-sixth of November, Eve, Pups, and Howard returned to Castle Carter feeling restless.

"I hope you have a decent whisky," Pups said, and Howard produced a Glenmorangie from a cupboard.

"I don't suppose you have the ingredients for a gin rickey?" Eve asked.

Howard didn't have any limes, only lemons, but she said that would be fine. The lemons in Egypt had a delicious sweetness.

Howard was thinking out loud as he poured their drinks. "It could be a cache of objects from the Amarna royal cemetery, where Akhenaten is buried. It certainly looks like some kind of storage facility."

Eve was crestfallen. "So it might not be Tutankhamun's tomb, even though it has his seal?"

"I'm not jumping to conclusions." Howard handed her the drink and she took a gulp. It was strong, making her sneeze, so she topped it up with more soda from his siphon. "I've come across his seal elsewhere."

"Normally tombs were carefully laid out, were they not?" Pups asked. "Perhaps those early robbers rummaged through this one and left it in disarray. That would help our case when arguing for a share."

"I didn't see a coffin, but I would expect that to be in a separate chamber, if it's there at all." Howard hadn't touched his whisky, which was balanced precariously on top of a book by his elbow.

Eve looked out the window. It was pitch-black now. Her stomach gurgled. "Are we going back to the hotel for dinner?" she asked Pups.

"I have a collection of tinned supplies," Howard said. "You're welcome to raid them if you like."

Eve wandered into his kitchen and opened the cupboards. She found jars of marmalade and jam, cans of mock turtle soup, tinned fruit, sardines, Brand's Essence of Chicken, a tin of water biscuits, and a pâté de fois gras. The Egyptian houseboy appeared in the doorway. She used mime to ask him to heat some soup and serve the fois gras on water biscuits. Essence of Chicken held no appeal.

When she returned, the men were talking about the legal procedures they must follow to register the find. She felt horribly frustrated. To know the treasures were there and not be able to explore them was cruel. When the food came, she had no appetite, and she noticed the men weren't eating either. Howard replenished their glasses instead.

"I definitely won't sleep tonight," Eve said. "It seems such a shame not to be able to go further. . . ."

"We don't want to get on the wrong side of the Egyptians," Pups cautioned. "Especially not at such a sensitive time, with independence less than a year old."

"No, of course not," Howard agreed. "All the same . . ." He paused, thinking out loud, and they both held their breath as they watched him. "How would you feel about slipping back for a quick look now, while no one else is around? We'll have to be careful, but . . ."

Before he could finish his sentence, they had both agreed.

Howard lent Eve one of his jackets to wear over her day dress. It was huge, the shoulders sagging to her elbows and the hem almost reaching her knees, but she was grateful for the warmth when they stepped out into the chilly desert air. Howard kept his own donkey tethered in the back garden, but it clearly thought it was off duty for the night and honked in angry protest, bucking and straining as he slipped a bridle over its head. He tied it to an old cart, then invited them to climb in. The Egyptian donkey cart drivers had a set of steps Eve could ascend but there were none here so she had to hitch up her skirts and clamber in any old how.

She felt nervous as a bank robber as they drove the two miles uphill, Howard's torch casting a long white beam that sliced through the darkness. Some wild creatures were howling in the desert, making her even more apprehensive.

"What's that noise?" she whispered.

"Jackals," Howard replied, and she shivered.

Once they turned into the Valley, the cart bumped erratically over the rough ground. Howard drove them right up to the tomb entrance, then tethered the donkey to a stake. He removed the key from his pocket and opened the metal gate, then they walked down the sloping corridor to the sealed doorway. Howard used a pick to chip a hole low down that was just big enough for a woman to crawl through.

"Ladies first." He turned to Eve and handed her

a torch. "You are the most impatient, as well as the smallest."

She hesitated. What might she find inside? Snakes? Bats? Angry spirits? "Could there be snakes?" she asked out loud.

"No." He shook his head. "It's been sealed for three millennia. Nothing will be alive in there."

He sounded very definite. It was on the tip of Eve's tongue to suggest that one of the men should lead the way, but then she steeled herself. It was an honor to be the first person to enter for three thousand years. She couldn't turn that down, especially not as a budding lady archaeologist.

Holding the torch in her teeth, she got down on her knees and crawled through the aperture, standing upright once she was inside. The temperature was hotter than the hottest Turkish bath, but it was a dry, oppressive heat that irritated her throat. The dusty air smelled faintly of perfume and, outside her torch beam, the darkness was impenetrable. Her heart was pounding so hard she thought she might faint and at first she didn't dare move. Behind her she heard Howard chipping away to widen the hole. One of the men was coming through, so she shuffled sideways, giving a startled yelp when her foot came into contact with an object.

She shone her torch around the chamber. The animal heads she had spotted through the aperture belonged to some strange elongated creatures; one reminded her of a leopard, another of a crocodile. The hairs on the back of her neck stood on end. To her left there was a pile of wheels and the body of a carriage; she guessed this was a vehicle designed to take the tomb's occupant to the afterlife, as was the Egyptian tradition. On the floor there were wooden chests and containers, footstools and jars, all higgledy-piggledy.

Her father appeared by her side, and she slipped her arm through his and clutched tight as they waited for Howard. Neither spoke. They were breathing air that had not been breathed for three millennia. She felt giddy, exhilarated, and nervous, all at the same time. It made her conscious of her physicality—the beating of her heart, the in-and-out movement of her ribs, the muscles of her eyes as they strained to peer through the darkness.

When Howard got inside, he began picking up objects and examining them by torchlight. "I think the animal-headed figures are couches," he told them, shining his beam along the length of one. He picked up a jar and turned it over to read the name engraved on the base: the first said Amenhophis, another read

Akhenaten, and then he came upon three in a row that said Tutankhamun.

"Why so many names?" he wondered out loud.

Eve stepped carefully toward the right side of the chamber and almost dropped her torch in astonishment when her beam alighted on a life-sized statue of a black-skinned boy wearing a gold headdress and holding a staff. The whites of his eyes gleamed. "Who's this fellow?" she asked, her voice shaky, and Howard came over.

"Good lord!" he exclaimed. "It looks like a guardian statue." He shone his torch along the wall it stood against and there, behind a low chest, was another statue that looked identical.

"What's a guardian statue?" Eve asked. The statue's gaze was uncannily lifelike. Every detail was perfect, from the pupils right down to the toes inside its golden sandals, as if it could spring to life at any minute and step toward her.

"It means the entry to the burial chamber must be here," he said. He knocked on the wall behind the statues. It was hollow.

Eve felt scared suddenly. "Perhaps we shouldn't go any farther," she whispered. She wrapped Howard's jacket more tightly around her, hoping they could leave soon. There was something that didn't feel right about this. Perhaps it was the thought that there could be a mummified corpse inside. It was like digging up someone's grave.

"We can't stop now," Howard said, and started chipping away at the lower part of the wall between the statues, as if he were a man possessed.

Eve realized that nothing she or Pups could say would stop him. Instead they stood, arms linked, holding their breath as they waited to find out what—or who—might lie beyond.

Chapter Twenty-Two

Valley of the Kings, November 26, 1922

Howard's pick soon reached the other side of the wall. He enlarged the hole, then patted his pockets, muttering, "Damnit, I forgot to bring a candle. I suppose a match will have to do." He struck a match and held it through the hole into the next chamber, waiting to see if the flame would be extinguished by gases inside. As he did so, a strange smell reached Eve: something oily and musky with a harshness that caught the back of her throat. She couldn't think of anything to compare it to: perhaps a mixture of Lysol, incense, and a sick horse's urine.

"Can you smell that?" she asked.

"It's extraordinary how the ancient oils retain their scent," Howard said. "The air seems safe in there. Do you want to be the first to go in again, little Eve?"

Goose bumps pricked her arms. She had strong mis-
givings, but she'd done it once and that had worked out
alright. Steeling herself, she got down on her hands and
knees and crawled through. The scent grew stronger,
making her cough and choke, and causing her eyes to
water.

Immediately when she reached the other side, even
before she stood up, her torch beam illuminated a wall
of brilliant gold carvings straight in front of her. It was
as tall as the chamber itself and there was a narrow corridor running around either side.

She shuffled to the left as her father came through,
then Howard. "By Jove, we've found it," he said. "This
is a shrine. The coffin will be inside." He shone his torch
at the seals on the side of the shrine facing them. "And
look. The ankh. The bird. I've got Tutankhamun . . .
and it is intact." His voice cracked, as if he were about
to weep.

Eve squeezed his arm in congratulations. "You
found it, Howard. This will make your name. You'll
be famous!" She was glad the coffin was sealed inside the shrine and she didn't have to look at it. It felt
creepy to think that a long-dead king's mummy lay in
there.

Howard gave a low laugh. "Theodore Davis came
within six feet of this very spot. He would have been

devastated to hear of our discovery! Just as well he passed away."

Eve shone her torch to the left and it lit an elaborate wall painting. "Look." She gestured and both men turned but it was impossible to make out the subject because the torch beam illuminated only a small area at a time.

"Careful where you put your feet," Howard said, and Eve realized there were several small items on the ground. She slid her feet as she moved rather than lifting them so she didn't risk breaking anything.

Over on the other side of the shrine there was a stack of golden oars. The perfume was still catching her throat and, combined with the stale air, the heat, and the stuffiness, it made her dizzy. She rested a hand against the shrine to catch her balance. Pups was coughing.

Behind the shrine she could see a doorway into another chamber. A figure she recognized as Anubis, the jackal-headed god who watched over the dead, was reclining on a plinth.

Howard picked something up from the ground and examined it. "I can't see any harm in taking a few mementos so long as we are discreet. What do you reckon, Lord C?"

Pups agreed. "Only small pieces. We'll have to keep

them for ourselves and not try to sell them on the open market, mind."

Eve was worried. It wasn't cheating the Egyptian government that bothered her, because they need never know. The thought in her head was that they shouldn't steal from Tutankhamun. Egyptians designed their tombs to contain everything the occupant would need in the afterlife, and it seemed wrong to take anything, like stealing flowers from a grave.

Howard slipped a couple of items into the pockets of the jacket she was wearing, and she saw Pups bending to retrieve more. Eve ran her fingers over the delicate gold filigree of the shrine. It felt like a holy place, with the incense smell and the absolute quiet.

"We'd better go soon," Howard said, consulting his pocket watch. "We need to get back well before first light."

He crawled out of the burial chamber first, followed by her father. Eve had a moment of panic when she was alone inside once more. What if there was a rock fall that trapped her there with Tutankhamun's mummy? She would die of terror long before she succumbed to suffocation.

As she knelt to crawl out, her fingers closed around an item on the floor. It looked glittery by torchlight. Should she take just one memento? Overcoming her reservations, she picked it up and stuffed it in her skirt pocket, then clambered through and stood up on the other side.

Eve and Pups watched as Howard rearranged chunks of plaster across the hole in the doorway to the burial chamber, then propped a basket and a bunch of reeds in front. "That will have to do," he said, checking his handiwork.

"If it looks like a recent break-in, all the better for our case to keep some of the finds," Pups said.

On the way through the antechamber Eve tripped over an object and it tumbled sideways with a deafening clatter, but she couldn't see clearly enough to set it right. She was in a hurry to get back out into the night air.

Howard took some time patching the hole in the outer doorway with dampened clay, and smoothing it down. He couldn't restore the broken seal but he made the surface around it look as authentic as he could, then locked the metal gate.

Eve took deep breaths, trying to clear her lungs of the stuffy, perfumed air from inside the tomb. Jackals were still howling in the hills behind and Eve thought it sounded as if they were in pain. It reminded her of the noise her father's dog Susie once made when a house-maid stood on her paw.

When they got back to Howard's house, he fetched a

bottle of brandy and three glasses, pouring them each a generous measure. Eve felt the warmth seep into her bones, its fruity scent cutting through the stale muskiness of the tomb that still lingered in her nostrils.

After a long swig, Pups started chuckling, then Howard joined him. It was infectious. Eve felt light-headed and almost hysterical as she laughed out loud. They had shared the most magnificent secret.

"Let's see what you've got then," Howard said, and Eve emptied the jacket pockets onto his table.

"That's a *shabti*," he said, looking at a small, human-shaped statue. "Do you know about them? They represent the workers that the king would need to perform tasks for him in the afterlife."

"I saw dozens of these, so he will be very well served," Eve remarked.

Howard picked up a long cylindrical object. "This was for holding reed pens," he said. "And my goodness, that's a wishing cup. A very fine example."

The item Eve had picked up at the last moment was a heavy gold box with a lotus-flower cartouche carved on the lid, and it smelled strongly of the unpleasant musky scent of the tomb. Howard pried off the lid with a metal ruler and showed her there was a sticky substance inside. The scent was overpowering now, making her eyes water.

"It's an unguent container," he said. "And the contents are still viscid. The tomb robbers would have taken this if they'd seen it. Unguents were more valuable than gold to the Ancient Egyptians."

"It looks rather valuable," Eve said. "It's heavy, so I'm guessing it's solid gold. Typical me! I always veer toward the most expensive items when I'm shopping, and now I've done the same thing in the tomb. Perhaps I should return it."

"Nonsense," Howard said, pushing it toward her. "It's yours now. Are you sure that's all you want?"

Her father had a wooden goose, an intricate collar made of beaten gold, and an elegant wine jar. Howard had a range of objects because he'd pocketed several from the antechamber too. The table was covered in them.

"Just this is fine," Eve said, closing the box and putting it back in her skirt pocket.

She couldn't believe how well preserved and intricately decorated everything was. Tutankhamun had clearly been a king with infinite wealth at his disposal.

"I hope you understand that we can't breathe a word about our adventure," Howard told them. "Not to anyone. It would undermine our legitimate claim and make it difficult to get another concession in Egypt."

They both agreed that they wouldn't tell a soul.

"I'm glad Theodore Davis didn't find the tomb," he said. "We will treat it with more care and respect than he would have done. I plan to keep the most meticulous records in the history of archaeology."

Eve noticed the sky was lightening outside. "Pups, we should go back to the hotel and get some rest."

"I don't think I'll be able to sleep tonight so I'll come across with you," Howard said. "I need to send telegrams informing the authorities that we've made a find that looks significant, and requesting their presence so we can proceed."

Eve took off his jacket and hung it on a coat stand in the hall, and Howard opened the front door.

"Bulldog is rather quiet this morning," Eve said, peering through the misty dawn toward the canary's cage. "Perhaps he decided to sleep late."

Howard followed her out and looked into the cage. "Oh no! Poor Bulldog!" he cried. "A cobra's got him."

The tail of a gray-brown snake was hanging through the bars, and the rest of it was coiled in the cage, with a canary-sized bump under its skin, about a third of the way down. Bulldog was slowly being digested.

Chapter Twenty-Three

London, January 1973

Eve woke with a start the morning after Ana Mansour's visit. She vaguely recalled she had been dreaming about the tomb but the details were foggy. Only one thing was clear: she had to give back the gold unguent container. She should never have taken it. Perhaps Ana could help her to do it anonymously, so she wouldn't need to reveal the illicit nighttime visit. Then it could be reunited with the other Tutankhamun treasures in the Cairo Museum, where it belonged.

She remembered the artifacts spread across Howard's table and wondered how much he had taken from the tomb over the years he worked on it. She didn't believe Ana's theory that he had already been inside when she and Pups arrived in November 1922. His astonishment at the sights that night was genuine, and besides, he'd had to chip through sealed doorways. However, it was possible he returned the day before the official opening, while she and Pups were resting at the Winter Palace. And after that, he was often alone inside the tomb, making his intricate drawings of the layout and then cataloguing everything. She didn't blame him for the items that found their way into his pockets. It was his discovery more than anyone else's, the crowning achievement of his career, and it was only natural that he wanted some mementos.

Had the Egyptian authorities stuck to the terms of the concession, he could have taken them legitimately, but in 1924 he fell out with them and was temporarily barred from the tomb. During his absence, one of their inspectors found a wooden head of Tutankhamun emerging from a lotus flower that had been packed for shipment without being itemized or catalogued. They accused Howard of attempting to steal it, but he maintained it was an administrative error. Maybe it was, maybe it wasn't. She clearly remembered seeing some Tutankhamun trinkets when she visited him at his London flat, the one around the corner from the Albert Hall. There was a blue *shabti* on his desk, and a tiny Anubis figure on the mantelpiece, but nothing that looked as valuable as her gold container.

Once Howard was finally allowed to continue his

work on the tomb in 1925, the terms of the concession had been changed, so all the contents belonged to the Egyptian state. Looking back from the 1970s, Eve could see that was only fair. It was part of their national heritage. Returning the gold unguent container would be her way of righting a wrong. That's what she should do, as long as she didn't get into trouble for taking it in the first place.

As soon as Brograve awoke, she told him her idea that they ask Ana to return it anonymously. He rubbed his eyes.

"I'm not sure that's a good idea," he said. "No matter how discreet Ana is, questions will be asked about how you came to have it. And remember, we don't know her very well." He stretched. "Besides, I haven't seen it for years."

That made her pause for thought. When had she last seen it?

When she and Pups returned from Egypt, she'd put it in a hat box in her closet at their Berkeley Square house. After a while she'd moved it to another closet because the unpleasant scent seemed to be impregnating her clothes. When she married Brograve she took it with her to their first home together, at 26 Charles Street, Mayfair, but she never put it on display. It was kept in a drawer in the spare room, as far as she remembered, wrapped in layers of cloth to try and contain the scent. And then, when they moved to Framfield, she'd stuck it in a box in the attic along with some other knickknacks. After that her mind went blank. She had a strange feeling she had put it somewhere in particular—but where?

She had never admitted to Brograve that she couldn't remember them leaving Framfield. She wished they hadn't; that house and garden had meant more to her even than Highclere and she missed them terribly. She hoped the new owners cherished them as much as she had.

Brograve brought her breakfast on a tray and helped her to sit up in bed and balance it on her knees. Since she had come home from Pine Trees, he had brought her breakfast in bed every morning. He would surprise her; she never knew whether it would be porridge, toast and honey, or an egg, but there was always a cup of milky tea. Today it was a boiled egg with toast soldiers arranged around it like the rays of the sun in a child's drawing.

While she ate, he sat on the bed beside her with his own tea.

"I need to find the unguent container today," she

told him. "If I don't, they'll say Howard took it, and once I'm gone, there will be no one left to defend him."

"The doctor said you were to take it easy," Brograve warned. "It doesn't have to be today."

She was undeterred. "If Sionead can lift boxes down for me, all I need do is sit on the sofa and sift through them. It probably won't take long. The container had such a curious smell I'll know as soon as I open the right box."

Brograve agreed, after cautioning that she mustn't overdo it. The telephone rang while she was still eating and he went out to the hall to answer it.

"She's much better, thank you," he said. There was a pause. "No, I'm afraid she can't talk to you today . . . I think we'd better leave it for a while . . . Why don't you give me your telephone number so we can ring you when it is convenient? . . . And your address? . . . Yes, I understand . . ."

The conversation went on for some time. Eve gathered that it was Ana Mansour and she was asking when they could resume their interview. She didn't want to talk to her again until she'd found the missing container and could tell her an edited version of the truth. It was too awkward being forced to lie.

Sionead came to take her blood pressure and dole

out her morning pills: so many pills she would rattle if you shook her. She said that out loud and Sionead smiled politely, whereupon Eve suddenly remembered she had said it before. Probably many times.

"The doctor's coming at eleven," Sionead said. "Just to check on you."

Eve felt bad for wasting his time. Everyone had made a big fuss about her feeling momentarily sleepy but she was fine now. Right as rain. She took a gulp of tea to get rid of the bitter aftertaste of the pills.

After breakfast, she got dressed. Sionead was on hand to help but Eve liked to do everything herself, no matter how long it took. The brassiere was especially tricky. She had to fasten the hooks at the front, then wriggle it around into position before forcing her arms through the straps. Pulling a sweater over her head could easily turn into a comedy routine, with her staggering around as if in a straitjacket.

When she was finally ready, she wandered through the flat, looking into cupboards and trying to decide where to start her search. There were cardboard boxes of photographs and letters, lots of mementos from her mother's last home, Brograve's files of financial documents, battered leather suitcases containing god-knows-what, and a bulging album of newspaper cuttings. On impulse, she lifted down the album and tucked it under her arm to take to the front room. A trip down memory lane.

The cuttings started with the first triumphant announcements of the find: "New Tomb Found: Egypt's Greatest," "Discovery of the Century," "Wonders Found in Luxor Tomb." The story had been on the front page of every newspaper in Britain and Egypt, probably around the world too.

The excitement hadn't died down by the time she and Pups returned to London in mid-December. Some canny manufacturers had already rushed out Tutankhamun-themed merchandise in time for Christmas: tins of biscuits with Egyptian-style patterns on the lid, bracelets like snakes coiling up your arm, even a face powder compact with the head of a cobra engraved on it. Tutankhamun was all the rage for the next few years, with every flapper worth her salt drawing kohl around her eyes with that little flick at the sides and learning the Tutankhamun shimmy. Eve had shimmied herself a few times, and received a tongue-lashing from Almina, who called it "the epitome of vulgarity."

Chapter Twenty-Four

Valley of the Kings, November 29, 1922

There weren't supposed to be any journalists at the official opening of the tomb. This was an occasion to be witnessed by dignitaries, both British and Egyptian, who had made their way to Luxor from Cairo. Pecky Callender had arranged a hook-up with the Valley's electricity supply so the interior could be lit and the visitors wouldn't have to scramble around in torchlight.

Howard had warned Eve and her father to be wary of talking to journalists. He didn't want the place overrun by curious sightseers before he'd had time to get adequate security in place. They would have to pretend they were entering the tomb for the first time, and they mustn't let slip about the existence of the burial chamber, because it wasn't going to be officially opened until after he had catalogued the antechamber.

Twenty-six of them were present when the gate was unlocked and the entrance was formally unblocked. Eve and Lady Allenby, wife of the British high commissioner, were the only women. Everyone was chattering with excitement as they waited in the sandy rubble field outside but Eve felt a tightening in her stomach as she worried that their previous entry might be detected.

They fell silent as they were led into the antechamber in twos. When Eve's turn came, she didn't need to fake astonishment at the sights. With better lighting, she could see the incredible jumble of objects more clearly—gilded thrones, a narrow golden bed, and the three bizarre animal couches. They took her breath away. She realized that the item she had knocked over in her haste must have been a chariot wheel, as one lay on its side.

"The couches have the heads of a cow goddess, a leopard, and an Ammut," Howard explained to the visitors, "a mythical creature that is part crocodile, part hippo, and part lioness."

"Golly! They look so modern," Lady Allenby exclaimed. "I'd love one for my parlor."

"And here"—Carter showed them—"we have some shoes with images of Nubian captives on the soles, so that Tutankhamun would quite literally have walked on his enemies."

Lying beneath the furniture there were falcon collars, alabaster vessels, and a white wishing cup that Eve blushed to see was the twin of the one they had smuggled out in Howard's jacket pocket. It was a huge storage room, brimful of objects the king might have needed in the afterlife. The sheer number of items, and the clear artistry of their design, made her shiver.

At the other end of the antechamber was the entrance to the burial chamber, guarded by the two life-size statues. Eve held her breath, hoping no one would spot the evidence of the hole Howard had chipped in the wall, but they were too overawed by what they could see.

"The guardian statues are similar but not identical," Howard said. "One shows Tutankhamun in life, the other in the afterlife."

"Are you quite convinced it is Tutankhamun's tomb?" Lady Allenby asked. "Not someone else's?"

"I am," Howard affirmed. "There are other names engraved here and there, but his is the main one."

Eve knew that he had been finally convinced only when he saw the name on the seal of the shrine, but he couldn't admit that. It didn't matter. He was the voice of authority now. Everyone present listened to his pronouncements with unquestioning respect. The Egyptian officials whispered to each other and Lady Allenby kept exclaiming, "Oh golly!"

Eve's nerves began to settle and she felt a buzz of excitement at the enormity of the events she was part of. Of course, they'd talked about the possibility of finding an undisturbed tomb, but the reality was overwhelming. She was desperately proud of Howard and Pups.

The following day brought more visitors: Pierre Lacau, director of the antiquities service, Paul Tottenham, adviser to the Ministry of Public Works, and Eve's uncle Mervyn, first secretary at the British Embassy. She was disappointed he hadn't brought his wife, Mary, and speculated that it might be because she was pregnant but Mervyn said no, it wasn't that.

"I'll bring her another time," he said. "For now, I'm here as a representative of His Majesty's government." He pulled a comic face, making Eve laugh.

"Dignified as always, Uncle Merv," she said. "I'm glad you are bringing suitable gravitas to your role."

"Talking of gravitas," he said, "I hear you're to become a respectable married lady. Congratulations, young Eve. When do I get to meet the man brave enough to take you on?"

"I can't risk you meeting him before the wedding in case you talk him out of it," Eve joked, poking him in the ribs. "But in all seriousness, I hope he'll be able to come and see the tomb before long, and I shall introduce you if you promise to be on best behavior."

Thinking about Brograve made her miss him terribly, but she busied herself handing around some of the heavy stone water bottles and helping to explain to visitors what they were about to see. In answer to their questions she told them there was no doubt this was the burial place of Tutankhamun, and that unlike every other tomb in the Valley, it had lain undisturbed since ancient times. She was enjoying her new role.

One man was firing more questions than any other and when she asked his name he told her he was Arthur Merton, a reporter from *The Times*.

Eve was nonplussed. There weren't supposed to be any press there.

"I wangled my way in," he admitted with a wink. "You do know how big this story is, don't you? Your name is going to be in the history books."

"All the credit goes to Howard Carter and my father," she said. "I just tagged along for the ride."

"But you must be interested in archaeology," he insisted. "You seem very knowledgeable."

As he probed, Eve's enthusiasm got the better of her. She told him about Howard's hunch years ago that Tutankhamun's tomb might be around here, and about his gridblock plan of the Valley identifying this spot beneath some old workmen's huts. She told him about Hussein the waterboy stumbling over the top step, and

Howard excavating the staircase, then sending them a telegram that made them rush out from England. Whenever she stopped talking, Arthur asked more questions, keeping her divulging more until it was his turn to be shown inside.

"Thank you. You've been very helpful," he said, and it was only then it occurred to Eve that perhaps she should have checked with Howard before letting her mouth run away with her. It was just too thrilling to keep to herself. Besides, the story would come out sooner or later.

After Uncle Mervyn had been shown around the tomb, she traveled back to the Winter Palace Hotel with him via donkey cart and then felucca. He was clearly impressed by what he had seen in the antechamber and kept asking questions.

"What makes Mr. Carter so convinced that Tutankhamun's coffin lies behind that wall?" he asked. "It looks to me more like a furniture repository than a king's burial place."

"Oh, he's very sure," Eve said. "There are all kinds of signs."

Mervyn was still puzzled. "But Tutankhamun artifacts have been found in other tombs over the years. I hope he is not going to be disappointed when he breaks through. Maybe it's another one of these red herrings you keep finding in archaeology."

"I promise you it's not a red herring . . ."

It was so frustrating not to be able to convince him that finally Eve couldn't keep quiet any longer. Mervyn was family. Surely it was safe to confess to him? "If I tell you a secret, do you promise you will never tell another soul for as long as you live?"

After he promised, she told him, in hushed tones, about their nighttime visit, when they had broken into the burial chamber and seen the shrine with Tutankhamun's seals intact. "Without a doubt," she told him, "it was the greatest moment of my life."

Mervyn stared at her, openmouthed. "Oh god, I hope that never comes out. It would be disastrous. Carter should have known better."

Straightaway, Eve regretted telling him. What was she thinking of? That was the second time she had been loose-tongued in the matter of a few hours, but she simply couldn't help herself.

"You won't say anything, will you?" she pleaded, clutching his arm. "My head would be on the chopping block."

"I promised, didn't I?" He drew a finger across his lips. "I want no part of it. As far as I'm concerned, this conversation never happened."

Chapter Twenty-Five

Luxor, December 1922

Two days later, when Lord Carnarvon was handed a copy of *The Times*, which had been shipped out from London, the discovery of the tomb was front-page news. He scanned the story, frowning, then looked up at Eve.

"Did you talk to this man, Arthur Merton?" he asked.

Eve blushed and admitted she had.

"Honestly, Evelyn!" he rebuked. "What did Howard tell us? You must exercise more discretion. It's a very delicate situation with the Egyptians and you could ruin things for all of us."

"What does it say?" she asked, shame-faced, and he handed her the paper. Arthur Merton hadn't taken notes while they were speaking but she recognized the passages he quoted as her own words exactly and was amazed at his memory. It was an object lesson in dealing with the press.

"I'm sorry, Pups. I've been an idiot. I'll apologize to Howard, and I promise it won't happen again." She blushed deeper, thinking of her even greater indiscretion with Uncle Mervyn and hoping fervently that never came to light.

Howard was working nonstop, constantly in meetings with officials, sending or receiving telegrams, and showing around the dignitaries who kept arriving in a continuous stream. He had approached the Metropolitan Museum asking for assistance and they sent Arthur Mace, their Australian-born assistant curator of Egyptian Art, and Harry Burton, an experienced photographer of antiquities. Both men were in Egypt already and they arrived in Luxor with their wives in early December. Although they were a generation older than Eve, she befriended the two women—Winifred and Minnie—and they became companions in the mêlée.

"Such a shame your mother couldn't be here," Winifred said, and Eve explained that Almina ran a private hospital in London so it was hard for her to get away. In fact, when Howard's telegram arrived she had telephoned her mother's London house and been told by the butler that Lady Carnarvon had gone to Paris. Eve had no idea why, but she sent word to the Ritz Hotel in Place Vendôme, since that's where she always stayed. Almina had many friends in Paris and thought nothing of traveling across the Channel for a party.

With Minnie and Winifred's help, Eve threw luncheon parties in the Valley, right next to the tomb. There was cold chicken and salads with Egyptian bread, and the local specialties of falafel, hummus, and pickled vegetables. She served fresh lemonade but no alcohol, not wishing to offend the Muslim workers, who were teetotalers.

Eve enjoyed playing hostess. Her mother was famous for the extravagant parties she threw, both at Highclere and at Seamore Place, and Eve had watched the ways she induced guests to mingle and made sure no one was excluded. If asked, she would say she had learned more from her father over the years, but from Almina she had inherited a love of entertaining.

Several guests asked her who Tutankhamun had been, and she explained that he had reigned from roughly 1332 to 1323 BC, and that he had unified the country after a split under his father, Akhenaten. Sometimes she amazed herself with the extent of her knowledge—there was seldom a question she couldn't answer—but she had been reading books on Egyptology since she was a child and had learned from Howard, the master.

On the thirteenth, Eve and Pups left Luxor to sail back to England. Eve couldn't wait to get back, to see Brograve and to tell her London friends about the tomb—the bits she was allowed to talk about, that is. Pups had arrangements to put in place: he must speak to his lawyers, arrange funding for the important task of securing and managing the tomb, and he had supplies to order and dispatch to help Howard, including a motorcar that would be shipped across to Luxor and placed at his disposal.

During the crossing, they were in celebratory mode, ordering champagne before dinner each evening and toasting Howard and Tutankhamun, the long-dead king. As they sailed past the north of Sicily, the volcanic island of Stromboli was erupting, providing an awe-inspiring display of red and orange flares shooting into the dark purple sky, as if nature itself were joining their festivities.

They got a fast steamer this time, and a week after leaving Egypt, they caught a taxicab from Charing Cross station to their Berkeley Square house. A mountain of post was stacked on the desk in Pups's study and he sat down to flick through it straightaway.

"Look, Eve!" he cried, and she came running into the room to find him reading a short note on monogrammed paper. "It's from the palace. King George and Queen Mary have invited us for afternoon tea so they can hear about the tomb firsthand. Who would have thought it?"

The telephone was ringing off the hook, and most of the callers were journalists wanting to talk to Eve or Lord Carnarvon about the discovery. They soon learned to let the butler deal with them; he had a knack for getting rid of unwanted callers.

Their visit to the palace was exhilarating. Eve remembered how apprehensive she had been at her presentation to Queen Mary two and a half years earlier, yet now she was there as an honored guest. They were ushered by liveried footmen into a private drawing room, and spent an hour regaling the royal couple with descriptions of their experiences. Eve did most of the talking, describing everything from the baking temperature in the tomb and its peculiar musky scent, to the animal couches and the lifelike guardian statues.

"It must feel rather a responsibility," the king remarked, and Pups agreed.

"One wants to do the right thing, for the sake of Anglo-Egyptian relations," he said, "and also for the history books."

"Of course, it comes at a sensitive moment in the country's history," Queen Mary said.

"I have every faith in Howard Carter," Pups replied. "He has been working with the Egyptians for twenty-five years, he speaks Arabic fluently, and I couldn't wish for a worthier ambassador."

"You are the one who made it possible," the king said. "I want you to know your country is proud of you. We're proud of you."

Eve was thrilled for Pups. He wasn't a man who sought the limelight, and wasn't especially relishing it, but she was glad his name would be in the history books. He deserved it.

Chapter Twenty-Six

London, January 1973

B rograve wakened Eve when the doctor came to
check up on her at eleven. It seemed she had fallen
asleep on the sofa with the Tutankhamun cuttings
folder on her lap.

The doctor pulled up a chair alongside her and
opened his bulky leather medical bag, rifling through
for the equipment he needed. Eve peered in at the jumble of stethoscope, tweezers, bandages, and syringes,
all in separate pockets and compartments. She had
missed his name when he came the day before and it
seemed too late to ask now, but he was friendly as he
carried out the routine tests, checking her reflexes, her
eyes, her heart, and so forth.

"Did I pass muster?" she asked as he packed up
again. "Not time for the knacker's yard yet, is it?"

"You've made a remarkable recovery from last year's stroke," he said. "You deserve a medal for effort. You're an inspiration."

But she caught snatches of the conversation as he talked to Brograve by the front door afterward. "It may have been a TIA," he said, and she knew that meant "transient ischemic attack," a kind of mini-stroke. "Keep an eye . . . avoid stressful situations . . ."

She'd been in a good mood earlier, looking through her Tutankhamun cuttings, but overhearing the doctor's words upset her. She knew TIAs were not a good sign. Her stupid brain! Why did it keep misbehaving? It was horrible to think another major stroke might be just around the corner and then she'd be back in the hospital, learning how to swallow all over again. Or worse. What if she died, and the truth about the tomb died with her?

Since she started having strokes, the possibility of dying had always been there. Each time could be the last. She tried not to dwell on it, because otherwise she would sit around feeling anxious, but it lent an urgency to her search for the gold container. She had to find it and return it to Egypt while she was still capable.

After the doctor left, Eve picked up the cuttings folder to take it back to the cupboard and a letter fell out. A handwritten letter, with large, loopy writing, dated December 1922. She checked the signature— Marie Corelli, a popular novelist who wrote mystical melodramas with titles like *The Sorrows of Satan* and *Treasure of Heaven*. She was much maligned by the literati of the day for her belief in reincarnation and out-of-body experiences, as well as her overblown writing style.

The letter had been waiting when Eve got to High- clere for Christmas Day 1922, flushed with triumph from her visit to the palace with Pups. A weird feeling had crept over her as she read the words:

> *I understand the excitement you must feel about your father's discovery but I am bound to warn you of the danger you and your loved ones could face if the pharaoh's burial chamber is disturbed. I'm sure you have read of the curses placed by an- cient priests on other tombs. In that of Khentika Ikhekhi were found the words "as for all men who shall enter this tomb, there will be judgment . . . an end will be made for him . . . I shall seize his neck like a bird."*

Eve thought of Howard Carter's canary and shivered. According to the letter, another curse read: "They

226 · GILL PAUL

that shall break the seal of this tomb shall meet death by a disease no doctor can diagnose."

She ran to the library, then the smoking room looking for Pups, and finally found him out by the stables. "Look!" she cried, and waited for him to read it. "What do you think?"

He rubbed his forehead with his knuckle. "Marie Corelli is seen as a fantasist in spiritualist circles, but I have certainly heard of curses of the pharaohs before now. Perhaps I should ask Sirenia's advice."

Eve winced. She had no faith in the histrionic clairvoyant her father used for his séances. "Howard has been entering pharaohs' tombs for over twenty years now without suffering ill effects. Perhaps we should consult him on our return to Egypt."

"Howard is bound to dismiss it," her father said. "He's a scientist to the core."

"Then perhaps we should dismiss it too," Eve said. "I can't imagine how an Ancient Egyptian could have cast a spell that would affect us three thousand years later."

"Their knowledge was advanced in many areas, so I wouldn't rule it out," he replied.

As it happened, other business got in the way and Pups was forced to return to London before he was able to consult Sirenia. Marie Corelli wrote to the newspapers about the "curse in the tomb" and soon after that, Arthur Weigall of the *Daily Mail* picked up the story and the other papers followed. Some speculated that microscopic spores in the air could cause fatal illnesses in those who visited it, or that there was a disease spread by bat droppings; others stuck to the supernatural interpretation.

Eve told herself it was all nonsense, but still she had a moment of trepidation when she caught a cold that January. Was it just a cold? Or her reaction to spores in the tomb? She had felt uneasy in the burial chamber, maybe for good reason.

Looking back now, at the age of . . . She hesitated. What age was she again? Seventy-one . . . As the first person in the chamber, she should have been the first victim of any curse, yet here she still was, fifty years later, having lived to tell the tale. And Howard had lived almost two decades after the tomb was opened.

Brograve came in to tell her luncheon was ready and asked what she was reading, so she handed it over.

"I remember this," he said, glancing at it. "What a load of tosh. The woman should have stuck to novels. She clearly had a lurid imagination."

Eve frowned, a memory coming to her. "That's exactly what you said at the time. Those exact words. Did I show it to you? Were we married in nineteen twenty-two?"

"Engaged," he said, taking the folder from her and slipping the letter back inside.

That puzzled Eve. She could remember them getting engaged but she couldn't remember Brograve being her fiancé when the tomb was discovered. Why hadn't he been there with her? Events had gotten shuffled in her head and now they were out of sequence, like a card index that has been dropped on the floor and hastily shoved back together.

"I've been trying to decide what to do about Ana Mansour," he said. "She's keen to talk to you again while she's in London, but I don't want you to be under any pressure. Why don't I write to her saying that we are looking through our family archives and that we'll get in touch when we have anything to share?"

"It's the truth. We are, aren't we?" Eve realized she had gotten waylaid. She'd meant to look for the gold container that morning and instead she'd lost herself in the cuttings folder. She closed her eyes, trying to picture where she had put her memento from the tomb. Fragments of memory floated around her brain, too vague to pin down. She had the impression she'd been in a rush. And she could remember thinking she wouldn't tell Brograve. But that didn't make sense. Why shouldn't he know?

Thinking about it gave her a creepy feeling, like a ghostly finger pressing on the back of her skull. It reminded her that after all the excitement of finding the tomb, events became darker and everything changed for the worse.

Chapter Twenty-Seven

London, January 1973

While Eve was taking an afternoon nap on the sofa, a plaid blanket draped over her, Brograve sat in the window seat to write to Ana Mansour. She had given him the address of a London hotel just off the Edgware Road. He kept it short, his fountain pen scratching across the Basildon Bond paper with their personal letterhead: the names Lord and Lady Beauchamp in fancy scroll and the family crest, parts of which dated back to his fourteenth-century ancestor Guy de Beauchamp.

It was snowing outside: gusty, horizontal snow that was settling on the roof of the townhouse opposite. The sky was so gray it felt almost like the middle of the night, although it was only three in the afternoon. Typical January weather.

He looked at Eve, sleeping peacefully, a fire glowing in the grate, and felt a fierce rush of protectiveness. During most of their married life she hadn't needed his protection because she was such an independent character, but these strokes were cruel. They made her fragile in a way she'd never been before.

He was glad he had been able to provide for her materially, although their lifestyle was nothing like as grand as the one she had grown up with at Highclere. He remembered being awestruck the first time they turned into the estate's twisting drive and the Italianate towers came into view. He hardly uttered a word as the butler greeted them at the front door and Eve led him through the hall into the gothic-style saloon at the center of the house. It had a vaulted ceiling two stories high, and a colonnaded gallery that ran around the first floor, with arches around the ground floor leading off to the other main rooms. Heraldic crests and ancestor portraits lined the walls, making it look more like a museum than a home.

Eve took him up a curved oak staircase and showed him to his room at a corner of the building, with a tall window looking out over the grounds and its own bathroom through a connecting door. "Where's your room?" he asked, hoping it was nearby, but she explained it was on an upper floor reached via the red staircase, not the oak. After she left, he unpacked and hung his clothes in the oak closet, then sat on the edge of the bed feeling nervous and unworthy. The purpose of the trip was for him to ask Lord Carnarvon's permission to marry his daughter, and he didn't have a clue what to say. He'd rehearsed several speeches in his head but none sounded right.

There was a knock on the door and a liveried footman asked if he could unpack his bags for him.

"It's already done," he said. "Thank you." Then he wondered if he had committed a faux pas by doing the man out of a job.

"Lord and Lady Carnarvon are having sherry in the drawing room. They invite you to join them when you are ready," he said, giving a little bow and starting to withdraw.

"Wait!" Brograve said. He checked his hair in the looking glass, smoothing it quickly with his hand. "Could you show me where the drawing room is? I'm afraid I'm hopelessly lost."

Lord and Lady Carnarvon were sitting opposite each other, and Eve was next to her father but she leaped to her feet and rushed over when she saw him, taking him by the arm and bringing him to greet his hosts. A footman handed him a glass of sherry from a silver tray and he lowered himself carefully into a chair, terrified of spilling a drop on the irreplaceable brocade or the plush Persian carpet. When he dared look around, his first impressions were of pistachio-green silk wallpaper and gilded moldings. Oil paintings lined the walls, and the furniture looked priceless, certainly far too grand to place a drink on, so he clutched his glass in his hand.

Porchy arrived soon after with his new wife, Catherine. Eve bombarded them with questions about married life, keen to hear every last detail. Everyone kept glancing at him, though, and he got the impression they knew why he was there, but it wasn't mentioned, as if there were protocols that must be observed.

They went through to the dining room for dinner and Brograve shivered as he looked up at the imposing equestrian portrait of Charles I, the king who lost his head after the English Civil War.

"It's a Van Dyck," Lady Carnarvon said, the first words she had spoken to him directly. Her expression was cold. She didn't approve of him.

After the meal, Lord Carnarvon rose and beckoned for Brograve to follow, saying, "Shall we?" It was time. Eve gave his hand a quick squeeze of encouragement.

They walked across the entrance hall and into a book-lined room with ornate wood-paneled ceilings and crimson velvet chairs. Two pillars separated this room from the main library, which stretched off into the distance. Lord Carnarvon poured him a snifter of brandy and he breathed in the rich aroma, then took a sip for Dutch courage, topping up the sherry and wine he'd already consumed.

"I understand you want to marry my daughter," Lord Carnarvon said, saving him from having to raise the subject himself. "And that she is in agreement with the plan." He raised an eyebrow. "Is that so?"

"Yes, I b-believe so," Brograve said, nerves making him stutter. "In fact, I was being altogether too slow in the matter so she p-proposed to me." Immediately he'd said it, he wondered if he was being ungallant, but Lord Carnarvon bellowed with laughter.

"That's my Eve! God bless her, you'll have your hands full, but I imagine you know that already."

He flicked open a silver table lighter and toasted a fat cigar over its flame, while Brograve pondered how to answer.

Lord Carnarvon puffed on his cigar until the tip glowed. "I've never done this before, but I imagine I had better ask how you plan to provide for my daughter. What is your profession?"

Brograve explained that he had started a company producing copper cables, and that he already had substantial orders. "I should also tell you that my father wants me to stand for parliament in his seat of Lowestoft at the next general election." He winced, sure that Lord Carnarvon was not a Liberal.

"Is that not somewhat of a suicide mission?" he replied. "The Liberal Party is in shambles, is it not? That Lloyd George coalition has well-nigh killed them off."

"It will be tricky," Brograve agreed. "I think the chances of winning are slim, but my father is retiring and it's his dearest wish that I should fight the seat, so . . ." He spread his hands. He knew he wouldn't win. In fact, it would be hugely inconvenient if he did because the new company took all his time, but he had to try for his father's sake.

"Your father's at Lloyd's of London, is he not? I look forward to meeting him. Perhaps we could all dine together at my club in the autumn?"

Brograve's heart gave a little leap. "Does that mean . . . ? Do you mean that I have your permission to marry Eve?"

"Good grief, man, of course you do! I would never go against Eve's wishes. She simply wouldn't have it."

Brograve heaved a sigh of relief and Lord Carnarvon laughed again. "Her mother might be a tad frosty because you weren't her first choice of candidate and Almina likes to be in charge, but my advice is to ride out the storm. When were you thinking of tying the knot?"

"Next April?" Brograve said, a question in his voice. "Eve wants a spring wedding."

"April it is, then." He put down his cigar and rose from his chair. Brograve rose as well, and Lord Carnarvon first of all shook his hand, then threw his arms around him and embraced him, patting his back. "Welcome to the family, young man."

Almina didn't say anything to Brograve's face but he heard that she berated Eve in private. "I offered you the son of an earl," she said, referring to Tommy Russell, "and instead you chose the son of a boring old baron." Eve imitated her mother's voice as she passed this on, doing an uncannily accurate impression. It didn't endear his future mother-in-law to him.

Still, April 1923 was decided on, and the women planned a trip to Paris to start researching wedding dresses. Almina rang to book the church, and spoke to her favorite florist and photographer. This was her forte. She loved organizing events and would oversee every detail with fierce perfectionism.

And then everything changed: an election was called for November fifteenth, and Brograve was in the midst of campaigning when Eve and Pups received the telegram from Howard Carter about the discovery of the tomb. Had it not been for politics, Brograve would have joined them, and he would have been there when they crawled into the burial chamber for that illicit nighttime visit instead of hearing about it secondhand. He wished he had been; Eve was raving about it afterward.

She and Pups were halfway to Egypt when the election result was announced: Brograve got a measly 25 percent of the vote in Lowestoft, and his Conservative opponent took 57 percent. Across the country, the Liberals were decimated and the fledgling Labour Party had its fortunes boosted.

Brograve wouldn't see the tomb until the following February, when he visited with his mother and father. And if he thought their wedding in April would be a straightforward matter, he had another think coming.

Chapter Twenty-Eight

London, January 1973

January drew to a close with a dramatic winter storm that brought down an ancient oak in the street outside Eve and Brograve's apartment. She was sad to see such a mighty creature felled and she took the lift down to the street to pick up a twisty twig with a shriveled acorn still attached to remember it by. She met the postman in the foyer and he handed her a letter addressed to her, in handwriting she didn't recognize.

"Glad to see you out and about again, Lady Eve!" he said. He always called her that and Eve never corrected him. In fact, the title should only be used with her surname, Lady Beauchamp or Lady Evelyn Beauchamp, but what did it matter?

"I'm greased lightning on my stick," she said, waving it. "Don't tell anyone but I'm training for the next Olympic Games."

"I'd put money on you in a heartbeat," he said.

Eve opened her letter over morning coffee. It was from Ana Mansour, and it was written on the stationery of a hotel off the Edgware Road.

Ana began by hoping that Eve was entirely recovered. "Please forgive me if my questioning upset you. It certainly wasn't my intention. Your husband has asked me to leave you in peace, and I fully understand that he wants to protect you. I just wanted you to know that I will remain at this address until I complete my research and you can contact me anytime if you think of anything that might help."

Ana wrote that she was sorry she hadn't had a chance to ask about Eve's recollections of the burial chamber. "Forgive me if I'm wrong, but I got the impression you remembered something about the wishing cup I showed you a picture of, and possibly the gold unguent container. If you did, I beg you to tell me whatever you know."

What on earth had she done with that gold container? Eve wondered yet again. *It must be somewhere in the flat. Surely she should be able to track it down by the scent?*

"I'm sorry to press you after your husband asked me not to," Ana wrote. "This winter is hard for me because my two children are in Cairo, with their father's family, and I can't return home until my research is finished. As a mother, I'm sure you will sympathize."

Eve was surprised. How could any woman leave her children for months on end? Perhaps they were at school and she had decided not to disrupt their education, but the separation must be heart-wrenching. Could she not fly home for a visit or two? Personally, she could never have left Patricia when she was young. The only time they spent a night apart was when Eve was in the hospital after her accident.

The second page of Ana's letter was a list of about twenty items whose whereabouts, she said, remained a mystery. The gold container and the wishing cup were among them. Eve recognized three of the others as the artifacts her father had taken from the tomb—the goose, the amulet, and the wine jar.

A thought struck her: where had her father's mementos gone? She remembered him putting them with the rest of his collection at Highclere when they were there at Christmas 1922. Sometime in the late 1920s, Howard had sold that collection to the Metropolitan Museum, but she was sure he wouldn't have included the three Tutankhamun items in the sale. He couldn't, because Pups should never have had them. Did that mean they were still at Highclere? She must telephone and ask Porchy. If she could help Ana to recover even three objects, perhaps she would be able to return to her children. She wanted to help if she could.

Eve decided not to show the letter to Brograve. He was being very protective of her, but there was no need. She felt absolutely fine now and just as soon as the weather improved, she looked forward to returning to life as it had been before the stroke. They could visit the horse races, starting with Newmarket in April; she enjoyed studying the form and having a "flutter," as her father used to call it. They liked eating out in London restaurants, and sometimes going to a casino afterward, where she used to be a demon at blackjack. And she hoped she would soon be well enough for a shopping trip with Maude, and lunch in the rooftop restaurant at Selfridges, which was their favorite haunt. It was almost a year since she'd bought any new clothes—an all-time record for her. Brograve would happily wear the same clothes for the rest of his life, so he couldn't understand the particular brand of joy that came from buying a chic new outfit.

That afternoon she wrote a reply to Ana's letter, sympathizing about the separation from her children. "What ages are they? Boys or girls?" she asked, doing her best to keep her writing legible. "Are they being well cared for? It must be a terrible worry."

She wrote that she did remember seeing a gold container in the burial chamber, but couldn't imagine what had happened to it—which was more or less the truth. She said there was a chance there might be a few items at Highclere, and promised: "I'm going to telephone my brother and ask him to hunt around."

She found a postage stamp in her purse and gazed at it: three pence. Was that what it cost? Money had changed from shillings and pennies to these new decimal "pence" and she couldn't get the hang of them at all. She stuck the stamp on the envelope and asked Mrs. Jarrold to post it on her way home from work.

The opening of the burial chamber took place on the afternoon of February seventeenth, 1923. Eve and Pups had arrived in Luxor two days earlier to be greeted with controversy. News had reached the Egyptian press that Lord Carnarvon had appointed *The Times* as the official newspaper covering the excavation of the tomb, a decision he made because their fee helped to offset his escalating costs. The Egyptians were infuriated by what they described as his "colonialist sense of entitlement," which kept their own journalists out of the loop. The rest of the British press were cross too. Arthur Weigall of the *Daily Mail* ambushed Eve whenever she walked through the lobby of the Winter Palace.

"What's happening?" he asked. "Can't you give me anything? I'll lose my job if I don't file stories every day."

She felt bad refusing, so tried to give him snippets of information while being careful to guard her tongue about the important stuff.

"A little bird told me that you and Howard Carter are an item," Arthur said with a cheeky grin. "Please tell me it's not true. An old curmudgeon like him can't have won the heart of a pretty young girl like you."

"For goodness' sake, Arthur, who on earth have you been listening to? Howard is twenty-seven years my senior and I've known him since I was a small child. Neither of us has a scrap of romantic interest in the other; that would be plain odd. Besides, my fiancé is arriving in Luxor any day now. I hope you will keep such tittle-tattle to yourself or he might have to challenge you to a duel."

"My lips are sealed," he said, with a smirk.

The group invited for the opening of the burial chamber assembled outside the tomb. Howard seemed tetchy, Eve thought, but she couldn't fathom why. Probably something to do with the press. If Arthur Weigall had asked *him* whether he'd had a romance with Eve, he'd have got his head bitten off.

Pierre Lacau, director of antiquities, was there, and an engineer called Sir William Garstin, who was an adviser to the Ministry of Public Works. The Met's Egyptologist Arthur Mace came with his wife, Winifred, and the photographer Harry Burton brought his wife, Minnie. Harry took some photographs of them all standing in the desert by the tomb entrance and promised to send a print to Eve.

At four in the afternoon, Howard stood in front of the assembled company and made a little speech, then Pups said a few words, before Howard gave the order for his workmen to go inside the tomb and break through the doorway into the burial chamber. When they pulled the rushes aside, they must have been able to see the section Howard had patched up, but none of the dignitaries were in the antechamber at that point and the workmen didn't comment.

The strong musky scent reached Eve before she was inside the antechamber, and it made her feel lightheaded. There was a pounding sensation right at the base of her skull that she put down to nerves. The words in Marie Corelli's letter came back to her: "death by a disease no doctor can diagnose," it had said. Should she be wary of going inside for a second time?

She and Pups had mentioned the curse story to Howard, and as predicted, he treated it with instant derision.

"The tomb was airtight," he explained, "and therefore nothing could possibly have been living inside: no bats, no insects, no fungi, no spores. The idea of a magical curse belongs in children's storybooks, along with enchanted castles and wicked witches."

Eve shook herself. Of course he was right. How could it be otherwise? She knew her father wasn't convinced, but he wisely kept his own counsel.

When it was her turn, she walked inside, paired with Sir William Garstin, curiosity overcoming her apprehension. She hadn't had a chance to examine the wall paintings last time they were inside, so she looked now, by the light of some arc lamps that had been set up. Were there any dire warnings inscribed there? She was no expert in translating hieroglyphics but it seemed there were just the traditional images depicting the journey of the soul through the skies to the other world. She spotted the opening of the mouth ceremony, which the Ancient Egyptians considered essential so that the deceased could still eat and drink, and the weighing of the heart ceremony; according to their beliefs, the deceased could only proceed to the afterlife if their heart weighed less than a feather.

Next she examined the intricate gilt carvings on the outer shrine, all set on a brilliant blue faience background. The artistry was staggering. She thought about the body preserved inside and said a silent Christian prayer for Tutankhamun that ended: "May he rest in eternal peace."

It would be months before Howard could start the delicate task of opening the shrine and exposing the inner coffin. It had to be handled with supreme care or the remains would crumble to dust on exposure to air. He would need a team of technical experts and lots of specialist equipment before they started breaking the seals.

When she emerged from the tomb, Eve staggered a little in the heat and brightness of the desert. Everyone seemed overawed. When they spoke, it was mostly gibberish, as if they'd had too much to drink.

Eve hugged her father tightly, then she hugged Howard too, before jumping back, remembering the absurd rumor about them and not wanting to give any watching pressmen a photograph that might fuel it.

"Is your mother not coming to see the tomb?" Arthur Weigall asked Eve when he came across her in the Winter Palace reception that evening. "She must be curious after all the Rothschild money that's been poured into the Egyptian desert."

"Of course she's curious!" Eve replied. "But, as I'm sure you know, she runs a private hospital in London that takes up much of her time."

Arthur looked sly. "I heard she's got a new friend, an ex–army officer called Ian Dennistoun. What's more, I heard his marriage has recently collapsed. Care to comment?"

Eve laughed at him. "Honestly, Arthur! Dorothy Dennistoun is a friend of my mother's and her husband was recently a patient in her hospital. You should write penny dreadfuls instead of reporting the news. Or go back to your curse stories! They seem more up your street."

She climbed the stairs to her suite, wondering where on earth he had dug up that story from. Perhaps her mother had accompanied Ian to some function or other and society columnists had leaped to put two and two together. What a sleazy bunch they were!

Two days after the official opening, Brograve arrived in Luxor with his parents. Eve went to the railway station to greet them and rushed into Brograve's arms. Although they'd been apart for only three weeks, it had felt like an eternity. She embraced Sir Edward and Betty too. As she got to know Brograve's father better, she realized he wasn't stern, as she'd first thought, but reserved, like his son. Beneath his exterior was a kind, hardworking, intensely moral man. Both he and Brograve were content to let the women do the talking, which was just as well because Eve and Betty always had plenty to say.

The morning after their arrival, Eve took them to the Valley, where Howard had agreed to give them a personal tour of the tomb. His mood seemed much improved and he was almost jovial as he greeted them.

"So you're Eve's young man," he said, shaking his hand vigorously. "I had no idea you were so tall! She told me all about you but omitted that detail." Howard wasn't short, but Brograve towered over him.

"You didn't ask," Eve replied.

The ceiling of the passageway into the antechamber was too low for Brograve and he had to stoop to walk down the slope. Eve clutched his arm, excited for him to see it. Once inside all three were visibly impressed by the treasures.

"You must be so proud," Betty gasped. "Everyone's saying it's the eighth wonder of the world. I'm honored that you were able to arrange for us to see it."

When they emerged, while Betty and Sir Edward were asking Howard questions, Eve led Brograve behind a sandy hillock so she could kiss him. She glanced around first to check that none of the Arab workers were watching, then stepped farther up the slope to even their height difference; otherwise he had to bend almost double to press his lips to hers.

"I love you, Pipsqueak," he whispered, and she giggled at the nickname he had recently coined for her.

"Love you too, Beanstalk," she replied.

"I like your young man," Howard told her later. "Even a romantically unschooled amateur like me can tell you've found yourself a good one."

Eve glowed. When she was with Brograve, it felt magical. She was a different person, a newer, shinier, happier, *better* version of her old self.

Chapter Twenty-Nine

London, February 1973

Eve couldn't help worrying about Ana Mansour. There had been no reply to her letter so she decided to try telephoning to ask how she was. Brograve wouldn't approve but she could call when he went out for his walk after luncheon. That was the time when she usually rang her friends, sitting at the telephone table in the hall with a cup of tea to have a good old natter.

The phone in the hotel rang out for a long time and Eve was about to give up when a man with a foreign accent answered. He knew who Ana Mansour was and Eve heard the creaking of stairs, then a knock on the door. There was a pause followed by the sound of feet hurrying down and the receiver being lifted.

"Lady Beauchamp?" Ana said, with hope in her voice.

"Please, at this point you should call me Eve," she replied. "I wanted to telephone to say I'm worried about you stuck here without your children, and to say please don't stay in London on my account. I *will* try to find some information for you but there are lots of gaps in my memory and I'm not sure if I will be able to help."

Ana didn't speak for a moment and when she did, she sounded deflated. It occurred to Eve that by telephoning she had raised her hopes, then torn them down again.

"I need to finish my research before I return to Egypt," Ana said, "but thank you for your thoughtfulness. I do sympathize with your memory loss. It must be hard."

Eve tried to shrug it off. "Most of the time it doesn't affect me. Life goes on, you know. But your questions made me stumble up against some of the blank spots, and I wanted to apologize if I seemed vague."

She heard the flare of a match as Ana lit a cigarette, then inhaled. Eve got a fleeting sense that she could smell the tobacco smoke wafting down the line.

"After my father's stroke, he found that writing down his memories helped. The more he wrote, the more he remembered little details that had escaped him. You might try that." Ana inhaled again.

"Yes, I suppose I could, but I don't seem to have the concentration for writing anymore. Besides, the difficulty lies in pinpointing exactly *what* I can't remember." She laughed, but it made her anxious. It was one thing knowing what she didn't remember; what about all the things she didn't *know* she wasn't remembering? There might be some important ones. "How is your father now?" she asked.

"He died over ten years ago," Ana said, "but I spent a lot of time with him after the stroke. Like you, he had gaps in his memory, and I came to the conclusion that his brain protected him from distressing memories, like his experiences in the war. It made me wonder if . . . Please stop me if you find this upsetting, but I wondered if you might have forgotten some things that happened around the opening of the tomb because of all the tragedies that came afterward. It must have been tough for you, and not helped by everyone saying they were caused by a curse." Eve heard a crackling sound as she took another draw on her cigarette.

"Ah, that old curse myth. Howard Carter used to say that sane people should dismiss such inventions with contempt. Those were his exact words."

"Did you never have a moment when you wondered if there might be any truth in it?" Ana asked.

Eve considered the question. "If I ever wondered,

Howard brought me back down to earth with a bump. And Brograve was always very scathing about it. So I had two rational people to hand."

Ana chuckled. "I can tell your husband wouldn't be the type to believe in the supernatural, but when you look at the list of all the bizarre deaths of people associated with the tomb, you can't help speculating. Maya's writings, the ones recently discovered at Saqqara, are full of blessings and curses and magic. Maybe some of the items from the tomb were cursed."

Were they? Suddenly the musky scent of the tomb filled Eve's nostrils. It used to linger around that gold box and now it seemed to be in the hall where she was sitting. The smell was so strong that she glanced around to see if the container had somehow appeared on the telephone table.

"It does make you question whether there's anything in it," Ana continued. "There are still mysteries surrounding how the Ancient Egyptians built the pyramids, and how they made their incredible observations of the stars without the aid of a telescope, so perhaps they did come up with a way of harming tomb robbers with their spells. I wouldn't want to keep anything from the tomb in my home, just in case."

Eve fell silent, thinking back to the weeks after they entered the burial chamber and took their souvenirs.

Everything began to go wrong from that moment, starting with Howard's canary. She shivered.

"Are you alright?" Ana asked. "I'm sorry. I didn't mean to upset you."

"I'm fine," Eve said, but she had an urge to get off the phone, so she made up a white lie. "It's just that I think I can hear my husband returning. He doesn't know I telephoned you. I'd better go. I'll be in touch if I think of anything that might help you."

She hung up, feeling alarmed. Why had she telephoned Ana? It didn't feel as if it had achieved anything. Instead, strange thoughts had been poured into her head, where they swirled around like Scotch mist.

What if the gold container was cursed, and that's why she kept having strokes? Where had she put it, and why had she not told Brograve? She had to find it and get rid of it as soon as possible before it finished her off completely.

Chapter Thirty

Luxor, February 19, 1923

Two days after the opening of the burial chamber, Eve's maid, Marcelle, developed excruciating stomach pains. A local doctor came to examine her and said he thought it might be appendicitis. Marcelle begged Eve to let her return to London; she was terrified at the thought of being operated on in a foreign country. Eve telegrammed her mother, who replied that Marcelle should come back as soon as possible for treatment at her hospital.

Brograve was sailing to London the following day to take care of business matters and said he would accompany her and make sure she was comfortable on the journey. Eve traveled on the train with them both to Alexandria and booked a first-class cabin on the steamer for Marcelle, then said her goodbyes. She would miss

Brograve terribly but at least she knew her maid was in safe hands.

Eve stayed overnight in Alexandria and when she returned to Luxor the following day, she found her father in his suite, stomping around in a foul mood.

"Bloody Howard has suddenly got airs above his station," he told her. "He thinks he's the only one in charge of the tomb and we're all supposed to bow to his will."

Eve was surprised. Howard and her father had never fallen out before, at least as far as she was aware. She sat in the armchair under his ceiling fan.

"This is not like you, Pups. What on earth did you argue about?"

Pups gave an exasperated sigh. "He thinks I shouldn't have done the deal with *The Times*, and complains it's made everything twice as hard for him because it's got the Egyptians' backs up. But I had no choice! Last September I told him I couldn't afford another season's excavation, and now there are many more expenses to cover than I ever dreamed of back then. It's my right to seek sources of revenue wherever I can find them."

"He must see the logic in that."

"You'd think so, wouldn't you?" He shook his head. "He's also complaining about the dignitaries who turn up wanting to be shown around the tomb, saying they interrupt his work. I replied that I'm afraid it is part of his role for the foreseeable future."

Pups was red in the face. The argument had clearly bothered him.

"I'm sure you'll kiss and make up tomorrow," she said. "It's just a spat, and it only happened because you're both under pressure."

"I think it might be rather more than a spat." Her father frowned. "He has banned me from setting foot in Castle Carter ever again."

"Oh dear," Eve said. "He has a fiery temper, but I expect he has calmed down and is already regretting his hasty words. I'll call on him later."

"Tell him he's an employee of mine and that he should bloody well know where his bread is buttered," her father snapped.

Eve decided she wouldn't pass on that exact message.

She traveled across to the Valley on her own for the first time, feeling slightly nervous about dealing with the Egyptians in a language she didn't understand. As it happened, she managed just fine, apart from being vastly overcharged by the donkey cart driver, but when she reached the tomb, Pecky Callender told her that Howard had gone home with a "gippy tummy." Eve got her driver to take her back down the road to Castle Carter.

Howard opened the door, looking rather green around the gills. In response to Eve's inquiry, he said he had been suffering from stomach problems for some months now and would seek a second opinion at her mother's hospital in the summer. Nevertheless he invited her into his sitting room and called for the houseboy to bring some tea.

"I'm sorry to hear you and Pups have fallen out," Eve began. "He can be a tad brusque when he is stressed and you seem to have borne the brunt, but you must know he doesn't mean anything by it. He has the greatest respect for you."

Howard leaned back in his chair, linking his hands in his lap. "You say that, Eve, but he is not showing me respect. I have given him my considered opinion, based on twenty-five years' working in Egypt, and he is dismissing it because it doesn't suit him." He shrugged. "I may have a certain responsibility as his employee—as he was at *pains* to remind me—but I have a greater responsibility to archaeology. I must make sure this tomb is properly preserved and recorded for posterity, and *that* is my top priority."

Eve hastened to reassure him. "It's Pups's top priority too. The difference between your positions is negligible. He's very upset about falling out with you."

Howard glanced out the window, his expression

stony. "I don't have time to be upset with him. I have work to do."

The houseboy brought in a tray with a pot of fresh mint tea and two tall glasses painted with gold and purple swirls. He poured one for each of them, then bowed before leaving the room.

"Can I assure Pups that you will carry on the good work?" Eve asked, picking up her glass and blowing on the tea.

"Of course! He knows I'm not the type to walk out on the job."

Eve struggled to find wording that would appease her father without making Howard feel as if he had backed down. "Can I say that you are sorry the argument happened?"

He glared. "Please don't report the word 'sorry' as coming from my lips. I stood up for what is right and I'm not sorry about that."

Eve decided it was going to be easier to get Pups to apologize. His temper cooled quickly after a flare-up and he never held a grudge.

"Is there anything I can send to help your stomach?" she asked. "I have some Andrews liver salts and Bayer aspirin in my medical chest."

"There's no need," he insisted. "But thank you all the same."

When Eve returned to the Winter Palace, she found her father in the salon chatting with Arthur Mace, the Egyptologist from the Met, and his charming wife, Winifred. Pups looked rather more relaxed than he had earlier.

"We've had a top-notch idea," he told her. "We thought the four of us might charter a boat and cruise up the Nile to Aswan, just for a week. I've never been that far upriver before. Will you join us, Eve?"

She clapped her hands. "I'd love to!" she cried. "How marvelously exciting!"

Arthur hired a boat with three luxury cabins, and staff on board to look after them.

"Before we go," she asked Pups, "please will you send a note to Howard? I suspect he is not the type who finds it easy to apologize, so why don't you do it?"

"You're right, little Eve," he said. "I will."

Later that evening he showed her the letter he'd written, and she was impressed by its warmth and humility: "Whatever your feelings are or will be for me in the future, my affection for you will never change," it said. "I'm a man with few friends and whatever happens, nothing will ever alter my feelings for you."

"Well done, Pups," she said, kissing his cheek before she took it to the concierge to be dispatched straightaway.

Chapter Thirty-One

The Nile, March 1923

Their cruise boat chugged slowly upriver through the stunning colorscapes of Egypt: the deep sapphire-blue of the Nile, the lush green of the date palms in the fertile strip irrigated by the river, and then the shimmery golden desert beyond. The weather was pleasantly warm with a slight breeze. Sitting on deck with a glass of guava juice, chatting with Arthur and Winifred, was a delightful way to spend a few days. Eve could see her father winding down. His complexion looked healthier and the sparkle was back in his eyes. He was only fifty-six years old but he'd suffered bouts of poor health since a car accident in 1909 when the Panhard rolled over, crushing his ribs.

They hired a guide to show them around the sites in Aswan: the Qubbet el-Hawa tombs of nobles from the Old Kingdom; the botanical garden on Kitchener's Island; the Aswan Dam, Kitchener's pet project to stop the Nile floods from destroying farmlands every year; and the temple complex of Isis, located on the island of Philae in the upper Nile.

While at Philae, Eve slipped away from their party and wandered down to the water's edge to look out across the lake formed by the dam. She knew some villages had been deliberately flooded and lay beneath the twinkling water, but there was no sign of them now— just a wide, choppy lake. Tiny waves made a slapping sound against the shingle where she stood.

Suddenly a shout rang out and she turned to see their guide running toward her, waving his arms wildly. *"Rujiet!"* he was repeating. *"Rujiet!"*

When he got close, he grabbed her arm and yanked her roughly back from the water's edge, hurting her. She gave a yelp. He had spoken English earlier but his words were incoherent in his agitation.

"What is it?" she cried, rubbing her wrenched shoulder. "What's the matter?"

"Crocodile!" he shouted in English and pointed to what she had thought was a log of wood floating on the surface of the water just a few yards away.

Eve started shaking. Now she looked closely, she could see the wide slit of the mouth and the languid blink of a yellow eye just above the waterline. It had been gliding toward her. One lunge and she would have been in its jaws. She turned and ran to her father and threw her arms around him.

"Let's get out of here," she begged. *"Please!"*

Pups was furious with the guide. "Incompetent fool! Why didn't you warn us? If anything had happened . . ." He didn't specify what he would have done, because he was too busy consoling Eve.

She just wanted to get as far away as she could in case the crocodile waddled ashore. The guide assured them it wouldn't but she didn't have much faith in him because he seemed very shaken.

As they got a carriage back to the Cataract Hotel, where they were staying in Aswan, she couldn't stop shivering despite the heat. If it had lunged at her and dragged her into the water, she doubted the men of the party would have been able to save her. She thought of that menacing yellow eye and knew she'd had a narrow escape.

When she wrote to Brograve that night she decided to turn the incident into a joke, so as not to alarm him, but that eye continued to haunt her.

It was hotter in Aswan than Luxor, a scorching heat that sapped their energy. The air cooled as soon as the sun set, but then mosquitoes surrounded them in a whining swarm. Their guide had taken Eve and Winifred to a market earlier where a stallholder sold them a lemon-scented oil that he guaranteed would keep mosquitoes away, and all of the party had applied it to their exposed skin. It seemed to work, because they sat out in the hotel garden for dinner without any of them getting bitten.

An old Bedouin man came to perform a coffee ceremony for them. He roasted the beans over an open flame, ground them, boiled, then sieved them, before pouring each of them a small cup from a spout held high in the air.

Eve sniffed her cup. There was some herbal ingredient besides coffee.

"Cardamom," Winifred told her, after taking a sip. "It's delicious!"

The old man explained through a translator that they must each drink three cups: one for the soul, one for the sword, and one because they were guests. It was tradition. He had brought a hookah and the men puffed on it while the women watched, amused. The smoke smelled sweetly herbal, like scented hay.

On their last night in Aswan, Pups was careless in closing his mosquito net when he went to bed and got a large, itchy mosquito bite on his cheek. Eve's lemon oil must have rubbed off on the pillow.

"It looks like a teenager's blemish!" Eve teased him over breakfast in the grand dining room. "At your age, Pups, you should be rather proud of that."

Chapter Thirty-Two

Cairo, March 16, 1923

From Aswan, Eve and Pups caught a train directly to Cairo, where he had plans to meet Pierre Lacau to discuss the management of the tomb. They checked into the Grand Continental Hotel overlooking Opera Square and Eve changed her clothes, ready to meet some friends of Pups's for dinner, then to watch a film. When she knocked on Pups's door, he said he couldn't face dinner.

"My face is aching where that dratted mosquito bit me," he said, cupping his palm over it.

Eve had a look close-up: the bite seemed inflamed, with a tiny cut at the edge where he had nicked it while shaving. She found some iodine in her medical kit and dabbed it on, staining the skin brown.

"I'll cancel our dinner," she said. "We can eat in the hotel. I'm sure you'll feel better after an early night."

The next morning, when she went to Pups's room to collect him for breakfast, he answered the door looking baggy-eyed. His forehead was burning, and when she touched the glands in his neck, as her mother had taught her to do, they were hard and swollen. Pups knew an English doctor in Cairo, by the name of Fletcher Barrett, so Eve telephoned and asked if he would stop by. It was probably just a mild infection, she told herself. He might need a few days' bed rest.

Dr. Barrett examined the mosquito bite, listened to her father's chest, checked his vital signs, and asked several questions about his health in recent days.

"That mosquito bite has become infected," he said at last, "and I fear it has caused blood poisoning."

Eve felt a cold chill of fear. "What should we do? How long will it take to heal?"

The doctor sat down and addressed them both, his tone serious. "A fit young man with a strong constitution would probably fight this off in no time, but I'm afraid your father's medical history could cause complications. I suggest you send your mother a telegram. She will be aware of the implications of blood poisoning."

There was a buzzing sound in Eve's ears and she was conscious of the beating of her heart. "What treatments can you give him? I put iodine on the bite last night. Shall I keep doing that?"

He nodded slowly. "Let me take a blood sample to confirm my diagnosis, and I'll return in a couple of hours with some medicine. Make sure he keeps sipping boiled water or light broths, and apply cloths soaked in tepid water to his brow and pulse points."

Eve was glad to be given tasks. First, she scribbled a telegram to her mother and got the concierge to send it, then she asked for plentiful boiled water to be brought to her father's room, along with some light chicken broth and a pot of tea for her. She would be his personal nurse, and she'd do everything in her power to make him well again. No patient would ever have been nursed as well as she would nurse him.

What if he dies? a voice in her head asked. She shook herself. It was unthinkable. She simply wouldn't let him.

While Pups slept that afternoon, she telephoned her uncle Mervyn, who promised to visit, and she sent telegrams to Howard Carter, to Lady Allenby, and to Brograve. To each of them she said that the illness was serious, but that he was receiving the best of care and no word should be leaked to the press. She knew her father would not want it to hit the headlines.

Her mother sent a telegram by return saying that she was flying out immediately in a De Havilland monoplane. They would have to refuel several times en route but it was by far the fastest way. That's when Eve knew it was a matter of life and death, because her mother was petrified of flying. A sob formed in her throat and wouldn't shift.

Brograve telegrammed offering to come to Cairo to support her. She replied that he should wait for now. She was spending all her time at her father's bedside and wouldn't be able to see him if he turned up.

Some friends visited the hotel, but Uncle Mervyn was the only one she admitted to Pups's sickroom. He was fevered and anxious, dozing fitfully, and often groaning in his sleep. Mervyn tried to talk to him but didn't get a coherent response.

"Call me, day or night," he told Eve. "Anything you need, I will arrange it."

"I need him to recover," Eve said, and Mervyn squeezed her hand hard.

The following morning, Pups seemed more lucid. Eve fed him spoonfuls of broth and they talked about the book Howard was planning to write about the tomb, along with Arthur Mace. It would be illustrated with Harry Burton's photographs, and Pups was to contribute a foreword. The public were crying out for information and this would be the first reliable source.

Pups fell asleep again, and when he wakened later, he was less coherent. "We shouldn't have disturbed the spirits," he murmured.

"What spirits?" Eve asked. "What are you talking about?"

"The spirits in the tomb," he said. "Malevolent spirits. We disturbed them."

"There weren't any spirits, Pups," she assured him, but she remembered the cloying scent that had irritated her throat, and that feeling like a finger poking at the back of her skull. And then Marie Corelli's warning came back to her: "A disease no doctor can diagnose." But that wasn't true because Fletcher Barrett *had* diagnosed it. What nonsense! She tried to wipe the thought from her brain.

The next morning, there was a brisk knock on the door and Almina bustled into the room, already in nurse mode despite the challenging journey. Eve had never been so glad to see her. Say what you liked about Almina, she was a talented nurse. All her ex-patients raved about her.

"What's his temperature?" she asked, and Eve told her the latest reading. She picked up his wrist to feel his pulse and tutted.

"Is it bad, Mama?" Eve whispered, trying not to let her panic show.

Her mother sucked air through her teeth. "Only time will tell."

Almina took over the task of making him sip liquids

and mopping his brow, her voice calm and soothing, but Eve didn't leave the room. She sat in an armchair, listening to every sound her father made in his sleep, and trying to communicate with him whenever he was awake. He developed an alarming cough, his lungs making a wheezing sound like an old water tank, and he was gasping for breath at times. Her mother arranged the pillows so that he was propped upright, and he seemed easier that way.

When Fletcher Barrett came, he examined the patient, then talked to Almina in a low voice. Eve could hardly hear, but she made out the words *pneumonia* and *critical* and dug her fingernails into her palms. This couldn't be happening.

After he left, Almina started to weep, very softly. That was a huge shock. Eve had never seen her mother cry before—not ever. She leaped to her feet and rushed to hug her. It felt odd, because she and Almina usually exchanged only the most cursory embraces, but now they clung to each other.

"Please don't cry, Mama. I'm sure he'll recover now you're here. Between us, we will save him."

That made her mother cry harder and Eve cried too. Who would have thought it? Almina didn't spend more than a few weeks a year with her husband, but she clearly cared deeply for him.

"Your father's a very dear man, who's been good to me," she said, dabbing her eyes with a lace handkerchief. "It wasn't ever a romantic match, not like you and Brograve . . ."

Eve was surprised by that. It almost sounded like grudging approval of her choice of husband.

"But we gave each other a lot of freedom in our marriage and it worked for us."

Eve was alarmed that she was talking in the past tense. "You could still have years ahead, Mama. No one dies of a mosquito bite. It's absurd!"

Almina looked at her sadly. "I hope you're right," she said, and turned to place a cloth on the patient's brow. Eve felt glad that Pups was with two women who loved him, and hoped the strength of their love would tether him to this world like invisible ropes.

A message was slipped under the door saying that Howard Carter was in the hotel, hoping to see Lord Carnarvon. Eve hurried downstairs to update him, but told him her father was too ill for visitors. She said the same to Lady Allenby, and Arthur Mace, and all the other friends who came, bearing flowers and fruit baskets and sympathy. Her father would hate for anyone to see him in this state. The only person she admitted was Porchy, who arrived on the fourth of April, posthaste from Alexandria.

"Thank goodness you're here," Eve said, jumping up to hug him. She didn't say, but she thought, *Thank goodness you made it in time.*

"I got the steamer from Marseilles. It took forever," he said, white-faced with shock when he saw the state of his father.

Pups was barely conscious, racked by coughing fits, vomiting up any liquid they could entice him to swallow. It was harrowing to watch. Eve, Porchy, and their mother sat by the bedside, stroking his hands and whispering reassurance.

"I'm scared," he croaked, his voice little more than a whisper.

"We love you, Pups," Eve told him. "You are the best father a girl could wish for. Please fight this. Please keep trying."

"We need you, Pups," Porchy said, anguish in his voice. Eve knew he must be thinking about the burden of the estate, which would fall on his shoulders if Pups died. He was only twenty-four, and must have hoped for much more time to learn how it all worked.

But in the early hours on the fifth, Pups's breathing slowed to a labored hiss and then stopped. Almina listened to his chest, felt the pulse in his neck, and her voice cracked as she said, "He's gone."

Eve wanted to scream, *No! He can't be!* He was far

too young to die. She needed him. Who would give her away at her wedding? It should have been taking place later that month, but she couldn't get married now, not without her father.

She bent to kiss his sweet face, on the side of his temple, and whispered, "Come back, Pups. Please come back." But there was no response. He wasn't there anymore.

She couldn't bear to stay in the room a moment longer. She ran outside, barging straight into some reporters who were hovering in the corridor like vultures. Someone must have tipped them off. She shoved through the midst of them, ignoring their questions, and slammed the door of her own room behind her before throwing herself on the bed.

With deep certainty, she knew she would never recover from this loss. She'd always thought of herself as a lucky person, but this was the very worst of luck. The innocent happiness of her youth had been destroyed overnight and it felt as though everything was going to change for the worse.

Chapter Thirty-Three

London, January 1973

The morning after her telephone conversation with Ana, Eve renewed her search for the gold unguent container. It preyed on her mind that it might be cursed and that's what was causing her strokes. Of course, she couldn't discuss it with Brograve—he would simply tease her—but she'd always had a creepy feeling about it because of the harsh, unpleasant smell. It seemed incredible that the contents still had an oily quality and a strong scent after three thousand years locked in an airless environment, and even more incredible that they retained them out in the open air. That alone made it feel sinister. Could the unguent have been cursed by Maya? She tried to cling to the rational view, but it was hard not to feel anxious.

If only she had never taken it from the tomb. It

hadn't brought her any pleasure. She had never put it on display in any of her homes but had hidden it away in cupboards and then the attic, to stop that strange smell pervading their living space.

A memory came to her of the day they moved from London to Framfield. What age had Patricia been? It was just before she started school, so probably four. She kept getting under the feet of the removal men as they carried furniture out to their van.

"Go and play in the sitting room," Eve told her. All the furniture had already been moved from there and only a few boxes remained. Patricia was quiet for ages so Eve left her alone, grateful for the peace. When she finally glanced in, she got the fright of her life. Patricia had found the unguent container and was playing with it.

"What are you doing?" she cried, rushing over. "Don't touch that!" She pried it from Patricia's hand and lifted her. The smell was especially strong when she buried her nose in her daughter's neck.

"I put the perfume on," Patricia said.

Irrational fear took hold. Eve rushed her to the bathroom and used a scratchy old towel that had been left behind to scrub at her daughter's hands, face, and neck. The scent was in her hair too. She hesitated. Was there time to wash it? There would have to be. She got Eve to crouch with her head over the side of the bath and rinsed her hair under the tap, lathering with a sliver of soap, then rinsing again. Patricia was crying, terrified by her mother's panic.

"What on earth are you doing?" Brograve asked, coming into the bathroom.

As Eve explained, she could hear how odd her actions sounded. What harm could it do? There couldn't be anything toxic in the unguent. It just had an unpleasant odor.

Brograve was looking at her as if worried she'd lost her mind, but when he spoke, he was his usual pragmatic self: "It will be nice to have clean hair for the new house," he said. "I'll open the car windows to help it dry on the way there."

"Silly Mummy," Eve said, hugging Patricia, and surreptitiously checking that no trace of the scent lingered. "Fancy me making a fuss over nothing!"

When they arrived at Framfield, Eve directed the removal men to put the cardboard box with the gold container directly into the attic. She could remember it said "Lyons Tea. Always the Best" on the side.

But there was no Lyons Tea box in their cupboards now. She established that quite quickly. Most of the remaining boxes had their contents written on labels on the sides. Perhaps the container was in one of the old suitcases. She asked Sionead to lift them down, recognizing the brown leather one she had taken on her honeymoon. The lock had rusted, but Sionead managed to prize it open using a chisel. Inside she found her wedding veil and a crumbling posy of dried flowers, on top of an embroidered silk bedspread that a cousin of Brograve's had given them as a wedding present. Eve had never liked the color, like spilled tea, so it hadn't been used. She picked it up and thought she caught a vague whiff of the scent of the tomb. Perhaps this was the cloth she had used to wrap the container in back in Charles Street, but it wasn't there anymore.

Another suitcase had some old toys of Patricia's—dolls with china faces, a miniature tea set, some dollhouse furniture. Yet another contained Brograve's model railway and a Meccano set from when he was a boy. He had never let her throw them away. But none contained the gold box.

Over lunch, she asked Brograve where he thought it might be.

"Do you remember about ten years ago we had to have the roof repaired at Framfield?" he asked.

She didn't, but nodded all the same.

"We gave a lot of things from the attic to jumble sales at that time. Maybe your Egyptian box was among them."

Eve had no memory of it, but she was sure she wouldn't have let it go to a jumble sale. It was far too valuable, its history too significant. Imagine if someone bought it for a shilling, not knowing what it was? She shivered. That couldn't be right. But where else might it be?

If it had begun to scare her, might she have wrapped it up and sent it back to the museum in Cairo, in an anonymous parcel, and not told Brograve? But if she had done that, Ana would know. It wouldn't be on her list of missing items.

Eve strained her memory, focusing on the image of the gold box and the Lyons Tea logo, trying to force her brain to remember, but nothing came. Whole years of her life—decades even—had been swallowed up by the strokes. She sometimes wondered if the memories were still there, hiding among the curls of gray matter in her brain, or if they had been wiped clean as a blackboard, without leaving the faintest impression. She hoped it was the former, hoped they would all reappear one day, the way the streets of London reappeared after the blanket of snow melted—first in patches and then altogether.

Chapter Thirty-Four

Cairo, April 5, 1923

Straight after Pups died, Almina took charge. She was used to dealing with death from her work in the hospital. She announced she would stay in Cairo to take care of the formalities and arrange to get Pups's body shipped home, while Eve and Porchy were to sail back and begin making preparations for the funeral.

Eve was crushed by grief and couldn't imagine how she would manage the journey. She lay on her bed sobbing so hard she made herself sick, then she huddled on the bathroom floor, shivering, her stomach in knots. How did anyone survive this? What could she do? She was twenty-one years old but felt like a helpless child.

Almina came in and crouched to comfort her. Stroking her daughter's hair, an arm tightly around her, she said, "We will get through this, Eve. You have to take it hour by hour. First I'm going to order breakfast to be brought to your room and you will eat something. I'll pack while you bathe and prepare for the journey. We will grit our teeth and keep putting one foot in front of the other, because that's all we can do."

When the breakfast tray arrived, Almina spread some toast with butter and honey—Eve's favorite when she was a child—and Eve managed a few bites, although her throat was so raw from crying it was hard to swallow.

Porchy was unnaturally quiet on the journey but had enough self-possession to purchase their travel tickets and hire porters to carry their luggage from the train to the steamer. Later, Eve couldn't remember any details of the voyage except that she spent a lot of time sobbing in her cabin. Eating felt like an impossible chore because it was as though there was a huge rock lodged in her chest that didn't leave space for food. Brograve met their train at Charing Cross and Eve clung to him, breathing his masculine scent and absorbing his steadiness.

As they walked arm in arm to the station entrance,

Eve's attention was caught by a newspaper kiosk. Pictures of Pups stared out from the front cover of almost every newspaper. "Killed by the curse of Tutankhamun" read a headline. "Writings in the tomb warned of tragedy" read another.

"Don't look," Brograve urged her. "There's been a lot of nonsense written. Best not pay it any mind."

It felt hateful that a family tragedy had been turned into sensational headlines. And they were wrong! There hadn't been any writings. Eve was tempted to buy a paper, to read the worst, but instead she let herself be helped into Brograve's car, glancing over her shoulder at the offensive kiosk.

On the journey to Highclere, Eve found that she was calmer if she stayed in physical contact with Brograve: resting her hand on his knee or her head on his shoulder. He didn't say much but was a calm, solid presence, and he loved her; after all they'd been through, she knew that with certainty.

The butler greeted them at the door, wearing a black armband and conveying sympathies on behalf of all the staff. Catherine met them in the drawing room and hugged Eve warmly. She'd had a fire laid and tea prepared for their arrival, already slipping into the role of lady of the house. Now that Porchy had inherited, Catherine took over the title Countess of Carnarvon from Almina, and Highclere became theirs. Eve looked around at the pistachio-green walls and the reality dawned on her that this wasn't her home anymore. Her mother's house at Seamore Place had never felt like home either, and Berkeley Square, Pups's London house, was to be sold. That made her technically homeless.

The four of them sat making a list of close friends who must be invited to the funeral. Eve went into Pups's library to fetch his address book from the drawer of the Napoleon desk, and it felt like trespassing. That had been his domain, where children were allowed only under supervision. She had never opened that drawer before, and was choked to see he'd kept a bag of toffees inside, the same toffees he used to slip her as a child when she fell and hurt her knee, or when she'd had a scolding from her mother.

Back in the drawing room, the butler was talking to Porchy. "One other matter, sir," he said. "I'm sorry to tell you that Lord Carnarvon's dog, Susie, has also died. In fact, she passed away on the night of the fifth of April, which I believe is the same night as his lordship."

"How strange!" Eve said. "Perhaps she had a sixth sense."

Porchy spoke in the condescending tone he saved

for his baby sister: "She was a twelve-year-old, three-legged mutt in poor health. She could have gone at any time."

Eve explained to Brograve: "She lost her leg in a fox snare. All the same, I think it's uncanny she died the same night as Pups. Rather touching even."

He smiled and reached over to ruffle her hair.

The funeral was a quiet affair with family and close friends. They decided that Susie should be buried alongside Pups on a hill overlooking the estate of which he had been so proud. Eve sobbed throughout and Brograve kept his arm firmly around her, propping her up.

That evening they had a special dinner, with Highclere's own beef and some rare wines from Lord Carnarvon's cellar, followed by his favorite Napoleon brandy. It was hushed and respectful, but as they sat in the drawing room after dinner, Eve became aware of raised voices from the corner where her mother and Porchy were sitting.

As she listened, she realized they were talking about the death duties that would have to be paid on the estate and her heart started to pound.

Brograve tried to intervene: "Tonight is not the

time for such a conversation," he said. "Save it for another day."

"When else?" Porchy demanded. "Mama is planning to disappear back to her London social life and her beloved hospital tomorrow, leaving me in the lurch."

"It's absurd," Almina said. "You can't really expect me to sink the remainder of my Rothschild inheritance into paying death duties to the government. What on earth would I live on?"

Eve's eyes filled with tears. "Please, both of you, not now." She felt too fragile to act as peacemaker.

"No!" Porchy slammed his glass on the table, some brandy sloshing over the side. "This place is mine now and if you're not planning to help me, Mama, you can get the hell off my bloody land!"

Brograve stood up and walked between them, his imposing height giving him authority. "Funerals are strange occasions," he said, turning from one to the other. "People say things they don't mean and later regret. Let's leave this subject for now and please—everyone—raise your glasses to Lord Carnarvon, who was the most decent of men."

Eve raised her glass—"To Pups"—and the others joined in. She was proud of Brograve; he was a beacon of strength, like a lighthouse in the eye of a storm.

Almina rose to go to her room and when Eve followed, she found her mother packing.

"I'm going to London first thing in the morning," she said. "Porchy and Catherine have made it very clear I'm not welcome."

Eve ran to hug her. "That's not true, Mama. Porchy is plastered. Don't pay any attention."

"It *is* true. Who am I anyway, now I'm no longer Countess of Carnarvon? I can't be the dowager countess because your grandfather's second wife has that title. I'm no one."

How like her mother to worry about the title, Eve thought. But it wasn't just that—it was what it symbolized: her hard-won acceptance in polite society after her illegitimate background. "You are a remarkable woman who runs a very successful hospital and you have dozens of friends who adore you. *I* adore you!"

"We must spend more time together, Evelyn." Her mother kissed her cheek. "I'd like that."

"Me too," Eve said. She had lost one parent and she desperately needed the one she had left.

Eve stayed a few more days at Highclere, finding comfort in riding around the estate with Brograve, telling him stories of her childhood, and visiting places she and Pups had loved: the stables, the lake, the farm, the circular Grotto Lodge. Every day she walked up Beacon Hill to sit by Pups's grave and she talked to him in her head as if he were there. It made her feel close to him.

"Did you ever talk to Edward?" she asked Brograve. "After he died, I mean."

"I still do," he said. "I've told him all about you, and that I can't wait to marry you." He gave a woeful smile.

"I'm sorry," Eve said. "We were supposed to be married this month." Almina had canceled the church for now.

"It's alright, my love," he said. "We will marry when you are ready, but not a moment before."

Among the deluge of condolence letters, Eve picked out one addressed to her, feeling as if she recognized the handwriting. When she opened it, she saw it was from the popular novelist Marie Corelli, the one who had written before Christmas. It began with her offering sympathy on Eve's loss, followed by her assurance that Lord Carnarvon was at peace in the spirit world.

"He came to me in a séance yesterday evening," she wrote, "and asked me to contact you. He said he doesn't want you to mourn because he died a happy man, having achieved his life's ambition with the discovery of the tomb. But he would like a chance to talk to you once more and asked that you consult a spirit medium. If it is at all possible, he promised he will be there with you."

Eve got goose bumps all over. Could it be true? Had Pups contacted Marie Corelli from the afterlife? Why would he, when he had never met her and hadn't held a high opinion of her? If he were going to contact any spiritual medium, surely it would have been Sirenia?

"Who's the letter from?" Brograve asked, and she made a snap decision not to tell him. She had a strong feeling he would try to talk her out of consulting a medium, and she already knew that she was going to give it a try.

Chapter Thirty-Five

London, May 1923

Eve considered contacting Sirenia, but decided against it. The woman was an actress who would say whatever she thought Eve wanted to hear, and she couldn't face the thought of all her moaning and wailing and regurgitating fake ectoplasm. If she was going to do this, she should consult the most reputable medium she could find and give it a serious chance, for Pups's sake. So, once she was back in London she telephoned Emily and asked her to seek advice from their family friend Sir Arthur Conan Doyle, since he was the country's best-known advocate of spiritualism.

Sir Arthur sent a message that he was glad to be of assistance and extended an invitation for Eve to join him for afternoon tea in the Ritz. She was nervous about the meeting, her grief still so raw that tears flowed at the slightest triggers. Sir Arthur had booked a private room, and greeted her with such warmth that she was dabbing her eyes even before they sat down.

He was a tall man with a silver moustache, and his old-school manners reminded her of Pups. Eve explained about the letter from Marie Corelli, saying she had never been a believer in spiritualism but that her father had. She said she felt she owed it to him to at least try to make contact but she did not want to risk being manipulated by charlatans.

Sir Arthur immediately understood. "I know just the place," he said. "At the Society for Psychical Research, based in Kensington, they conduct scientific investigations into psychic phenomena. You can trust them to be honest and avoid histrionics."

That sounded encouraging but Eve was still wary. "Would they be discreet? Not a whiff of this can end up in the press."

"I can personally vouch for their discretion," he assured her. "Would you like me to make an appointment for you and accompany you there?"

"Please," Eve begged. "I would be ever so grateful."

Over tea, he explained a little more to her about his own beliefs, and about the comfort it had given him to be able to contact his beloved son and brother. He told her that in the spiritualists' view, death is a mere transition into another realm where spirits can evolve to a higher plane, and that they continue to watch over their loved ones on earth.

"They come to us in idle moments," he said, "as a voice in our heads, or a beam of light traveling across a mirror, or sometimes by making a much-loved scent appear. The terrifying ghosts of popular imagination are a far cry from the much gentler truth."

By the time they parted, Eve couldn't wait for the appointment. She yearned to speak to Pups again and know that he heard her. If only it were possible!

Sir Arthur picked her up from Seamore Place in his motorcar, a Daimler Landaulette with bright blue paintwork. She admired it, and told him that Pups had taught her to drive after the war. All the way to South Kensington they chatted about cars, which helped take her mind off her nervousness about the appointment.

The Society was based in a tall, dark-stone terraced house, with a library on the raised ground floor. Eve was glad of Sir Arthur's steadying arm as they announced themselves at reception. Nerves were jangling in the pit of her stomach. They were ushered straight up to the first floor, and into a room where a small, bearded man of indeterminate age sat in an armchair. He rose to shake her hand and introduced himself as Leonard

Farinelli, but all the while he seemed, disconcertingly, to be looking at something over her left shoulder.

"Would you like me to wait downstairs?" Sir Arthur asked.

"No, please stay," Eve said. She glanced around, looking for a table at which the séance might be held, but there was no furniture other than some worn armchairs.

"I'll make notes, if you like," Sir Arthur offered. "To remind you afterward." He guided Eve into the chair opposite Leonard Farinelli, and took a seat off to the side. She swallowed hard.

"Pups is with you," the man began abruptly, his eyes unfocused. "He came into the room with you."

Eve was startled and tears sprang to her eyes. How did he know she had called her father Pups? Was he really there? She turned but couldn't see anything.

Still looking over her shoulder, Leonard Farinelli described Pups's appearance. He said he was wearing a tweed suit with a waistcoat and bow tie and a hat with a wide ribbon around it. It sounded like the way he always dressed. Her skin prickled. He described Pups's complexion, pitted from a bout of smallpox in his teens, and his neat moustache.

Eve looked behind her again but there was nothing there. "Why can you see him but I can't?" she asked.

"I only see a vague shadow," he told her. "It takes

a lot of energy for spirits to make themselves visible. They can't maintain it for long."

Suddenly, Eve felt sure she could smell the brand of cigar Pups smoked. She sniffed the air. It was definitely there. He was with her. She gasped. "Pups? Is it really you?" She sniffed in one direction, then another, trying to find the source of the smell. "Can he hear me?"

"Of course," the psychic said. "He senses your thoughts too."

Eve closed her eyes and thought about how much she loved him, how much she missed him, praying he could sense that.

"He wants to tell you he is at peace," the man said. "It was his time to pass, and he has no regrets."

Eve shook her head. That was hard to believe. Surely he must be frustrated to die before the opening of Tutankhamun's shrine, without seeing all the wonders it might contain? She dabbed her eyes with a handkerchief.

The man's eyes were closed now as he concentrated on hearing the messages. "He wants you to tell your mother that he loves her very much, and that he is grateful for their long and happy marriage."

That was odd. She couldn't imagine her father saying that. But perhaps that's the kind of thing he might say after death, once he was a spirit.

"And he says to tell your brother that he will be with him, to guide him, as he works to preserve the estate."

The man was scarcely moving, scarcely breathing. Eve was grateful to be spared the dramatic displays she heard other mediums practiced—the table tilting, the ghostly apparitions. This, at least, was peaceful and dignified.

"Pups says he wants you to marry Brograve as soon as possible, and is only sad he will not be able to walk you down the aisle. He said he is a good man and you have chosen wisely."

A sob burst from Eve's throat. Sir Arthur leaned across to grip her forearm briefly.

In his low, accentless voice, Leonard Farinelli talked of Pups's love of motorcars and horses, of his dog, Susie, now with him in the spirit world, and he mentioned others from the past with whom Pups had been reunited: an old friend of his, Prince Victor, who had died in 1918; his mother, Evelyn, after whom she was named. Eve felt a warm glow. All she had wanted was to know that her father was at peace, and not troubled by the sudden manner of his death. It seemed that was the case.

Then the man's expression changed. He gasped out loud as if he had seen something that terrified him. "Your father says it was foolish of your party to enter the tomb of Tutankhamun. He says the spirits within were disturbed and he worries that harm could come to those who ventured inside. He insists that no goods should be taken from the tomb, to avoid the worst of the pharaoh's curse."

Eve frowned. That didn't ring true. Pups knew they had already taken goods from the tomb—and he would never have called Tutankhamun a pharaoh, a term that was not used about kings of that dynasty. Perhaps the man had misunderstood.

"Could you ask Pups what we should do about the tomb, now that it is open?" she asked.

There was a long pause before the answer came. "He suggests you consult holy men who may be able to exorcise the evil."

Eve shivered at the word *evil*. Her father had mentioned malevolent spirits when he was hallucinating during the fever of his final days. It didn't mean it was true, though. How could it be?

When the session was over, she shook Leonard Farinelli's hand and thanked him for his insights. Sir Arthur led her downstairs to the library, and someone produced a pot of tea. She felt very shaken. She was convinced that Pups had been present in the room in some form, but overall it wasn't the reassuring experience she had hoped for.

"How could a tomb retain a spell placed upon it three thousand years ago?" she asked.

"We don't know," Sir Arthur said. "Much of the ancient knowledge has been lost, but I do know Egyptians used to cast spells by creating unguents imbued with elemental powers."

"Mr. Farinelli seems to think that evil spirits were disturbed when we entered. Do you believe that? Could Tutankhamun's spirit still be there?" The thought made her shiver.

"Any spirits from the ancient world will long since have passed to another realm," Sir Arthur assured her. "But it could be that their negative emotions were absorbed into the stones themselves. We have proved that walls can hold the memories of deeds that have been committed in buildings centuries earlier. I'm sure you must have sensed the history of Highclere as you walk around."

Eve considered that. She grew up knowing the history of Highclere; it was hard to decide what she might have sensed if she had not already known about it.

"How would we find a holy man to exorcise the tomb in Egypt?" she asked. "And what about those of us who have already set foot in it without such protection? Are we in danger?"

"I will ask around for you," Sir Arthur said. "If the

tomb is not desecrated, but is treated with the respect it deserves as a burial ground, I am sure you will be spared."

"But Pups wasn't spared," Eve reminded him. "He died of a mosquito bite. What kind of a senseless death is that?" She remembered something else. "And just before he fell ill, I came close to ending up in the jaws of a crocodile. Could that have been caused by evil spirits? Howard Carter's canary was eaten by a snake, and he has since had stomach problems. My maid Marcelle fell ill too. Might they all be connected?" She felt hysterical at the thought.

"Please don't let your fears carry you away," Sir Arthur urged. "I want you to focus on the knowledge that your father came to you today, and that he is at peace. As for the rest . . . I'm sure all will be well."

He drove Eve back to Seamore Place, trying to reassure her, but she was deeply troubled by the experience. Had her father been there? Were all the words his? When Brograve came to visit that evening, she couldn't hide her distress, and she blurted out what she had done.

He listened to the whole story without interrupting, then read the notes that Sir Arthur had taken. When he'd finished, he spoke calmly. "The man told you nothing that he could not have read in the newspapers.

He knew you were coming so he did his research beforehand and combined it with a few lucky guesses."

Eve argued with him: "But how could he know I called my father Pups?"

"You may have called him that in front of a journalist, and it appeared in a news story. Or perhaps Sir Arthur had briefed him before your visit, based on what you told him when you had tea at the Ritz."

That hadn't occurred to Eve. "Do you think he would have done that? He told me the Society is there to promote research into whether or not the spirit world exists, but it seems to me that he and Leonard Farinelli already believe."

"Of course they do. There's nothing remotely scientific about their methods."

Had she been conned? If so, it meant Pups hadn't been there. But if there was any truth in it, then the whole thing must be accurate, including the warnings about evil spirits.

"What if it is true that Pups, Howard, and I were cursed because we broke into the tomb? I can't risk you catching any bad luck through your association with me. I give you full permission to terminate our engagement forthwith and save yourself from any danger." A sob burst from her throat. She couldn't bear to think of life without Brograve, but she also couldn't bear to think he might come to harm because of her.

"Oh, Eve," he said, profound sadness in his voice. He reached out and lifted her onto his lap, then wrapped his arms around her, so their faces were inches apart. "Don't you know yet that I would do anything for you? I'd go anywhere, and take any risk to be with you. If it is true that you are cursed, then you need me more than ever so that I can protect you." He kissed her and held her close. "I love you, Pipsqueak, and I want to be your husband. No matter what."

Chapter Thirty-Six

London, March 1973

During his constitutional around Regent's Park, Brograve worried about Eve. She had become obsessed with finding that wretched gold box she brought back from the tomb. It clearly wasn't in the flat but still she insisted on pulling down every last box from every last cupboard, and moving ornaments from surface to surface as if that might make it magically appear. He had overheard her muttering to herself and realized she thought it had some kind of supernatural power, although she would never say as much to him. She knew his views on the matter.

Back in 1923, he had been astonished at her decision to consult a clairvoyant after Pups died. She was normally a rational woman, and he had thought they saw eye to eye on the absurd notion of "spirits getting in touch," but it seemed that she had been desperate for any crumbs of comfort.

Of course, contacting spirits was all the rage in the 1920s, with lots of folk providing Ouija boards and Tarot readings as entertainments at parties. Spiritualists had been around long before the war, but they became more respectable after authority figures who should have known better—like Sir Arthur Conan Doyle—gave them credibility. Stories appeared in the papers about some mystical "angels" said to have protected British troops in the Battle of Mons, and clairvoyants sprang up on every street corner pandering to those who had lost husbands and sons in the trenches. Poppycock, all of it!

Growing up with a father who held séances at Highclere must have affected Eve's thinking somewhat. She had disparaged them as over-the-top theatrical performances, but it was as if the notion of spiritualism had crept into the corners of her mind, the way a religious upbringing still colors the thoughts of those who claim to be atheist as adults. If asked directly, Eve would say that of course she didn't believe spirits could communicate with us, and of course she didn't believe there was a curse on Tutankhamun's tomb, but at gut level she was suggestible.

That's why he was worried when she became obsessed with finding the gold container from the tomb.

It wouldn't help her recovery. He wished he could think of something to distract her—and then an idea occurred to him.

Over lunch, he made his suggestion. "Did you realize that in April it will be fifty years since Pups died? Fifty whole years! I thought it might be nice if we go to Highclere for a visit around the anniversary, so you can spend time with Porchy, and walk around all the places you and your father used to love. It's a fitting way to remember him."

A smile lit up her face and her eyes sparkled. "I would *adore* that!" she said. She reached over to kiss him.

"I'll telephone and arrange it," he promised, pleased to have cheered her up. His primary goal in life was to make her happy.

Every marriage has its secrets, Eve supposed. Some men had mistresses and she guessed there were women who had lovers too, although she didn't know any. She and Brograve had no secrets on that scale, but there were a few things she didn't share with him: the cost of a new dress, sometimes, or the confidences of friends. She hadn't told him about telephoning Ana Mansour because he seemed to have taken against the woman, whereas Eve felt sorry she hadn't been able to

help her. She was curious too; Ana was a lady archaeologist, just as Eve had always longed to be, and she
wondered what it was like.

She telephoned her again, a couple of weeks later,
and Ana came to the phone more quickly this time, almost as if expecting the call.

"I hope you're not lonely in London?" Eve asked. "I
think you said you have friends here?"

"I know a few people," Ana replied. "Thank you for
asking. It's kind of you to take an interest."

Her Egyptian accent was almost undetectable, Eve
thought. Occasionally a vowel sounded vaguely foreign,
but she never stumbled on a word or failed to understand anything that was said. "Your English is perfect.
Did you learn it at school?"

"I had an English mother," Ana replied. "She only
ever spoke English to me so I became fluent quite young.
It's been useful over the years because many digs are
multicultural and English is the common language."

"Does your mother live in England now?" Eve loved
hearing other people's life stories, and Ana's sounded
exotic, crisscrossing two continents and two cultures.

"She died when I was fifteen." Ana gave a sad laugh.
"A long time ago."

"Fifteen! I lost my father at twenty-one and thought

I should never recover from the grief. It must have been so much harder at fifteen. . . ." Eve remembered feeling as if the bedrock on which her life was built had shifted and she was sliding off the edge and being swallowed up by an abyss. And then Brograve caught her, thank goodness.

"It was a time of great challenges . . ." Ana said. Speaking slowly, she explained that her father had immersed himself in religion after his wife's death. Ana had grown up with religious freedom till then but suddenly he wanted her to take Quranic lessons from an imam, and wear a veil. "Needless to say, I rebelled. We argued for the next three years, but I managed to persuade him to let me study at university. I had always wanted to be an archaeologist, and he had encouraged me, so he could hardly refuse."

"Me too!" Eve said. "It was my dearest wish to be a lady archaeologist when I was younger." A memory came back to her of finding an old coin while digging in the grounds at Highclere. She'd pretended to anyone who would listen that it was the most significant find ever known to mankind, even after Porchy scornfully told her it was just a Victorian farthing. She must have been very young.

"So why didn't you?" Ana asked. "You clearly enjoyed the time you spent in the Valley. Why weren't you involved while Howard Carter was dismantling the tomb?"

Eve swallowed. "I couldn't face going back there after Pups died. Egypt would always have reminded me of him dying."

It wasn't just that, she thought. She had loved Egypt so passionately—the baking heat, the vibrant colors, the culture, the sheer foreignness—then that love had turned to horror almost overnight. Suddenly she associated it with danger: the crocodiles floating in the Nile, looking like logs of wood; the cobras that hid in trees, camouflaged against the bark; the whining mosquitoes and strange flying insects that transmitted disease and infection; and the militant nationalists shooting people in the street.

"When I married Brograve, I decided to start a new chapter, being a wife and mother instead of a lady archaeologist."

"That's a shame," Ana said. "There are so few women in our profession, even now. You could have been a trailblazer."

"I would have loved Patricia to take up archaeology, but she had different interests. You can't force it, can you? They either take to something or they don't. Do you have a daughter who could follow in your footsteps one day?"

There was a long pause and Eve thought Ana's voice sounded shaky when she replied. "I don't think my daughter, Layla, is interested in archaeology."

There was something odd about the way she said it. Why didn't she know her own daughter's interests? Was it because they'd been separated for so long? "What age is she?" Eve asked. "Maybe she will grow into it."

"Layla is eleven and my son, Masud, is eight."

"You're lucky to have two," Eve said. "I would have loved a son. You must miss them terribly."

"*Do you think she knows?*" said a voice that was neither Ana's nor Eve's. It was a crossed line. They often got crossed lines in that apartment block. It unsettled Eve to think that their neighbors might be listening in anytime she was on the phone.

"Hello?" she called into the ether. "If you can hear me, please hang up." There was no reply and the muffled conversation continued, barely audible. "How annoying! I suppose we'd better say goodbye," she said to Ana. "But I'll call you again soon."

"Before you go, did you remember where the gold unguent container is?" Ana asked.

Her tone sounded as if she knew that Eve had it, and Eve tried to remember if she had admitted that. She didn't think she had.

"I honestly don't *know*," Eve replied, frustrated with herself. "The truth is that I can't remember."

"It was taken out of the tomb, wasn't it?" Ana persevered. "When did you see it last?"

"If I knew that, I'd know where it was." It upset her that she couldn't find it. It was starting to scare her.

Sionead glanced out into the hall and gave her a concerned look. "You OK?" she whispered.

"I'm fine," Eve said, but she had that funny headache again, like a finger pressing the back of her skull. "Perhaps you could fetch me a paracetamol? Sorry, Ana, I have to go. Goodbye."

She placed the receiver on the hall table and rested her head in her hands, completely forgetting that Ana was still on the line. It was only half an hour later, when Brograve got home, that he noticed the whining noise and put it back on the hook.

Sionead's contract had been for three months and the time was drawing to a close. During Eve's afternoon nap, she asked Brograve whether he was ready to manage without her. There was another job her agency could put her forward for, now that Eve didn't need help with personal care. A plumber had come to replace the bath with a walk-in shower so she didn't need help washing herself anymore. She hadn't had a choking incident since before Christmas, and the TIA in January had been very mild, so Sionead's role lay largely in dispensing pills and checking blood pressure.

"You don't need me," she said. "Not really."

Brograve felt tightness in his chest. What if something happened that he couldn't cope with?

Sionead sensed his uneasiness. "Before I go, I could teach you some techniques to use if the need arises. We can practice together. I'm not going to leave you in the lurch. It's just that there are other households where I could be of more use."

"What kind of techniques?" His voice was hoarse, so he cleared his throat.

"You already know what to do in the event of choking," she said. "I could show you what to do if Eve has a funny turn. Explain when you might need an ambulance, and when you just need a doctor."

"I'll talk to Eve about it," he said, but he already knew her views: she didn't think she needed Sionead and felt he shouldn't be wasting all that money. It *was* expensive. "But I'd be grateful if you could explain the techniques."

She began with the worst-case scenario—what to do if he found Eve unconscious and not breathing. She demonstrated how to attempt resuscitation while waiting for an ambulance, and he practiced on a long cylindrical sofa cushion. A tear slid from the corner of his eye as he imagined having to do this in real life, and he turned his head so Sionead wouldn't see.

Next she showed him the recovery position, to be used if Eve was unconscious but still breathing. And finally she explained some tests to perform if Eve was conscious but seemed muddled, or had slurred speech or a drooping face. Brograve was so choked up he could barely speak.

"I could write everything down for you," Sionead offered, "and leave the list by the phone."

He nodded and mumbled, "Yes, please do that."

"You've saved her life before," she told him. "The last stroke would have been much worse if you hadn't gotten her to hospital so quickly."

He knew time was of the essence. He hadn't told Eve in so many words, but that was why they had to leave Framfield. After an incident in 1971, it took over an hour for the ambulance to find them, then another hour to reach St. George's. That time it was just a TIA, but if it had been a stroke, the damage didn't bear thinking about.

As soon as Sionead left the room more tears came to his eyes. What if he were the only person there when Eve collapsed and his actions made all the difference between her living or dying, but he failed her? How would he live with himself? It would be like the guilt he'd felt about his friend Oliver, but multiplied many times over.

All elderly couples must live with this fear, he rationalized. Sionead had given him some control over the situation. He would keep the list handy, and if the time came, he would do the very best he could.

Chapter Thirty-Seven

London, March 1973

Eve and Brograve met Maude and Cuthbert for afternoon tea in the Savoy Hotel River Room. It was nice to have a reason to dress up, Eve thought. Even when they were spending the day at home, she wore a smart skirt and blouse, and chose a necklace to match. She had never taken to trousers; they made her look like one of the seven dwarfs.

It was a sparkling spring day—warm in the sun and chilly in the shade—and she had put on an ice-blue flowered dress, fitted around the bodice, swishy at the hem, a tea dress they used to call them. Her favorite pearls were clasped around her neck and she tottered into the River Room on blue leather Mary Janes, leaning on her tripod stick. She couldn't wear high heels for now while she was still getting her balance back.

"Don't you look lovely!" Maude said, embracing her. "I'm still in my winter woollies because I feel the cold now I'm an old biddy."

They ordered the full afternoon tea: finger sandwiches, slices of cake, scones with cream and jam, homemade shortbread. They'd never eat it all, but it looked storybook pretty in its tiered cake stand.

"We had our golden wedding anniversary party here," Cuthbert said, and Maude nudged him with a quick frown.

"Golden! That's fifty years!" Eve exclaimed. "Has it really been that long?"

"I'm sorry," Maude said. "It was last September, while you were in the hospital. I wasn't going to mention it because I didn't want you to feel you missed out. Yours is coming up later this year, isn't it?"

"Is it?" Eve looked at Brograve. "When's our anniversary?"

"The eighth of October," he said.

"It's usually women who remember dates," Eve said, "but Brograve is our keeper of memories now. I suppose we should celebrate our fiftieth, but we got married during one of the lowest points of my life, so anniversaries have always felt rather bittersweet."

"Fifty years is an achievement!" Maude said. "You

should have a party. We could get the old gang together, see who's still around."

Eve wasn't sure about that. Parties were difficult for her now that she had a rotten memory. She hated to hurt people's feelings by forgetting who they were. Maybe she could ask Brograve to stand at her elbow and whisper names, the way the Queen's lady-in-waiting did for Her Majesty.

"You always threw the best parties," Cuthbert said. "I loved those ones on the terrace at the House of Commons, or in the owners' bar at Newmarket, or your picnics at Glyndebourne. You're a consummate hostess."

Eve stared blankly. She didn't remember any of those occasions. Not a single one.

"Perhaps it would be too much pressure to host a party this year," Brograve said, seeming to sense her bewilderment. "Maybe I should take you to Paris instead. We could have a second honeymoon."

She beamed at him. "That would be lovely," she said, then turned to Maude and Cuthbert. "Now, I want to hear all about this party you secretly held behind my back. How many guests? What did you serve? Was there music and dancing? Spill the beans so I can at least imagine I was there."

Eve had been in no mood for a wedding in 1923, the year Pups died, but she felt she owed it to Brograve. They had waited long enough to be man and wife. Their engagement was announced in *The Times* on the seventeenth of July, and Almina took Eve to Paris for their long-delayed trip to choose a wedding dress, both of them garbed head to toe in black mourning clothes.

They settled on a beautiful drop-waisted gown of ivory chanteuse and a full-length veil of old Brussels lace. Eve couldn't raise any enthusiasm for the process. Her limbs felt heavy. Everything was difficult: making conversation, eating, getting dressed in the morning—it all took Olympian effort.

Almina was in better spirits than she had been at Highclere, almost her old self again. She'd decided she wanted to be addressed as Almina, Countess of Carnarvon, and had placed an announcement on *The Times* court page to that effect. Having her identity clarified seemed to boost her confidence. She chatted to the women at the fashion houses, and with their help selected dozens of new outfits for Eve's honeymoon, charging them all to her personal account.

Back in London, Maude, Emily, and Lois, the unholy quadrumvirate, rallied around. They would be her matrons of honor and would make sure the day went smoothly, looking after the flowers, the decoration of the church, the guest list. All she had to do was turn up and repeat her vows.

"We'll even help you with that if you like," Maude joked.

Most of the summer Almina was preoccupied with work at the hospital, which was now located in Portland Place. It was the hospital of choice for her aristocratic friends, and all the beds were full. Among the patients was Pups's half brother Aubrey, who had long suffered from ill health and very poor eyesight. On top of that, a dental operation had gone wrong, causing blood poisoning. When Eve visited him she found he was very poorly indeed, drifting in and out of fevered consciousness. It took her viscerally back to the hotel room in Cairo where Pups had died five months earlier, and she was in floods of tears as she left. Aubrey was only forty-three and he had four children, the youngest just a year old; how could life be so cruel?

Uncle Mervyn arrived from Cairo on the twenty-sixth of September—the day before his brother Aubrey died, and just twelve days before Eve's wedding was due to take place.

"We have to postpone the wedding," Eve said, at a

family wake in Seamore Place. "As a mark of respect, if nothing else. Many of the guests will be in mourning. We're still in mourning."

"Nonsense! It has to go ahead," Almina insisted. "We can't change the arrangements a second time or the rector will give up on us."

"It's supposed to be the happiest day of my life but I feel so sad," Eve said. "I don't want my wedding day to be a day of mourning."

Brograve was consulted but he said he would do whatever Eve wanted. Eve knew his parents were keen for the wedding to proceed—Betty had more than once dropped hints about the patter of tiny feet, and expressed a wish that if the baby were a boy he be named Edward, after Brograve's brother.

Uncle Mervyn urged her to marry as planned. "There is great comfort to be had in marriage and I want that for you," he said. "Into the darkest time of your life, Brograve will bring light."

But still it felt wrong.

"Couldn't we just have a slight delay, till December perhaps?" Eve asked Almina. "I like winter weddings, with snow and fur muffs."

"December's out of the question," Almina said immediately. Her tone was so adamant that Eve was puzzled.

"What difference does it make?" she asked. "I don't understand."

"I have other plans in December," Almina said but wouldn't explain what they were. "Later," she said, glancing sideways at Mervyn.

When Eve went to her mother's room at bedtime, Almina blurted out the truth: "I'm getting married to Ian Dennistoun in December, and I don't want our weddings to clash."

"Ian Dennistoun?" Eve stared in disbelief. "Your friend Dorothy's ex-husband?"

Her mother nodded, biting her lip to restrain a smile that was twitching the corners of her mouth.

"But . . ." Eve was flabbergasted. Ian was a charmless middle-aged man with a paunch who had neither money nor profession. He had become a member of her mother's social circle lately, but *marriage*? How *could* she? "December will only be eight months since Pups died. It would be an insult to his memory."

"Oh, Eve, you're so sentimental." Almina turned to her mirror and began to smear cold cream on her neck. "I have as much right to be happy as you do. I love Ian and he loves me. We'll keep the wedding low-key, I promise."

"Couldn't you at least mourn Pups for a year? Is that too much to ask?" The haste felt indecent.

"You're so young, Eve. I can't explain it to you but I need this, and I deserve it, so it's happening in December and that's that."

Eve couldn't think how to reply. She ran from the room and rushed downstairs to tell Brograve.

"What is wrong with my family?" she cried. It felt as if everything was falling apart now that Pups had gone, like a book without any binding. "Porchy and Mama are at loggerheads, and she says she is marrying Ian Dennistoun. *Ian,* of all people!" She was too shocked and irate to cry. "Porchy will be incandescent when he hears. The press will have a field day . . ." She remembered Arthur Weigall hinting about it earlier in the year, and she hadn't believed him.

"Families are tricky constructs," Brograve said. "It's not the first time we've had this conversation. We can't change what the others do, but we *can* make decisions for ourselves. And I propose that you and I get married on the eighth of October as planned, then I will be your family. Let the rest of them do as they wish."

Eve sat in his lap and rested her head on his shoulder. In that position they were an exact fit. He was the only person she felt safe around now that Pups was gone. When she was in his arms, breathing the scent of him, she felt protected and wholly loved.

"You're right. I've waited four years to become Evelyn Beauchamp and there's no point waiting a moment longer."

To herself, she thought, *Best get it done before anything else can go wrong.*

Chapter Thirty-Eight

London, October 1923

Sun streamed through the ancient stained-glass windows above the altar as Eve walked down the aisle on Porchy's arm. He was kind to her that day when he stepped into his father's shoes to give her away. St. Margaret's was an elegant church with pretty stone arches running along either side of the pews. She was aware of the whispers and giggles of the little flower girls behind, who looked like Botticelli cherubs. She imagined Pups's spirit was there, floating somewhere in the atmosphere, wishing her well. If it were at all possible, she knew he wouldn't miss his daughter's wedding day.

Brograve looked taller and lankier than ever as he stood at the altar, and she smiled. Although she was wearing the most vertiginous high heels she could find, their height difference made them look as if they were different species—like a giraffe marrying a deer. She grinned at Maude, Emily, and Lois, all dressed in matching mauve satin gowns and looking beautiful, each in their own way.

When she reached the front of the church, Brograve took her hand and held it throughout the ceremony, as if to anchor her. All the same, tears came when the minister pronounced them man and wife. Pups would have been so proud. She could hear Almina sniffling in the front row—only the second time Eve had ever heard her mother cry.

Next it was time for photographs: group ones, family ones, individual ones; the photographer herded them around till he had all the pictures he wanted. They had decided not to hang around for a party but to catch a boat train to Paris that evening. Eve changed into a cream linen traveling outfit, knocked back a glass of champagne, and tossed her orange blossom bouquet over her shoulder. It was caught by a young cousin of Brograve's, who looked a little unnerved.

Then at last they were alone together in a private carriage, legally wedded man and wife.

Brograve had arranged for some Bollinger and a light supper to be served in the train carriage, which had a table, armchairs, and a fold-down bed in the corner by the window. They sat and picked at the food, sipping champagne, and Eve felt nervous. Would he want to make love to her here, on the train, or would he wait till they reached Paris? Emily had told her what to expect, in some detail, and had warned her that it would hurt the first time but that the pain passed quickly, to be replaced by "indescribable" pleasure.

He held out his hand to pull her onto his lap and when they kissed, he seemed tentative, although there was no doubting the lust they felt for each other. She pressed herself against his body and kissed him till she was in a frenzy of desire. She could feel that he had stiffened beneath his trousers, but she was nervous that the guard might interrupt them, so she pulled away and reached for her champagne glass.

"I have a wedding present for you," he said. "I couldn't bring it with me but I have a photograph."

He pulled it from his jacket pocket and handed it over. It showed a foal, a newborn by the looks of things, its twig-like legs bowed, unused to bearing weight.

Eve stared at him in astonishment. "Did you buy him? Or is it a her?"

"Yes. Porchy helped me choose. He's a bay, born to the Derby winner Endicott. I thought you might stable him at Highclere, and that will give you lots of opportunities to visit. I know how much you miss it."

"You bought me a horse!" It was such a magnificent gift, she couldn't take it in.

"We can visit him as soon as we get back from Paris. I left it for you to name him."

Eve looked from the photograph to her husband's grinning face and felt tears coming. It was the most thoughtful gift she'd ever received. The name flashed into her head: "Miraculous," she said. "Because he's a little miracle."

"So are you," Brograve said, touching her cheek. "You are my little miracle."

The honeymoon was not the romantic idyll Eve had dreamed of when they first got engaged because she couldn't shed her sadness. They ate some wonderful French food and drank fine wines, and every night they had a flutter in a casino, just as she knew Pups used to do when he was in Paris. By day they caught a steamboat along the Seine, climbed the Eiffel Tower, strolled in the Tuileries, and visited Sacré-Coeur in Montmartre. Eve had to trot to keep up with Brograve because one of his steps was equivalent to two or three of hers.

The biggest shock was that, despite the passion she felt for her new husband, the physical side of marriage did not come easily. On the first night in their hotel suite, in a four-poster bed with hangings embroidered in gold thread, they attempted to make love, but it was so painful for Eve that they had to give up. It wasn't a slight pain, like a headache after drinking too much gin, or a finger accidentally slashed on a kitchen knife; this was excruciating, as though her flesh were being ripped apart, and she screamed out loud.

Brograve was distraught to have hurt her so badly, while Eve was distressed to have failed at the first hurdle in her new role as his wife. Something must be wrong with her. Married couples the world over performed this act; why couldn't she?

"We're both tired," Brograve said, kissing her forehead. "And there's no rush. We have all the time in the world."

She insisted on trying again the following night, and the next, but it was too painful to proceed. By their last night in Paris, two weeks later, they had still not managed to consummate their marriage and it cast a cloud on the romance. Over a quiet dinner in Montmartre, Eve asked Brograve a question that had been on her mind.

"Have you ever made love to a girl before? You can tell me the truth. I don't mind if you say yes."

"No." He shook his head straightaway. "I always wanted to wait till I was married. During the war there were opportunities—French girls who would do it for food or money—but the men who tried usually ended up with syphilis."

"Good. I'm glad we will be each other's only lovers," she said, squeezing his knee under the table.

"Maybe if I had more experience . . ." he began, but didn't finish the sentence.

"It's not you, it's me," Eve said. She had been experimenting in their bathroom and realized there was enough room inside her. "I seem to tense up when you try to enter."

"You're still traumatized by your father's death," he said. "I'm in no rush. We're both young and healthy, and I'm sure it will simply happen one day."

Eve wasn't so sure. If the problem lay in her being too tense, perhaps there was a solution. She gulped down her glass of Saint-Émilion and gestured for the waiter to refill it. When the bottle was empty, she motioned for him to bring another. Brograve looked bemused but didn't attempt to stop her.

Eve was so plastered she had to cling to his arm as she staggered back to the hotel. As soon as they were in their room, she stripped off her gown and pushed him backward onto the bed, unfastening the buttons at the front of his trousers.

"Now!" she said. "Do it to me now!"

It still hurt a lot, and there was blood on the gold

coverlet, but she and Brograve were joined properly for the first time. As she lay in his arms afterward, with a throbbing between her legs and the beginnings of a hangover jabbing her temples, she was happy. There were times in life, she thought, when you just had to push through pain in order to get to the other side.

Brograve sensed that Eve wasn't listening to the conversation with Maude and Cuthbert. She was staring out the Savoy River Room's window, watching the boats go by on the Thames, and hadn't touched the finger sandwiches on her plate.

"I can still speak French," she announced suddenly. "*Je peux encore parler français.* I just realized that. It means I'll be able to talk to people when we go to Paris."

She was excited and Brograve felt warm inside. "Those years of childhood lessons with a French tutor paid off. You've always been more fluent than I am."

He noticed Maude and Cuthbert glancing at each other, just quickly, and he knew what they were thinking: Eve wasn't herself again, not yet. Maybe she never would be. But in all the ways that mattered she was still the woman he'd married, and he loved her more than ever.

Chapter Thirty-Nine

London, March 1973

Patricia took Eve out for an afternoon while Brograve attended a formal lunch at the gentlemen-only Garrick Club. She had managed to get them an appointment with Leonard of Mayfair, hairdresser to the stars. Eve knew he cut the hair of Elizabeth Taylor and Jackie Kennedy, but when she tried to get him to gossip about his celebrity clients, he refused with a smile, meeting her eyes in the mirror.

"Let's talk about you instead," he said. "What's happening in your life?"

Eve found herself telling him about her latest stroke, and about how hard it was to have memory lapses, and, as she talked, Leonard quietly worked miracles. Afterward she wished she had watched his technique instead of chatting away. He cut layers into the hair that had always been so frizzy and wayward, and when he finished it sat effortlessly around her face in a style that made her look years younger. She gasped with delight.

Patricia asked for a sculpted bob, like the signature look Leonard had created for Twiggy. While Eve waited, a young girl filed her nails, painting them a pretty peach color and massaging her hands with hand cream. She felt thoroughly spoiled.

Afterward they went to an Italian restaurant in Shepherd Market for a salad and a glass of champagne. Eve gazed at her daughter, so pretty with her new haircut, and felt grateful that she lived nearby. Mrs. Jarrold's daughter had emigrated to Australia and tears came to her eyes whenever she mentioned her.

"Dad told me you've been talking to an Egyptian academic about Tutankhamun," Patricia commented. "It's nice they still want your knowledge after all these years."

"I know," Eve replied. "I think they're trying to make sure I tell them everything before I kick the bucket."

"Mum!" Patricia tutted dismissively, but it was true.

"She wants me to find that gold container with the smelly unguent inside, the one that came from the tomb. Do you remember it?"

"How could I forget?" Patricia exclaimed. "I was traumatized that time you dragged me into the bathroom and washed my hair in cold water and soap just because I had touched the damn thing."

"Was it cold?" Eve made a face. "I'm sorry."

"You totally overreacted and scared the life out of me." Patricia sipped her champagne. "Thinking back, that container must be valuable. From the weight of it, I reckon it was solid gold."

"Any idea where it might be?" Eve asked.

Her daughter shrugged. "I haven't seen it since the day of the hair-washing trauma. Didn't you think it might be cursed? I remember you muttering something to that effect."

"Of course not!" Eve shook her head for emphasis. "But you never know what the Egyptians put in those unguents. It could have burned your skin."

She felt ashamed, thinking back, but she'd done what mothers do—protected her child from possible danger. That instinct to keep Patricia from harm was as strong as ever, even now that she was in her forties. There had been four car bombs in London the previous month, planted by the IRA, and she had been unable to think or speak until she got Patricia on the phone and knew that she, Michael, and her grandsons were safe.

Eve was ringing Ana Mansour regularly now. She was curious about this woman with whom she shared a love of archaeology, and enjoyed hearing about her life. It was rare to make a new friend at her age, especially with the sheltered life she and Brograve were living while she recuperated. One day she asked about the discovery of the Lighthouse of Alexandria, and Ana told her that exploration was an exception in that it had been led by a woman, Honor Frost.

"I'm not a diver," Ana said, "so I wasn't down there on the seabed when she identified parts of the ruins in the eastern harbor. It wasn't a dramatic moment in the way the opening of Tutankhamun's tomb was—rather, it was the result of forensic examination over a period of months, and lots of cross-checking with existing records, which is where I came in. But I was thrilled to be part of it, of course." She laughed. "Not nearly as thrilled as when I managed to meet you."

"I've been wondering how you tracked me down," Eve said. "It can't have been easy."

"On the contrary," Ana replied. "I saw your interview in *The Times* after the British Museum exhibition opened, so I knew your married name, and then I found your Framfield address in *Who's Who*."

Eve was puzzled. *What interview? What exhibition?* "Is the exhibition still on?" she asked, testing the water.

"No, it closed in December, but it was the most popular exhibition in their history. Over a million people came to see it. Tutankhamun clearly still has the power to draw a crowd."

There had been a Tutankhamun exhibition in London? "I wish I'd seen it," Eve said.

There was a long pause. "You did," Ana said. "You were at the opening ceremony, with the Queen. That's when the *Times* journalist interviewed you and loads of papers ran your photograph, posing alongside the funeral mask."

"Really? What year was that?"

"Last year. March 1972."

Eve sighed. Her stupid memory. "I expect I've got the article in my cuttings book," she said, then she cast around for a way to change the subject, embarrassed by her lapse. "How are your children? Have you spoken to them recently?"

"No." Ana sounded forlorn. "My husband's mother has asked me not to telephone or write to them anymore. She said it's upsetting for them."

"What?" Eve was horrified. "She can't do that! Children need their mothers. Can't your husband have a word?"

There was a pause. "It's more complicated than that."

Eve heard her strike a match. She'd always liked the smell of matches. Was it sulfur? She couldn't remember.

"My husband and I are divorced," Ana said. "I didn't plan to tell you because lots of people don't approve of divorce, but I feel as though I can confide in you."

"Of *course* you can!" Eve exclaimed. "Gosh, I'm so sorry to hear that."

"He got custody of the children and took them to live in his mother's house so she can raise them while he runs his business."

"But they'd be far better off with you than their grandma," Eve protested. "What judge made such a crazy decision?" She didn't know anyone who was divorced, hadn't even realized it was possible in a Muslim country.

Ana inhaled her cigarette and blew out before replying. "It's the way things are in Egypt. If I behave myself I'm allowed to see them from time to time. When I have enough money, I plan to hire a lawyer and fight for more access."

Eve was scandalized. "I've never heard the like! In this country, judges almost always give custody to the mother. It's the natural way of things. Oh, I'm so sorry, my dear. I wish I could help."

"Well . . ." Ana took another drag on her cigarette. "I'm hoping you find some of the lost Tutankhamun pieces; then I'll be able to return to Egypt and press on with my case."

"Gosh, I hope so," Eve said. "I'll do my absolute best. We're visiting Highclere in the first week of April and I'll have a look there too."

Afterward, she couldn't stop thinking about Ana's situation. It must be heart-breaking. She considered telling Brograve when he got back from his walk, to see if he knew anyone who might be able to help, but something stopped her. He didn't have so many contacts in government since he'd retired, and besides, she had a feeling he wouldn't approve of her telephone conversations with Ana.

Instead she went to look in her cuttings book, which was in the cupboard in Sionead's old room, empty now that she had gone to live with some other people. The *Times* interview Ana had spoken of was at the back of the book.

The first thing Eve noticed was that the photo they'd used wasn't too bad. Her hair had behaved itself for a change, and the suit she'd chosen showed off her trim figure. They had printed some lovely old pictures of her, Pups, and Howard Carter standing outside the tomb. Harry Burton must have taken them.

She had a pang of missing Pups. She'd never stopped missing him but sometimes it came back with a sudden intensity. Spiritualists would probably say his spirit was visiting her at those times. It was a nice thought.

The director of the British Museum was in one of the photos, and Eve remembered his face. He looked nice. Might she have given him the gold container for his exhibition? That would have been a logical thing to do . . . But if she had, Brograve would know about it, so that couldn't be right. Funny that Patricia remembered her thinking it was cursed.

She left the cuttings book out on the spare bed, open to the page, planning to read the article later, but then she forgot and when she next came to look for it, it was gone. It was infuriating the way she kept losing things these days, as if objects in their flat had a life of their own. She rearranged the ornaments one day and the next they were all in the wrong places again. Maybe Mrs. Jarrold was moving them. That must be it.

Chapter Forty

Highclere Castle, April 3, 1973

Brograve decided to drive them to Highclere. Sometimes they caught the train but Eve's walking was still unsteady. Besides, they were going for a week and had a suitcase each. The weather was unpredictable, switching from sunshine to showers in the blink of an eye, and they needed clothes for all eventualities because they tended to spend a lot of time outdoors. These days there were never any porters in railway stations to help with your luggage so it was tricky for elderly folk like them.

"I still miss driving," Eve remarked, as she watched him switch on the ignition. She could feel the vibrations, hear the change in engine noise as he raised the clutch and pressed on the accelerator. She used to love being behind the wheel, but she'd gotten tunnel vision after one of her strokes and the doctors said it wasn't safe for her to drive. It had been a bitter disappointment.

After they married, Brograve had bought a Ford Model T, which was a practical car for driving around town. She used it more than he did, because he was at work during the day. She sped around shopping and visiting friends, or driving to Highclere to visit Miraculous, then going to race meets once he was ready for the track.

In 1929, Brograve had given her the best birthday present ever—a car of her own, an Austin Seven with dark green paintwork and leather seats. She couldn't stop grinning as she took it out for a test drive. It was smooth to run, with an engine noise like the purr of a big cat, and the top speed was said to be seventy miles per hour. No one was allowed to drop so much as a crumb in that car. When she collected Patricia from school, she put a piece of carpet in the footwell to protect it from muddy feet.

Eve sucked in her lips to stop herself criticizing Brograve's driving on the way to Highclere. He was too cautious in London traffic; you had to be decisive and push your nose out or it took all day to get anywhere. He rode the clutch too, which would wear out the gearbox.

"Do you know if Porchy has a lady friend at the moment?" Brograve asked, with merriment in his eyes. "One of his boozy floozies?"

Eve tried to remember. She spoke to her brother on the telephone every week or so but he rarely confided in her about his women. Catherine, his first wife, the mother of his two children, had left him back in the 1930s. Their great love affair, conducted against a background of parental disapproval, had not survived his philandering and her fondness for the bottle. Which came first, Eve wasn't sure. To her great sadness they divorced and Catherine lived in Switzerland now, from where she sent them a Christmas card every year.

His second marriage to an American actress called Tilly hadn't lasted long at all—Eve and Brograve scarcely got to know her—before she fled back to the States. Since then there had been a string of mistresses but Eve could never remember their names. Mabel? Ivy? They didn't stick around. Happiness in love was something her brother struggled with.

"We'll find out soon enough," she said.

She felt emotional heading back to Highclere. Being there made her think about Pups's funeral, and about her mother's sudden death just three years earlier. Almina had choked on a piece of chicken, of all things. Both her parents had died unexpectedly, and it made her sad to dwell on them. Of course, there were happy memories at

Highclere too, if she delved further back: parties on the lawn during long summer evenings, cantering around the estate on her pony, swimming in the lake with Porchy. As they turned into the twisting driveway and the turreted towers came into view, she felt a quickening of her pulse. Although she had loved Framfield dearly, in many ways Highclere was still home.

The butler, Taylor, showed them through the saloon into the drawing room, where Porchy was sitting, whisky in hand, by the windows that looked out toward the stables. She noticed he'd hung a painting of Catherine above the fireplace, looking as beautiful and luminous as when they first met, before the booze marred her looks.

The butler poured them each a sherry and gave Porchy a generous refill of whisky, adding a splash of water before returning the jug to the sideboard.

Porchy took a swig. "Do you know, I'm still getting begging letters from Almina's creditors?" he complained almost as soon as they sat down. "I got one yesterday. She seems to have promised all kinds of hangers-on that she would leave them money in her will, and instead all she left was debt. But try getting them to believe that . . ."

"It wasn't her fault." Eve had spent years trying to broker peace between the two without success. "She was brought up with money on tap and could never reconcile herself to it drying up after Alfred de Rothschild died. She was too generous, always a sucker for an underdog story."

"She was hideously irresponsible!" he exclaimed. "We could have lost Highclere because of her. I'm still negotiating with the tax office, signing over paintings right, left, and center." He glanced up at his ex-wife hanging on the wall.

"At least you won't have to pay death duty on Almina's estate if she left only debt," Brograve commented. "The rates are sky-high under Harold Wilson's government."

Eve knew he was trying to steer conversation away from a contentious area. Her brother's arguments with her mother had been a source of great sadness to her. She picked up a silver table lighter that had belonged to Pups, and ran her finger over the engraving of his initials: GESMH. It was complicated when an estate was inherited by the eldest son while the wife was still alive, but there was no doubt that if she'd been in charge, Almina would have run the place into the ground. She never had any sense when it came to money.

All the same, it had been cruel of Porchy to force her to declare bankruptcy. Brograve took his side, saying it was the only prudent course of action, but Eve used to slip her mother money in secret. Poor Mama. She had been a rather distant mother but it wasn't her fault. The train of thought brought to mind Ana Mansour and her separation from her children.

"I wonder if you ever found any Tutankhamun relics lying around at Highclere?" she asked Porchy, interrupting a conversation about the shortcomings of the Wilson government. "I think there may be a few bits and pieces Pups brought back from the tomb."

He snorted like a horse. "You ask me this every bloody time we talk on the phone, Baby Sis. You're getting senile. I told you his entire collection went to the Met."

"Are you sure it all went?" she asked. "Was nothing left behind?"

Her father's Egyptian collection used to be housed in two cupboards built into the wall cavities between the drawing room and the smoking room. There were shelves inside, and artifacts were kept in old tobacco tins. As a child, Eve loved to explore the treasures, which she knew off by heart. "Test me!" she'd demand, and Pups would choose a tin at random and show Eve the contents. Without fail, she would be able to relate the provenance of the item, the dates, and the symbolism of the ancient imagery of gods, ritual ceremonies, and strange composite animals that were part this and part that.

"I wouldn't swear to it in a court of law," Porchy

backtracked. "There are three hundred bloody rooms here, so maybe the odd Egyptian knickknack is gathering dust somewhere."

"Would you mind if I have a poke around tomorrow? Just out of interest?"

Before Porchy could answer, Taylor cleared his throat. "Pardon me for interrupting, sir. I believe there are some small items in the old cupboards, behind the panels." He pointed toward the wall adjoining the smoking room. "They were boarded up during the war, when we heard evacuee children were coming to stay. I assumed you knew about them, sir."

Eve's stomach gave a lurch. She got up and went to the spot where the cupboards had been, in the doorway between the two rooms. When she knocked on the panels, she could hear it was hollow behind.

"Good god," Porchy said. "I suppose we had better have a look, in that case. I'll get a man to remove those panels tomorrow morning. Maybe you can help to identify things, Baby Sis. You were always more interested in those crumbling old relics than I was."

Eve glanced at the walls, feeling a mixture of curiosity and apprehension. Maybe there would be something there to help Ana Mansour get back to see her children. She shivered. It felt as if there might be a ghost or two lurking inside.

Chapter Forty-One

Highclere Castle, April 1973

As soon as the first corner of the paneling was re-moved, Eve caught a whiff of musky scent. It made her cough.

"Can you smell that?" she asked Brograve. "Doesn't it remind you of the tomb?"

He sniffed, then shook his head. "To me, it smells of damp."

The panel splintered as Porchy's man used a chisel to pry it from the wall, nails popping out and scattering on the parquet floor. Behind, Eve could see the old cupboard door. It wasn't locked, thank goodness, and when he pulled it open she saw rusting tins on the shelves: Lambert & Butler Gold Leaf; Player's Navy Cut. She stretched an arm out and grabbed the first tin she could reach. Nestling on some yellowing cotton inside was part of a blue faience necklace.

"I know this," she said. "It's from the tomb of Amenhotep III. KV22." She was delighted her memory hadn't let her down. "It's broken. Perhaps that's why Howard didn't include it in the sale to the Met."

She reached for another tin. This one had a sand-colored scarab beetle inside, just an inch long. "Did you know that walking anticlockwise around scarabs is supposed to make wishes come true?" she told the men. "I think it's five times around to get a husband and seven times for a child."

"Well, it worked for you," Brograve replied, but Porchy rolled his eyes in a derogatory manner and said, "Honestly, what tosh!"

"Oh look!" she cried, pointing to the top shelf. "That's one of Merneptah's embalming oil jugs. I found them, you know. My claim to fame!"

"The handle's broken," Porchy commented. "Couldn't you have found an intact one?"

Brograve smiled and rolled his eyes.

Eve didn't mind; she was delighted to see the jug again. "We found thirteen, actually. The Egyptian government got seven and we got six. I suppose the intact ones went to the Met."

Porchy's man turned his attention to the cupboard on the other side. Once again the door behind the paneling was unlocked and there were cigarette tins on the shelves. It took Eve right back to childhood, when she used to love looking through these treasures with Pups. It was their special place.

"Don't touch anything with your bare hands," she warned the men. "You need to wear gloves. The sweat on our skin can cause decomposition."

"Do you think there's anything valuable?" Porchy asked.

"Maybe." Eve opened another tin and looked in to see three carnelian bracelet plaques. She remembered when Howard brought them, before the war. The First World War, that was. They were also from the tomb of Amenhotep III, and were inscribed with the name of his wife, Queen Tiye.

"His principal wife," she heard Pups's voice correcting her. She felt close to her father in there, as if his spirit was lingering in the air. She was glad they had come here to mark the fiftieth anniversary of his death. It was the right place to be.

"It's definitely worth getting an expert to check them," she said. "If you call the British Museum, I expect they'll send someone. Meanwhile, do you mind if I have a poke around?"

"Be my guest," Porchy said. "Brograve and I are going to the stables to look at the new bloodstock. We'll see you for luncheon at one."

As soon as they left, Eve began to hunt for Tutankhamun relics. She had a crystal-clear memory of the items Pups had pulled from his pockets in Castle Carter the night they crept into the tomb. There had been an amulet of Wadjet, the cobra goddess, made out of beaten gold, a clay wine jar, and that wooden goose varnished with resin. She asked Taylor to bring her a stepladder and a pair of gloves and he returned with both, but insisted he should be the one to climb the ladder.

They worked methodically through the shelves and Eve discovered many items she hadn't seen in decades. A lot had been left behind when Howard sold the collection to the Met, and not all of it was damaged. Perhaps he had wanted Highclere to keep its links with Egypt.

Howard had become quite the celebrity in the 1920s, in demand all over the world, but he and Eve remained close and every time he passed through London he would visit her. At first he tried to persuade her to return to Egypt, but when he realized she was adamantly against it, he brought her the firsthand news from the Valley of the Kings instead.

It was February 1924 when he finally opened the

lid of the stone sarcophagus that had been inside the blue and gold shrine. It was cracked, he told her, and the crack had been hurriedly filled with gypsum, as if there had been an accident while it was being lowered into place. It made the job of lifting it more difficult, in case it fell apart at the weak joint.

Inside they found the first of the anthropoid coffins, its solid gold mask shimmering in the arc lamps Harry Burton had set up. From its size, Howard guessed there must be several more coffins, and so it turned out, each one tucked inside the last like a set of babushka dolls. There was enough solid gold to fill Fort Knox, he told her. Security had to be tight.

The funerary mask was the image most people associated with the tomb now: the striped headcloth with a uraeus on top, the lifelike kohl-lined eyes, painted with white calcite, the pupils made of obsidian, and the beard of lapis-colored glass. Howard had sounded overawed when he described it to her.

"Truly phenomenal. You know I'm not much given to displays of emotion, Eve, but I had to sit down because my knees were trembling. I only hope you'll see it sometime . . ."

She was glad not to have been present for the uncovering of the mummy; the very thought made her shiver. She heard from Howard that the resins poured over the corpse had meant it was stuck to the inside of the coffin and had to be examined where it lay, in an autopsy that began in November 1925.

The results were fascinating. Tutankhamun had been short, just five foot four and one-eighth inches, and he had a club foot. They could tell that he died around the age of eighteen, which fitted with what they knew from other sources. Experts couldn't agree on the cause of death. Could it have been tuberculosis, which was rife in Ancient Egypt? Or malaria? Was the head injury they could see the result of heavy-handedness during the embalming process or a fatal blow to the head? Did he break his leg in a chariot accident, then catch blood poisoning from the wound?

It was all too morbid for Eve. Death had been everywhere in the 1920s. First there had been Pups, then his half brother Aubrey, and so many other people who visited the tomb started to succumb. A railroad millionaire caught pneumonia and died just a month after Pups. An Egyptian prince was shot dead by his wife later that same year. A high-ranking official in Egyptian military intelligence was assassinated in Cairo while his car was stuck in traffic. An Oxford scholar, the author of numerous books on Egypt, hanged himself in a hotel room, leaving a suicide note written in his own blood that read "I have succumbed to a curse."

The professor of Egyptology at Johns Hopkins University in Maryland burned to death in a house fire.

Then there were some victims she knew well. Poor Arthur Mace, who had accompanied them on the Aswan cruise, had died of unexplained arsenic poisoning. And Richard Bethell, Howard's private secretary, had been smothered in bed in a Mayfair club and his murderer never found. His distraught father threw himself from a seventh-floor window, unable to cope with the loss, and on the way to the father's funeral, the hearse ran over and killed an eight-year-old boy. Eve had been aghast when she read of this tragedy in the *Express*.

She remembered Howard's dismissive answer when she asked him if he thought there could be a link among the deaths.

"Do you know how many thousands of visitors I showed around the tomb?" he asked. "Statistically, *fewer* of them have died than might have been expected in a random sample of the population."

Always the scientist, Eve thought. Always an answer for everything, just like Brograve. To her mind, his explanation addressed the *number* of deaths, but not the sheer oddness of some of them.

Chapter Forty-Two

Highclere Castle, April 1973

When she had finished checking the cupboard on one side of the doorway, Eve turned to the other. One item there was swaddled in a length of discolored cotton and she unwrapped it to find the wooden goose Pups had taken from the tomb, its black resin coat daubed with gold on the breast, its neck curved in swan-like fashion, and a white beak pointed coyly downward. Heart beating a little faster, she laid it, still in its cotton, on the coffee table between the sofas in the drawing room.

The amulet of Wadjet turned up next, its beaten gold gleaming. It was covered in intricate carvings showing the segments of the snake's body, the feathered wings, and the human head wearing a headdress. It was in mint condition, as if the artist had buffed up his work that very morning. She placed it beside the goose.

Several clay wine jars were stacked together on an upper shelf and Taylor lifted them all down for her. They looked similar and Eve couldn't decide which one might have come from the tomb. She squinted at the tiny cartouches carved on the bases but couldn't make them out. Fortunately Porchy had left a pair of reading glasses lying around, so she put them on to examine the jars, soon spotting the hieroglyphic letters that spelled Tutankhamun on one of them. She was sure the jar had a hint of the cloying muskiness of the unguent container. Arthur Conan Doyle had told her the Ancient Egyptians used unguents and oils imbued with elemental spirits, or so she remembered.

"Mr. Conan Doyle also believes in fairies," Howard had scoffed when she mentioned that. "Did you see the article he wrote for *Strand Magazine* about the little girls in Cottingley who claimed to have photographed fairies? The man's a gullible fool!"

Looking back, Eve remembered being convinced by Conan Doyle when she first met him. He had seemed like an authority. But afterward, when he kept writing to her with dire warnings about the curse, trying to get her to agree to exorcisms and such like, it grew rather wearisome. Howard would never have agreed to an exorcism in the tomb. He would have mocked the notion.

Eve searched through the remainder of the objects Taylor brought down from the shelves, but there was no sign of the gold container, so she hadn't hidden it there. It was disappointing but she hoped Ana Mansour would be pleased to receive three of the artifacts from her list. With any luck, she could take them back to Cairo and get her job back, then start her legal battle for access to her children. Eve hated to think it was her fault Ana hadn't been able to return sooner.

When she met Brograve and Porchy for luncheon in the dining room, Eve told them of her finds. Porchy's reaction—entirely predictably—was to ask whether they could sell them at auction to the highest bidder.

"I don't think so," Eve said, "given that they are stolen goods. Pups shouldn't have taken them from the tomb. It seems to me we should give them to Ana Mansour to return to the Cairo Museum, where most of the other Tutankhamun relics are kept along with his sarcophagus."

Brograve objected: "You can't just hand over priceless artifacts to a woman we've only met twice. We don't know anything about her. It should be done officially. I'll ask Cuthbert to inquire through the British Council."

"Who's Ana Mansour?" Porchy asked. "If we're giving them to anyone, it should be the British Museum, then I can claim tax relief on the gifts. They are mine, after all—contents of the house, and all that."

Eve began to wish she had just sneaked them into her suitcase without mentioning them. She wanted to give them to Ana, but it would be difficult now that the cat was out of the bag.

After lunch, Brograve telephoned Cuthbert and explained the sensitive nature of the find. "We think they are missing artifacts from Tutankhamun's tomb," he said. "Dr. Ana Mansour from Cairo University gave us a list of items that were mentioned in Maya's tomb in Saqqara, and these appear to be three of them."

Cuthbert asked a few questions, then promised to make inquiries and get back to him.

"Maude sends her love," Brograve told Eve afterward. "She wants to have lunch with you when you get back and—her words—'hit the sales.'" He raised an eyebrow in a comical manner that made her laugh.

Money had never been an issue between them. She knew lots of men just gave their wives an allowance to cover the housekeeping, but right from the start Brograve insisted they have a joint account and said she could spend whatever she liked. In fifty years, she couldn't remember a single occasion when he had criticized her spending—not even when she gave money to Almina. He had a generous soul.

Over dinner that evening, once he'd sunk a few whiskies, Porchy returned to his familiar rant about their mother. He seemed obsessed. Eve suspected her presence had rekindled his anger and the booze was stoking it.

"Do you know what Almina said to me when I got back from the war?" he asked Brograve. "I walked in the door and went to embrace her—as any son might—but she shrank away from me, saying, 'Have you been deloused yet?' I'll never forget that. Not 'Welcome back!' or 'Good to see you!' or 'Glad you survived' but 'Have you been deloused?'"

"It's not fair to criticize her when she's not around to defend herself," Eve argued. "Almina and Pups were distant parents but that wasn't unusual for the era." It's true she had brought Patricia up with a lot more love and one-on-one attention, but times had changed, and so had attitudes on parenting.

"You always want to think well of everyone," Porchy said, "even when it's not justified. Don't you remember us being bundled from house to house—or off to Eton in my case—like inconvenient pieces of baggage, never seeing our parents from one month to the next? Don't you remember spending Christmas with Nanny Moss and only being allowed in their 'sacred presence' for half an hour?"

Eve shook her head. That wasn't how she remembered it at all. They hadn't eaten Christmas dinner together because Pups and Almina generally had guests, but they always opened presents with them on Christmas morning.

Porchy continued: "You weren't beaten by Pups the way I was. Birch twigs, he used, on my bare backside, and bloody painful they were too."

"No, he never beat me," she agreed. She couldn't imagine Pups hitting anyone, but she remembered Porchy showing her the stripes on his backside once. They had looked so sore they made her cry.

"I've got a good mind to write a memoir one day in which I describe the true nature of the man behind the discovery of Tutankhamun's tomb, and his stony-hearted wife. I'd probably make a bit of money." He slurped his drink noisily.

"You wouldn't!" Eve cried.

"I might." He cackled. "Whyever not?"

"It would be cruel. Besides, you never went to the Valley of the Kings. You don't know the first thing

about the tomb, and that was the high point of his life."
She felt possessive; it was *her* legacy, not his.

"I'm entitled to let the world know what *my* life has
been like. I'm sure I'll find a publisher." He lit a cigarette and threw his lighter on the table with an air of
defiance, clearly ready to escalate the argument.

Brograve did his usual trick of veering the conversation in another direction entirely. "I was looking through that wonderful book the British Museum
published last year to coincide with the exhibition. The
photographic reproductions are excellent. They did a
grand job."

Talk turned to the exhibition, the one Eve had forgotten about, but she couldn't stop worrying about Porchy's idea of writing a book. She hoped he wouldn't.
There were too many hurtful bits of family history that
he could mention, in particular his destructive feud
with Almina. Fifty years after Pups's death they should
be celebrating him, not maligning him.

Her heart fluttered like a butterfly trapped beneath
her ribs. It was ridiculous how anxious she got sometimes. She never used to be like that. When did it start?
After the accident? Or was it to do with getting older
and her memory being unreliable? She hated to think
that she might hurt someone's feelings due to forgetful-
ness. Or go out for a walk and not be able to remember

the way home. Or leave the gas on and blow up the house.

"Think of your worries as little birds," Brograve said to her once. "Flap your wings"—he waved his hands up and down—"and let them fly away."

She tried but it wasn't much use. In her imagination, the little bird flew straight into a closed window and fell unconscious to the floor.

Chapter Forty-Three

London, October 1923

When they returned from their honeymoon, Eve and Brograve moved into a four-bedroom townhouse at 26 Charles Street in Mayfair, not far from her mother's Seamore Place house. Brograve opened accounts at Heal's and Harrods and Eve had fun choosing furniture and fittings there. She liked the Art Deco style, with its sweeping curves and colored inlays, its starbursts and elegant patterns in bold shades. They had only one maid and a cook to attend to their needs but Eve claimed to like doing domestic chores herself. She learned a few simple recipes to make on the cook's night off—Brograve particularly loved her "chicken à la king," a casserole of chicken with mushrooms in a sherry and cream sauce. Most of all, he liked coming home from his office to find her there every evening, waiting for him. He still couldn't believe his luck that Eve had married him. Just looking at her made him smile.

In early December, he and Eve were the only guests at the registry office wedding of Almina to Ian Dennistoun, since Porchy had refused to attend. They signed the register as witnesses, then the four went for luncheon in an Italian restaurant in Knightsbridge, an awkward occasion when the conversation was stilted and the gaiety seemed forced. Almina was giggly and girlish, and couldn't stop pawing her groom, in a way that was embarrassing. Brograve agreed with Eve that she should have waited at least a year after her first husband's death before remarrying. Their hurry left a bad taste in the mouth.

He didn't say as much to Eve, but he didn't like Ian. The man was a divorcé who, since leaving the army under a cloud, had made no attempt to find gainful employment. Now it seemed he planned to live off Almina's Rothschild inheritance. For Brograve, it was hard to respect a man who fleeced his wife. It was certainly not the way he'd been brought up. Eve had inherited twenty-five thousand pounds from Alfred de Rothschild but that was her nest egg. Brograve would never have dreamed of touching it. His income from the copper cable company subsidized their lifestyle perfectly well; they were even planning to buy a bigger house before long.

Almina was still at loggerheads with Porchy over the death duties to be paid on Lord Carnarvon's estate. The longer it dragged on, the more both became entrenched. Brograve warned Eve not to get involved, but she couldn't help trying to "fix" things—that was her all over. She was terribly upset when Porchy refused to invite Almina to the christening of her first grandchild, a boy they named Henry, who was born in January 1924. Eve doted on the little lad. She couldn't stop picking him up and cradling him, cooing and smiling, letting him grip her finger, tug her hair, and leave patches of dribble on her shoulder. It was clear she was desperate to have a child herself and Brograve was determined to give her one. He hoped nature would soon take its course.

They still had some difficulty in their marital relations: Eve was so small-boned, he had to be very gentle and restrained when they made love. Sometimes she flinched when he reached out to initiate lovemaking and he felt terrible about that. Occasionally he still wished he'd had some experience before marriage, enough to learn what women liked . . . but on the whole he was glad they had kept this most intimate of acts between the two of them.

Finally, in November 1924, the doctor telephoned with news that Eve was pregnant. She shrieked at the top of her lungs, then pranced around the sitting room singing, "You're just as sweet as an angel." Brograve cherished the memory; he could still picture it when he closed his eyes. She had been wearing a cornflower-blue dress and her expression was radiant, her dancing a mixture of foxtrot, tango, and her own made-up steps, her singing sweet and true.

Right from the start Eve was determined to be the best of mothers. She told Brograve she planned to shower their children with love, and let them pursue their own interests and become their own people, the way Pups had with her, and he agreed completely. She was already filled with love for this babe in the womb and overwhelmed by fierce protectiveness. As he stroked her belly, Brograve found it hard to think of the fetus as a human being, but he knew he would have killed with his bare hands if anyone threatened to harm Eve. It was his job to keep her safe—to keep them both safe.

Within a week of receiving the news, though, Eve complained of feeling nauseous. Soon she was throwing up from dawn till dusk and could scarcely keep any food or water down. Christmas Day was a wash-out, as the aroma of roasting goose made her retch uncontrollably and she had to withdraw to her bedroom with the door closed while he ate alone. She couldn't leave the house, but lay on the sofa from morning till night with a bowl by her side. Brograve was helpless and frustrated. There was little he could do except hold her hair, rub her back, fetch glasses of water, and mutter reassurances. It was unbearable to watch her suffer. He would gladly have taken on the sickness himself, were that possible in some peculiar twist of nature.

The doctor was concerned as her weight started to drop. He prescribed meat jellies to build her up but she found the smell repulsive. Even the scent of flowers made her queasy. "The nausea will pass," everyone kept saying, and Brograve knew it would eventually, but he worried that the baby might be harmed if she couldn't keep down enough food to nourish it.

While all this was going on, any normal mother would have been expected to support her daughter, to reassure and encourage her. Instead, Almina was wrapped up in her own affairs. It transpired that—surprise, surprise—Ian Dennistoun had never been able to pay his first wife, Dorothy, the alimony a divorce court had determined he should pay. Once he married Almina, Dorothy saw her chance and demanded that she be recompensed from Almina's fortune. Backed by Ian, Almina refused to give her a penny, and they both hired lawyers. Every evening, Almina telephoned Eve complaining about Dorothy's latest demands, and never once considering her daughter's fragile state.

It made Brograve increasingly furious as he watched Eve, gaunt and gray, trying to comfort her mother. He had to bite back acid comments on many an occasion. It wasn't right that he should criticize Eve's mother. It would only make things harder for Eve. And yet, there were times when he could cheerfully have throttled Almina.

Chapter Forty-Four

London, February 1925

When Eve was seventeen weeks pregnant, a telegram arrived from Brograve's mother saying that his father had died, suddenly, in the South of France after catching a chill while on holiday. Although Sir Edward had been in frail health for some time, it came as a shock.

Brograve had no time to mourn because he had to rush out to attend the funeral, which was being held at the English cemetery in Nice two days hence. Eve wanted to go with him—she'd grown very fond of her father-in-law—but it was out of the question. Travel sickness on top of pregnancy sickness would finish her off. On the journey there he worried about leaving her behind, and he worried about how his mother would cope with the loss of his father. He had to step up and be head of the family now, the patriarch. It was his turn to protect everyone, and deep down he wasn't sure if he was capable. But he had to be; he had no choice in the matter.

After the funeral, Brograve brought Betty back to London and, at Eve's suggestion, she moved in with them rather than go home alone. Brograve well remembered her uncontrollable grief after his brother died and was wary that her distress might upset Eve, but this time she was quiet and contained in her mourning. She proved to be good company for Eve, offering the kind of woman-to-woman advice that Almina had singularly failed to give during this pregnancy.

Brograve was frantically busy. He couldn't sleep at night for making lists in his head of all the things he had to do: talking to obituarists about Sir Edward's illustrious career and sending photographs to accompany their articles; sorting out his father's financial affairs and taking charge of his mother's, because she had never so much as paid a bill in her life and wouldn't know where to start. Friends and family who had been unable to travel to Nice were agitating for a memorial service to pay their respects to his father, so he organized one in St. Margaret's, the church where he and Eve had been married. It was standing room only, and afterward everyone told Brograve he'd done his father proud, but the strain of the day exhausted him.

It was a difficult period, made a hundred times worse when Almina's case, *Dennistoun v. Dennistoun,* came to the High Court in March.

All of Almina's and Dorothy's friends had urged the women to back down, but they were headstrong characters, incapable of compromise. Proceedings were vitriolic from the start, with accusations of promiscuity and infidelity flung around and names dragged through the mud. Almina's barrister leaked a story doing the rounds that Dorothy had slept with her husband's superior in the army to win him a promotion, and it became headline news. There were strong hints that Almina had been having an affair with Ian before the death of her first husband, the Earl of Carnarvon. It was also revealed that Almina had been the illegitimate child of Alfred de Rothschild, something most of her society friends already knew but not the nation at large. Every sordid detail of their lives became fodder for the opposition's barrister and a gift for the journalists covering the trial.

Each evening, Almina telephoned Eve to rant about the day's proceedings, never once stopping to ask how she was feeling, or how Betty or Brograve were faring after their bereavement. Eve clearly found it draining but she would never refuse to take the telephone calls, and Brograve's fury grew by the day.

One evening, when Eve was weak from prolonged vomiting, he could hold back no longer. He grabbed the receiver and spoke to Almina directly: "My wife is ill and vulnerable, and I would ask you to please refrain from distressing her further with your calls."

"How dare you come between me and my daughter!" she shrieked. "Hand back the telephone immediately."

Brograve prided himself on never losing his temper, but suddenly he felt rage welling up, boiling and unstoppable: "Strange as it may seem, not everything is about you, Almina," he shouted. "Did you ever stop to consider how it would affect Eve that you are dragging the family name through the mud? No, I don't suppose you did. You are the most *selfish* woman it has ever been my misfortune to come across!"

"I've never heard such impertinence!" Almina replied, sounding shocked. "Unless you apologize, I will never speak to you again."

In response Brograve hung up the phone. He turned to Eve and his mother. "She says she won't speak to me again unless I apologize. And since I have no intention of apologizing, we may not be seeing her for a while."

He left the room, grabbed his coat, and charged out

the front door before either could stop him. He stamped down the darkened street, muttering under his breath, not even looking where he was going, and kept moving until he had walked off the worst of his rage.

On his return, Eve didn't berate him for losing his temper with her mother. Instead she got up and hugged him. He didn't expect her to stop taking her mother's telephone calls. That wouldn't be fair. But it would suit him right down to the ground if he never had to see Almina again.

All in all, Brograve could sympathize with the fact that Porchy was still furious with Almina three years after her death. She'd been the kind of woman who aroused fury. It was testament to Eve's easygoing personality that she never had a serious falling-out with her mother, but continued to be the family peacemaker, the one who got on with everyone.

In his summing-up at the end of the Dennistoun case, the judge had called it "the most bitterly contested litigation" he had ever known. The jury decided that Almina need not pay alimony to Dorothy—but costs were awarded against her, so she would have to pay the substantial legal fees herself. It took a large dent out of her fortune and led directly to the financial mishaps and hardship of her later years. In Brograve's opinion, the dispute should never have been allowed to go to court.

After Ian Dennistoun died in 1938, Almina was lonely. Eve lunched with her in London from time to time, and they kept up to date by telephone, but she never came to stay at Framfield because that would have meant accepting hospitality from Brograve, and his name was still mud.

When her money ran out, Almina used to call regularly with some sob story or other, and Eve would write her a check. She knew that Brograve knew, because he was the one who checked the bank statements, but it was never mentioned.

Before they left Highclere, Brograve succeeded in persuading Porchy not to write an indiscreet memoir.

"There's no benefit to be served in reliving the bad old days," he said. "And it would be undignified."

Porchy agreed. "If only Pups had lived. He could control Almina's impulsive nature, just about, but I never stood a chance. You're right—best draw a line under it."

On their last day at Highclere, Taylor handed Brograve a telephone message. His friend Cuthbert had rung and asked if he would call back.

"I got in touch with the university in Cairo," Cuthbert said, "and I have some unsettling news for you. Ana

Mansour is no longer employed there. She used to work for them but she was sacked more than a year ago."

"Good god!" Brograve exclaimed, shocked. "Whatever for?"

"I don't know the precise circumstances—they were cagey about it—but I get the impression it was quite a scandal. If she was trying to get your wife to hand over Tutankhamun artifacts by impersonating a university employee, then she was committing fraud."

Brograve was horrified. The woman had been in his house. He'd taken her to meet Eve while she was in a vulnerable condition. Why hadn't he checked up on her? He had trusted her simply because she wrote on university notepaper, but she must have had some left over from when she worked there. What a fool he had been!

"I suppose there's no harm done if you didn't give her anything," Cuthbert said.

"No, we didn't, thank god. I imagine she planned to take our heirlooms and sell them to the highest bidder." He remembered something. "She said her father used to be an antiquities dealer so I suppose she could have learned the business from him."

"Some of the world's biggest auction houses turn a blind eye when it comes to the provenance of antiquities. You'd be amazed," Cuthbert said.

"So what do you suggest we do with the artifacts we've found at Highclere? I want it to be entirely aboveboard."

"Perhaps talking to the British Museum is the best option," Cuthbert replied. "I'm told Lord Carnarvon left a stipulation in his will that they be given first call on his collection, but his widow decided to go with the Met in New York, since they were the highest bidder."

"Of course she did," Brograve said wearily. "That was my mother-in-law all over. Many thanks for your help, Cuthbert."

He hung up the phone feeling stunned. You read about people who preyed on the elderly. Could Ana be one of them? Might she have taken anything of theirs? Why, oh why, had he ever let her in his home?

Chapter Forty-Five

London, May 1973

E ve was astonished when Brograve broke the news that Ana Mansour was not an employee of Cairo University. She tried to remember their conversations. Had she ever claimed directly that she worked for them? If she didn't, then who *did* she work for?

"I don't think she expected me to give her the artifacts," she told Brograve. "She just wanted information, to set the record straight."

"But which record would she be setting straight if she doesn't have an official capacity? It doesn't make sense."

Eve was baffled. Why had Ana tape-recorded her story? Why was she so keen to find the gold container?

"The tape recording was a ruse," Brograve said, "and she wanted the gold container because it sounds valuable. The Egyptians used solid gold, not gold plate. Remember how heavy that container was."

Eve couldn't believe it. Ana was kind. She brought her lotus flowers. They'd become friends.

"When we get back to London I'm going to telephone her hotel," Brograve said, "and give her a piece of my mind."

Eve kept quiet. She still hadn't told him that she and Ana had been chatting. Should she say so now? He would think she had been gullible—he often told her she was too trusting—but she couldn't bring herself to believe Ana had deliberately deceived her. She decided that when they got back to London, she would ring first and hear her side of the story. She and Ana had become friends, and you should always give friends the benefit of the doubt.

The note with her hotel number was in the drawer of the telephone table. As soon as they got home, while Brograve was taking their cases to the bedroom, she slipped it into her skirt pocket. She hoped it was a simple misunderstanding. Maybe Ana worked at a different university, or at the Cairo Museum. All the same, she wondered what kind of "scandal" might have led to her dismissal.

As soon as Brograve left for his walk the next day, she telephoned Ana's hotel.

"How was your trip?" Ana asked straightaway. "Did you find any Tutankhamun relics at Highclere?"

"There's something I need to ask you first," Eve began. "Brograve's been told that you no longer work at Cairo University and that you were sacked from your job. Has someone made a terrible mistake?"

There was a pause and when she spoke, Ana sounded indignant. "Did your husband write to them? Was he checking up on me?"

"Not at all," Eve assured her. "He asked his friend at the British Council about the proper protocols for returning antiquities. He wanted to do things by the book." Ana didn't say anything. "You understand, he's cross now because he feels you lied to him."

"I didn't lie, but . . . it's embarrassing." Ana sounded very hesitant. "I was hoping I wouldn't have to tell you this. . . . The truth is that I was sacked for having an affair with a colleague. He was married, I was married, and when it came out, I was the one who got sacked."

"That's not fair!" Eve exclaimed. "Everyone has affairs nowadays. It's hardly a sacking offense."

"It's the way things work in Egypt, I'm afraid." Ana spoke matter-of-factly. "But I was sad because I loved my university job, so I came up with a plan. I thought if I could track down some of the missing Tutankhamun artifacts and return them to my homeland, I might be reinstated. The colonialist powers who are hanging on to our ancient heritage is a political hot potato in Egypt. And after talking to you, I sensed you would agree. So that's what I've been pinning my hopes on."

"But your children!" Eve was surprised. "Surely being with them is more important than getting your job back?"

Eve heard the flare of a match and the gasp as smoke was inhaled. It made her wish she hadn't given up smoking. When was that? Eons ago. She had never smoked much, just the odd puff at parties, but she still got the urge sometimes.

"I told you, my husband won't let me see them. Until I get my job back, I can't afford to pay for legal advice, so I'm trapped."

"I wish I could help." Eve wanted to take back the words as soon as she said them. Brograve would never let her help, not now that he knew Ana had misled them. "You're a sucker for a hard-luck story," he had said to her on more than one occasion, and she supposed it was true.

"*Did* you find anything at Highclere, Lady Beauchamp?" Ana demanded.

"We did," Eve said. "Three items from your list. But my husband and brother have decided to give them to the British Museum."

There was a long silence punctuated by cigarette smoke being exhaled, then Ana asked: "Was the gold unguent container among them?"

Eve shook her head. "No, I've got no idea where that is."

"Are you sure?" Ana asked. "Did you look everywhere? Surely if you found *some* artifacts, it means there could be more?"

"I'm afraid if anything else turns up, my brother will also give it to the British Museum. He's asking one of their experts to come and look through the items that remain there. I'm sorry not to be more helpful." Eve felt bad for dashing Ana's hopes so thoroughly.

"Do you think it's fair they remain in Britain?" Ana asked, sounding angry. "How would you feel if Egypt had stolen the Sutton Hoo burial treasures and was refusing to return them? Or what if we had invaded your country and made off with your Crown Jewels?"

"I do see your point," Eve said, feeling uncomfortable, "but it's out of my hands now. Wrong decisions were made in the past, but this is now, and if I could do anything about it, I would."

"I believe you would." Ana sighed.

"What will you do next?" Eve asked.

"I honestly don't know." She sounded defeated. "I

had staked everything on this plan and now I've run out of ideas."

In the days that followed, Eve's thoughts often returned to Ana Mansour. How could she bear to be separated from her children? Wasn't being with them more important than getting her job back? If it had been her, Eve wouldn't have waited for the law to run its course. She would have snatched them from their grandmother at the first opportunity and run away with them as fast and as far as she could.

Chapter Forty-Six

London, July 10, 1925

Betty assured Eve that a difficult pregnancy was always followed by an easy birth. "It's common knowledge," she said, with a wave of her hand. "Take my word for it."

So when Eve started to have contractions two days after the due date the doctor had calculated, she was excited and hardly fearful at all. It wasn't painful at first—just a gripping sensation. Brograve telephoned the doctor and midwife and they appeared at the house within the hour.

"My cake is baked!" Eve greeted them cheerfully. "I'm still not sure how I'm going to get it out, but I believe that's your department."

And then the contractions got worse. "I hope it doesn't go on like this much longer," she groaned, and saw them glance at each other, a look that told her there was a long night ahead. Soon she was slicked in sweat, and the pains were coming every few minutes. Goodness, it was uncomfortable. "Hurry up, little one," she urged. Poor Brograve was in the sitting room waiting for news. She hoped he didn't hear when she gave an involuntary scream.

In the early hours of the morning, Eve heard the doctor whispering to the midwife that the labor was not progressing and she began to get scared. What if the baby was stuck inside her? What if its little heart stopped with all the strain?

Suddenly she remembered the macabre discovery Howard had made in the treasury section of the tomb: a Canopic jar containing the skeletons of two stillborn babies.

"We are assuming they must have been Tutankhamun's babies with his wife Ankhesenamun," Howard had told her. "Had one of them lived, it would have changed the entire order of succession in Egypt."

Eve shivered. What an odd thing to keep in your tomb, and for them to be preserved for millennia. All she could think of was poor Ankhesenamun. "She must have been distraught to lose two babies."

"Life was more fragile then," Howard replied,

"and loss common, especially since there was so much inbreeding. Ankhesenamun was Tutankhamun's half sister."

As she struggled to give birth to her own baby, Eve's mind kept returning to those stillborn babies. How could any woman bear to go through the whole nine months, and labor too, and be told her baby was dead? She couldn't shake thoughts of doom, increasingly convinced something was badly wrong.

Twenty-four hours after her contractions began, when Eve felt as if her insides had been torn to smithereens, the doctor finally ripped the baby out of her using a gigantic pair of metal forceps. The midwife caught it—a slippery creature covered in blood and white mucus—and began patting it urgently. The wait seemed interminable. Eve couldn't breathe, craning her neck to see if her baby was alive, but too scared to ask. And finally there was a mewl, like a kitten, and tears rolled down Eve's cheeks.

"It's a girl," the midwife said.

The doctor was busy between Eve's legs. Everything hurt. But she was alive, and her daughter was alive, and that's all that mattered. They gave her a shot of morphine and she slid into a dreamless sleep.

When she opened her eyes, Brograve was sitting

by her bedside with the baby in his arms—a perfect child with a fluff of dark hair and a wrinkled face, eyes screwed shut against the light.

"Look what we made," he said, holding her out, the words catching in his throat.

Eve was filled with a rush of emotions: relief that she had survived and the child was alive after all the trauma; a massive surge of love for her daughter; and awe at this miracle. People had been having babies since the dawn of time, but until now she had never realized quite how *extraordinary* it was that an entire new person had grown inside her.

From the minute Patricia was born, Eve wanted to keep her within earshot at all times. The cradle stayed in their bedroom until she was six months old, and Eve never left the house without her in those early months. She was overwhelmed by the responsibility for this tiny creature. It was up to them to mold the type of human being she became, and that felt like magic of the most profound kind possible.

Chapter Forty-Seven

London, May 1973

"I can't find that slip of paper with Ana Mansour's telephone number," Brograve said over dinner. "Do you know where it is?"

They had started eating their meals at the kitchen table. There seemed no point in carrying dishes through to the dining room only to carry them back again afterward. Besides, Eve liked her kitchen. Unruly houseplants grew on a broad sunny windowsill, alongside which sat a little cabinet painted to look like a chocolate-box cottage that contained a range of dried herbs in jars. Most were past their best, but it was a pretty object.

"I already telephoned her," Eve said. "She told me she was sacked for having an affair with a colleague. Hardly a hanging offense in this day and age!" She raised an eyebrow and smiled at him. "She was hoping that if she solved the mystery of the missing items from the tomb and perhaps took some back to Cairo, they might consider reinstating her."

Brograve grunted, still suspicious. "What about all the time you spent answering her questions? Will the tape recording be given to the museum, as she promised?"

Eve hadn't thought to ask about that. "I'm sure it will," she said, then told him the story of Ana's husband getting custody of her children and even denying her access.

"She should have thought of that before she had an affair," Brograve said. "Sharia law is very much on the side of men. I believe they can divorce their wives simply by saying 'I divorce you' three times, but women don't have the same right."

"Goodness! So they could blurt it out in the heat of an argument one night, then wake up divorced the next morning? That seems harsh." She had a sip of sherry, her favorite medium-dry one. "I feel sorry for her. I wish we could have helped."

"I don't like being lied to," Brograve grumbled. "I've got a good mind to contact the university and tell them she's still sending out letters on their notepaper and pretending to be an employee."

"Please don't do that," Eve said. "After all, no harm has been done."

"She might be trying to trick someone else. Maybe we weren't the only targets. And you only have her word for it that she was planning to return the items to Egypt."

He finished his meal and put his knife and fork together. He ate at twice the speed of Eve so his plate was always empty when she was just halfway through. She cut off half her remaining chicken breast and passed it across.

"I can't help wondering what happened to that gold unguent container," she said, in an attempt to distract him from his annoyance about Ana. "Do you think there's any chance we might have left it in Framfield, in a forgotten corner? What about the hollow behind the panel in the bathroom, where we used to hide my jewelry when we went on holiday? Or in the storage space under the window seat in the library?"

It was a funny old house. The corridors had unexpected twists and turns, so you could easily lose your bearings. Even after living there for years, Eve would glance out a window expecting to see the front garden and instead she'd be facing the kitchen yard.

"I checked both of those before we left," Brograve assured her. "And now the new owners have gutted it. Knocked down walls, added extra bathrooms, created an open-plan kitchen-diner out the back. If there was anything hidden away, I'm sure it would have been found by their builders."

Eve's heart ached to think of that house—*her* house—being ripped apart. She still mourned for it. Why did they have to leave? She pined for the garden in particular. May was one of her favorite months; the trees would be in leaf, there would be a shimmering carpet of bluebells in the orchard, and a few early roses might have put in an appearance.

"Talking about things that are missing, have you seen my father's gold clock?" Brograve asked. "It used to be on the mantelpiece in the sitting room. It crossed my mind that Ana could have taken it when I left her in there, the day Sionead and I had to help you to bed."

"Goodness, you *have* taken against her!" Eve raised her eyebrows. "I've been rearranging the ornaments in there so I've probably moved it somewhere safe. I'll have a hunt later."

She'd been trying to return objects to the groupings they used to have in Framfield. Where had the clock been? She was pretty sure it used to be on the mantelpiece, so why wasn't it there now?

After they finished their meal, she walked all around the apartment, checking every shelf, but couldn't see the clock anywhere. What might she have done with it? She had a vague memory of putting it somewhere useful, but where?

She went to the cupboard where they kept the photo albums and dug out some Framfield ones, mostly from the late 1920s and early 1930s, soon after they moved in. They might confirm where the clock used to be. Brograve was watching a detective show on television, but Eve sat by the drawing-room window, under a standard lamp, and began to leaf through pictures of the house she had loved so much. If she spotted the clock in one of the photos, then she could work out where it was now and stop Brograve from blaming Ana for something she didn't do. That was her plan, at least.

Chapter Forty-Eight

Framfield, 1929

Eve hadn't married Brograve for his money. He only launched his copper cable company in 1922 and she had no idea whether he would turn out to be any good at business, but it was already thriving by the time Patricia was born in 1925. Eve was nervous when he invited Porchy to invest, worried that mixing family and business would be a mistake, but, as it turned out, Porchy made rather a lot of money from his stake and was delighted.

"Are we rich?" she asked Brograve, when he suggested they buy a country house.

"Comfortable," he replied.

Eve liked that word. It made her feel secure.

They drove around the Home Counties, viewing properties that were in their price range and close enough to be an easy commute from town. Patricia sat in the back seat, singing happily, always a contented child.

As soon as they drove into the village of Framfield, Eve had a good feeling about it. There was a pretty old church, a pub, a few shops, a row of thatched and half-timbered cottages, and a large lake on the outskirts: it was the idyllic country village of her imagination. The house for sale was T-shaped, with a sixteenth-century main section and two wings that had been added in the seventeenth century, in a mixture of half-timbering and red brick. One of the best things, from Eve's point of view, was that it was set on a remote lane, without through traffic, and she could see a group of children playing in the garden of a neighboring house.

Patricia was an only child and Eve was keen for her to have as many friends as possible, to compensate. She would love to have given her a sibling but the damage done to her insides during the birth had made the doctor advise Eve to avoid another pregnancy. It had been a blow at the time. She desperately wanted to give Brograve a son, not least because the baronetcy would become extinct if she didn't. He was a man who *should* have a son. But he accepted the decision with equanimity, and Patricia was such a delightful child, Eve couldn't harbor any regrets.

As they walked into the front hall, Eve had a curious sense of feeling at home immediately. She remembered Sir Arthur Conan Doyle saying that houses held memories in their stones. If that were the case, she felt sure the previous occupants had been happy here. It had a welcoming atmosphere. There was plenty of room to invite visitors for weekend house parties, the garden was a full acre, and there was good walking around about. It wasn't palatial, but it felt more like a family home than Highclere ever had.

Brograve put in an offer and they hugged each other in glee when it was accepted. After they moved in, they discovered that the roof leaked, the bathroom plumbing drained into the cavity above the kitchen ceiling, and there were moles in the lawn, but right from the start they loved it dearly. They made friends with the neighbors in the lane, inviting each other for gin and tonics on long summer evenings. When they heard that the local school had an excellent reputation, Eve put Patricia's name down.

Brograve became increasingly irate as the disastrous policies of Ramsay MacDonald's Labour Party following the Wall Street Crash led the country into acute financial crisis. He often slammed his morning paper on the table in disgust or grumbled through the evening news on television. Still, Eve was astounded when he announced he was going to stand for parliament in the general election of October 1931.

"But the Liberal Party is dead as a dodo," she replied. "Are you sure it's a good idea?"

"I'm going to stand for the Conservatives," he said. "They've offered me the seat of Walthamstow East. I'm sure if my father were alive, he would also switch allegiance since it seems the party most likely to save the country from ruin."

When she got over her surprise, Eve was thrilled. She had time on her hands now that Patricia was at school, and she would relish going on the campaign trail with him.

She and Brograve drove out to explore Walthamstow in northeast London, and found a largely working-class constituency, enclosed by the Lea Valley to the west and Epping Forest to the east, with some picturesque historic areas and a mile-long street market full of bustle and color.

"I'm told that unemployment is an issue," Brograve said, "and the people feel they have suffered unfairly under the Labour budget cuts. Our message is that we will promote business and create wealth for all."

He had grown in confidence since the Lowestoft defeat. On the hustings, he spoke with a certainty that made people listen. He sounded like a man who had the answers. Eve wandered the streets, chatting to the market traders and women shoppers, and they told her about their desperation for decent housing and a secure living. It surely wasn't too much to ask.

A journalist from the local paper requested an interview with Eve and she agreed, meeting him at campaign headquarters one late September morning. He was an eager lad who came armed with sheaves of notes, and—as she had anticipated—he quickly veered away from Brograve's policies to question her about her family history. How did she feel about her mother's notorious court case against Dorothy Dennistoun?

"That's *ancient* history," she told him. "I'm sure your readers have far more pressing issues to worry about."

Did she feel her family had been cursed by its connection with Tutankhamun?

She laughed. "Yes, I broke a nail this morning, and I hold the Egyptian king entirely responsible."

"Seriously, though," he said, "your family seems to have had more than your fair share of tragedy, most recently with the sudden death of your brother-in-law."

Eve took a calming breath before replying. Catherine's brother had dropped dead at the age of twenty-nine while playing tennis on the court at Highclere. It seemed there had been an undiagnosed heart condition. Catherine went quite mad with grief. She came to Framfield to stay for a week after the funeral, and the only consolation she found was in the gin bottle.

"Catherine's brother never entered Tutankhamun's tomb, and had never even been to Egypt," she told him. "Are you suggesting that anyone remotely associated with my family might be cursed, despite the fact that I myself remain mysteriously unscathed? In that case, are you sure you are not putting yourself at risk simply by being in my presence?"

He grinned at that. "Sorry. I had to ask. The editor insisted."

"Don't worry, I'm used to it."

"There's one more question of a delicate nature that he wants me to put to you. We've heard that your mother arranges abortions for upper-class girls at her private hospital. Would you care to comment?"

Eve flinched. "Blimey, which gutter did you trawl that nonsense from?"

"Shall I record that as 'no comment'?" he asked.

"No, record exactly what I said. And remember that my mother knows her way around the law courts should you be tempted to print anything slanderous."

He laughed. "Fair point."

"Could it be true?" she asked Brograve as they drove home that evening.

"Very likely," he replied. "Nothing your mother gets up to would surprise me. Why don't you ask her?"

Eve closed her eyes. They were friends, she and Almina, but mainly because Eve never challenged her. Ian had proved an unreliable sort of husband and Almina had no one else to turn to, so Eve didn't want them to fall out.

Perhaps she would pretend she'd never heard the abortion rumor. She hoped with all her heart it wasn't true.

On the twenty-seventh of October, 1931, Brograve won a resounding victory over his Labour and Liberal counterparts, getting almost sixty percent of the vote in Walthamstow East. It reflected a national landslide for the Conservatives and a new era in British politics. As she watched him make his acceptance speech, Eve felt fit to burst with pride. If only Pups could have witnessed this!

She thought about the man Brograve had become since she first met him as a quiet, traumatized soldier at the Residency Christmas party in Cairo. Had she somehow sensed back then that he would turn out to have such inner strength? Or had it been the luck of the draw when she picked him as her husband-to-be? She felt a surge of lust for him. Winning an election was extremely sexy.

Eve was excited to explore the new opportunities that opened up for her as an MP's wife. Before Brograve made his maiden speech, she had joined dozens of social committees at the House of Commons. She got involved in organizing charity fundraisers, volunteered to entertain the wives of politicians visiting from overseas, and took on umpteen other unpaid roles, simply because she loved meeting new people.

Every morning she drove Brograve to Uckfield station to catch the London train before she dropped Patricia at school, then she got on with her commitments for the day. She often drove to Walthamstow to help Brograve on constituency business, or to Putney to visit his mother. Some days she would be at the House or in one of the meeting rooms around Parliament Square. If she had time, she drove to Newmarket or Kempton Park, Cheltenham or Newbury when one of their horses was racing—they had bought another foal, named Hot Flash after the white flash on her nose.

It was the most fulfilling period of her life, she reflected. Eve had not accomplished her childhood dream to be a lady archaeologist, but she had no regrets about that. Her time was filled with pursuits that used her personality and skills, a family she cherished, and a home she loved.

Chapter Forty-Nine

London, May 1973

E ve flicked through the old black-and-white photographs of the Framfield house. There was one of
Patricia dancing on the lawn, wearing a summer frock
with a ruched bodice; it had been rose pink with sprigs
of green leaves, she remembered. Another showed the
giant Christmas tree they installed in the front hall
every year with an explosion of presents underneath.
Next there was Patricia bouncing on the four-poster in
cotton pajamas.

There weren't any pictures of her mother or Porchy at Framfield. Her mother wouldn't come because
she had never forgiven Brograve for his outburst on the
telephone when Eve was pregnant. Her brother didn't
come because he was lazy; he was happy for them to
visit Highclere, and he met Brograve for long lunches

at his London club, but he couldn't be bothered to drive the extra sixty miles or so to her country house—not even to see his little niece.

Howard Carter came, though. There was a glorious photograph of him reclining on the lawn wearing a daisy chain Patricia had made for him, pretending to sip tea from a doll's teacup. Another showed him crouched in front of Patricia's dollhouse helping her to arrange the furniture. Who would have thought that a childless man could have such a knack with children?

"They used to gossip about you and Howard," Brograve said, glancing over her shoulder when he came to top up her sherry. "Said I should keep an eye on the pair of you because you seemed rather too close."

Eve chuckled. "A *Daily Mail* journalist tried to get that rumor off the ground, but nothing could have been further from the truth. Poor, dear Howard. He was like a friendly uncle, I suppose."

She remembered one occasion when he came to stay for the weekend of their annual summer picnic. Most of the village was invited—all their closest neighbors and the parents of Patricia's school friends too—and they treated Howard as a celebrity. All day long he was surrounded by folk asking about the tomb, and he never tired of answering them. Eve brought him a plate of sandwiches and cold cuts because he'd been so busy talking he hadn't had a chance to visit the long trestle tables laid out around the lawn, laden with food she'd spent the best part of a week preparing.

"Have you retired from archaeology now that work on the tomb is finished?" she heard one neighbor asking.

Eve knew that Howard would never retire. After he finished dismantling the tomb and overseeing the installation of its contents in the Cairo Museum, he had spent several years on the lecture circuit. Lots of countries bestowed honors upon him, and he wrote well-received books on Tutankhamun.

"Far from retiring, I am looking forward to my next challenge. I have a secret ambition to search for the tomb of Alexander the Great." He turned to Eve with a grin. "Care to accompany me?"

"Definitely," she said, trying to remember if they thought it was in Alexandria, Babylon, or Greece. There was a mystery surrounding it, that much she knew.

Before she could ask, one of the school mothers interrupted. "I know you take a dim view of stories about the curse of Tutankhamun, but I recently read an article by Sir Bruce Ingram in the *Illustrated London News* about disasters that befell him after you gave him a mummified hand from the tomb. He says that soon after he placed it in his country house, the building burned to the ground—yet the hand survived. Then after he had the house rebuilt, it was badly damaged by flooding. He wrote that since he donated the hand to the Cairo Museum, there have been no further misfortunes. How do you explain that?"

Eve thought Howard might rebuke her, but he smiled and answered politely.

"Sir Bruce is a good friend of mine and we have agreed to differ on this. I see his misfortunes as pure coincidence and his blaming the mummified hand I gave him as superstition. Perhaps you have seen the Boris Karloff film *The Mummy*, which came out last year? I suggested to Sir Bruce he should get in touch with the script writers to give them material for the follow-up."

There was general laughter at that, and Eve left them to fetch the first of the desserts from the kitchen: a sherry trifle, Brograve's favorite.

Eve looked up from the photograph album, trying to remember if Howard had ever begun his hunt for the tomb of Alexander. She couldn't remember seeing him again after that summer picnic.

"When did Howard die?" she asked Brograve.

"Nineteen thirty-nine. You, Almina, and Porchy went to the funeral in Putney Vale. I was busy in the House that day."

Eve couldn't remember. "What did he die of?"

"Hodgkin's disease. His last years were difficult because of the side effects of the radiation treatments. His niece, Phyllis, moved in to take care of him, but you visited often. We took him for dinner at the Savoy one evening when he felt a little better, but I remember he scarcely ate anything. He got very thin toward the end."

"Poor Howard. I miss him." It sounded silly to miss someone more than thirty years after their death, but she did.

She turned the page of the album and there were some photographs of Betty, Brograve's mother, someone else she missed. She had come to stay at Framfield for the last three years of her life, once she was too frail to live alone. They gave her a wing of the house, so she had her own sitting room, bedroom, bathroom, and a small kitchen, but she invariably dined with them. She was never any trouble, Eve thought. Had Almina lived with them, every arrangement would have had to revolve around her, but Betty quietly fitted in, the way she had when she stayed with them for six months after her husband's death.

There were few pictures of Brograve in the album because he was usually the one wielding the camera, but she stopped at one that showed him standing in front of the mantelpiece in Framfield with the gold clock behind him. That's where it should have been. Why had she moved it?

"I can't find anything anymore," she complained to Brograve. "I don't know why. It's as if things move around on their own."

He looked up. "What else is lost?"

"Your father's clock and the gold container from the tomb. Maybe other things, I'm not sure."

He pursed his lips. "Are you still convinced Ana Mansour didn't take the clock?"

Eve shook her head firmly. "She's not like that."

He gave her an inquisitive look, as if to ask how she knew what Ana was like, but she turned back to the album before he could question her further.

On the last page, there was a photograph of a brown bear grazing by the side of a river. Clearly it hadn't been taken at Framfield. She squinted, trying to remember where it was, and suddenly it came to her.

"This bear was in Canada, wasn't it?" she asked, holding it up so he could see.

He turned to look, and surprise spread across his face. "You remember that?"

"Of course I do. I was petrified. You kept saying the bear was on the other side of the river and it was safe to stop and take a photograph, but I wanted to get back in the car and drive away. I knew bears could swim and they are faster than humans too." She chuckled. "Then you took ages lining up the shot, getting as close as you could. . . ." She stopped. "When was it?"

He seemed boyishly excited by her answer. "Patricia was ten. It was just four months after your accident and we went there so you could see a rehabilitation specialist, but we made a holiday out of it too. Do you remember now? You've never been able to remember that holiday before. You were still recuperating."

Eve thought hard, but Patricia wasn't in the image in her mind—just the bear, the river, and her husband.

Brograve came to stand beside her and pointed to some other photographs on the same page. "That's Niagara Falls," he said. "Do you remember being there? The deafening roar of the water?"

She looked at the image of the three of them against a railing in front of a wall of grayish misty water but nothing came back to her.

"We went out on a boat called the *Maid of the Mist,*" he said, "and we all got soaked by the spray. It ruined your hairstyle. Look!"

He pointed to a picture of Eve with her hair plastered to her head. She stared hard, willing her brain to work, but it wouldn't.

"It was perishing cold that day," he persevered.

"We only had summer clothes with us and had to buy Patricia a warm coat in a shop."

Eve considered lying, pretending she could remember just to please him, but there was nothing there. Maybe she didn't even remember the bear. Maybe she just remembered the photograph and her mind had created a memory around it.

"Doesn't matter," he said, disappointment in his voice. "It's wonderful that you've got one memory back from that trip."

Looking at him, Eve realized in a burst of insight how sad it must be to have a wife who couldn't remember huge chunks of your shared past. They were old now, him and her. Every morning she listened to him coughing and hacking in the bathroom, saw the exertion it took for him to bend and pull on his socks, watched him rubbing his lower back after bringing in the coal scuttle—the tiny signs of a body wearing out. But that was nothing compared to what he had to put up with from her as her mind wore out.

"It must be ghastly for you," she said. "Me not remembering. I'm sorry. I wish I could."

"It's not ghastly at all," he said, with a fond smile. "You're still you and that's what counts. That's the *only* thing that counts."

Chapter Fifty

London, July 1973

Eve walked around the apartment opening all the windows to try to get a breeze blowing through. Brograve had gone for his walk but she found it too hot to venture out these days until late afternoon when the sun was less intense. It wasn't like the heat in Egypt, the dangerous kind that pressed down on you like a lead weight, but it still gave her a headache if she stayed out for long. She felt anxious when he went outdoors, in case anything happened, but he was never gone for more than an hour.

The buzzer rang and she answered the entry phone, but it seemed to have a loose wire and all she could hear was muffled crackling. The buzzer rang again. It was probably the postman. She pressed the door entry button to let him leave any post in the hall downstairs.

Next she heard the clank of the lift approaching their floor. Could it be Patricia? But she had her own keys and wouldn't have needed to ring the buzzer. None of their friends dropped by unannounced. They'd always telephone first. She froze on hearing a knock on the door. The visitor was just a few feet away.

Eve opened the door, remembering as she did so that Patricia had told her always to look through the peephole first.

"My goodness!" she exclaimed. Ana Mansour was standing outside, wearing a tailored white summer dress, with sunglasses balanced on her head and a tan leather shoulder bag hanging by her side.

"Lady Beauchamp," she said, with a smile that looked forced. "I wonder if I might have a word."

There was no apology for turning up without warning, no explanation. Eve thought the intrusion was odd but she couldn't think of a polite reason not to invite her inside. If only Brograve were there, or Mrs. Jarrold . . . but she was entirely alone.

"I was about to have a nap," she prevaricated. "This heat is exhausting."

"It won't take long," Ana replied, and swept past her, heading for the sitting room.

Eve followed and hovered near the doorway, reasoning that if she sat down, it would take longer to persuade

Ana to leave. She had a brisk air about her today that was making Eve feel uneasy. Ana didn't sit down either but stopped by the window and turned to face Eve.

"I thought you and I were friends," Ana said. "I confided in you about my problems. I trusted you. But I found out recently that most of what you told me is a pack of lies."

Eve gasped. "That's not true." Feeling suddenly wobbly, she edged toward the nearest chair and sank onto it with a bump. "What makes you say that?"

Ana spoke with an accusing tone. "Your uncle, Mervyn Herbert, left his journals to Oxford University, where they became available to scholars last week. In one journal entry he writes that you told him that you, your father, and Howard Carter sneaked back to the tomb in November 1922, two days before the official opening, and that the three of you entered the burial chamber that night."

Eve was stricken with horror. She had expressly told Mervyn that her confession was to remain confidential. Could this get her into trouble? Might she be arrested? She couldn't decide how best to answer without incriminating herself.

Ana folded her arms. "According to Mervyn Herbert, you all took souvenirs from the burial chamber that night. I suppose that explains the items you found at Highclere, but where are the rest, Eve? And why didn't you tell me about this?"

Eve couldn't think of what to say. If only Brograve were there. "I don't know what you're talking about," she said in a whisper, and could feel her cheeks flush at the lie.

"When I described the gold unguent container, you seemed startled, as if you recognized it. Was that because you know where it is? Maybe you have it here, hidden away somewhere." Ana glanced at the corner cabinet that contained some china knickknacks.

Eve began to feel giddy and became aware of a pounding in her right temple. "Please, I can't talk to you today," she said. "I'm not well. Can you come back another day?"

Ana sighed in exasperation. "You've already wasted enough of my time, Lady Beauchamp. According to Mervyn Herbert's papers, you were the first person to squeeze into the burial chamber. Didn't you think to tell me that? You've made me look a fool. The very least you can do is be honest now."

"I don't know where the container is," Eve whispered. "That's the honest truth."

"What else did you take, Eve?" Her tone softened. "You can tell me. No one is going to mind after all this time. We just want the truth."

"That was all I took," Eve said. "Just that. Please, I don't feel well. I need to lie down." The headache was worsening by the second, making it hard to think or speak.

Ana walked over to the mantelpiece and picked up a photograph. "Are these your grandsons?" She turned it around so Eve could see. "Handsome boys. The elder looks like your father, don't you think?"

To Eve, it sounded as though she was threatening the boys. "Is that a trick question?" she asked.

Ana shook her head. "I was just trying to be friendly. Look." She pulled a wallet from her shoulder bag, extracted a photograph, and came over to show Eve: a girl and a boy with dark hair and brown skin. "These are my children, Layla and Masud."

Eve nodded, not sure what she was supposed to say.

"I haven't seen them for over a year now," Ana said. "I thought you wanted to help me be reunited with them, but instead your lies have wasted my time and kept me from them."

"If I knew anything, I would tell you," Eve said. "I'm sorry. Thank you for stopping by. If you don't mind . . ." She pushed herself up from the chair and staggered out to the hall. Where was her walking stick? She must have put it down somewhere. She was always mislaying it.

Ana didn't follow straightaway. When Eve glanced back, she could see her checking inside the china cabinet, then perusing the shelves in the alcove. Was she planning to steal something? Had Brograve been right about that? How could she stop her? Should she ring the police? She couldn't remember the number, although she knew it was a really obvious one with three digits.

Eve opened the front door and held it wide. "Thank you for shtopping by," she said, and noticed that her tongue was heavy in her mouth. "I hope you have a g-good journey."

Ana came out to the hall and there was a moment when she considered saying something else. Eve saw the thought flicker across her face.

"Are you alright?" she asked instead. "You look a little strange."

"G-go!" Eve said. "P-please."

Ana turned on the threshold, as if she had another question, but Eve was too quick for her and slammed the door shut. Her heart was beating hard and she felt as if she might throw up. She meant to try and reach the sitting room sofa for a lie-down but suddenly her legs gave way and she slid down the door onto the hall carpet. The pattern in the wallpaper was dancing in a most peculiar fashion and she felt as if she were seasick, or tipsy. It was the oddest sensation.

There was a little jug of sweet peas on the hall table and she could smell their scent, a strong, choking sweetness. The grandfather clock chimed. And then she had a vivid memory of holding the gold unguent container, trying not to inhale that strange musky scent, her heart racing as she decided where to put it so it couldn't do any harm.

Eve felt very odd now and opened her mouth to shout for Brograve but her face was too heavy and the sound wouldn't come. She tried to push herself along the floor but her arms had no strength. Blackness was closing in like thick fog and she had no choice but to let it engulf her.

Chapter Fifty-One

London, July 1973

Brograve was overheated when he got back from his walk. He could feel his face was red as a ripe tomato. In the lift, he used his handkerchief to wipe the perspiration from his brow, then took out his keys.

When he pushed on the door to their apartment, it opened only a crack. He frowned. Something was in the way. Carefully, he eased it far enough to peer around the edge and his whole body went rigid with shock when he saw Eve crumpled on the floor. "Eve!" he called, but there was no response. He glanced around. There wasn't time to fetch a neighbor to help.

Taking a deep breath, he crouched down and slid his hand around the edge of the door, bending his arm so that he could cradle Eve's head as he gently pushed the door open. Once the gap was wide enough, he squeezed through and dropped to his knees beside her. She was breathing, thank god! He rolled her onto her side, out of the way of the door, and bent her legs into recovery position before grabbing the hall telephone.

The ambulance operator was kind. "They'll be with you shortly," she said. "I'll stay on the line."

Sionead's list of instructions was on the telephone table, underneath a vase of sweet peas, but Brograve couldn't reach it because a sudden pain in his chest knocked the breath out of him.

"Not now," he whispered. "No!"

Still holding the receiver to his ear, he slumped on the floor beside Eve. The operator told him to check her pulse, so he did. The beats seemed normal; she was definitely alive. He bent to kiss her cheek and whispered: "Pipsqueak? Are you there? Please wake up."

What was going on inside that head of hers? Which bit of brain was affected? Would it be a TIA or a devastating, life-changing stroke? Might this be the one that killed her?

The woman on the phone was still talking but he bent double as another pain crushed his chest. How would the ambulancemen get through the street door? He'd have to stand up to answer the buzzer, and he wasn't sure he was capable.

There was no choice. He'd have to manage somehow.

"They're nearly there," the operator was saying. "Any minute now."

And then he heard the clang of the lift door and two men appeared, carrying medical bags and a stretcher. Someone else must have let them in, thank god! He stammered out Eve's history of strokes, hoping he hadn't forgotten anything.

"Are you alright, sir?" one of the men asked.

He nodded, and leaned back against the wall while they carried out some tests on Eve and strapped an oxygen mask over her face.

They lifted her onto the stretcher, then one of them helped him to his feet. Pain in his back stopped him from straightening up and he felt giddy as the blood rushed from his head. Somehow he managed to stagger to the lift, surprisingly shaky on his feet.

The ambulance was parked on double yellow lines right outside the building. He climbed in and sat in the passenger seat by Eve's feet. He knew the drill; they'd been here before.

"Are you her next of kin?" the man who was sitting in the back with them asked, filling out a form on his lap, and Brograve remembered he should have called Patricia. He gave her phone number in case he was having a heart attack and might be about to lose consciousness.

As they drove through the sun-baked city streets, he

couldn't take his eyes off Eve's face. It was stuffy in the back of the ambulance. Shards of white light pierced the slits above the darkened blinds and dust motes danced.

Suddenly her eyelids twitched and fluttered, then she opened her eyes and looked straight at him. Amber eyes she had, the prettiest he had ever seen. She gave him a crooked smile, then went back to sleep again.

When they reached the hospital, Brograve was too dizzy to walk and he felt sick as well. He was furious with himself, because he wanted to stay by Eve's side, but instead one of the ambulancemen helped him into a wheelchair and wheeled him to a cubicle, where a nurse took some blood, strapped a monitor to his chest, and told him to rest.

He lay back. Was this what a heart attack felt like? He was seventy-six now, a year older than his father had been when he died. Maybe his time was drawing to a close, but he couldn't go while Eve still needed him. He had to hang on for her.

It was one of his greatest regrets that his father had passed away so early. He never met his only grandchild. He never knew that Brograve became a member of parliament and a parliamentary private secretary in both the Ministry of Transport and the Foreign Office. His copper cable company had made him independently wealthy, and he had been a good son, taking care of his mother till the end. She and Eve had always been close, and Betty had been a doting grandma. His father would have been proud of him, he was sure.

Thinking back on his achievements, Brograve knew without doubt that the one he was proudest of was marrying Eve. She was far too good for him; after all these years, he still couldn't believe his luck. When he accompanied her to charity balls and parliamentary teas and all the other events she got involved in, people gravitated toward her, wanting to be in her orbit. She sparkled in company, making everyone feel at ease, from grand diplomats and overseas politicians' wives who barely spoke English through to the tea ladies and waiters who served them, whom she never forgot to thank. He often stood back and watched the energy she exuded, the friendly words she had for everyone, her natural talent for socializing, and he swelled with pride.

A doctor arrived at his bedside, asking questions. Brograve told him about the chest pains and dizziness, adding that they seemed to have passed.

"The good news is that it wasn't a heart attack," the doctor told him. "I suspect it was angina, brought on by the shock of finding your wife unconscious. I hear you had also been out walking in the heat, which I wouldn't advise, not at your age. This is a warning. You need to take it a bit easier."

Brograve closed his eyes, relief making him emotional. "Can I see my wife now?" he asked.

The doctor told him to wait while they got some medicine from the hospital pharmacy: a pill he would have to take daily and a spray to squirt under his tongue if he had any more chest pains.

Brograve sat on the edge of the bed, impatient to be with Eve, watching the minutes tick around on his watch. It seemed to take forever until a nurse brought his medicines, then accompanied him upstairs to the ward where Eve had been taken. As he got close to her bed, he saw she was awake and his eyes filled with tears. He walked straight over and kissed her full on the lips, stroking her hair.

The nurse pulled up a plastic chair for him and offered to fetch a cup of tea. "Your daughter's on the way, and the doctor will be round to have a word shortly."

"Hello," Eve said, looking at him and smiling, her speech clear and her mouth hardly lopsided at all.

"Hello you," he said and kissed her again. "What a fright you gave me! How are you feeling?"

"Fine," she said, still smiling.

"Patricia's on the way," he told her, and she smiled

without comment. "I hope she gets parked. It's always difficult in visiting hours."

"Yes," Eve said.

There was something disconcerting about her monosyllabic answers and a blankness in her expression. He wanted to ask her questions, to test her, but knew it would be cruel at this stage. Instead, he put his arms around her and laid his head on her shoulder, giddy with gratitude that she was alive.

Later, the doctor asked Brograve and Patricia to join him in a relatives' room down the corridor. Brograve liked the respectful way he spoke to them, assuming they understood the issues from previous occasions.

"It's not a massive stroke," he said, "and she came around quickly, which is a plus. Her hand movement is unimpaired and her speech is clear, but you need to be prepared for a certain amount of confusion in the aftermath."

"Of course," Brograve said, and Patricia squeezed his hand.

"She may be unusually emotional, or forgetful, or simply fail to understand things she used to understand perfectly well."

Brograve's throat felt too tight to speak, so he just nodded.

"I know from past experience that she is a very determined lady," the doctor said, "but her age will count against her. I warn you: don't expect too much straightaway."

"When can I take her home?" Brograve asked. "Should I hire a live-in nurse like I did last time? I'll have to check if the agency has someone available." His mind leaped ahead to all the arrangements he would have to make.

"I suggest you leave her with us for the next few days and we'll assess her more fully," the doctor said.

"Come and stay with me, Dad," Patricia said.

She asked the doctor some questions but Brograve wasn't listening. He just wanted his wife home again and for everything to go back to the way it had been the previous day. And he had a sinking feeling in the pit of his stomach that it wasn't going to be like that, not this time.

Chapter Fifty-Two

London, July 1973

Eve thought everyone was very kind in the hospital. There seemed to be a never-ending supply of tea in plastic beakers, and they brought her little meals on trays with lovely puddings like sponge and custard. On the morning she was due to leave, one of the nurses brushed her hair and smoothed Pond's cold cream on her cheeks.

"We're making you look nice for going home," she said.

"That's lovely. I must come here again," Eve said.

"No offense, but I hope you don't," the nurse replied, and Eve laughed.

"Framfield," Eve said. "I live in Framfield." She was excited about seeing her house. All the flowers would be out in her garden.

Her husband collected her and they caught a taxi together, the black kind where you sit in the back seat and feel the vibrations of the engine and hear a kind of rattling, humming sound. It stopped in the wrong place, outside an apartment block, but she let her husband lead her into a lift and up to the third floor.

When he unlocked the door of an apartment, she walked in and recognized that she had been there before but she couldn't remember whose apartment it was. That telephone table was familiar, but now it had some wilted sweet peas collapsed over the side of a vase. In the sitting room she recognized the royal blue sofa in front of the TV and the table by the window. She sat down, quite content to be there.

Her husband brought her a cup of coffee. He said their daughter, Patricia, was in the kitchen, putting some shopping in the refrigerator. She was staying for supper, he said, and had bought some nice fish for them.

"Lemon sole—your favorite," he said.

Eve smiled and thanked him, although she couldn't remember having had lemon sole before. Did it taste of lemon?

After a while she went to the bathroom and looked in the cabinet: it was full of shampoos and creams and talcum powder. She opened the talcum and sniffed its sweet powderiness; it reminded her of babies. Nice soft towels hung on the rail. You could walk into the shower, like the ones in the hospital, and there was a little stool for sitting down.

I should remember this, a voice in her head nagged. *Something is wrong.* But then she decided it didn't particularly matter because it all seemed very nice.

When she went back to the sitting room, her husband asked if she wanted a sherry and she said, "Yes, please," although she couldn't remember what sherry tasted like.

"Are we married?" she asked him. The question just slipped out and straightaway she regretted it. She could tell from the look that flashed across his face that she'd hurt his feelings, although he was quick to turn it into a joke.

"I'm not the type to make a girl live in sin," he quipped. "We got married on the eighth of October nineteen twenty-three, fifty years ago this year."

"Course we did." She nodded, sad to have upset him. She hated upsetting people but sometimes words came out of her mouth without her having thought about them properly first. She watched him pouring two glasses of sherry, careful to make the liquid the same level in each, and felt a rush of love for him.

"Would you like me to show you pictures of our wedding day?" he asked as he handed her a glass.

"I'd love that," she said. She sipped the sherry and found it was delicious.

He went out into the hall and when he came back he was holding an album. He sat on the sofa beside her and opened to the first page. It showed a photograph of a bridal couple but they looked funny. The top of the lady's head was only just level with the man's shoulder. The height difference was comic. She chuckled.

"That's us, Pipsqueak," he said, and she touched the picture with a finger. The girl looked nothing like the face she saw in the mirror but she recognized it was her all the same. She had dark wavy hair cut in a bob shape, and she was quite pretty, with owl eyes set in a round face, but she was not smiling. She looked very serious.

"You wore an ivory chanteuse dress," he said, "and your train was trimmed with old Brussels lace. That was your 'something old.' Look how long it was!"

Eve turned to her husband, then back to the photo, and she could see the similarities between him and the man pictured. He already had receding hair in the photograph, and that high forehead and his trim moustache were almost exactly the same. The only difference was that his hair was now gray instead of dark.

"Your bouquet was made of orange blossoms and they had the most glorious scent," he said. Suddenly

Eve could smell it. It was so strong she looked around to see if there were flowers in the room, but there weren't. They hadn't brought home the flowers she had in the hospital because Patricia said it was bad luck.

Brograve turned another page and began to name their wedding guests: lots of names, lots of faces, and she didn't remember any of them. Didn't matter. They were probably dead. She was glad to see she'd been popular once, although it made her melancholy that she wasn't now.

"That's your brother, Porchy," he said. She thought she recognized him. "And there's Howard Carter."

Eve remembered Howard. "He found Tutankhamun," she said. "And then there was a curse."

"No." Brograve smiled and shook his head. "There was no curse. That was just a fairy story."

"Really?" She was sure there had been a curse. That's what had caused her to lose her memories.

"Far from being cursed, we've been very lucky, you and I," he said. "We have each other, as well as a beautiful daughter and two dashing grandsons. We have a comfortable home; and we've had lots of foreign holidays. Most people aren't as lucky as us."

"Why were we lucky?" she asked, and he kissed her on the lips before he replied.

"Because of your sunny personality. I was in the

glooms when we met and you brought me the gift of happiness. You still do."

"You're very welcome," she said, and kissed him back, but it made her feel sad that she kept getting things wrong. A wave of emotion brought tears to her eyes.

"Don't cry," he said in a soothing voice. "Everything's fine. You had a funny turn but you'll soon be right as rain."

She couldn't help it; the tears rolled down her cheeks. Her husband took out a handkerchief and dabbed at them.

"I know how to cheer you up," he said. "Would you like me to sing the national anthem?"

"Yes, please," she said, although it seemed an odd thing to do.

"God save our gracious queen," he began, and Eve giggled. He had a terrible voice, singing it all on the same flat note. Then she stopped abruptly, hoping he wouldn't be upset that she was laughing at him.

"Oh Lord our God arise, scatter our enemies," he continued.

Her daughter came into the room saying that dinner was ready and she started laughing too. It must be a joke. Eve laughed even louder than before, glad they were all laughing at the same thing.

Chapter Fifty-Three

London, July 1973

Over the next few days, Eve often spoke of the curse of Tutankhamun and told Brograve that's what had caused her memory loss. She didn't seem upset, just repeated it as fact. Brograve corrected her every time but it had stuck in her head for some reason.

"You were in an accident," he said. "A long time ago. That's why you have funny turns."

He didn't like to tell her the medical details: about the head injury that caused severe trauma to her brain, and the strokes she had been prone to since then, which the doctors thought were linked to that injury. He didn't want to remind her of the accident at all, for fear of distressing her, but it didn't seem right to let her keep thinking the curse of Tutankhamun had caused her to lose her memory. It was strange that in her confusion she had locked onto that ridiculous piece of mythology that used to obsess the press. She hadn't believed it before. They'd both scoffed at the news reports that blamed the curse for the deaths of anyone who ever visited the tomb. But then everything changed on that awful summer's day in 1935.

Brograve was in his office at the House of Commons when a policeman rang, very deferential, apologizing that he had bad news. He said Eve had been in a serious road accident and she'd been taken to Addenbrooke's Hospital in Cambridge. He didn't know how bad it was but said she hadn't regained consciousness.

Panic took hold, a rushing, gripping feeling of terror, before he shook himself and leaped into action. First he telephoned their housekeeper to check that she could collect Patricia from school, then he borrowed a car from a chap in the office next door to his and set off for the hospital.

Eve was one of the best drivers he knew—much better than he was. Someone must have crashed into her, and he guessed it must have been at speed for her to be injured so badly as to be unconscious. Earlier that year a speed limit of thirty miles per hour had been introduced in built-up areas but it wasn't popular. Around the country, speed-limit signs had been torn down and tossed into rivers or village ponds. The Englishman liked the freedom to press the accelerator to the floor in his own car. If this turned out to be a case of dangerous driving, Brograve would press for the full weight of the law to be brought to bear. His knuckles were bony ridges as he gripped the steering wheel.

All the way to Cambridge he tried to focus on practicalities. It was nearly the summer recess so he was sure he could take compassionate leave from the House. The health secretary was a friend and he would ask his advice if they needed a second opinion on Eve's injuries. They might have to cancel their holiday in the South of France; they'd rented a villa for the month of August and invited different sets of friends to join them for a week each. Maybe Eve wouldn't be well enough now. All these matters occupied his brain, but he refused to let himself think she might not make it. She had to; that's all there was to it.

When he reached the hospital, a doctor told him that Eve had sustained a head injury and was in a coma. Brograve's brain froze at the word *coma*, terrified of the connotations. His ears were ringing so hard he couldn't hear anything else, then had to ask a nurse to repeat it all later.

When he got to Eve's bedside, he gripped the rail, watching her tiny face swathed in bandages, the tubes brutally puncturing her skin, the purple bruising already visible on exposed flesh, and he felt totally lost. Could she hear anything? There was no response when he whispered her name.

"Do you want me to telephone someone for you?" a nurse asked. "Any relatives?"

Brograve couldn't bear to have Porchy there or, even worse, Almina, so he said, "No, thank you." There was only one person he wanted to talk to and she was lying in front of him, deeply unconscious.

"What happened, Eve?" he whispered, but there was no reply. It was only when two policemen came to the ward to check on her that he learned about the chain of events that had led to the collision.

One of them was Scottish, a tall man with sandy hair; the other was lean and dark with shaggy eyebrows. They spoke to him respectfully, choosing their words with care, helmets on their laps, a little nervous perhaps. They knew he was a government minister.

Brograve looked from one to the other. Though they were trying their best, he knew they didn't begin to understand. This wasn't just another traffic accident, just another victim. This was *Eve! His* Eve! He wanted to shake them to get the urgency across. But instead he sat, and nodded, and listened quietly, wondering if they could feel his desperation, wondering if they cared.

Chapter Fifty-Four

London, July 1, 1935

Eve visited Howard Carter, in a flat he had bought around the corner from the Albert Hall. Howard still dressed just as her father used to, in a three-piece suit and bow tie, but he was stooped and needed a walking stick to get around now. He looked ghastly, she thought, as they sat chatting; his skin was gray, the whites of his eyes pale yellow, and his cheeks hollow.

"I've been having X-ray treatments for a problem with my glands," he said. "Jolly unpleasant. Can't say I recommend it." He touched his stomach lightly and kept his hand there, as if to hold back queasiness.

"It will be worth it in the end, I dare say," Eve replied, wondering if he had cancer. Since childhood she'd always spoken her mind with Howard, and he with her, but it seemed rude to mention the word *cancer* if he didn't volunteer it. "Are you happy with your doctors? More to the point, is Mama happy?"

Although Almina never had formal training in medicine, she considered herself more expert than the vast majority of doctors.

"She's arranged the best of care and given me a strict diet," he said. "I am, of course, following it to the letter." They exchanged complicit smiles.

"How are the Egyptians? Still giving you grief?" Eve asked. There had been a long history of grievances on Howard's side and on theirs, but on the whole she hoped the authorities appreciated what an astounding job he had done in preserving the tomb. He'd got the world's top experts involved, and had left a record that was the most thorough of any archaeological dig in history.

"They'll always find something to complain about." He sniffed. "Do you remember that funny smell when we broke into the burial chamber?"

"I certainly do," she said. "It was horrid."

"They tell me that staff working with the objects from the burial chamber complain of headaches and giddiness. One man has an asthma attack if he goes near them. And it reminded me that I used to feel very odd if I worked in there for long . . ."

"I did too," Eve interrupted. "I remember feeling dizzy the night we first broke in."

Howard closed his eyes for a second, as if waiting for a spasm of pain to pass. "I couldn't work out what was causing the smell," he said, "But then I wondered if it might have been the unguent in that container you took?"

Straightaway, Eve knew he was right. She shuddered. "I never liked that smell. I keep the container hidden away in the attic because otherwise the scent seeps out and impregnates my clothes."

"I'm glad you keep it in the attic, my dear. I've come to suspect it may be some kind of poison that Maya left as a trap for tomb robbers."

"Poison!" She was shocked. That unguent had been on Patricia's skin, in her hair!

"If the robbers had managed to access the burial chamber, that's the first item they would have stolen, because unguents were so valuable," Howard explained. "That's why Maya designed one that would make them ill. Perhaps it could even have proved fatal three thousand years ago. He might have called it 'magic' but the toxins they used then were very real."

Eve clutched her throat. "Do you think it could still be dangerous?"

"Probably not." He smiled. "But I certainly wouldn't want to breathe it in, day in, day out. You are wise to keep it in the attic."

Eve was shaken, but tried to make light of it. "There was me thinking I'd taken the most valuable object that night, and instead I took the most lethal!"

"It would be interesting to have scientists analyze it and find out what the poison is, but I'm torn because that would mean confessing our little secret." He gave her a rueful smile. "I've never regretted what we did, have you?"

"Absolutely not. It was thrilling! I'm glad it was just us three. Well, four: you, me, Pups, and Tutankhamun." She glanced at the clock and realized she was running late.

He had a fond smile as he regarded her. "Where are you hurtling off to this afternoon?"

Eve bit her lip, glancing at the clock again. "I'm hoping to get to Newmarket, where Hot Flash is running in the three-fifteen." Howard looked blank so she reminded him. "You know, our filly. She took the St. Leger last year, and has a feel for speed."

"Like her owner," Howard said. "I've never known you to sit still for long, not since you were a nipper of—what were you, seven when I met you?"

"Six. You came to Highclere with some bits and pieces for Pups's collection and I bored you to death with the entire extent of my knowledge of Ancient Egypt. I'm cringing at the memory."

"You have never bored me, Eve. You never will. Now go—go and see your horse and come back to visit me soon."

His niece, Phyllis, came into the hall to bid Eve goodbye.

"Is he going to be alright?" Eve asked. "Is there anything I can do?" It was on the tip of her tongue to ask if they needed money, but she stopped herself. Howard had done well over the years from buying and selling Egyptian artifacts, and from his lecture tours and books. He must be comfortable.

"Don't worry," Phyllis said. "We're fine. I'd tell you if we weren't."

Not fine at all, Eve thought, as she left the London suburbs behind and headed into the countryside. He was only sixty-one and should have been in better health. Poor Howard!

She hoped the press didn't get wind of his illness or they'd claim it was the curse of Tutankhamun. Every chance they got, they wheeled out the old trope. Howard had calculated that ten years after the official opening of the tomb, only six of the twenty-six present had died, which wasn't bad odds considering the average age of the guests was probably around sixty.

She took the Great Cambridge Road. As it crossed the River Lea, sun glinted off the water and the sky was a bright cloudless blue, making it feel like the South of France rather than England. She tried to shake off her gloom and focus on their trip to Montpellier in three weeks' time. She couldn't wait. Still, a kernel of worry nagged at her.

It was horrid to think of an Ancient Egyptian poison rotting away in her attic. Sometimes she wished Tutankhamun's tomb had never been found, but had been left undisturbed beneath the rock and sand of the Egyptian desert.

The clock on the dashboard read twenty to three. Time was tight but Eve could still make it to the starting gate if she kept up her present speed. Just as that thought crossed her mind, a tractor turned out of a field into the road in front. *No*, she groaned. She beeped her horn, but there was nowhere for the driver to pull over because there were dry-stone walls lining the fields on either side. As luck would have it, this was the only twisty stretch in an otherwise ruler-straight road that dated back to the Romans. Eve pulled the car's nose out in an attempt to pass, but another car was hurtling toward her so she drew back again.

She tried several times to pass the tractor but each time had to abandon the attempt. It was too risky. A queue of cars built up behind her and she hoped the tractor driver felt guilty at least. Some of the other drivers beeped their horns, but it did nothing but raise their blood pressure, Eve thought. It looked as though she was going to miss the race after all. Too bad.

Straight after a tight bend, a clear stretch beckoned: her chance at last. She accelerated into the other side of the road. The car directly behind her also pulled out. And then, like a mirage, a country bus turned out of a lane up ahead that had been hidden among trees. It was heading straight for her.

Adrenaline kicked in. Eve pressed her accelerator to the floor, taking the Austin up to its top speed, but quickly realized she wouldn't get past the tractor in time to avoid crashing headlong into the bus. She couldn't brake and pull back because the car behind was hemming her in. There was a field to the right but a dry-stone wall stood in the way. A million thoughts flooded her brain in split seconds as she tried to think how to save herself. *Patricia!* she screamed silently. *Brograve!*

Just before the bus hit, she spun the steering wheel hard right toward the wall and braced herself. Metal exploded on metal and glass shattered on her passenger side, the impact throwing her hard against the driver's door. She was still conscious when the car filled with a musky fragrance that caught the back of her throat. It was a scent she knew from long ago, the scent of Tut-ankhamun's tomb. An image flashed into her mind of the boy king's striped funeral mask, with the uraeus on top, its cobra head poised to strike.

It got me, she thought with surprise, just before there was a second explosion as the car behind smashed into her, followed by silence.

Chapter Fifty-Five

London, July 1973

Brograve tried to count how many strokes Eve had suffered in the thirty-eight years that had passed since her car accident. Was it four? Maybe five? Each of them had stolen something. The first took her peripheral vision, meaning she was no longer allowed to drive. The second and third had been mild but they still took chunks of memory, and left her fatigued for a long time afterward; she had never regained the fizzling energy she had possessed in her twenties. The fourth, the previous year, had taken months for her to bounce back from, and had affected her mobility, her balance, and the strength in her right hand, as well as sucking up more swathes of memory. But this latest one was different, he soon came to realize. It was as if a bomb had gone off in her head, laying waste to her intelligence and leaving her brain full of craters, like no-man's-land.

He watched her one afternoon, sitting in an armchair, gazing into space, and saw a blankness in her expression, a haziness. It wasn't the expression of someone who was lost in thought. Her eyes were open but there was nothing behind them.

"What are you thinking about?" he asked, and she was startled. She frowned, trying to remember.

"Nothing much," she said, and he suspected that was the truth. He turned his head so she couldn't see the tears glinting behind his glasses.

Patricia stayed for the first week after Eve came out of hospital, making all their meals and helping her to wash and dress. "Keep her calm," the doctor had said, and together they tried to work out a routine that would be easy for her.

She loved comedy programs on television, especially the ones with canned laughter. Brograve wasn't sure she got the jokes but she chortled along quite happily. She didn't like violence, flinching and trying to cover her face as if terrified, so they learned to avoid crime shows and war films. Once when Patricia raised her voice to an insurance salesman on the telephone, Eve became distressed and rushed out to the hall screaming, "No! Stop it! Stop!," and only calmed down when she had hung up.

Emotions washed over her at random, without any obvious cause, but if she got sad, the national anthem always worked its magic, and she loved kisses and hugs.

Patricia tried to persuade him to hire a live-in caregiver. "How will you cope once I've gone home again, Dad? Won't you get lonely when it's just the two of you?"

He was surprised at the question. "Of course not! I've got Eve for company."

"But it's not her anymore, is it? Not really."

"It *is* her!" He was adamant. She was still his Eve. Her personality was the same. She wanted everyone in the room to be happy just as she always had. He loved her more than ever now that she was newly helpless.

Once Patricia left, the two of them got into new routines together. Most of the morning was taken up with getting her dressed and eating breakfast, but they usually went out somewhere in the afternoon. On fine days he drove her to Kew Gardens or Hampton Court or stately homes with pretty gardens where they could walk and admire the trees and flowers. If it was raining they had afternoon tea in a smart hotel, or saw Patricia and their grandsons, or visited Maude and Cuthbert. In the evenings they had a picnic in front of the television, with cheese and crackers, biscuits and cakes, a sherry for her and a whisky for him. Who cared about eating a proper meal at their age, for goodness' sake?

Brograve wasn't unhappy. He found he could focus on the present most of the time. It did no good thinking back on what they had lost. He wasn't going to start grieving for Eve when she was still there beside him, still his loving, sunny wife. But sometimes, as he lay in bed listening to her breathing, he couldn't help comparing her mind now to the way it was before the last two strokes, just over a year earlier. They had been the cruelest.

In March 1972, she'd been invited to the opening of the Tutankhamun exhibition at the British Museum. The director walked her around the exhibits and she chatted knowledgeably about the iconic funeral mask made of sheet gold and the four anthropoid coffins that had been slotted inside the sarcophagus, about the *shabti* figures, the boat and the carriages, the guardian statues and the animal couches.

Some photographers persuaded her to pose for photographs next to the funeral mask. As she stood there, flashbulbs clicking, a journalist called out the standard question.

"You're one of the only people who entered the tomb yet managed to avoid the curse. Why do you think that is?"

"Good genes," Eve had replied, quick as a flash, making Brograve chuckle.

The Queen arrived and Eve chatted with her for a

few moments—they knew each other because Porchy's son trained her horses. Then she was interviewed by a journalist from *The Times,* and she was lucid and funny and articulate. Her memory had not let her down once. He'd been so proud of her that day.

She couldn't have done that now. When the doctor came to see her at home, he asked her a series of simple questions.

"Where are we?" he asked.

"Framfield, of course," she replied with certainty.

"What year is it?"

"Nineteen twenty-two. Maybe nineteen twenty-three." She glanced at Brograve and he smiled and nodded.

"And who is the prime minister?"

She looked at Brograve again before answering, "Lloyd George?"

"Well done," he said, nodding and writing something in his notes. "You're doing just fine, Lady Beauchamp."

Eve beamed, seeming pleased with herself, and Brograve smiled too, although there was an ache in his heart that never went away.

One morning, he pulled out the lavishly illustrated book that had been published to coincide with the British Museum exhibition, then sat beside Eve to show it to her. He didn't mean to test her, just thought she might enjoy it. She touched some of the pictures with her finger, and watching closely, he convinced himself there was recognition in her eyes.

"Beautiful," she said about an image of the gold and blue faience shrine.

There was a black-and-white photograph of her standing outside the tomb with Howard Carter and her father and she lingered over that for a long time. It was clearly ringing bells for her.

"That's Pups," Brograve said, pointing. "And Howard."

"How is Howard?" she asked.

"He died a long time ago," Brograve said, hoping it wouldn't upset her. "You went to the funeral, with Porchy and your mother."

"Yes, of course." She nodded, calmly, and turned to the next page.

All morning she sat with that book, flicking the pages one way, then the other, and Brograve was sure she was remembering some of it. She seemed animated. He didn't ask her any questions, though. That would have been cruel.

Maude often rang for a chat, and Brograve was glad of it because she was the one person he could tell the truth to: "Her memory's shot to pieces, but sometimes there's a flash of recognition. Like when you are tuning the channel on the television and it's all fuzzy until suddenly a clear picture comes through. You twiddle the knob a little more to try and make it clearer and it vanishes again. But at least she's happy."

"I can tell she's happy," Maude replied. "You're doing a wonderful job. I love seeing the two of you, although it sometimes makes me melancholy. If only she hadn't had that car accident, she probably wouldn't have had the strokes. . . ."

"You can't think that way," Brograve interrupted. "It does no one any good. We're all at an age where bits of us are malfunctioning—although you seem to have gotten off lightly. You're still as sharp and agile as ever."

"Hardly!" she exclaimed. "Oh hang on, Cuthbert wants a word. He's holding out his hand for the receiver, waving as if it's something urgent. I'll call again soon. Give Eve a kiss from me."

Cuthbert's voice came on the line. "Did you hear any more from that Egyptian woman, Ana Mansour?" he asked, without preamble.

"We haven't heard since last May," Brograve replied. "She took to her heels when she realized she wasn't getting anywhere with us."

"I have some news from a colleague in Cairo,"

Cuthbert said. "It turns out the real reason she was sacked from the university was for being overzealous in tracking down and reclaiming Egyptian artifacts held in private collections overseas. She tried to black-mail a German millionaire and he called the police."

Brograve wasn't surprised. Deep down, he had al-ways felt as if Ana didn't fit the profile of an academic trying to make the history books accurate. "What did she do with the artifacts she reclaimed? Was she trying to sell them?"

"No, everything she found went to Egyptian muse-ums. She had access to information about private col-lectors through her father's old dealership, as well as through her own research. But the university couldn't be seen to condone her methods, and that's why she was sacked."

"My father's gold clock has been missing since her visit," Brograve said. "It did cross my mind to wonder if she might have taken it, but Eve talked me out of it."

"I don't have any evidence that she was a thief," Cuthbert said. "My informant said she sees herself as a patriot doing the right thing for her country."

Brograve remembered Eve's disappointment that Porchy wouldn't let her hand over the Tutankhamun items they found at Highclere. It had been obvious then that Eve had spoken to Ana since her last visit, and he wondered what had been agreed between them. Had Eve seen the woman again? Had she handed anything over? Was anything else missing from the apartment, besides his clock? It was hard to tell the way Eve moved things around. She was doing it more than ever now, like a nervous tic.

When he came off the phone he went into the sitting room and asked her: "Do you remember that Egyptian woman, Ana Mansour? The one who came here asking questions about the tomb."

She nodded, but he wasn't sure if he believed her. She often said whatever she thought he wanted to hear.

"Did you give her anything?" he persevered. "A present maybe?"

"No," she said. "I think she was cross with me."

Brograve replied, "*I* was cross with *her.* She lied to us. Did she ever come here when I wasn't at home? Can you remember?"

Eve looked up at him, her eyes wide and childlike. "Did who come?"

"Ana Mansour."

"Who's that?"

He tried explaining, but her thoughts had wandered elsewhere, her fingers playing with the fringe of a blanket he'd draped over her knees.

"Do you believe in ghosts?" she asked.

444 • GILL PAUL

"Not the kind that haunt you," he said. "Not the scary kind you see in films. But I suppose we all carry the people we have loved in our memories. I still think of my brother, Edward, sometimes, and wonder what his life would have been like if he had lived."

"Your brother died in the war," she said. "You told me about it the night we met."

Brograve shook his head, feeling choked at the window of lucidity. Such moments were rare now.

"I never met him, did I?" she said. "I wish I had. If he was anything like you, he must have been wonderful."

"Why did you ask me about ghosts?" he asked.

She had a faint smile on her face. "Oh, just because . . ." she said.

Chapter Fifty-Six

London, August 25, 1976

E ve woke to the dawn chorus. It seemed as if it had never been so loud and urgent. She used to have a knack for identifying birdsong when they lived in the countryside, but you didn't hear it so much in the city.

She listened hard, trying to separate the different calls: the tuneful melody of a blackbird, the chatter of jays, the cawing of a crow. "Get up, get up!" they were saying, but she and her husband had a routine. He always brought her breakfast in bed so she had to wait for him to get up first. This morning he was still sleeping soundly, so she decided to wait.

There was a heatwave that summer, and they slept with just a sheet on top and the windows flung wide to catch any breath of air. It hadn't rained for months. There was a ban on watering gardens and Eve hoped her poor plants at the old house were not suffering too badly. She often thought about that garden, where she had spent so much time. The hollyhocks, the roses, the lupines . . . It had been so pretty, with the most delicious scents. They sometimes went to stately homes to look at the plants, but they hadn't been since spring because of the heat. It could be dangerous for old people, according to the leaflet that came through the door.

She had discovered a gold clock hidden away in her bedside cabinet, buried among the unread books and tubes of hand cream. It seemed an odd place to keep it, she thought, but now it came in handy because she could simply open the door and check the time. Almost eight o'clock. He'd probably wake soon. He was lying on his back with his mouth slightly open, the way he did when he'd been snoring. It was lucky she slept soundly because he could snore like a bull.

A ladybug landed on the sheet and she recited the old rhyme in a whisper: "Ladybird, ladybird, fly away home. Your house is on fire and your children are gone." She was pleased with herself for remembering this and turned to see if her husband had heard, but he was still sleeping.

Eve was starting to get hungry so she decided to waken him. She slid her head onto his shoulder and eased her body so she was pressing against his side, but he didn't respond. He felt cooler than her, although he was usually the hotter of the two of them—like a hot water bottle in winter. He was very still. He must be in a deep sleep. Maybe he was dreaming.

Gradually she got a creeping sensation that something was wrong. She hugged him tight, kissing his neck, but there was no response, and somehow he didn't feel right. She called, "Waken up!" No response. Had something very, very bad happened?

Fear gripped her. Why was he so cool? So still? She didn't know what to do. Panic was nudging her brain. She tried flapping her hands to make it fly away. "You'll be fine," she said out loud. "Just be calm." She decided she would keep lying by his side, without moving, until he woke up.

She must have dozed off because she wakened a while later to the sound of a key turning in the front door.

"Hellooooo . . ." a woman called, singing the word. It was her daughter. Eve heard her go into the living room, then the kitchen, looking for them.

When she pushed open the bedroom door, Eve whispered, "He's still asleep."

"Dad?" her daughter said with a question in her

voice, and came over to look at him. She shook his shoulders and touched his forehead, then bent her head to listen to his chest.

That panicky feeling came back and Eve held her breath, trying to drown out the noise in her head. *Please no, please no, please no.*

"I'm going to make a phone call," her daughter said in a strangled voice and disappeared from the room with a hand over her mouth. When she returned several minutes later, she was composed. She came around to Eve's side of the bed and kissed her cheek, then gently pulled her away from her husband, saying, "Let me help you get dressed, Mum."

Eve didn't want to get up. She wanted to stay in bed, holding her husband, but she allowed her daughter to pull off her nightie and put on some underclothes, then a long cotton dress with a summery print. There was no need for stockings in the heat. She wanted to cry, but it was nice that her daughter was being so kind.

Her husband was still in bed, still in the same position. Now she looked at him, she could see he looked the way Pups had looked at the end: as if he wasn't there anymore. *He's gone and died,* the voice in Eve's head told her. *Your husband is dead. You're all alone. What will become of you?*

She tried not to listen but the voice was getting

louder and more insistent so she could hardly hear what her daughter was saying. Something about the doctor.

They walked through to the kitchen together and her daughter filled the kettle and put it on the stove, then she made a little choking sound and rushed out of the room. She must be upset. Eve was upset too. She tried not to cry because once she started, she didn't know how she would ever stop.

And then she heard a voice.

"What's up, Pipsqueak?" it said. *"Are you sad because I didn't bring you breakfast? Don't worry— there's nothing to worry about."*

It was definitely his voice. She turned and couldn't see him but there was no doubt he was there.

"What shall we have for breakfast, Pipsqueak?" he asked.

It had to be him. No one else called her that.

"Toast?" she said cautiously.

"Good choice," he said, so she got up to turn on the grill.

When her daughter returned, Eve said to her, "Don't worry. It's going to be OK. Would you like some toast?"

The doctor went into the bedroom to see Brograve first, then he came to talk to Eve in the sitting room. Her daughter brought them all some coffee. Eve thought she should have laid out a plate of biscuits, even though the doctor said he didn't want any. He was too thin for a young man, probably working too hard.

"You're doing really well," he told Eve, making a steeple with his fingers. "I've been talking to Patricia and we think it would be best if you go and stay with her for a while, to give us time to make arrangements."

"Alright," Eve agreed. "Him too?" She gestured over her left shoulder to where she could sense her husband was sitting, out of sight.

Her daughter caught eyes with the doctor, looking worried. "I'll pack a bag for you, Mum," she said.

"Will the boys be there?" Eve asked. She couldn't remember their names for the life of her.

"They're grown up now. They've got their own homes, but I'm sure they'll come and visit. And they'll be at the funeral." Her daughter's voice cracked on the word.

"Whose funeral is it?" Eve asked. They told her, but her mind was wandering and she didn't listen. She'd been to so many funerals. Friends were dropping like flies, her husband said. The church services were terribly solemn but she liked the parties afterward, where you got sandwiches cut in triangles and with any luck a glass of sherry, and everyone said lovely things about the dead person.

"Will there be sherry?" she asked, and her daughter said she would make sure of it, and gave her a hug. She was in a very emotional mood.

There were lots of people at the funeral. Eve glanced around, trying to estimate the numbers, but it was a big church and she couldn't even see all the way to the back. It was terribly grand. The coffin was carried in by soldiers in smart red tunics and there were white lilies on top, with a very strong scent that was a bit like burning rubber.

The minister said his bit, then lots of people went up to the lectern to speak, including one of her grandsons, bless him. He got an appreciative laugh from the crowd with a story involving a waiter in a restaurant. Eve was numb. None of it felt real, until they sang the hymn "Abide with Me," with that mournful old tune. A wave of grief crashed over her and she began to sob noisily. Her daughter put an arm around her and offered a handkerchief, but Eve couldn't stop. She wanted to scream and wail, but through her sobbing she heard her husband's voice.

"Pull yourself together, Pipsqueak. Put on a good show, that's a girl."

Eve hadn't realized he was there, but it seemed he was. She couldn't see him but suddenly she could feel the warmth and pressure of his arms around her. He was so big he could wrap her up completely in his limbs. She could smell the scent of him: masculine and extraordinarily comforting. She dried her tears and sat up straight, balling the handkerchief in her fist.

She remembered doubting it as a girl when her father told her he got in touch with his mother at séances. She hadn't believed that Sherlock Holmes author and the psychic man's words, and she felt guilty now because it turned out they had been right after all. Spirits *did* return, and you *could* talk to them.

"Good turnout today," she commented to Brograve, and he agreed: *"Jolly good."*

When it was over, Eve and her daughter stood by the church exit and everyone filed past and shook her hand and stopped for a few words. Her daughter did most of the talking while Eve said, "Lovely to see you," and "Thank you for coming," and "How kind!" They all seemed to know her, so she smiled as if she knew them too.

Afterward they went to her daughter's house and there was a lovely spread of afternoon tea, with sandwiches, scones and jam, and a Victoria sponge. She'd gone to a lot of trouble. Eve got quite tipsy on the sherry but resisted when they tried to make her go to bed. She was enjoying chatting with all these lovely people and didn't want the party to end.

Besides, she hated going to bed at her daughter's because it meant waking up alone. There was no warm body in the bed. Her husband didn't bring her breakfast anymore. She lay there with a big ball of tears in her throat, feeling empty and lost and worried, until her daughter came to help her get dressed.

Her husband wasn't there, at least not so she could actually see him, and she didn't want to think about that too much. Maybe when she went back to her own house, he'd be waiting for her. He'd have to be, because she didn't think she could manage on her own.

Chapter Fifty-Seven

London, January 6, 1980

Eve had no idea where she was. The room was unfamiliar and it was full of strangers. She mostly sat at the window watching the rain. It was bucketing down, dripping off the eaves, gushing down the drainpipe, and bouncing off the surface of puddles on the path. She was pretty sure it was afternoon but they had the overhead lights on, and a television set was blaring away.

She shifted in her chair to look around. Some very old-looking people were watching television, hunched silently in their chairs. How dull they must be, not even making conversation. Earlier, a jolly girl had made them sit in a circle and asked them to throw a ball to one another, but Eve couldn't be bothered. She didn't even try to catch it, so after a while they stopped throwing to her.

Her husband came and went and she never knew when he would be there again. It made her sad when she thought about him. Why did he leave her? She knew he loved her, so why did he go?

"There's a visitor to see you," said one of the young ladies who worked there. "Her name is Ana Mansour. She says she's a friend of yours. Shall I show her in? I could bring tea and biscuits."

The name meant absolutely nothing to Eve. Was it her daughter? One of her grandsons' girlfriends? Perhaps one of her brother's children . . . They'd gotten married and she could never remember their married names.

"Alright." She nodded. "Tea and biscuits would be nice." Her voice was croaky and she realized it had been a long time since she'd spoken out loud, although there was a constant conversation in her head, going on and on until it tired her so much she dozed off.

She didn't recognize the woman who was walking toward her, not even a flicker. Long dark hair, brown eyes, a black trouser suit. She'd never gotten used to women in trousers, showing their bottoms so clearly. This woman's trousers were tight around plumpish thighs. A flowing skirt would have looked so much nicer.

"I never wore trousers," Eve told her after they'd

said hello. "We left that to the men. They're not very flattering, are they?"

The woman seemed amused. "My generation is doing everything men used to do, and doing it better most of the time."

"Not everything," Eve said. There were things her husband could do that she could never have attempted, but she couldn't think of an example at that precise moment.

A lady in a light blue uniform brought the tea trolley and poured cups for both of them. "Careful. It's hot," she said as she put one down beside Eve.

Eve found that rather patronizing. Of course tea was hot! But she didn't comment. People often said things like that when you were elderly.

"Lady Beauchamp," her visitor said. "One of your old neighbors told me you were living here now. Do you remember eight years ago I used to come to your house to ask you questions about your life?"

"Of course," she said, although she didn't. She had learned it didn't matter what she said because people told her what they wanted her to know.

"We talked about you visiting Tutankhamun's tomb. We were recording your memories, do you remember?"

Eve watched her talking, a look of studied concentration on her face. "Yes, of course."

"Do you remember we talked about the missing gold container from the tomb, and I asked if you knew where it was? I think you did know. I wonder if you can remember now. Maybe you hid it somewhere?"

Had she? Eve was baffled. *Why would she hide it?*

"Or maybe you brought it here with you?"

"I very much doubt that," Eve replied, looking around. "But I'll have a think and let you know." She had a gulp of tea but it burned her mouth so she spat it back into the cup. The scorched feeling on her tongue was unpleasant.

"I wanted to ask you more questions and see if I can jog your memory about that lovely gold container you took from Tutankhamun's tomb. It would be nice to know where it went, don't you think?"

The visitor seemed keen to ingratiate herself. She had good skin, Eve thought, with no pimples, so she couldn't understand why it was coated in thick pancake makeup, like actors wore onstage. And those black smudges above and below her eyes made her look half-dead. Maybe it was the new fashion.

"I'm afraid I won't be able to," she replied, when she realized the visitor was waiting for an answer. "I don't remember anymore."

The visitor mulled this over. "Could we at least try? Maybe something will jog your memory."

"I won't be much help," Eve warned. "I know nothing now."

It was true. She could remember that she used to know a lot of things, and that she'd had a busy life, but the details had gone. It didn't make her sad; it was just a fact, like rain being wet and tea being hot.

"You don't remember Tutankhamun?" the woman asked.

Eve shook her head. "No, dear."

She seemed very disappointed at that. "Howard Carter? Do you remember him?"

Eve pretended to scan her memory. "No, sorry."

She sighed. "If I show you some pictures, do you think it would help? Or I could read out to you the memories you told me last time."

That sounded nice. Her daughter read to her sometimes. Eve found it impossible to concentrate on the story but she liked listening to her voice.

"I'm a bit tired today. Come back tomorrow. And could you bring some sherry?" she asked. "They don't serve it here. I've no idea why not."

The woman smiled. "I'll come back tomorrow and bring some sherry, and read to you. That would be lovely."

When she came the next day they sat in Eve's bedroom—so no one could spy on them, the woman said. She had brought a bottle of sherry and a glass in her leather shoulder bag and Eve sipped it while she listened to the story. It was very relaxing.

When the woman had finished, she said: "I wonder if you remember anything about that gold container you took from the tomb. It's very important you try to remember."

Eve wanted to help, she really did. She had a trick of sliding her brain sideways; that sometimes worked. She thought about what she was trying to remember and let her mind drift away from it, and sometimes the answer came. "I might know," she said. "Yes, it's possible."

"Where is it now? Can you tell me?" Her tone was urgent.

Eve tried sliding her brain, but she got distracted by the smell in the room.

"What's that perfume you're wearing?" she asked. "It reminds me of something."

"Patchouli," the woman replied and held out her wrist so Eve could smell it up close.

"It smells like my old rose garden in the rain," Eve said. Another waft of perfume reached her nostrils. Then she remembered the thing that she'd been trying so hard to remember. She remembered where the gold container was. There was a picture in her head, clear as anything.

In the memory, she was climbing up to the attic and searching frantically through boxes until she found it. The scent was overwhelming, making her giddy as she paused at the top of the attic ladder, one of those extending metal ones that slid down with a thud. She probably shouldn't have been climbing ladders but she knew she had to get rid of the gold box because it was cursed.

She climbed back down the ladder, clinging on for dear life, and took the container out to the garden, where she dug a hole right in the middle of the rose bed and threw it in. That way, her family would be safe. Everyone would be safe. She covered it with soil and patted it down firmly.

Suddenly Eve became aware that her husband was in the room with them. *"Don't tell her where it is,"* he said. *"She's trying to trick you."*

The visitor was giving her an odd look and she wondered if she was muttering to herself. She did that sometimes.

"She brought me sherry," Eve told him. "She seems nice."

"She lied to us," he said. *"She's not who she says she is."*

"It's in the rose garden. Don't forget," Eve said out loud.

The woman blinked. "What about the rose garden?"

"You know . . . the thing we were talking about." *Damn! What was the name of it?*

Light dawned in the woman's eyes. "The gold container is in the rose garden. Which rose garden?"

"I buried it." She could hear her husband sighing. He was exasperated with her.

The woman cleared her throat. "You didn't have a garden in London. Do you mean at your house in Framfield?"

Eve didn't recognize the name, but she said yes all the same.

"Why did you bury it?"

"To make us safe." She was surprised the woman didn't understand.

Her face lit up. She was clearly very pleased. "You mean because of the curse?"

Eve smiled back. "Of course. Why else?"

"But that's wonderful! Thank you for telling me." She stood up as if she couldn't wait to leave. "Would you like me to leave the rest of the sherry with you? You can hide it and have a drink whenever you like."

Eve thought that was a splendid idea. "Thank you.

Perhaps you could put it in there." She pointed to a cupboard by the bed.

The woman put the bottle inside. "Thank *you*, Lady Beauchamp," she said, shaking her hand. "It's been a great pleasure talking to you."

"Silly old Pipsqueak," her husband said, as the visitor walked off into the corridor and turned toward the swinging doors that led to the outside world.

Chapter Fifty-Eight

London, January 29, 1980

Her daughter came to visit Eve one afternoon. As she walked over from the entrance, Eve noticed her umbrella was leaving a trail of drips across the gray-blue linoleum. She hugged her tight, almost too tight, and held on for ages, but Eve liked it. She didn't get enough hugs these days.

"Are you OK, Mum?" she asked. "Are they treating you well?"

"It's very nice," Eve said. "They're all very kind."

Her daughter glanced around. "I still feel awful about putting you in here, but you needed more care than I could give you. Nursing care."

"It's fine. I don't mind at all." That seemed to be what she wanted to hear.

Patricia took her coat off and folded it over the back

of a chair, tossing her umbrella underneath, then she sat down by Eve.

"There's something I need to ask you," her daughter said, pulling a newspaper cutting from her handbag. It had a black-and-white picture at the top. There were four people in the picture: a man, a woman, and two children, all of them dark-haired and foreign-looking, smiling at the camera. "Do you remember that woman?" she asked, pointing.

Eve took it and held it close to her face so she could see better. "Oh, yes," she said, although she didn't.

"Her name was Ana Mansour," her daughter told her. "It says in the story that you gave her something. Is that right?"

Eve shook her head. "No, dear. I wouldn't do that."

"A gold container from Tutankhamun's tomb, it says. I wondered if it was the one I was playing with one day and you dragged me off to wash my hair. Do you remember? I was only four."

"I wouldn't do that." Eve was very sure of herself.

"Shall I read the story to you anyway?"

Eve looked around for the sherry. She liked a sherry while someone was reading to her but the bottle wasn't in her cupboard anymore. They must have moved it. Or maybe she had finished it. "Alright," she said.

"The headline is: 'The Curse of Tutankhamun

Strikes Again.'" Her daughter made a funny face, rolling her eyes, and Eve laughed. She carried on reading:

> A woman found dead in a London hotel room last week is being claimed as the latest victim of the curse of Tutankhamun. Forensic scientists have been unable to find a cause for the death of the forty-eight-year-old Egyptian national, who has been named as Ana Mansour, an archaeologist from Cairo. Some believe she could be the latest in the dozens of people associated with the Ancient Egyptian king's tomb who died unusual or unexplained deaths.
>
> Mrs. Mansour was in London to collect a rare and priceless solid gold ointment container that came from the burial chamber of Tutankhamun. It was given to her by Lady Evelyn Beauchamp, née Herbert, the daughter of Lord Carnarvon, who funded the exploration that led to the discovery of the tomb in November 1922.

Her daughter smiled at her and said, "That's you, Mum," before she carried on.

> The ointment container was in the hotel room when Mrs. Mansour's body was found by a chambermaid. Authorities at the Egyptian Museum in Cairo say

*that a pungent scent in artifacts that came from the
burial chamber has caused breathing difficulties
when staff are exposed to it, but the director said it
was ridiculous to claim it could have any supernatural qualities. Is he right, or could it be that the
ancient king's curse is still effective after more than
three millennia?*

Her daughter looked up. "She was the woman who
used to come and ask you questions about the tomb,
wasn't she?"

Eve looked at the photo again. They were on a beach
and the man had his arm around the woman's shoulders. "Who is the man?" she asked.

"The caption says: 'Mrs. Ana Mansour with her
husband, Muhammad, and their two children on holiday at the Red Sea resort of Hurghada last month.'"

Eve didn't know the man or the children but she
remembered the woman. They used to talk about important things from the past, back in the days when
she could still remember it.

"I liked her," she said. "She was my friend."

Acknowledgments

This novel is dedicated to Karen Sullivan, publisher of Orenda Books and one of my closest friends. She suggested I write about Tutankhamun, read and commented on an early draft, gave me advice on the structure when it wasn't working, then read and commented on a final draft, all the while dispensing encouragement as needed. She's been an indispensable beta reader for every one of my novels, but this time she totally went beyond the call!

Lucia Macro, my New York editor (I love saying that), has also been a big influence on the direction the novel took, with her witty emails and wise edits. The entire crew at William Morrow are totally professional yet warm and approachable. Huge thanks to Liate Stehlik, Asanté Simons, Amelia Wood, Danielle

Bartlett, Sophie Normil, Jennifer Hart, Jean Marie Kelly, and Jessica Rozler. My copy editor, Kim Lewis, caught some howlers in the manuscript, for which I am incredibly grateful. And Diahann Sturge did a wonderful job with the design.

I love knowing that Vivien Green, Gaia Banks, and Alba Arnau at Sheil Land Associates have my back. Vivien has represented me for the last twenty-one years, and I hope there are many more to come. I love the enthusiasm and flair of the Avon UK team: Molly Walker-Sharp, Ellie Pilcher, Oli Malcolm, Helen Huthwaite, and Phoebe Morgan are sparky "ideas people" and a sheer joy to work with.

I need different types of experts to check facts in each novel. This time I particularly want to thank Linda Jones, who worked as a physio with stroke patients in the 1970s, and who made lots of valuable contributions to the way I dealt with those sections. Tara Draper-Stumm checked the Egyptology content and made some useful additions. Ralph Atkins checked the bits on vintage cars; Rosie de Guzman clarified a couple of points about horse racing; and David Boyle, one of the most knowledgeable people I know, read the whole novel for historical accuracy. However, if any errors have crept in, I should stress they are entirely mine.

Huge love to my traveling pal Louise Kerr, who

came to Egypt with me and is always the perfect person to have an adventure with. Thanks also to Richard Hughes for accompanying me on a research trip to Highclere, which involved drinking cocktails on the lawn on a glorious summer's day. Love to Tracy Rees for reading the final draft and making suggestions, as well as to my wonderful friend Lor Bingham for research, editorial, and enthusiastic social media support.

I have met many British book bloggers in person at launches and events over the years. They are a lively bunch, united by their love of reading, and I'm constantly amazed at the work they put into reviewing and promoting their reviews. Huge thanks to them, as always.

This time I would also like to thank the American bloggers and podcasters who have reached out and welcomed me onto their sites: Ashley Hasty of Hasty Book List; Sharlene Martin Moore and Bobbi Dumas of Romance of Reading; Tammy Meadal Underhill of Peace Love Books; Kristy Barrett of A Novel Bee; Cindy Burnett of *Thoughts from a Page*; Hank Garner of *Author Stories*; Michelle Marie Dunton Cronauer; Melody Hawkins of Oh the Books She Will Read; Victoria Wood of BiblioLifestyle; Barbara Bos of Women Writers, Women's Books; and bookstagrammers too numerous to mention—grateful thanks to you all.

Thank you to the Historical Writers Association, especially Imogen Robertson and Frances Owen, for their generous support, and to the Historical Novel Society for making their conferences such a fun place to connect with other historical authors.

During the time of Covid, friendships were more important than ever, so I'm sending love to all the author pals and non-author pals who have made the months pass more quickly. And to Karel Bata: I can't think of anyone I would rather have been in lockdown with.